Evarance

Rise of the Shadows

Evarance

Rise of the Shadows

BONNIE M. CLARK

STEALTH BOOKS

EVARANCE – RISE OF THE SHADOWS

Copyright © 2016 by Bonnie M. Clark

Stealth Books®

www.stealthbooks.com

Cover Design by Renata Lechner

http://thelemadreamsart.deviantart.com

ISBN-13: 978-1-939398-63-5

Published in the United States of America

This book is dedicated to my loving husband, Frank, without whom this story may have never been told. Thank you for loving me and supporting me through this momentous project and always believing in me, even when I wasn't always able to believe in myself.

CONTENTS

PREFACE

"Wake up! Just wake up already!" Rachel's head screamed as the monstrous black creature approached, growling low and viciously, his lips curled up showing razor sharp teeth dripping with saliva and blood.

"You have nowhere left to run, little girl," he snarled with a wicked grin, crouching low, readying for the attack.

Rachel took one step backward before her back pressed hard against the solid rock wall. She closed her eyes tightly, waiting for the blow that would certainly end her life.

There was a time, before the horrible nightmares began, that she found solace in her dreams. To Rachel, her dreams were an exciting escape from the boring life she once lived. But now, more than anything, she just wanted the dream she had become trapped in for so long to end.

CHAPTER 1. PATH OF ASH

The air in the forest was crisp and clean with delicate scents of bark and foliage wafting about. The surrounding trees were painted in brilliant autumn hues of yellow, red, and orange, their branches dancing gently in a passing breeze, releasing several dead or dying leaves to float and twist in elegant downward spirals toward the forest floor. The ground now had a thin covering of such leaves, many which were still too fresh to have become brown and crackly with dehydration.

Moving forward around trees and shrubs, it was hard not to notice the eerie quiet aside from the slight rustle of leaves and branches in the breeze. There were no birds, no bugs, no animals visible, and no telltale noises that suggested the presence of any such creatures. Everything was unnaturally still. Even more peculiar were the leaves on the forest floor, though they were still fresh and vibrant with color, many of the leaves scattered across the ground were partially singed with black, or crumbled into an ashen dust. *I wonder what happened to those . . .*

Before the thought could be completed, a loud male voice broke through.

"Hey, Rae! Time to get up! Ya know how Mom gets when you're late for breakfast."

Rachel struggled to open her unfocused, green eyes. The

weight of her eyelids felt dreadfully heavy, and the light peeking through the blinds forced her to blink several times before her eyes were willing to adjust to the brightness of her room. *What a strange dream,* she thought, recalling the charred leaves on the ground and the strange silence that accompanied them.

She turned over in bed, yawning widely before burying her face in her pillow, shaking her shoulder-length, strawberry-blonde hair as she did. She stretched her legs and arms long and tightly before rolling back over, half dazed, half conscious, fighting to heave herself out of the snuggly warm bed.

Another voice carried through her bedroom door, a mature female voice, this time traveling up from the floor below.

"Rachel honey, I hope you're getting up. The table is nearly set. . . ."

It was Mom, and Rachel didn't particularly want to get into trouble this early in the morning. She grumbled briefly to herself about the absurdity of having breakfast so early, before mustering all the strength she could to kick the covers off and roll out of bed.

"Coming, Mom . . ." she yelled back as she fumbled across her room, stumbling over piles of clothes and books before finally reaching her dresser, which she rummaged through to find something half decent to wear.

Her dresser was filled mostly with hand-me-down clothes that came from her older sister Evalyn, who had just barely turned sweet sixteen. Rachel was twelve, so the clothes were several years old, some a bit outdated, which would matter if Rachel cared about that sort of thing, but she didn't. She didn't mind hand-me-downs really, so long as they fit okay and didn't look too terrible on her.

The really cool thing about having a sixteen-year-old sister was the freedom that came with it. Evalyn had just received her driver's license, which meant Rachel didn't have to rely as much on Mom and Dad to go places, especially since they were almost never home anyway. She had already accompanied Evalyn on several drives and knew she could count on her sister to drop her off somewhere or pick her up in a pinch.

Pulling on a worn T-shirt, dark-gray hoodie, and some jeans, Rachel made her way down the hall, passing her older brother Christian's room. He preferred being called "Chris" and had recently dyed the tips of his short, spiky, dark-brown hair blond just because he could. Mom was terribly upset when she found out what he had done to his hair, but Dad quickly calmed her down, reminding her that there are worse things a fourteen year old might do in his spare time.

His door sported a big BIOHAZARD sign with the menacing words ENTER AT YOUR OWN RISK written below. The remainder of his door was sloppily decorated with crisscrossing yellow caution tape. His room always gave Rachel the creeps so she rushed by it.

Unlike Evalyn and Chris, Rachel didn't look like the rest of the family. She didn't have dark-brown hair and blue eyes like her mom, dad, brother, and sister, and was the only one with freckles dotting her nose and cheeks. Her strawberry-blond hair and green eyes made her feel like a sore thumb sticking out in every family photo. Sometimes she wondered if she truly belonged in the family at all or if she had really been adopted all along.

Whenever she voiced her doubts Mom and Dad always insisted that Rachel really was their daughter. They would even remind her they had the baby pictures to prove it. But she still wondered at times. Supposedly she favored her Aunt Jenny, which was what all the relatives kept telling her, but no one had been able to substantiate that fact with a single picture of her aunt, which, in Rachel's mind, made the whole issue all the more suspicious.

They said all the pictures of her aunt burned up in a house fire. Grandma lost everything she owned in that fire, including all the pictures of Aunt Jenny and Dad when they were growing up. As the story goes, Aunt Jenny went missing when Rachel was very small, but to this day, no one would talk about what happened to her. Rachel knew better than to bring it up anymore. It had become one of those taboo family topics no one would discuss.

Stepping down the stairs past all the family photos that everyday served as a reminder of just how very different she was from everyone else, Rachel inhaled deeply, cracking a smile as she did. The house was filled with tantalizing smells of frying bacon and freshly made pancakes. The aroma dissolved any lingering bits of sleepiness she was still fighting.

Rachel especially enjoyed Saturday morning breakfast with the family, despite how early Mom would make it. It was one of the few times during the week she could enjoy a home-cooked meal. Both Mom and Dad worked long hours so she, her brother, and her sister rarely saw their parents during the workweek. Most of their meals came from boxes or cans, but the weekend was different. Every weekend, Mom would try to cook a couple of special homemade meals so everyone could sit down, eat, and reconnect as a family, whatever that meant.

As Rachel neared the table she could already see Chris,

Evalyn and Mom sitting down, waiting patiently to start breakfast. Mom tried to ignore Chris as he breathed onto his spoon and stuck it to his nose over and over again. Evalyn worked on manipulating her long, wavy, lush brown hair into a loose half-braid before noticing Rachel walk up to the table.

"Morning sleepyhead," Evalyn teased, smiling as she pulled out the chair next to her.

"Yeah, yeah . . ." Rachel replied, sitting down in the chair with an awkward scoot. "I'm not the *only* one who sleeps in, you know." She gave Chris a sharp glance, watching the spoon fall yet again off his nose and onto the table. He left the spoon where it had fallen, directing his attention to Rachel instead.

"Hey now, who woke up who today, huh? For all the trouble I went through gettin' you out of bed, how about you thank me by cleaning my room?"

"Trouble?" Rachel snapped. "You barely did *anything*. Besides, I wouldn't touch your room with a ten-foot pole."

"You're kiddin', right?" Chris said, with almost a hint of genuine shock in his voice. "Entering *my* room is like a super privilege. You should feel honored I asked you to clean it."

"Ha, yeah right! Privilege is *not* the word I would use."

"*Enough!*" yelled Mom, glaring around the table and then slowly calming down. She was a slender woman with deep-blue eyes and dark hair cut in a short professional style. It seemed obvious, to her kids at least, that she must be quite the businesswoman because she always carried a strong, commanding presence that demanded respect.

"Evalyn, honey," Mom's voice was calm and sweet again, "would you please say grace?"

"Of course," Evalyn said cheerily, acting as though she

had been completely unaffected by her brother and sister bickering.

Everyone at the table bowed their heads just long enough for Evalyn to bless the food.

"Yo, pass the pancakes, Rae," Chris insisted, well aware that he'd already put Rachel in a terrible mood.

"Only, if you clean *my* room," she shot back at him, stubbornly folding her arms.

"Really?" Evalyn sighed, passing the pancake platter over to Chris. "Can't you guys get along just once?"

Mom raised her eyebrow at Rachel and Chris who promptly settled down, and breakfast continued with very little arguing, which was usually how meals ended up when Mom's patience was wearing thin.

"Where's Dad?" asked Chris, nodding slightly toward the empty seat where Dad usually sits.

"He's out in the garage cleaning up *your* mess, Christian." Mom did not sound very happy. "Honestly, why is the lawn mower in pieces again? You know you're supposed to mow the lawn today. But how you plan on doing that with the lawn mower sprawled out all over the floor is beyond me."

"Well, it was actin' funny so I thought I'd have a look," Chris said defensively.

"Don't take apart what you can't put back together." Mom's voice was stern.

"I was gonna put it back together today, honest."

"Well, after you finish eating, bring your father his breakfast. Heaven knows he must be starving by now!"

"No need, honey," Dad broke in as he entered the room, placing his arm gently on Mom's shoulder. "I put the lawn mower back together. A little oil and gas and it should be good as new."

Dad was a tall, medium build man with dark, short hair parted loosely on one side. His glasses rested slightly crooked on his nose and a few beads of sweat dripped down his forehead. He was an engineer by profession and always seemed to figure out how to fix whatever Chris dismantled during the week.

"So . . ." Dad continued, smiling, "who's ready for the big camping trip next week?" Soft groans replaced the awkward silence. "I see, I see . . . Well, you'd better make the most of this week and get yourselves packed. I'll print out a supply list for each of you and post them on your bedroom doors." He sat down and began his breakfast while everyone else, at the request of Mom, quietly cleared their dishes off the table.

Even though Mom and Dad were off work, it was going to be another busy day for them. They had a list full of errands to run and most likely wouldn't be back until dinnertime. Evalyn had already finished all her weekend chores. She was always on top of everything. It was just one of the many traits Rachel envied. So Evalyn's plans for the day consisted mainly of hanging out with a few of her friends at the mall, window shopping, and undoubtedly checking out the boys. Chris had already gone outside to begin mowing the lawn, leaving Rachel with the laundry to take care of.

"Ugh, laundry . . ." Rachel mumbled to herself after Mom and Dad's friendly reminder to her before they headed out the door. She hated folding and putting away laundry about as much as a person can hate anything, but it was her week to take care of it, and it wasn't the sort of task she could exactly skip doing. Her parents were sure to notice if they didn't have clean clothes to wear for work, so even though she hated doing it, she threw a load in the washer and pulled out a pile of clothes from the dryer that Mom had been *kind* enough to wash already. Though Rachel on principle didn't really believe it was kind to give her work to do so early in the morning.

She folded the clothes from the load Mom had run, which were, of course, Mom and Dad's work clothes. They were always washed first so Mom and Dad were sure to have clean, unwrinkled clothing to wear. She carried the clean clothes up to her parents' bedroom and opened the door to their large, walk-in closet. The closet was dark, despite the sun peeking in through the blinds, flooding the rest of the room with the morning light.

As she reached toward the light switch with her free hand an unusual orange glow caught her eye, keeping her from flipping on the switch. The light, which looked more like a thin glowing line, hovered above the shelf on her dad's side of the closet. She had been in Mom's and Dad's closet plenty of times to hang up clothes or put something away for them, and she had never seen anything out of the ordinary let alone *glowing* in the closet before.

"*Gotcha!*" Chris said from behind her, poking a finger into her side and making her jump just enough to hit the light switch on while simultaneously dropping the basket full of freshly folded clothes all over the floor.

"Hey!" Rachel snapped angrily, looking at the mess of unfolded clothes. "What'd you do that for?"

"I dunno," Chris said with a shrug. "I came upstairs to grab some music to mow the lawn to and saw you just standing there frozen inside the closet with the light off." He pushed Rachel aside, poking his head in to take a look around, but didn't see anything of interest.

"It was kind of creepy," he added, before Rachel shoved him out of the room.

"Just leave me alone, Chris!" she said. It was still morning, but she'd already had enough of him for one day. "You and I both have chores to do and now mine will take even longer thanks to you."

"Alright, alright . . ." Chris said half apologetically and half sarcastically. "I'll leave you to your laundry."

Rachel shut the door in his face, ignoring the mumblings she could still hear through it.

She walked cautiously back to the closet, but with the light on nothing looked out of the ordinary. Gathering up the clothes on the floor she quickly put them away. Just as she was about to leave, she wondered if the strange glow would come back when the light went out, so she watched the closet carefully as she turned off the light switch.

Once her eyes adjusted to the darkness, she could definitely see the faint orange glow again. Flipping the switch on while keeping her eyes fixated on the spot where the glow was, she noticed a small, dusty, brown wooden box, only slightly larger than her hand, which looked like it hadn't been opened in ages.

She pulled the box down off the shelf, wiping off years of dust that had accumulated on top. Under the layers of dust one word was etched deeply into the wood. It was a name she had heard mostly in passing as she grew, but one that had also been as foreign and elusive to her as the person it belonged to. The box simply read *Jenny*.

She knew this box must have belonged to her Aunt Jenny, the one who had disappeared so long ago. It was probably the only remaining piece of proof that Aunt Jenny actually had existed and wasn't just a fairy tale everyone insisted on repeating when commenting on Rachel's unusual appearance compared to everyone else in the family.

She looked around briefly on the off chance Chris was going to try to sneak up on her again. But Chris was nowhere to be seen, and she could hear the distant hum of a lawn mower, so she knew she was completely alone.

The box was hinged on one side with a clasp holding it shut on the other. Popping open the clasp, she slowly lifted the lid to take a peek inside. Loose on the bottom of the box was a silver charm bracelet that reflected back the bits of the light that touched it. She gently took out the bracelet, gazing at it in wonder. It was fitted with an adjustable clasp, allowing her to size it perfectly onto her wrist.

It was the most beautiful thing she had ever seen, made of an intricately detailed silver chain with little dangling charms that looked as though they had been expertly carved out of many different materials. One of the charms resembled a fire that appeared to be made from red, orange, and yellow crystals. It shimmered in the sunlight and looked as if it were really burning. There was a tree charm, which of course was made of wood, a water drop charm that shimmered with a beautiful aquamarine color, and a brown jagged rock that was broken, revealing metal pieces protruding from its center. There was even a charm made up of white swirls that reminded Rachel of clouds or wind. The last of the charms Rachel instantly recognized as a Chinese yin-yang made of black and white polished stones. The two stones swirled around each other as if they were frozen in a neverending dance.

She pulled the sleeve of her hoodie over the bracelet and quickly closed the box. Something about the bracelet mesmerized Rachel in a way that made her feel leaving it in that dusty old box would be a sort of travesty, since she, as well as everyone else in the family, knew that Aunt Jenny was never coming back. By the looks of the box, she felt certain no one would even notice the bracelet was missing.

She slipped the box back up onto the shelf and slinked out of the room, making sure everything looked exactly the same as before. Mom and Dad would have a fit if they knew Rachel had been in their closet going through Aunt Jenny's old things, but she was tired of the stories or lack of them, and she was even more tired of feeling so different from the rest of the family. If she really did take after her Aunt Jenny, like everyone said she did, wasn't she more entitled than anyone else in the family to wear Aunt Jenny's bracelet? Besides, now that she had it on, she couldn't bear the thought of taking it off. It felt almost as though the bracelet had become a part of her in some weird sort of way, and now that she wore it she had to keep it safe—and more importantly hidden from her parents who would undoubtedly unleash some sort of awful punishment on her if they found out she'd taken it.

She went back to her room, and after admiring the bracelet a little longer, she spent the better part of the day reading in between putting away loads of laundry. She loved books and enjoyed experiencing all the fantastic places her mind took her as she read. In fact, she often wished her life were a lot more exciting, like the stories she read. Finding the box with the bracelet was admittedly pretty thrilling compared to most days in her boring life, but it was still a far cry from the sort of adventures she longed for.

The day slipped by swiftly. Mom and Dad made it home in time to cook dinner, and Evalyn walked in just in time to eat. Rachel wasn't sure what Chris had been up to all day, but then she didn't really care. The important thing was that he'd left her alone, which was a welcome change from his usual irritating interruptions. Dinner was also quiet partly because Rachel didn't let Chris get to her the way he had at breakfast. She had more important things to do that night than waste her time with him.

After wolfing down her meal and abruptly excusing herself from the table, she went back to her room, this time not to read, but to gaze longingly at the bracelet dangling from her wrist. She wondered where Aunt Jenny could have gotten it. There were no *Made in Anywhere* engravings etched onto it, making its origin a complete mystery. All the charms were lovely, but the one that fascinated her most was the one that looked like fire. She still swore the fire looked as though it were burning, even though the crystals that made up the little charm were hard and cool to the touch.

The day was growing dark, and it was nearly time for bed when Rachel noticed that the fiery glow of the little charm was getting brighter and brighter. She quickly closed her blinds to make her room pitch black, but instead of her room succumbing to the darkness, everything around her glowed with a brilliant orange light. The light shone brightly from the little fire charm. It was the same light that had led her to the bracelet's hiding place in her parents' closet in the first place.

She didn't know how the little fire was able to glow the way it did. It wasn't just unusual . . . it was almost magical. Rachel had seen glow-in-the-dark stickers, glow necklaces, and even glow sticks before, but none of those came close to the light the little fire charm was producing.

Suddenly she heard a soft knock on the door. She quickly pulled her sleeve back over the bracelet stifling the light until the room was again dark.

"Yes?" she asked, hoping it wasn't Chris. He'd been doing such a great job of leaving her alone most of the day.

"It's Mom. Can I come in?"

"Sure," said Rachel, double-checking her wrist to make sure the bracelet was still completely covered.

Mom opened the door and flicked on the light. "Why is it so dark in here? You going to bed already?" Mom asked.

"Yeah, I think so," Rachel replied, trying to defuse any suspicions her mom might have. "It's been a long day, and I'm really tired."

"Alright, honey," Mom said with a smile. "I'm going to bed, too. Thank you for doing the laundry today."

"No problem," Rachel said, feeling a twinge of guilt about taking the bracelet while doing the laundry, but not quite enough guilt to come clean about it. "See you tomorrow."

"Bright and early," Mom said before shutting the door, leaving Rachel to her thoughts.

After staying up a bit longer to get into pajamas, Rachel finally let sleep overcome her.

Suddenly she awoke, fully expecting Chris to burst through her door at any moment to pester her again or at the very least hear Mom shouting to coax her downstairs for another early morning breakfast. But instead, and to her utter astonishment, she wasn't home at all. In fact, she was in an autumn forest bursting with colors and the fresh, crisp scent of outdoor fall air. Many of the leaves on the ground were singed and burned, disintegrated into a gray ash that created a path through the woods, winding out of her sight.

"Where am I?" she asked aloud, taking in the unusual

but almost familiar surroundings. She felt as though she had been here before, though she couldn't quite remember when.

She stepped carefully around the sections of burnt leaves and ash. Closer and closer she looked at the peculiar patterns and shapes burned here and there, but couldn't make out what they were from. She walked forward, slowly at first, following the singed and burned path. With each step her curiosity grew and her pace quickened until she was speeding ahead in a full-blown sprint, dodging bushes, touching trees as she went, snapping twigs and knocking off dying leaves that brushed by her. The path weaved on through the forest like a long and winding snake.

Rachel slowed down to a halt and leaned over trying to catch her breath. She wasn't sure how far she had run, but now she could see no beginning or end to the path she was following. Listening and looking, she couldn't see or hear anything but the trees as the wind gently blew through them.

"How strange," she muttered, then yelled out a strong "*Hello!* Is anybody there?" But still there was only silence. A cold chill ran up her spine. But there was nothing, nothing but trees, leaves, forest, ash, and shadows dancing on the forest floor as the sun peeked through the leafy canopy.

The sun was high in the sky now, telling her it was about midday. And although the forest seemed peaceful enough, she began to feel a bit uneasy, her stomach turning a notch. She continued down the path of ash, this time at a much more manageable pace, but now she couldn't shake the feeling that she was being watched. It began making her feel a little paranoid.

It wasn't long before she could clearly hear the sounds of water trickling, and as she continued to follow the ashen path, the sounds became louder and louder until she came to a small ledge no more than two feet above a thin stream. The water was smooth like a sheet of glass yet flowing steadily.

Rachel crouched on the edge of the ledge. Looking deep into the water, she could see herself, strawberry-blonde hair, green eyes, freckles — all on the water's surface. Through her reflection she caught a glimpse of something moving in the water, but she couldn't make it out.

Squinting, she saw it dart past her again. It was almost fish-like the way it swam, but it was also clear and airy looking, like nothing she had ever seen before. Whatever it was, it swam up fast and leapt high out of the water before popping mid-air just like a bubble. Rachel could feel the slight wetness of the bubble from the creature tickle her face. Moments later, she heard a splash and saw the fish-like creature reform as it plunged back into the water.

"What . . . ?" she began to say. That was before she saw them. There were dozens of these unusual fish swimming back and forth through the moving water. She hadn't noticed them at first because they blended almost perfectly with the water. But now that she knew what to look for it was clear the stream was bustling with life.

Leaning down farther, she stretched out her hand, letting her fingers lightly touch the water, forming ripples on the surface. For a moment, the bubble fish nipped gently at her fingertips, before a loud snapping of branches caused them to quickly scatter. What was hidden in the trees on the other side of the stream? She stood still, waiting, listening for whatever was going to happen next. But the forest lay silent.

Over the stream, a broken down tree acted as a natural bridge. Its trunk was round and fat, and it too was charred and covered in ash much like the path etched into the forest floor. The burns on the fallen tree were much clearer, however, than those lining the forest floor, and Rachel spied paw prints burned onto the wood leading directly across the stream from where she stood.

She wasn't sure if she should follow the path any longer. Dad had always told her that if she were ever lost in the woods, she should wait right where she was, and in time he'd be sure to find her. But she had already strayed so far from where she began, and she had no memory of coming here in the first place. Was she already on the family camping trip? Were they looking for her right now? She couldn't tell.

A few more branches crackled, and then she saw it. On the other side of the stream a fire was peeking out from behind one of the trees. It was low to the ground, burning bright orange, bursting with flecks of yellow, outlined in hints of red that danced at the edge of the flames before disappearing into the air. Something about this fire seemed different from all the other fires she had seen before. There was no smoke billowing from the flames, and even though there were trees nearby there were no sparks to ignite them.

It was bizarre, but something about the fire captivated her much in the same way the bracelet had. Fire could be dangerous, and the thought of running away while she still could briefly crossed her mind, but she couldn't run even if she wanted to, not yet, not until she knew a little more about the mesmerizing flame. After all, what *had* she expected to find at the end of a burned forest path if not a fire?

The fire grew bigger as it moved out from behind the sheltering tree. As it stepped out, Rachel could see a fox-shaped body and face looking out through the flames. The eyes were outlined in a rich black and glowed golden. The ears burned blue-black, as did the paws and nose. The mouth, chest, and tail-tip blazed with an almost blinding white flame, and the rest of the body burned mostly orange with bits of yellow and red highlighting the coat as the flames pulsed all over the body, completing the unmistakable markings of a red fox. Only this fox appeared to be on fire.

It was an unnaturally tall and slender-looking fox, almost as tall as a wolf, and of course the fire that engulfed its fur was anything but normal.

"Why are you here?" a female voice said gently as the mouth of the creature moved in sync. Rachel couldn't believe her ears. Had the burning fox just spoken to her?

"I . . . I'm not really sure," Rachel uttered clumsily in reply. "I just sort of woke up here. What are you, anyway?" This unusual creature had to be the most beautiful Rachel had ever seen.

The creature's ear perked up slightly, and with a hint of surprise she replied, "Isn't it obvious? I'm a firefox."

"It's just," Rachel continued, "I've never seen anything like you before."

"And I've never seen a human wander so deep into our forest before," the firefox replied. "A child no less . . ."

"I'm not a child," Rachel shot back a bit defensively, her cheeks burning red hot. She would be thirteen soon enough and was annoyed at always being treated like a kid.

"You're an adult then?" the female firefox asked.

"Well, not exactly," Rachel admitted. "I suppose I'm somewhere in between."

"This forest is not safe, young one," the firefox warned, stepping warily closer to Rachel, while remaining on her side of the stream. Rachel could see the ground wilting beneath the feet of the firefox with each step it took. "You should return home as swiftly as your feet will carry you."

"And what if I don't know where home is?" Rachel asked, looking around but still not recognizing anything she saw.

"Then follow me," the firefox instructed. "My name is Incindia. I can bring you safely out of the forest, but from there, you will be on your own. The darkness is moving again, and with it will come the Shadai."

Incindia bowed her head low to Rachel from across the stream as a way of introduction.

"And my name is Rachel," Rachel said with a slight bow of her head in return. "What do you mean the darkness is coming? And what exactly is the Shadai?"

Rachel's head began reeling with questions. This couldn't be real, could it? The bubble fish were strange enough, but to be talking with a firefox about some sort of darkness and something called a Shadai was a little crazy.

"The darkness," Incindia repeated, "would be easier to show you than to explain. As for the Shadai, some also refer to them as the shadows. They are evil, bloodthirsty creatures that live under the cloud of darkness that hovers over many parts of this land. The shadow wolves are one of many species of Shadai and are our sworn enemy. Believe me, you don't ever want to come face to face with a shadow wolf. Now let us leave quickly while there is still time."

Incindia turned her back to Rachel, waiting for her to cross over the fallen tree. Rachel wasn't sure what to think of everything, with doom and gloom of the darkness heading their way, followed by some horrible creatures that from the sound of it would surely harm her if they got the chance. And then there was Incindia's promise to lead her to safety — or at least safely out of the forest. What choice did she have but to follow this firefox? Incindia *seemed* nice enough.

As Rachel walked carefully across the tree trunk joining both banks of the stream, she hoped the firefox really *was* as nice as she seemed. Stepping nearer to Incindia, she could feel the intensifying warmth emanating from her fiery coat. She could also feel a slight lightheadedness come over her. Then the world around her dissolved into darkness.

"Incindia?" she cried out.

And then everything turned black.

CHAPTER 2. DREAM CHASING

Rachel opened her eyes feeling dazed and confused. She was once again in her room sprawled out across her bed. Had that all just been a dream? It didn't feel like a dream. In fact, she could still feel the lingering warmth of the firefox flame on her skin. Or was that just her blanket playing tricks on her?

Even if it was just a dream, Rachel still couldn't believe how vivid, how real the whole incident had seemed. She couldn't be sure exactly what was going on, but she did sense she was becoming part of something very special, even if she couldn't quite put those feelings into words. She wanted to dream again, to return to that strange world. She wanted to return to the pages in her mind and watch the story of her dreams unfold.

It was such a peculiar feeling, to dream with such crispness and clarity; it really didn't feel like it had been a dream at all. Should she tell anyone about her dreams? Even if she tried, she knew Evalyn and Chris wouldn't take her seriously. So for now the dreams would remain a secret. A secret world she would keep hidden in her mind, safe from the ridicule of those who would think she was weird or maybe even a little insane.

She quickly got dressed and grabbed her diary off her nightstand, flipping through the empty pages. She had been meaning to write in it for some time, but hadn't had anything she felt was really worth it. Until now.

She opened the cover and stared at the blank page for a moment before grabbing a pencil from her nightstand drawer. At the top of the page, she wrote just one word, *Firefox* . . . before hearing a loud *Thud! Thud!* against her bedroom door.

"What do you want?" Rachel shouted, annoyed she was interrupted.

"Ryan's here to see you," Chris said in a muffled voice through the door.

"Not him again . . ." Rachel muttered, walking to the door, flinging it open. "Why couldn't you just have told him I'm not home??"

"And miss out on the fun?" Chris chuckled as Rachel pushed him aside, stomping toward the front door.

Ryan was a kid from school who, during the school year, would always *accidently* bump into Rachel at her locker when she was least expecting it. His clothes were dirty, his jeans holey, his hair a mess. Rachel doubted he'd ever brushed it in his life. And he had the worst breath of anyone she had ever met!

It didn't help that Ryan would somehow magically appear right behind her just as she had finished filling her backpack with books for her next class. And then, as if that wasn't bad enough, he'd stand so close to her as she turned around she'd nearly be pinned to her locker by his dragon breath.

Ryan was one of the reasons Rachel was dreading the new school year, which was why she answered the door with it only slightly cracked open, while at the same time standing as far back from the opening as she could. She did not want to find out how disgusting his breath was today.

"I was wondering what classes you're taking this year," Ryan said, smiling. Rachel cringed, looking at the breakfast still in his teeth. "School's going to start again soon so I was just curious."

"Well, I haven't gotten my school schedule yet," Rachel lied. "And I'm sort of busy right now. So . . . later."

With that, she shut the door and turned around leaning against it. *I'm such a wimp* was the only thought running through her mind. She wished she could tell him to leave her alone. Or possibly even tell him that he was kind of creepy, and she wanted him to stop stalking her. But as much as she wanted to, she also felt a little bad for him. After all, he really was just trying to be nice to her, and all she ever offered him in return was the cold shoulder.

She waited a moment for Ryan to knock on the door again and was relieved to hear nothing but silence. He must have left.

"*Chris!*" she yelled up the stairs, infuriated at her brother for putting her in such an awkward situation. "*Next time just tell him I'm not home!*"

"Not gonna happen, Rae," Chris yelled back. "I'm not lyin' for you."

"Why not?" Rachel growled, marching upstairs.

"Well, for one, Mom and Dad told us not to lie. But seriously, you need to learn to take care of your own problems and stop hiding from them. If you want him to leave you alone you need to *tell* him. Yourself."

"Can't he just get a clue?" Rachel snapped angrily, though she wasn't sure who she was madder at: Chris or herself.

"Afraid not, Rae. He's a guy who obviously likes you.

Guys don't take hints. They have to be *told*. Tell you what, next time, *you* answer the door so I won't have to wonder whether I should lie for you."

That just infuriated Rachel more as she stormed back to her room, being sure to give Chris a shove with her shoulder as she walked past him before slamming the bedroom door.

Chris can be such a jerk, she thought. *It's not like I'm asking him to rob a bank for me. I just want him to protect me from stalkers. Isn't that the kind of thing a big brother should do?*

She plopped down on her bed in frustration before seeing the diary lying open next to her. *Firefox . . .* it read, and as she read that one word, her frustration instantly melted away.

"Well, here goes nothing," she said aloud to herself, and then picking up the pencil she began writing.

She wrote down every detail she could remember about her dream. The ashen forest floor, the bobbing bubble fish, even the uneasy feeling of being watched that overcame her as she was walking through those autumn woods. She didn't want to forget a thing, so she wrote and wrote until her hand started to hurt.

The day passed quickly, and as Rachel slipped into her pajamas to get ready for bed, she hoped she would have more dreams tonight like the one the night before. A quick brush of her teeth and hair, and out went the bedroom light. Her bracelet glowed orange once again and as it did, she tucked her arm under a pillow, stifling the light on the off chance Mom or Dad checked on her as she slept. In what felt like only moments after her head hit the pillow, she found herself wide awake once more, once again back in the forest.

The leaves were as stunning as ever, with the sun shining through the canopy accenting the already vibrant colors. Incindia was nowhere to be found, but Rachel was certain this was where they had met in her last dream. The log she had walked across lay behind her, still marked with firefox footprints, as she now stood in the same spot Incindia had when they first were introduced. The ground beneath her feet was completely scorched, with a new path leading deeper into the forest or possibly out of it—she couldn't tell which.

She followed the new path only a short distance before she noticed a change in the forest. It buzzed with unusual life all around her, and even the trees had a different look and feel about them. The autumn colors faded as she walked, shifting to various hues of green.

A rock-like snake suddenly came to life and crossed her path, looking up at her briefly before slithering merrily on its way. Large crystalline vines wrapped around some of the trees bearing large, translucent flowers in dazzling colors.

Little rodents that looked very much like flying white squirrels hopped from tree to tree, vanishing into a vaporous mist mid-leap, only to reappear on adjacent trees. They almost reminded her of little ninjas vanishing into puffs of white smoke, which made her laugh to herself.

Laughing felt good, and so did the freedom of being back inside her dreams. Here she wasn't tied down by the worries and cares of the real world. And here there were so many wonderful sights and sounds to experience, which beat being in the real world any day. In fact, she was having such a good time as she walked, she had completely forgotten about Incindia's warning to her about the dangers of lingering in the forest. It felt so peaceful and at the same time so alive.

It didn't take her long to reach the end of the newly

burned path and when she did, she spied a burning fire with the unmistakable white-tipped tail and hot black-blue ears of a firefox.

"Incindia!" Rachel yelled, anxious to continue where she had left off in her last dream. It was reassuring to know Incindia hadn't strayed too far from where Rachel had last seen her. At least that's what Rachel had thought, but as the foxlike creature turned its head Rachel's way, Rachel was surprised to see it wasn't Incindia's face that stared back at her. This firefox's face looked a lot less gentle, sleek, and refined when compared to Incindia.

"I'm sorry. I thought you were someone else," Rachel said, smiling nervously.

"Are you, Rachel?" the firefox replied in a tone much more masculine than Incindia's. "I'm Torrens."

After the initial startle of hearing her name come out of this new firefox's mouth, Rachel let out a sigh of relief. The only one who knew her name was Incindia, so surely this firefox must know Incindia as well.

"Nice to meet you, Torrens," Rachel replied with a nod of her head. "Sorry about the mixup. Did Incindia tell you about me?"

"Actually, she sent me to find you," Torrens said, a little to Rachel's surprise. Just how much time had passed in this dream since the last time she was in it?

"So she was expecting me then?" Rachel asked.

"She was certain you'd be back," Torrens replied, lifting his head. "She just wasn't sure when."

"Well, I'm back," Rachel said, stating the obvious. How could Incindia have known Rachel would return the next time she fell asleep? Then again, why was Rachel even entertaining that sort of thought in the first place? This was just a dream after all, nothing more. Wasn't it? "So do you think you could take me to her?"

Torrens didn't answer. Instead he turned his body away from hers and looking back said, "Follow me. There's something I need to show you."

She obeyed, following the flaming fox up a path that ended at a cliff's edge. From there she could see what looked like a neverending expanse of forest covered in an enormous black cloud that stretched as far as her eyes could see. Was this the darkness Incindia had warned her about? The forest trees looked very dull under the shadow of the darkness, like their very essence was being sucked out of them.

"How terrible," Rachel said, soaking in just how much of the forest the darkness covered. The time she had spent in these unusual dreams so far was filled primarily with beauty and wonder, but what she now saw was just the opposite. It looked like it brought with it a sort of death to everything it touched. "That's . . ."

". . . the darkness," Torrens replied, finishing her sentence. "It will be here soon. Incindia asked that I show it to you, though I don't dare take you any closer. It's a dangerous place, and Incindia is waiting for us."

Rachel moved closer to Torrens, appreciating the warmth of his flames. The darkness was sickening, infecting everything it touched. For a moment she imagined herself in the shadowy forest without Torrens' warmth and guidance. Already he was beginning to feel like family to her, like a big brother who actually cared.

"Why is the darkness taking over the forest?" Rachel asked.

"That's not for me to say," Torrens replied solemnly. "But I'm sure Incindia will be able to answer at least some of your questions. Follow me, and I will take you to her now."

"Thank you, Torrens, for showing me this," Rachel said, even though in the back of her mind she almost wished she hadn't seen the blackness heading their way. It made her stomach feel queasy realizing just how much truth was in the warning Incindia had given her during their first meeting.

"My pleasure, Rachel," Torrens said, politely bowing his head. "Please follow me. Incindia awaits."

"*Rachel!*" Chris's voice echoed through the forest as everything began fading away. "*Time to get up!*"

"Torrens . . ." Rachel muttered to herself as she lay sleepily in her bed. Morning had come much too soon. There was a loud thumping against her door and she knew it was Chris still trying to wake her up.

"*I'm up!*" she yelled, hoping that would be enough for her brother to leave her alone.

That dream didn't feel at all as long as the one she'd had before it. But then dreams could be funny like that: speeding up and slowing down time depending on what the dreamer was dreaming.

She grabbed her diary and wrote more. She wrote about Torrens, the crystalline vines on the trees, and everything else she could remember, including the darkness hanging over the land. She wrote page after page around meal times and kept to herself for most of the day.

Evalyn and Chris might have been a little concerned with how much time Rachel was spending in her room. That is if they weren't so busy with their own summer vacation plans.

Another day had come and gone leaving Rachel with one less day of freedom before school started, and one less day before she'd have to come up with more creative excuses to avoid Ryan in school. She couldn't wait for another night of sleep to see where her dreams would take her.

As she lay in bed waiting for sleep to overcome her, she wondered if she would dream of Torrens or Incindia again. Would she still be in the forest or somewhere completely new? It wasn't long before her thoughts melted into a peaceful slumber. When she awoke this time, she didn't see an ashen path on the forest floor. There were no trees wrapped in crystal vines and no darkness in any direction. Instead she stood at the edge of a steep, tree-covered slope overlooking a dazzling blue ocean.

Looking down at the water's edge, she saw beautiful white sandy beaches that stretched for miles and miles, the shoreline glistening in the sunlight. The beaches looked as though they were alive, rising and sinking like waves in the ocean. It was such a curious sight Rachel just had to see more. Down the rocky slopes she slid, hopping, running, and weaving through the trees as she did.

When she reached the bottom she couldn't help but feel as if something, or someone, was watching her again. She looked all around, and although she couldn't see anything suspicious, she couldn't immediately shake the uneasy feeling that settled in the pit of her stomach. Twisting the bracelet on her wrist as she looked around, she began wondering why every time she dreamed she felt like she was being watched. Was the guilt of taking Aunt Jenny's bracelet finally getting to her? And were her dreams subconsciously telling her to put it back where she found it? Regardless of what the feeling meant, she chose again to ignore it.

The beach was close now, and as she walked nearer, she could hear a chorus of meows. The sand moved and swayed in a melodic wave that sounded just like cats. Her first impression wasn't far from the truth, for as she finally reached the soft, sandy earth, she could see them jumping and pouncing on one another. They were definitely kittens . . . well, sort of. Only they looked more like sand castles that had been formed into the shape of kittens. They chased each other playfully on the granular surface, tumbling back into the sand, breaking into millions of pieces before resurfacing and reforming much like the bubble fish had reformed once they hit the water. It was quite a sight to behold.

"Here kitty, kitty, kitty . . ." Rachel called to one of the kittens chasing flecks of sand near the forest edge where Rachel stood. The sandy kitten took one cautious look at Rachel and scampered away as fast as it could, wary of the stranger from the woods.

Rachel followed the kitten across the beach, drawing closer and closer to the mass of kitties jumping in and out of the soft white sand. As she approached them, some began to hiss at her, backing away before permanently disappearing into piles of sand. Others walked farther down the beach, keeping a watchful distance from Rachel.

What a strange place this is, Rachel thought, and as quickly as she did, the dream began fading away. Rachel woke up in a daze, sprawled across her bed with the covers kicked half off. Grabbing her diary again, she added everything she could remember from this dream.

The next couple of nights flew by at a similar pace. Each night was special and unique, bringing with it sights, sounds and smells Rachel had never imagined herself to be clever enough to dream up. One night she saw flaming bats burning streaks across the night sky. The next night there were lizards that leapt into the air and blew away like gusts of wind. Every dream was carefully added to her diary the following morning.

As exciting as each dream was, Rachel began to wonder if she would see Incindia or Torrens again. She wanted to know more about the firefoxes, and every time she thought she would have a chance to learn more about them she'd wake up.

After many nights in unfamiliar places she finally found herself waking up in a familiar one. This time Incindia was standing right in front of Rachel, as magnificent as ever.

"You've returned," Incindia said with a pleasantly surprised tone in her voice.

"Seems that way," Rachel said with a smile.

"How many times have you been here?" Incindia asked.

"Well, lets see . . . three, I think," Rachel replied.

"Only three times?" Incindia looked puzzled.

"Sure," Rachel replied, "I met you once, then I met Torrens, and now, well, here I am again."

"Oh," Incindia said, a glimmer of understanding in her eyes, "I meant, how many times have you been to Calim?"

"Calim?" Rachel asked. "What's Calim?"

Incindia's voice was calm and soothing, sounding almost like that of a mother teaching her child. "Calim is the name of *this* world."

"What do you mean?" Rachel asked, looking very confused. "You don't mean an *actual* world. This's just a dream, right?"

"No," Incindia's voice was soft and warm like the flames engulfing her body. "Calim is a world, a planet, much like the one you come from. It is true that to you this may *seem* like a dream, but it's all real."

Rachel couldn't help but feel like her dreams were getting weirder by the minute—as if flaming animals weren't weird enough.

"So you're telling me I'm on an entirely different planet right now?" She asked the question, but really didn't think it could be true. She was just dreaming. She must be. That was the only logical explanation.

"Yes," Incindia said firmly.

"And how exactly did I get here? How is that even possible?"

"Through the Evarance," Incindia replied, her eyes burning with such a wizened look it was hard for Rachel not to believe every word that she said, no matter how insane it sounded.

"But this is just a dream. I'm just dreaming, aren't I?"

"In a sense this is a dream to you, I suppose. But that's what the Evarance does, after all."

Rachel was completely lost even though she was trying hard to understand. "What do you mean Evarance? It does what exactly?"

"The Evarance," Incindia spoke slow and direct. "It's the veil or barrier between your world and ours. It's the reason you're here." Incindia's eyes burned with intensity.

"The veil between worlds?" Rachel asked.

"The path of dreams some call it," Incindia clarified. "It's the portal through which dreams are seen. The same portal through which you have come here to us."

"So am I dreaming or am I really here?" A puzzled expression engulfed Rachel's face.

"I believe the answer to that question is both."

"Well, that's about as clear as mud," Rachel muttered.

"So," Incindia asked again, "how many times have you come to this world?"

"I don't know really," Rachel replied. She had a detailed record of her dreams now, so assuming that they were connected in some way, she gave Incindia her best guess. "Five or six times? Something like that anyway."

"Just as I suspected," Incindia said, looking up to the heavens then again at Rachel.

"Do you remember the darkness I told you about?" Incindia asked, perhaps trying to gauge what Rachel had learned about in her other dreams or visits to Calim.

"Sure, Torrens showed it to me once," Rachel said, remembering the dying forest shadowed by a dark sky covering the land.

"Look up," Incindia instructed, and Rachel obeyed. The sky was sunny with sparse clouds, but off in the distance she could see dark, blackened clouds, almost like storm clouds only much blacker, hovering in the sky. They were the same clouds Torrens had shown her, only now they were much, much closer.

"See the darkness over there?" Incindia asked, pointing her nose toward the dark sky.

"Yeah," Rachel replied, "looks like a storm is coming."

"It's much worse than a storm, Rachel. The darkness is slowly engulfing the planet."

"What will happen when it gets here?"

"It will block out all light in the sky. It will kill many of the plants and animals that live here, and it will bring with it unspeakable horrors."

The shadow wolves . . . Rachel remembered Incindia's warning about the Shadai. "Isn't there something you can do to stop it?"

"I'm not sure," Incindia said, pausing briefly in thought, "but we certainly won't stop trying to find a way. The fire-foxes won't go down without a fight and neither will the other species the darkness threatens to extinguish."

"How soon will the darkness be here?" Rachel asked, looking up once again at the sky. The blackened clouds didn't seem to be moving very fast, but the longer Rachel stared at them, the more she noticed a slight change coming over them. The clouds were definitely headed their way.

"We don't know," Incindia replied. "The growth doesn't really seem to be stable at all. What we do know is that so far, the darkness has only grown bigger, never smaller. It's only a matter of time . . ."

"A matter of time, unless . . ." Rachel corrected, "unless, of course, you find a way to stop it from growing larger or better yet, find a way to get rid of it entirely. I mean, there's got to be a way, right?"

"I believe there is," Incindia said before lifting a paw off the ground and licking it, fire sticking to her fireproof tongue for only a moment before fizzling out.

Her ear perked up suddenly, and she turned her head sharply to follow a sound inaudible to Rachel's ears but crystal clear in her own.

"We better get a move on," Incindia said as she began walking away from the direction of the silent noise.

"Where are we going?" Rachel asked as she followed, glancing back several times, wondering what it was that Incindia had heard.

"I want you to meet someone," was all that Incindia said before Rachel felt the familiar fading all around her that meant this dream was coming to a close.

"I'm sorry, Incindia—" was all she could get out before

her world faded, and she opened her eyes to find herself once again back home. She had wanted to tell Incindia what was happening, that the dream was coming to a close, but there just hadn't been enough time.

"Oh well," she sighed, "Incindia will find out soon enough that I'm not there anymore."

Was she crazy? She was talking to herself like it all had been real. Like Incindia was real. But dreams just aren't real, no matter what Incindia said. She grabbed her diary and added to it what she had learned about Calim and the darkness. She was still sort of foggy on what the Evarance was but she wrote down what she could before hauling herself out of bed to get ready for yet another day.

School would be starting soon. Only two more weeks to go before she'd be walking the hallways, trying to keep her eyes open during the more boring lessons, and attempting to avoid Ryan. He really wasn't a bad person, but he was still creepy, no matter how hard he tried to be nice to her. She wondered if he would be less creepy if he actually practiced good hygiene. Did he even realize just how gross it was to be around him sometimes? Maybe the poor guy didn't know any better.

Rachel went to the bathroom to brush her hair. In the mirror it looked flat and boring, no matter what she tried to do with it. She looked at her green eyes, her nose, her freckles, and her ears in the mirror. She was outright dull all over. She'd never look anything like Evalyn, whose bouncy rich-brown locks and ocean blue eyes could melt any boy's heart.

Rachel smiled at herself which, she thought, was not much of an improvement. Then she frowned as she looked over the rest of her scraggly body, too old and awkward for a child, yet still much too young to be a woman.

There was a knock on the bathroom door. To her surprise it wasn't Chris just trying to be obnoxious as usual; it was Evalyn.

"Rachel, are you almost done in there?" Evalyn said through the door.

Evalyn had been so busy spending time with her friends over the summer Rachel had scarcely seen her at all. The fact that she could now drive gave her all the more reason to spend her days away from home hanging out with friends and running errands for Mom and Dad.

"I need to take a shower and get ready to leave," Evalyn's sweet yet insistent voice pressed.

"Yeah, alright," Rachel replied, opening the door to Evalyn, slipping out past her. "It's all yours."

Rachel's tummy growled, prompting her to head down to the kitchen. As she went, she couldn't help but wonder if what Incindia had said was true. What if these dreams were real?

CHAPTER 3. KOBOLD CAPERS

Rachel wasn't the only one who was having strange dreams. A few days after Rachel's dreams began, Chris found himself waking up in a dark, cold place shortly after going to bed. The ground was covered in loose dirt, and the walls felt cold, rough, and hard. A faint glow emitted from torches down a long hallway.

After letting his eyes adjust to the low light, Chris could see the rocky ceiling and walls of what looked liked a cave. He walked down the tunnel cautiously and quietly until he noticed a faint hammering sound farther down. He could hear rocks shattering and falling to the ground in pieces with each stroke of a hammer that pounded away in a rhythmic pattern. As he walked forward, he came to a large, wooden, wheeled cart sitting on top of a kind of railroad track. The cart, which Chris recognized at once to be a mining cart, was overflowing with chunks of rock, crystal, and metal. He heard a long, low snarl coming from an adjacent corridor and ducked quickly behind the wooden cart so as not to be seen.

"Did you find it yet?" one voice grumbled.

Chris could hear two sets of footsteps stop right in front of the cart he was squatting behind. He also noticed a foul stench that reeked of wet, sweaty dog, only much, much worse.

"Not yet," the other gruff voice replied, "but I think we're getting close."

"We need to find it before the ceremony begins. Without the offering, the dragons can't assimilate, and you know how nasty Adamas can be. We don't want another massacre," the first creature snapped.

Chris tried to breathe as slowly and quietly as he could while listening hard to the two rough voices on the other side of the cart.

"Why do we work so hard for those dragons anyway?" the second creature growled. "We kobolds outnumber them a hundred to one or more." The creature, or kobold, as he called himself, spoke in a continuous series of growls. He reminded Chris of what a dog or a wolf or some other kind of canine would sound like if those types of animals could actually talk.

"Patience," the first kobold said, lowering his voice as if he were trying not to be overheard. "You know our numbers grow every day, but one dragon could easily kill hundreds of us. Their scaly armor is strong, made even stronger through the sweat and blood we pour into this neverending work."

"But if we all attacked at once—" the second kobold said almost defiantly.

"No!" the first kobold broke in, almost hushing the second as he spoke. "It would be nearly impossible to rally all the kobolds together without the dragons finding out. They have spies everywhere."

The kobolds stopped speaking for a moment, perhaps looking around to make sure no one was listening. Chris couldn't see them and dared not move. The kobolds continued talking even more softly than before.

"I have a plan, Kobir," the first kobold said darkly, sounding as though he was grinning with delight at himself.

"What is it?" the second kobold asked quietly but anxiously.

"You know Adamas, the dragon king?" the first kobold asked.

"Of course I do," Kobir replied.

"He's not like the other dragons, not made of metal, that is," the first kobold continued.

"Everyone knows that, Tarik. He's a *diamond* dragon, and a nasty one, too." Kobir growled. "So what?"

"So," Tarik continued, "I overheard the other dragons talking about him during the last ceremony. They seem to think Adamas can still assimilate with a piece of metal since he doesn't have a metal coat of armor yet."

"If that's true, why hasn't he assimilated already? It can only make him stronger, right?" Chris could hear by the tone of Kobir's voice that he was growing frustrated.

"Think, Kobir, think," Tarik snarled angrily. "He probably hasn't found the *right* metal yet. A dragon is only as powerful as the metal he assimilates with. And he only has one chance to do it."

There was that word *assimilate* again. Chris wasn't sure what it meant exactly, but he had a feeling joining in on the conversation to find out wouldn't be a very good idea.

"I know of a metal," Tarik went on, "so powerful and rare even the mighty Adamas couldn't turn it down. It is said to be the strongest metal on all of Calim. Only a fool would let it slip through his claws. And Adamas is no fool."

"If Adamas assimilated with a metal like that," Kobir squeaked in sheer terror at the thought, "it would create a monster. How could we become free then?"

"Quiet fool, quiet!" Tarik snapped, hushing Kobir who had been steadily talking louder as the conversation progressed. "The offering will be tainted with a poison dug from deep within this mine. I've been collecting it. Very soon I'll have more than enough to ensure the dragon king's demise. Of course, Adamas will expect the metal to make him stronger than any other dragon in existence. And it certainly would, if not for the poison."

"A poisoned offering?" Kobir's voice grew with excitement. "But what if the poison doesn't work?"

"It will," Tarik said confidently. "I've already tested it."

"So we offer a precious metal laced with poison to the king?"

"Exactly," mused Tarik. "The last laugh will be ours. Adamas will fall. And I want to be there when he does."

"But what about the other dragons?" Kobir said.

"We build an army."

"A kobold army? But you said —" Kobir grumbled.

"Not a kobold army!" Tarik snapped. "We need others to help us. The shadow wolves, for instance, have wanted this territory for some time. They may help us with the proper persuasion . . ." Tarik broke off speaking, seemingly distracted by something. He began sniffing the air heavily.

Chris could feel the cart move slightly as if the kobold were leaning over it in search of something.

"What is it?" Kobir asked, and he too began sniffing the air.

Before Tarik had a chance to answer, the sound of footsteps echoed from a nearby corridor.

"You two, over there!" a new, but equally gruff voice called out. "Back to work! The ceremony is nearly upon us. Can't have you two loafing about with an offering still to prepare."

The kobolds grabbed the cart Chris was hiding behind and began jiggling it ever so slightly on the track. Chris held his breath and braced himself.

"What do you think you're doing with that cart?" the third voice yelled across the room.

"We're clearing it out!" Tarik snarled. "Got a problem with that?"

"No time," the gruff voice came again, "we need more diggers. Both of you, down into the mines. *Now!*"

Tarik and Kobir reluctantly let go of the cart and staggered away. When Chris was certain the kobolds were out of earshot, he peeked his head up over the cart and for the first time saw what they looked like.

They were short, skinny, wolf-like creatures, probably only four feet tall, standing upright on two legs. They looked almost humanoid in their appearance, carrying pickaxes with their front paws, which had some surprising similarities to human hands, only with longer fingers and a lot more hair. Their snouts were long like a wolf's and their ears were very similar to a wolf's as well, only larger with a slight bend at the tips.

Their fur was brown and wiry, their tails long and slightly arced. They wore hooded, torn, dark-brown cloth tunics for shirts with rugged medium-brown sashes tied around their waists, holding their tunics together. They had no pants to cover their furry legs, but the tunics were long, draping down past their tails.

Although they were shorter than Chris, they looked downright dangerous holding their sharpened mining pickaxes while exposing their pointy canine teeth to speak with one another as they vanished down a distant corridor.

Chris normally enjoyed stirring up trouble whenever he could, but something about this place made him think that might not be such a good idea. He resolved to stay out of sight for as long as possible.

The coast was clear. Chris stood up all the way and stretched. He had hidden frozen behind the cart for so long his legs were aching with pain. "Man, that hurts!" he remarked, rubbing his thighs. "I wonder which way leads out . . ."

Looking over the mining cart, he saw a large cavern from which several mining tunnels branched out in different directions down unknown paths. The kobolds had vanished down a tunnel to the left, the same tunnel from which Chris could hear the pounding of pickaxes. He listened to the right side of the cavern, which lay quiet, and saw that the path down one of the corridors trailed upward. With any luck the path would keep going up until he found his way out of this strange place.

He began walking down the right-hand corridor, feeling the wall as he went while catching his balance here and there. The tunnel twisted slowly as it angled upward. "This is good," Chris said with a smile. "If this keeps up, I'll be outta here in no time!" But he had spoken too soon. In the tunnel ahead of him he heard footsteps and grumbling noises heading his way, and coming fast!

Frantically he looked around, spying a dark passageway off to the side that had no torches lining the walls, making it the perfect place to keep out of sight. He quickly ducked into the darkness, scooting far enough back to remain well hidden in the shadows.

Four kobolds hustled along, talking about dragons, metals, and mining. After the chattering had died down and the kobolds had disappeared, Chris heard heavy breathing behind him and felt hot, dry air circle up and around him. He turned slowly, almost robotically, and looked into the darkness.

Behind him stood the largest lizard he'd ever seen. Its body was smoky-brown, scaly, and about as big as a large dog. The lizard also had two large horns protruding from the back of its head, spines running down its back and tail, fat sharp claws on its feet, and what looked a little like enormous brown bat wings sticking out of its back.

"No way!" Chris breathed, his eyes widening in both amazement and shock as he stumbled back a few steps. "You're no lizard, you're a dragon!" His heart thumped hard in his chest as the dragon lifted its head, tilted it to the side, and looked at Chris coolly.

"Why are you here?" the dragon asked sharply, his tail whipping behind him in the darkness as it chipped off pieces of rock from the wall.

"I don't really know," Chris replied, taken aback. Sure, the kobolds had been talking about dragons, but Chris didn't think he'd actually see, let alone talk, to one.

"You don't belong here," the dragon snorted, squinting its beady eyes as it examined Chris.

"Obviously," Chris retorted, wondering if he wouldn't have been better off staying in the lit corridor with the kobolds as the dragon's face inched closer to him.

"If they find you," the dragon said sounding stern and cold, "they'll kill you."

"Who, the kobolds?" Chris asked, still uncertain whether this creature was a friend or foe.

"Kobolds, dragons, it doesn't matter. They don't tolerate *your* kind here."

Chris gulped hard. "If that's true, then why am I still alive? I mean, *you're* a dragon, aren't you?"

"I am . . ." the dragon said slowly, analyzing Chris. "In truth, I'm not supposed to be here, either."

Chris was relieved. At least he and the dragon had something in common. They both were somewhere they apparently shouldn't be. Maybe he could use that to his advantage and persuade the dragon to leave him alone. Or better yet, convince the dragon to help him find a way out of the mines.

"What's your name?" Chris asked, hoping to keep the dragon on semi-friendly terms.

"I don't have my true name yet," the dragon replied. "I'm only a youngling. But for now they call me Rucknar."

"Ruck," Chris nodded his head in approval, smiling, "I like that!"

Rucknar tilted his head again, this time in the other direction, and eyed Chris, squinting as if Chris was something very hard for him to read. "You're not like the other humans, are you?" Rucknar asked.

"Why aren't you supposed to be here, Ruck?" Chris asked, quickly changing subjects to try and keep the focus away from himself.

Rucknar didn't answer. Instead he began backing away from Chris and the lit tunnel, going deeper into the darkness. "More are coming. We need to move now," Rucknar said, turning away.

Was it wise to follow a dragon into a dark tunnel? Probably not, but Chris wasn't going to let that stop him.

"Can I trust you?" Chris asked, wondering if he could somehow expose a bit of the dragon's true intentions before following him into the dark unknown.

"No, not really," the dragon replied nonchalantly, continuing into the blackness. "It's your choice, but I would stay as far away from those kobolds as I could if I were you." Rucknar's voice echoed as he disappeared into the shadows.

Chris could hear the kobolds drawing closer. This wasn't a small group like the four kobolds that had passed by earlier. The sounds of rumbling feet traveling up the corridor sounded almost like a small army was marching his way, making Chris feel even more certain that following Rucknar was the right thing to do.

"Wait up, Ruck!" Chris called quietly down the tunnel, following the dragon into the dark.

The farther he walked, the more Chris's eyes adjusted to the darkness and the better he was able to see, or so he thought, until he realized the walls were actually glowing with a faint white light that was gradually getting brighter. Rucknar walked steadily ahead, paying no attention to the white lights dotting the walls. Chris, on the other hand, couldn't ignore them. As he looked closer at the walls, he discovered moth-like insects sitting on the rocky surface, glowing with light much like fireflies did, only whiter and brighter.

"Those are amazing," Chris said, staring in awe at the little winged insects. Their wings sparkled with light as the air in the tunnel became thick and humid with moisture.

"What are those things?" he asked Rucknar, brushing a few of them off of the wall and causing them to flutter away.

"Just some Luminary," Rucknar replied in an unimpressed tone, before he stopped and turned around to face Chris with a puzzled expression on his face. "You *do* know what Luminaries are, don't you?" Rucknar asked.

Chris just shrugged, shaking his head no. Was he

supposed to know what they were? Rucknar's puzzled expression changed from confusion into shock as he looked over this strange human.

"What about the Ai're or the Shadai?" Rucknar pressed.

"The what?" Chris asked. "Never heard of them."

"Are all humans this clueless?" Rucknar wondered aloud, shaking his head in disbelief. He'd heard about humans, but had never actually met one before Chris. Even so, Chris was absolutely nothing at all like the stories he'd been told by the elders.

"I'm not clueless, Ruck," Chris said a bit defensively.

"Rucknar!" the dragon corrected, growing agitated with Chris's insistence on saying his name wrong.

"Alright, Ruck, I get it," Chris said, completely missing the point. "I may not know what the lumi-whatevers are, but that doesn't mean I'm clueless. It just means I've got some things to learn still, that's all."

"Stupid human . . ." Rucknar hissed turning back around to continue down the tunnel. Chris pretended he hadn't heard that and followed down the path as well. Only this time he was trailing behind at what he considered to be a safer distance then before, seeing how Rucknar was becoming increasingly irritated. Walking, Chris watched as the dragon's tail now whipped regularly back and forth, chipping off rocks from each wall as it swung, scaring the nearby luminary moths in the process.

As they continued to walk through the tunnel in the cool glow of the moths, Chris could hear the sound of crashing water growing closer. Not much farther down, light also began flooding into the tunnel, no longer from the Luminary, but from sunlight shining through a cascading waterfall. The falls poured down right outside the mine, blocking both the view out and undoubtedly the view in, concealing the opening in the mountainside where Rucknar and Chris now stood.

The air directly behind the falls smelled clean and pure. It wasn't until he smelled the fresh air that Chris truly appreciated what clean air smelled like when compared with the awful stench of the mine, which reeked of sweaty kobolds. He grabbed his shirt, taking a whiff to see if that nasty smell had rubbed off onto him. Unfortunately, it had.

"Whew, those kobolds sure are potent!" Chris remarked, shaking the bottom of his shirt to try and air it out.

Rucknar didn't seem to notice or care how bad Chris smelled, but rather seemed distracted by something, acting almost as if Chris wasn't there at all.

"It's starting soon," Rucknar said anxiously as he walked down a path that led out from behind the waterfall.

"What's starting?" Chris asked, following behind into the warm rays of the sun. Rucknar wouldn't answer. The path continued downward just a short distance, opening up to a small grassy field, which surrounded a sizable pool at the base of the waterfall. The field was surrounded with beautiful woodlands, and the mountainside was covered in a mixture of tree and rock. The path leading back up to the mine was well concealed by the landscape and the waterfall.

Standing on the soft green grass at the base of the falls, Rucknar turned to Chris, looking over him one last time.

"Leave," Rucknar said sternly, "before one of the others finds you."

"That's it, then?" Chris asked, both a bit relieved he had made it safely out of the mine and surprised Rucknar was letting him go, just like that. Chris didn't want to leave

Rucknar yet. He wanted to know more about him. He also wanted to learn more about the other dragons and this unusual place.

Rucknar, perceiving Chris's thoughts, said again, this time more forcefully, "Go away, strange human. Go away, and don't even think about following me unless you want to die."

"Yeah, alright," Chris conceded, a little disappointed his time with Rucknar had been so short. "It was really cool meetin' you, Ruck. I hope I'll be able to see you again sometime."

"I don't," Rucknar snorted, scampering into the woods.

As Rucknar vanished out of sight, something shimmered on the ground, catching Chris's attention. He leaned over to look, picking up a thin, flat, hard piece of crystal colored a smoky-brown hue. It was a little rough to the touch as Chris rubbed it between his fingers, trying to figure out what it was. Then it dawned on him: He was holding a dragon scale, one that must have fallen off of Rucknar after the many whips of his tail against the rock wall of the kobold mine. He put the scale in the side pocket of his cargo pants before looking out once more at the mountain and the waterfall.

This was a truly beautiful place. The waterfall glistened in the sunlight as it poured into the most pure pool of water Chris had ever seen. Anyone who stumbled here by chance would never guess what lay just behind the falls, deep within the mountain. But Chris knew, and it was time for him to leave before some of those kobolds made their way out.

He turned and focused his attention instead toward the spot in the woods where Ruckar had scurried off.

"Should I?" Chris asked himself, a big grin spreading across his face as he began walking toward the dragon's invisible path.

And then, he was awake. Back in his room in bed with eyes wide open staring at the ceiling.

"That was weird," Chris said, looking around his room. It was all just a dream, but not just any dream. It had to have been one of the strangest and most real dreams he had ever had.

"That was freakin' awesome!" he shouted excitedly as he sat up in bed. He pulled off his shirt to get dressed for the day, and noticed it had a foul smell. Not quite as bad as the kobolds, but still pretty close.

"Phew," he said, briefly sniffing his shirt. "Definitely time for a shower."

As he stood up to make his way toward the bathroom, something fell next to him onto the floor. It was a flat piece of smoky-brown crystal, and as far as Chris could tell, it looked exactly like the dragon scale he found in the grass after Rucknar had run off into the woods.

"But that's impossible . . ." Chris gasped as he reached down to pick it up.

He turned it over several times in his hand. Looking at it, he wondered if this was just some sort of joke Rachel was playing on him. But how could it be? Rachel couldn't possibly know about his dream. It definitely looked like the same crystal scale, and it was rough to the touch, too, just like the scale in his dream. He mulled it over but couldn't come up with a logical explanation of how it had ended up in his pocket. It was so bizarre.

He set the crystal piece down on his desk, not quite certain what to make of it. One thing was for sure though, he needed a shower—and badly. The crystal would have to wait.

CHAPTER 4. SHADOWY NIGHTMARE

It had been nearly a week since Rachel started having incredible dreams about another world, a world filled with unusual animals and beautiful forests. She could scarcely concentrate on anything else. The smells of the trees and the flowers, the warmth of the firefox flames against her body — it all created images so vivid and vibrant in her head that she felt like she was truly alive for the first time in her life. Though crazy, the dream world seemed more real to her then the real world.

Rachel could hardly wait for her dreams to begin again that night. As she lay in bed, she looked thoughtfully down at the charm bracelet hanging from her wrist, thinking about Incindia and Torrens as she rubbed the little fire charm. She imagined with crystal clarity the dream world, her world, which Incindia had told her was really the world of a planet named Calim. She didn't have to imagine for very long because in no time she was fast asleep, back in her dreams. But this time the world looked *very* different.

There was no sun shining. The sky was dark, heavy, and thick with black clouds. Wind was blowing all around Rachel, whistling eerily as it whipped past, nipping at her sharply with a chilling sting. The trees were dead, or at least dying, strangled by what Rachel assumed was the lack of light.

Black vines crawled up the tree trunks like black leeches sucking the life out of what was once probably a very beautiful forest. The grass and foliage covering the forest floor lay discolored and mostly dead, although a few sparse plants still fought to live.

Where am I? Rachel thought, but the thought only tickled her mind for a moment. She already knew where she was, though she didn't want to admit it. She was underneath the shadow of darkness Incindia and Torrens had warned her about and pretty deep in as far as she could tell. There was no light visible in the sky, no matter which direction she faced.

She shivered, wrapping her arms tightly across her chest to fend off the cold. Could this be the home of the firefoxes? Was it already overtaken by the darkness? She couldn't tell.

Nothing looked familiar, although she doubted it would, even if this were a place she had dreamed about before. According to Incindia, the darkness would kill almost everything it touched, transforming the world with a deathly sickness, much like a plague sweeping across the land. Perhaps it was too late to save anyone or anything.

Rachel couldn't bear the thought of losing all those beautiful dreams so soon after having discovered them. And what about Torrens and Incindia? She hoped they had made it safely out of this awful place before it was too late. She walked on, hoping to find more signs of life in this dark, cold, creepy place.

A few miles away from her three shadow wolves were patrolling the woods.

"Have you picked up a scent yet?" one shadow wolf asked while running alongside a companion, his voice deep and a little slow. He was large, black, and especially hairy, with a thick coat of fur covering an overfed, hefty body that looked much more like an oversized wolf than a shadow. One of his ears, partially torn off in a fight, hung down the side of his head.

"Nothing yet," the other shadow wolf replied anxiously, taking an occasional whiff of the ground as he ran. His paws were only slightly smaller and his body much more ragged and slender.

"We had better find something soon," the larger shadow wolf snorted back. "Umbra's not exactly patient."

"No, he's not," the scraggly one agreed. "It'll be our hides if we don't find something soon."

The third shadow wolf caught up from behind with the other two. This one was neither overly large nor lanky. He was muscular and solid with a trim waist and wicked smile showing razor sharp canines. His eyes were cold and calculating. "I found something." The third shadow wolf grinned darkly as the other two other shadow wolves slowed down, flanking him on both sides while keeping stride with him.

"What is it, Trebax?" the large shadow wolf with the torn ear growled as they ran.

"It's not what you expect," Trebax said, his wicked grin widening as he lead the two other wolves to the location where the unusual scent still lingered.

"A female?" the skinny one asked, sniffing the air and then the ground.

"A human female," Trebax corrected, an evil hunger filling his inhuman eyes.

The large shadow wolf sniffed around as well, concluding, "It's a young one, too, only a child."

"Exactly!" Trebax agreed, greedily licking his lips. "This

job will be easy, but before we go catch our prey, scour the area for any other human scents. They often travel in packs, and we need to be sure she's alone."

On their leader's command, the two wire-haired shadow wolves bounded off to search the surrounding woods for other signs of human disturbance, surveying the area much like law enforcement would a crime scene.

Trebax, leaving his underlings to sniff out the scents of other humans that may be with the girl, instead honed in on her scent, walking cautiously in the direction it traveled. He dared not chase after her until he knew with certainty there was only one human they'd be dealing with. Curiously, the girl's scent zigzagged through the trees, on a few occasions circling back to where it came from before taking off in an entirely different direction. Was she intentionally trying to throw them off her trail? Trebax wondered.

It was only a few minutes before the other two shadow wolves bounded back into view to report.

"Drenar," Trebax said, facing the large black shadow wolf with the torn ear, "did you find any other human scents?"

"No," Drenar replied, grinning.

"Sanshir?" Trebax asked, now focusing his attention on the malnourished looking one.

"No other humans, just the girl." Sanshir cackled happily.

"Looks like we're going hunting," Trebax said with a hint of anxious delight resonating in his voice. He sprinted off into the forest with Drenar and Sanshir following closely behind.

Despite all her walking, Rachel felt like she was getting nowhere fast. It's not that she wasn't trying hard to find a way out of the dark woods, but her efforts seemed more and more useless the farther she walked. She had thought about crying out for help on the off chance Torrens or Incindia would be able to hear her, but she silenced the thought almost as quickly as it had come.

She couldn't imagine something as stunning as a firefox lurking around in a dark, creepy forest such as this one. Then again, she couldn't really imagine a firefox lurking anywhere at all. They were the type of creatures, in her mind at least, that stood proud and tall, blazing in a stunning fiery light. And there was no brilliant light like that shining anywhere in this bleak and dismal place.

There was also another thought that pricked at the back of Rachel's mind and kept her from calling out. That thought wasn't nearly as nice as the beautiful images of firefoxes dancing around in her head. No, if she really was beneath the shadow of darkness and Incindia was right about the sorts of things that lived here, Rachel knew better than to draw attention to herself.

The shadow wolves were much closer to Rachel now, flying through the darkness with stealth and ease. They came around a bend in hot pursuit of the girl who was intruding on their territory, their paws beating heavily on the ground as they ran, exploding into a chorus of howls signifying they were very close to closing in on their prey.

Rachel heard the howls echoing through the air. Her heart felt as though it had stopped beating in her chest, terror momentarily crippling her body. She knew what was making those harrowing sounds, and they were closing in *fast*. Her eyes widened. Seconds felt like minutes. She looked frantically around for anything, anything that could save her from what was headed her way.

Not far from where she stood was an overhanging brush of vines and dying flowers that looked as though it were rotting into a putrid mass. It was all she had. Willing her body to break free of its frozen state, she lunged, pummeling through the layer of thick vines before falling to her knees on the ground just behind them in a dark enclosed space no larger than her closet.

The stench of the flowers was almost unbearable, rotten and vile. It was worse than anything Rachel had ever smelled in her entire life, even worse than Ryan's breath. But she dared not move. No sooner did the vines stop swaying from her forceful intrusion then the outline of the shadow wolves came into view through the vines.

They were very close now. Rachel could hear their breathing and see their bodies inching her way as she peered out from behind the vines. There were three of them with pitch black, wiry hair and razor sharp teeth dripping with saliva. They sniffed the air, trying, no doubt, to catch a whiff of her scent. Rachel held her breath and froze perfectly still. Drenar, the biggest of the shadow wolves, came right up to the brush, his nose poking through the vines right near Rachel's shoes, sniffing hard.

He stopped sniffing a moment before quickly pulling his nose back out. Rachel began to panic. Her heart, which had stopped beating the first time she heard the shadow wolves howl, was now beating entirely too fast. She could feel the pounding in her chest, beating so loudly in her own head she felt certain they could hear it, too. He must have smelled her. What could she do? She was trapped with nowhere to go.

Drenar, standing right outside the rotting flowers, began to let out several loud and violent sneezes, putting his head to the ground while rubbing his nose with both paws, frantically trying to remove the foul odor of the putrid vine from his nostrils. The other two shadow wolves looked at him with disgust as he began rolling on the ground away from where Rachel hid, continuing to scrape his face with the pads of his feet.

"Sanshir!" Trabax barked, directing the overly skinny shadow wolf to continue scouring the area Drenar had unsuccessfully checked. As Sanshir made his way toward Rachel, sniffing the ground feverishly, something caught his attention. Drenar, who was no longer sneezing having successfully rolled far enough away from the irritating brush to regain control of his nose noticed it at the same time.

Rachel could smell it, too, even through the sewage-like stench that surrounded her. It smelled just like a campfire. Just like a . . . firefox!

"What's that?" Drenar asked slowly, sniffing the air.

"A firefox," Trebax snapped angrily, pacing the ground.

Sanshir sniffed the ground just outside Rachel's hiding spot a few more times before whimpering impatiently, "The girl's not here. Let's go get that firefox!"

Sniffing the air a couple more times, Trebax, the meanest looking shadow wolf in the group, agreed. "We'll pick up her scent again after we've dealt with the Fi'eri. She can't have gotten very far. Let's get ourselves a firefox!"

The three shadow wolves bounded away, off to pursue another prey. It was several minutes before Rachel felt like it was safe enough to move around. She lifted the sleeve of her hoodie, exposing her bracelet and the light of the little fire charm to get a better view of the tiny space she was holed up in, but just as she was about to stand, she could see the vines jiggling in front of her. Wiggling though the vines was a black nose similar to the shadow wolf Drenar's, only much, much smaller. A black muzzle popped though, followed by a black canine face and two ears that stood straight up.

Rachel doused the light of the bracelet with her sleeve and froze, holding her breath. But it was too late. She'd been seen.

"There you are!" said a young, carefree voice coming from the little creature's mouth.

It didn't sound at all like a shadow wolf. In fact, now that she looked at it, it didn't really look much like a shadow wolf, either, though the pitch-black fur was certainly unnerving. The animal climbed all the way into the small space, sitting down next to Rachel. It was small, much smaller than Torrens or Incindia, but had a definite foxlike appearance. Were there shadow foxes? Incindia had never mentioned anything like that to Rachel.

"A-are you a Shadai?" Rachel asked with a stutter, nervously looking down at it. Even if it was some sort of fox, Incindia had made it very clear that Shadai were bad news, and what could it be if not a Shadai?

Looking at her confused face, the furry black creature let out a laugh. "Of course I'm not a Shadai!" he said, grinning widely. "I'm a firefox. Name's Ember."

He took a paw and rubbed black ash off the tips of his ears, which ignited into a low, white flame, the familiar smell of campfire diminishing the potency of the awful vines. He brushed ash off his feet and tail tip as well, allowing them to glow with the same white light.

"Well, that totally makes you look more foxlike," Rachel said with a smile, feeling the calming warmth emanating from his body. "But you don't really look like a firefox," Rachel added, surveying his black body with white flames, "at least not any I've seen before."

"Yeah, I get that a lot," Ember said, grinning even wider, "and it confuses the snot out of those shadow wolves!"

"Shadow wolves!" Rachel said with a shiver. "I almost forgot. Do you think we're safe here?"

"We'll need to move soon, I think. I burned a trail that's bound to keep them busy for a little while, but they'll come back this way. Good thinking ducking behind these vines," Ember said, wrinkling his nose. "They're really potent! Just the thing to throw a shadow wolf off the hunt!"

"More like dumb luck," Rachel said with a sigh.

"Well, I'd take dumb luck over being caught by a shadow wolf any day," Ember said with a wink.

"Incindia, Torrens, where are they?" Rachel asked, remembering how worried she was about them. Since this little firefox had made it, maybe they had, too.

"They're fine," Ember said with a smile. "In fact, Incindia asked me to keep an eye out for you."

"She did?" Rachel asked, relieved to hear that both Incindia and Torrens were okay.

Ember didn't answer. Instead, he perked his ears straight up listening intently to something going on way off in the forest, too far away for Rachel to hear.

"They're coming back," he said, his carefree manner instantly disappearing. He took his paws and snuffed out the glowing white flames on his body with black ash. "Stay here! I'll try to lead them away again."

Rachel didn't want to be left all alone in this horrible place, but before she could protest, Ember had slipped through the vines and was gone. Her body felt cold again as the lingering warmth of Ember's body and the unmistakable scent of a smoky campfire dissolved, again leaving the unbearably terrible stench of the rotting flowers.

She heard the now familiar pounding of feet heading her way, and in no time the shadow wolves came into view.

"It went that way," Drenar said slowly, sniffing the air while pointing his nose in the direction Ember had run.

"You two go on ahead," Trebax said darkly, sniffing suspiciously at the ground. "I'll catch up."

"If you insist!" Sanshir howled with delight, eagerly running off into the woods, followed by Drenar. Rachel could tell they both had just one thing on their minds and that was to catch Ember. She hoped he'd be okay.

Trebax inhaled deeply, a wicked smile creeping across his face. He faced the putrid vines Rachel hid behind and took a few steps in her direction. Rachel felt a rush of panic wash over her body. He knew.

Trebax bent his head down low, staring into the vines as though he had X-ray vision. Rachel could feel that cold, hungry stare pierce right through her.

"Do you think I'm dumb, girl?" he asked, savoring the panic he knew he was instilling in her. "You may have been able to fool Sanshir and Drenar, but you cannot fool me," his voice was dark and resonant. "I know where you are," he said, taking another terrifying step closer, licking his lip, "and I know exactly what I'm going to do with you, little trespasser."

He bent his head even lower to the ground and began to growl viciously, the wicked smile replaced by a maddened, bloodthirsty look. Rachel was scared. She could feel wet pools of tears well up in the corners of her eyes. Was this the end?

"You're mine!" he yelled, violently crashing through the vines, his razor sharp fangs snapping right at her face as she screamed, waking up in a cold sweat on her bed shaking. *It was a dream. It was all just a dream.* The tears started pouring down her cheeks.

Moments later, her bedroom door flung open as her mother rushed to her bedside looking intently over her.

"Rachel, are you okay?" she asked, putting one hand on Rachel's shoulder while wiping Rachel's brow with the other. "I heard a scream."

"I'm fine," Rachel lied, still shaken, wiping away the tears with the back of her bracelet-free hand while keeping her other hand tucked under the blanket.

"You sure didn't sound fine," Mom said, sitting down on the bed next to her.

"I just had a bad dream," Rachel admitted sheepishly. As awful as the dream was, she didn't want her mom babying her, but at the same time, the sooner she let her mom know what happened, the sooner her mom would leave her alone.

"It sounded more like a nightmare to me," Mom replied.

"A nightmare then," Rachel agreed, trying to hide how upset she was still feeling inside. "But I'm okay now."

"Are you sure?" Mom asked.

"Yeah Mom, I'm fine, *really*."

"Do you want to talk to me about it?"

"No," Rachel insisted.

"Alright," Mom conceded, giving Rachel a hug before walking to her door. "You know I love you, right?"

"Mom . . ." Rachel groaned.

"Okay, I'll be going now. Try to get some more sleep if you can," Mom said, closing the door behind her as she went back to her own room.

But how could Rachel fall back asleep again after

something like that? She was too shaken. But even worse, she was afraid. Afraid of what would happen if the nightmare continued when she closed her eyes.

Morning couldn't come soon enough. And once it did, the day went by entirely too fast. Rachel didn't mention her nightmare to anyone else. She didn't feel like she could. What she experienced when she dreamed was so unbelievable and *real*, no one else could possibly understand what she was going through. So what was the point of trying to explain it to anyone?

As night approached, she didn't go to sleep right away. She couldn't. Instead, after the rest of the house lay quiet in the darkness of the night, she pulled out her diary, and despite not wanting to write what she had gone through the night before, she felt compelled to do so. She hoped that maybe writing down her fears would help her keep them under control, but it didn't. It just allowed her to relive the fear all over again.

She tucked the diary under her pillow and lay in bed listening to the stillness, trying to free her mind of the nightmares that consumed it. She tried to stay awake the entire night, but her body just wouldn't let her. Sleep came and with it, the ice-cold chill of the shadowy world she had left behind.

CHAPTER 5. ECHOES OF DREAMS

Evalyn didn't know about the dreams Rachel or Chris were having, but she also wasn't immune to them. As she lay her head down on her fluffed-up pillow in her tidy room, she slipped into a peaceful slumber. Soon she was in a field of flowers in the middle of a large valley surrounded by deep-green forests. Bright flashes of light darted across the brilliant blue sky, and a very short distance away, a village of small cottages lay next to a lovely pond dotted with cattails and covered in lily pads.

After making her way through the field to the village, she saw people busily wandering around a marketplace full of goods ranging from fresh fruits and vegetables to clothing and trinkets. The baked goods stand looked especially enticing with its desserts and sweet breads. A man behind the stand shouted loudly, "Fresh bread for sale!" as he proudly showed off his wares to the passersby.

Another stand was filled with beautiful flowers, which Evalyn stopped in front to admire. The flowers were artfully displayed in eye-catching arrangements that varied from simple to complex designs. A little farther down was a blacksmith's forge decorated in an assortment of swords, shields, and other masterfully detailed weaponry. Across from the forge was a stable housing several horses. It was as though she had stepped back into a time long ago, a time before cars, cellphones, and all the other modern conveniences to which Evalyn was accustomed.

As she watched, mesmerized by the bustling activity in the little village, she didn't notice the horse and rider galloping her way in the middle of the busy street. A woman carrying a basket of herbs rushed hurriedly past, making way for the horse and its rider, nearly knocking Evalyn over in the process. Evalyn dodged the woman just in time to avoid the impact, only to place herself squarely in the path of the horse, which was nearly upon her.

"Watch out!" a young man yelled, leaping between the horse and Evalyn and grabbing her arm to pull her away just in time. They both tumbled to the ground, landing hard on the edge of the dirt road.

"That one was *real*," he said, trying to catch his breath as he rolled off Evalyn and stood back up. Evalyn stared up at the stranger from where she lay, still a little bit dazed by the fall. He was tall and handsome, looking about 18 or 19, with light-brown, clean-cut hair and chocolate-brown eyes. He wore a white collared, loosely fitting long-sleeved shirt overlaid with a dark, olive-green waistcoat. His legs were covered in dark-brown pants with knee high brown leather boots.

"Are you all right?" he asked, reaching toward Evalyn, offering to help her up.

"I think so," Evalyn said, blushing a faint pink as she grabbed his hand and stood up, brushing the dust off her clothes then quickly combing her fingers through her hair.

"You really should be more careful," he scolded lightly but with a smile. "Wouldn't want something bad happening to a beautiful girl such as yourself."

Evalyn's face blushed even more as she smiled, half

embarrassed and half flattered by the handsome stranger who had just saved her life.

"I'm Kendrick, by the way."

"Oh, and I'm Evalyn," she said, casually twisting a lock of wavy brown hair around her finger and smiling back.

"Well, it's a pleasure meeting you, Evalyn," Kendrick said, bowing slightly.

"What did you mean when you said 'that one was *real*'?" she asked, looking down the road on which she had nearly been trampled.

"What I meant was that the man riding the horse wasn't an Echo."

"Not an echo?" Evalyn asked, the flesh colored tone finally returning to her cheeks. "What is an *Echo*?"

Kendrick's face, though still smiling, showed a hint of surprise at the question. "You don't know what an Echo is?"

"Well, sure, I guess," Evayln replied. "It's when someone yells something and what they yell gets repeated back to them. It has something to do with the way sound travels, doesn't it?"

Kendrick laughed. "That's true, but that's not the type of Echo I'm talking about."

"No?" Evalyn said, the blush in her cheeks returning again, more from embarrassment this time.

"Where are you from?" Kendrick probed, noticing for the first time her unusual attire.

"Well, not from around here," Evalyn said, glancing around at the beautiful little village. "This is a really pretty place," she added admiringly.

"They don't have Echoes where you come from?"

"I don't know," Evalyn replied. "You haven't told me what one is yet!"

"Oh, right," Kendrick said, rubbing the back of his neck. It was not something he'd ever really had to explain before. "Well, an Echo is like a reflection of a being from another world."

"Another world?" Evalyn asked. She'd certainly never heard of anything like that before.

Looking at the confused expression on Evalyn's face, he decided to take a different approach. "Mmm, maybe I should show you first," he said as he reached out toward her hand, gently taking hold of it. They walked over to a vegetable stand surrounded by a crowd of people filling their baskets with food. He pulled Evalyn straight into the crowd, walking *through* several people in a ghostlike manner before walking straight *through* the vegetable stand as if it weren't even there. When they came out on the other side, Evalyn's eyes became very wide.

"What just happened?" she asked nervously, letting go of Kendrick's hand.

"Those are Echoes," Kendrick said, grinning widely as he gestured one hand toward the vegetable stand still surrounded with people.

"But we just walked *through* them," Evalyn gasped, feeling a little sick to her stomach. Was this some sort of ghost town?

"It's like I said, they're not real, just reflections. In fact most of this market is just Echoes doing their thing."

Evalyn backed away a few steps from Kendrick and the mass of Echoes going about their business, only to accidently walk into another group of people at the neighboring stand, who, like the first group, were also nothing more than a ghost-like illusion. She could feel the blood drain from her face as she watched the people walk right through her body, carrying on with their shopping like she wasn't even there.

"Evalyn?" Kendrick asked, walking over to her, his grin fading to an expression of concern. "Are you alright? You don't look so good."

Evalyn only half heard him as she swooned, the lightheadedness washing down her body as she fell to the ground.

When she awoke she was in a house with wooden walls, a wooden floor, and an old fashioned fireplace with a cast-iron pot hanging inside it. She was in a bed she'd never seen before, and as she sat up to put her feet on the floor, a cool, damp cloth fell off her forehead and onto her lap. Where was she?

Next to the bed on a small plate were a roll and some fruit. And next to the plate, a clear glass of water had been placed on top of a note that read: *Please eat if you're feeling hungry. I'll be back soon. Kendrick*

Evalyn grabbed the roll and took a bite. It felt good going down into her empty stomach. Was this where Kendrick lived? It was a small home, but well kept, and the delicious aroma of some sort of soup or stew filled the air as the pot hanging in the fireplace simmered over a dying flame. Before Evalyn had the chance to get up and look around, the door swung open. It was Kendrick, carrying a handful of wood, which he promptly added to the fire.

"Feeling any better?" he asked, turning his attention to Evalyn as he sat down in a chair near the bed.

"I'm feeling much better," Evalyn blushed, vaguely remembering how she had fainted in the marketplace.

"That's good to hear," Kendrick said, smiling. "I was worried about you."

"You were?" Evalyn asked.

"Of course! Isn't it obvious?"

Evalyn picked up the damp cloth on her lap. She looked over again at the little plate of food and the note he had left for her, both making it clear to her that his concern was genuine.

"They're gone now," Kendrick said, changing the subject. "The market closed, and the Echoes have left."

"Are you sure those Echoes aren't actually ghosts?" Evalyn asked, still slightly unnerved by having watched them walk right through her.

"Sure I'm sure," Kendrick replied with confidence. "There's another one I want to show you. That is, of course, if you think you can handle it. They're not all that bad, once you understand them. But we have to hurry. I don't know how long this one will hang around."

Evalyn was feeling a bit better, and she did feel like she would be able to handle whatever it was that he wanted to show her.

She followed him out of the little house then back through the marketplace which now only had a sparse few remaining storefronts, including the blacksmith, stables and bakery stand. Those must have all been real and not Echoes. Leaving the village Kendrick continued on, walking next to Evalyn, leading her right back into the field of flowers where she had first found herself.

The sun was still bright, but hanging much lower on the horizon than before the marketplace fiasco. The air was warm with a gentle breeze. In the middle of the flowery clearing, she saw a young girl, maybe four or five years old, in a vibrant lilac dress with matching ribbons in her auburn hair, picking flowers into a bouquet. Kendrick stopped walking and watched the girl for a moment. Evalyn did the same.

After picking several flowers, still unaware of Evalyn and Kendrick's presence, the girl closed her eyes, letting the wind blow through her hair.

"She looks so happy," Evalyn remarked, watching the girl slowly breathe in and out as the wind gently caressed her skin.

Kendrick nodded. "She is. This field is her happy place. She visits here often."

The girl opened her eyes, but didn't look Evalyn's or Kendrick's way. Instead, she smiled widely, waving her hand at a woman Evalyn hadn't noticed before who was walking straight toward the little girl.

"Is she an Echo, too?" Evalyn asked, looking at the woman who was wearing a long, flowing dress and a wide-brimmed hat with flowers on it that matched the little girl's ribbons.

"Yes," Kendrick said solemnly, his demeanor overcome with a sort of reverence, "that's the little girl's mother."

"Can they hear us?" Evalyn asked, watching the mother walk up to the little girl who was beaming with excitement as she proudly showed off the lovely bouquet she had made.

"No, they can't hear us, and we can't hear them, either," he said. "Although sometimes I wish I could."

It was both sweet and strange, almost like watching a movie. These two beings in front of them were completely unaware they were being watched. It was as though they were living in their own little world, oblivious.

As Evalyn watched, she could see a large blanket materialize on the ground near the girl and woman. It was covered in a wonderful spread of picnic foods. There were fruits, cheeses, and crackers neatly set out in an artistic array.

There was also a pasta salad, what looked like a potato salad, and a green leaf salad next to neatly wrapped square packages with beautifully tied bows.

Evalyn watched with curiosity as the little girl handed the woman the flowers she had picked, which were also just a part of the elaborate illusion.

"Mommy, these are for you," the girl said, beaming happily at the woman.

"Why, aren't those just the loveliest flowers I've ever seen!" the woman replied excitedly, picking up the girl and spinning her around in a tight hug.

They both sat down on the blanket and began eating the food. As they did, Evalyn watched them fade away into a transparent nothingness, disappearing entirely, leaving her to stand alone next to Kendrick in an empty field of flowers.

"I thought you said we couldn't hear them," Evalyn remarked, knowing full well she had just heard what the mother and daughter had said to each other.

"I didn't hear anything," Kendrick said, looking toward Evalyn with a curious expression. "Did you?"

"I'm pretty sure I did," Evalyn said, second-guessing herself. Did she really hear the little girl and the woman or was her mind just playing tricks on her?

"What did they say?" Kendrick asked, a hint of excitement rising in his voice.

"Well, the girl said something about picking flowers for her mother, and her mother told her how beautiful they were or something like that," Evalyn responded clumsily, taken a bit off guard. Had she known she was going to be quizzed on the conversation she would have paid better attention.

"That's really amazing, Evalyn," he said, looking deeply

into her blue eyes, "that you could hear what they were saying. My whole life I've watched and wondered what sorts of things the Echoes talked about, and no one I've ever met before could hear them the way you just did."

Evalyn could feel her heart beat as the blood rushed again into her now rose-colored cheeks. Why did he have this effect on her? She averted her eyes from his gaze to regain control of her heart, which had begun beating faster. Seeing Evalyn become a bit flustered, Kendrick redirected his gaze as well, looking out over the beautiful field of flowers.

"They say the Echoes are really dreamers from another world. They are the reflection of people like you and me, and sometimes even animals, who travel here through their dreams to escape the realities of their own world for a little while. They come here to enjoy this world as a part of their dreams. Our village acts as a backdrop in which the Echoes play out the deepest and purest desires of their hearts."

He looked back at Evalyn to see if she was following what he was telling her. She glanced at him a moment, saying nothing, so he continued.

"That girl we just saw has come here for a couple of years now. She loves this field of flowers. She often comes to run and play here, and sometimes she brings others with her to be a part of her beautiful dreams. Like today, when we saw her mother here with her. Sometimes the Echoes that join her are other dreamers just like she is, sharing in her dreams. Other times, they're just illusions conjured up by her imagination to help her act out the dreams she's having. I don't know whether or not the woman was a true Echo or a dreamer from another world, or if she was just an imaginary part of the little girl's dream. But I know for a fact the girl is one of them, and we just got to be part of a very special moment for her."

Evalyn looked at Kendrick as he stared off into the distance, obviously deep in thought. *What is it about these things, these Echoes, that touched him the way they did?* She thought about the little girl and the mother. They both seemed so happy to spend time with each other. *Were the images she saw really just reflections of the imagination of a little girl sound asleep in a bed in some far off world? A girl whose deepest, purest desire, at least for today, was just to spend time with her mother going on a picnic?*

"So," Kendrick smiled, looking at Evalyn, whatever deep thoughts he had been thinking now momentarily set aside, "do you have Echoes where you're from?"

Evalyn had been so absorbed with what was happening around her, it almost felt strange for her to think about home. When she did it brought to mind more questions than answers. *Where was she? How did she get here? Where was her family? Are there Echoes where she came from?* She didn't know. She didn't think so, but just because she'd never seen them before didn't mean they didn't exist.

"No?" she answered, wavering in uncertainty. "I don't know. I've never seen anything like them before."

Kendrick nodded, saying nothing.

"My turn to ask a question now," Evalyn said. "What is this place? I mean, where are we exactly?" She knew she was in some sort of town or village, but that was about it.

"That was two questions," Kendrick grinned teasingly, "but I'll answer both. We're in my hometown, the village of Teran, just south of Maldin and east of the windlands. Our village is best known for the flowers and herbs we grow. We grind them up to make medicine and ointments for the neighboring cities."

Evalyn had never heard of any of those places before, and by the expression on her face, Kendrick knew it, too.

"How did you end up here in my village?" Kendrick asked.

Evalyn thought a moment, but the truth was she had no idea. The last thing she remembered doing before coming here was going to sleep.

Her jaw dropped. She was in a dream. This was all just some crazy dream about a handsome boy, which really wasn't all that unusual. Kendrick stood waiting in quiet anticipation for her answer.

"I-I think this is just a dream," Evalyn blurted out. "The last thing I remember before coming here was falling asleep on my bed."

Kendrick stared at Evalyn, his eyes wide with fascination.

"You're one of the dreamers?" he asked.

Evalyn almost didn't believe it herself. Everything seemed much too real to be a dream, but it just had to be. Nothing else made sense.

"Tell me," Kendrick pressed, "what's the name of the world you come from?"

By *world* Evalyn assumed he meant planet.

"Earth," Evalyn replied. The word sounded funny as it rolled off her tongue. She never would have thought she would one day be telling someone the name of her planet as a place of origin.

"This world is Calim," Kendrick said, confirming what they now had both suspected. Evalyn was one of the dreamers, visiting this unusual world through her dreams.

"There's one thing I don't get, though," Kendrick

continued, reaching for one of her hands, which he clasped gently as his eyes looked deeply into hers. Her hand tingled at the sensation of his soft skin touching hers.

"What's that?" she asked, her eyes focused on his, unable to break free.

"Isn't it obvious?" Kendrick replied with a smile that nearly melted her heart.

Evalyn began to blush again; she couldn't help it despite trying not to. "It's not obvious to me!"

Kendrick took her other hand into his and held both hands up between them, lacing his fingers in hers and squeezing slightly. "You're here, Evalyn. You're not an Echo, at least not like any I've seen. I can't figure out how you can physically be here when you're not from here. But somehow you are. You're here, and you're real."

Evalyn gently pulled her hands away from his, looking down toward the flowers swaying in a gentle breeze.

"This all feels real," she said, glancing up at him again, watching him as he leaned down to pick a white and red flower.

"It is real, Evalyn," he assured her, handing her the flower. The flower was breathtaking. It had a long thin stem, rich green leaves, and perfect white petals with tips dusted a deep red color that opened in a twisted, spiraling pattern. It had a delicate yet rich aroma that was unlike anything Evalyn had ever smelled before.

"What is it?" she asked, as she looked over the beautiful flower, breathing in the intoxicating scent.

"It's an andalyn," Kendrick said. "They're really rare."

Evalyn surveyed the field a moment looking for other flowers like the one she was holding, but she didn't see any.

"It's lovely," she remarked, trying to hand back the

precious flower.

"It's for you," Kendrick insisted, pushing Evalyn's hand gently back along with the flower. "Please, keep it."

He watched Evalyn with quiet anticipation on his face to see if she would accept the gift.

"Thanks," she smiled, twirling the flower stem between her fingers as she took another sniff.

"The andalyn is special because it communicates the feelings of the person who picked it. And so long as that person is alive, the flower will remain alive, too. If the person is happy, the flower will become more beautiful and fragrant in direct proportion to those feelings. If the person is upset or sad, the flower will wilt and darken. It changes colors, too, in response to those feelings."

"Sort of like a mood ring?" Evalyn asked, watching a puzzled expression come over Kendrick's face. "You know, a ring that changes color depending on the mood of the person wearing it. They sell tons of those in the mall at home, but if you ask me I don't think they work that well."

"I've never heard of anything like that before," Kendrick replied.

"You're not missing much." Now that she thought about it, a mood ring was a poor comparison with the exquisite flower she held. She looked at it in wonder. It was absolutely stunning. Was this how Kendrick was truly feeling inside? If so, it was clear just how lovely a person he was, both inside and out.

"So," she said, wanting to be certain she understood, "since you picked this flower for me . . ."

". . . it means it will show you how I feel," Kendrick smiled, finishing her sentence, his hair and clothing moving gently in the passing breeze as the sun began to set on the horizon.

"Andalyns are rare because they only grow in places where an Echo has experienced a life altering event while dreaming. An event so powerful, it continues to affect them even after they've woken up from their dreams and returned home. When this world leaves that strong an impression on the dreamer, the dreamer in return leaves their own sort of impression or echoprint on Calim, releasing a piece of their essence here to grow and flourish in the form of a flower. This flower has been growing and flourishing here ever since that little girl came to visit two years ago."

Evalyn looked down at the flower in her hand. According to Kendrick, it was a part of the little girl they saw, a part of her essence, her being. Why would he give her such a precious gift? He barely even knew her.

"How do the Echoes come here?" she asked, still trying to understand why and how she was there.

"They travel through something called the Evarance," Kendrick said, pointing at the sky, which had now faded into a dark blue as night approached.

"Is that a place?" Evalyn asked.

"No, more like a path," Kendrick replied. "It's a pathway that carries the dreamers from one world to another. And not just to this world, but as far as I've been taught, it can carry the dreamers to any world."

"How do you know so much about all of this?" Evalyn asked, looking at Kendrick as he observed the stars beginning to light up the night sky.

He turned his head back toward her, giving her his complete and undivided attention. "I learned about the Evarance and the Echoes from stories I heard as a child—though I'm not sure where the stories came from."

A cool chill began to fall over the field as the last traces of light finally faded from the horizon. Evalyn shivered slightly as she and Kendrick stood under the dazzling night sky.

"Are you cold?" he asked, watching her fold her arms to try to retain some of the warmth from her body.

"A little bit," she said, rubbing the sides of her arms with her hands.

"Let's get back to my place. It'll be a lot warmer than staying out here."

Evalyn nodded her head.

As they made their way back to his home, Evalyn could see people, no, Echoes, appearing in the field to gaze longingly at the stars.

"Echoes like to stargaze, too," Kendrick said with a wink, laughing lightly. His smile, his laugh—everything about him—warmed Evalyn's heart, even though her arms and face were still a little cold.

As he opened the door to his house to let Evalyn in, she felt a rush of warm air surround her body. Stepping inside, she closed her eyes a moment to soak in the heat of the fire. When she reopened them, she found herself back in her room, lying on her bed, an unusual flower clasped in one hand.

CHAPTER 6. THE CAMPOUT

Walking under the shadow of darkness, Rachel cried quietly to herself. Why did she have to return to this terrible place? Though she was safe for the moment and the shadow wolves were nowhere in sight, she knew it was only a matter of time before they found her again. After all, this was their territory. What would happen to her when they did find her? Surely Trebax would finish what he started. The fact that she had so narrowly escaped was nothing short of a miracle, one she felt certain must have only enraged him more, if that was even possible.

She wondered what happened to Ember. Did they catch him? Did they kill him? He had been brave trying to lead the Shadai away while she remained hidden, masked by the terrible smelling plants. He was so small, so young, probably only a kit, not yet fully grown or matured into a full-fledged firefox like Incindia or Torrens. Was he okay?

Rachel heard the rustle of dead leaves coming from somewhere behind a patch of trees encircled by black, leechlike vines that had drained the life out of the whole group, leaving them dull, lifeless, and brittle. She ducked behind another seemingly dead tree to hide until she was certain it was safe. The black vines on the tree pulsed and moved, visibly still sucking the life out of the tree while oozing black sludge down its bark.

She glanced around the trunk to see what it was that had made the unexpected noise. Her heart beat fast as she watched a black haired shadow wolf slowly walk into view, sniffing the ground and the air. It wasn't Trebax, Drenar, or Sanshir, but rather a female that was a bit smaller than the others, but solidly built. Although small by shadow wolf standards, she still stood at about the same height as a full-grown firefox. Lifting up her head she spied Rachel and began to growl with lips curled upward as she lowered her head.

Rachel ducked behind the tree, knowing that it would only deter the shadow wolf an extra moment at best. A howl pierced the air, no doubt signaling other shadow wolves in the vicinity. There was another rustle of leaves, this time coming behind her. She pressed her back against the gooey black vines on the tree sandwiched between the shadow wolf and the unknown creature making its way toward her.

As the shadow wolf rounded the trunk of the tree, aiming straight for Rachel, Ember leapt out from a cluster of bushes, landing between her and the startled shadow wolf.

"Run!" Ember yelled, white flames bursting from beneath an ashy covering on his ears, paws, and tail tip. His body crackled a slight gray-orange, like coals on a dying fire, not quite igniting into a flame.

Rachel obeyed. She ran, listening to the chorus of howls that gathered where Ember had stayed to protect her.

"Please be okay. Please be okay," she pleaded as she ran, hoping beyond hope that Ember would find a safe way out.

The howls grew louder behind her, and the pounding of feet became audible as the shadow wolves came into view. Rachel quickly thrust her body forward, but she was no match for their speed; in only moments they were at her heels. She reached her arms out in one last desperate attempt to grab onto some black vines, which draped low between two of the trees, with the hope that somehow she would be able to pull herself safely out of the shadow wolves' reach.

As she stretched out her hands to grab for the vines, she awoke, rolling off her bed onto the floor, still reaching out. Climbing back onto her bed, shaken, she saw the alarm clock blaring at her mockingly as it read 4:30 A.M. She had only slept for one hour, but as tired as she was, she was determined not to fall asleep again. She grabbed her diary and wrote, slipping it under her pillow when she was done. Then, waiting for the rest of the family to stir before making her way downstairs for breakfast, she got up and slipped on a pair of jeans, one of her nicer T-shirts, and a dark gray hoodie.

Today they were leaving to go on their annual camping trip. This was the last place Rachel wanted to go, but she didn't have a choice. Making her way down the stairs at about 5:30 A.M., she found Mom and Dad already awake, beginning to load up the car with camping gear.

Evalyn walked down the stairs twirling a beautiful white and red flower between her fingers, followed by Chris.

"Who's that from?" Chris asked, reaching to pluck one of the petals before Evalyn moved it out of his reach. "I don't know," she replied, gazing longingly at it. It looked an awful lot like the flower in her dreams, but that was impossible.

"Ooo . . . Eva's got a secret admirer," Chris teased, though Evalyn paid no attention. She walked over to the breakfast table where Rachel was seated, already devouring a bowl of cereal.

"Bad night?" Evalyn asked, noticing Rachel's ragged hair and overly tired face.

"You have no idea," Rachel grumbled, shoving another bite of cereal into her mouth.

While the kids ate breakfast, Dad and Mom continued busily loading the car. Since Dad wanted to make sure everyone got the most out of the family campout, leaving at the crack of dawn was a must. After eating, Chris helped Dad load a cooler into the back of the car, checking the last item off Dad's packing list.

After Evalyn finished eating, she went upstairs to put the flower she'd been fiddling with throughout breakfast into a vase on her nightstand. Then she made a quick stop in front of the bathroom mirror before strolling out to the car. She was as beautiful as ever, her long, dark locks bouncing lightly with each step. Even though Evalyn wasn't likely to meet anyone in the middle of the woods, it was obvious she had taken the time to get her hair and makeup just right for the trip.

Next to Evalyn, Rachel felt like a toad. She'd completely forgotten to brush her hair. Her clothes, although used, were still very nice thanks to Evalyn's good taste. But they didn't quite compliment Rachel's light hair and green eyes. Rachel's hoodie looked a bit more ragged than the rest of her clothes, but that's because it was one of the few pieces of clothing that wasn't a hand-me-down from Evalyn, and she wore it every chance she got. Before heading out to the car, Rachel grabbed a baseball cap from the coat closet and slid it on.

As Dad pushed the trunk door shut, Mom, Evalyn, Chris, and Rachel climbed into the car. Dad hurried over to the driver's side, and in no time they were on their way. The ride was quiet. Everyone was too tired from waking up so early to be very social, and Rachel was tired in general from barely having slept. Chris slouched against his window, dozing on and off. Occasionally he'd let out a loud snore, which Rachel corrected with a swift jab of her elbow.

Rachel was still very sleepy, but unlike Evalyn and Chris she couldn't take a nap, and the car ride was about as uneventful as watching paint peel. She couldn't stop thinking about the nightmares. She wished she'd brought some music to play to drown out the memories. But Dad forbade all electronics during the campout. Except, of course, the camera for taking pictures to capture the memories.

"This is our chance to get in touch with nature and spend some quality time together as a family," she remembered her dad lecturing. "No electronics. I mean it!"

It was bad enough that her dreams were now consumed by dark and terrible things, but to have her days consumed by them, too, was almost unbearable. No matter how hard she tried to block those images out of her mind the scenes kept playing back over and over again in agonizing detail.

She stared out her window pretending to be interested in the scenery. The trees lining the road looked black against the awakening sky as the car sped smoothly along the winding road. The sun was going to rise soon, the horizon already dancing with shades of blue, lavender, and pink as sunkissed clouds stretched across the sky. In a matter of minutes the sun would finally peek out over the horizon, dissolving all the darkness from the sky. Rachel wished she could dissolve all her nightmares as easily.

As the hours passed and they neared their destination, Dad decided to look for a rest stop for food and a bathroom break.

"Anyone hungry?" Dad's abnormally cheery voice called back as lunchtime approached, interrupting the dark thoughts that had lasted for just about the entire drive.

"I am," Evalyn called back.

"How about you, Christian?" Mom inquired. Rachel gave the snoozing Chris another sharp jab.

"Wha? Huh?" Chris popped back to life.

"Are you hungry yet?" Mom asked again.

"Totally!" Chris replied, grinning widely. "You know I won't turn down food!"

"How about you, Rachel honey?" Mom asked. Of course, Rachel knew no matter what she said, they'd be stopping to eat lunch, but she humored her mom by replying anyway.

"Sure, Mom." She tried to sound as normal as she could, despite her bad mood and tired body.

"It's settled then!" Dad said, pulling into the first drive-thru he could find.

The food was surprisingly good, and having something in her belly helped her perk up a bit. Maybe she would make it through another sleep-deprived day after all. At least that was the hope.

The sun was now out in full force as they pulled onto a gravel road that led deep into the woods. Rachel's uncle owned acres upon acres of woodland that he let the family use for their yearly campouts. The car turned off the gravel road and pulled into a clearing, which showed signs of prior use. There was a fire pit already dug out with wooden stumps around it forming some makeshift seating, perfect for sitting on while roasting marshmallows and telling ghost stories. There was also a level area designated for the tents.

"We're here!" Dad announced, looking back in the rearview mirror to see if anyone else was excited as he was, but, of course, no one was. "Chris, I'll need your help unloading the car. And sweetheart," Dad turned his head toward Mom, smiling, "if you and the girls could, I'd really like you to gather some firewood for tonight."

"Sure, honey," Mom said, smiling back. "Evalyn, Rachel . . ." Mom began, as Rachel broke in, "Yeah, yeah . . . we know."

"Well, let's get to it!" Dad said enthusiastically as everyone vacated the car. Chris popped the hatch on the trunk and began unloading all of the camping equipment with Dad. Rachel didn't like being in the forest, not after the nightmares. She reluctantly followed Evalyn and Mom into the surrounding woods but stayed unusually close to them as they gathered armfuls of wood.

"That should do it," Mom said, wiping her brow before picking up one last sizable stick to add to the pile in her arms. "Let's head back to camp and help Dad and Christian with those tents."

By the time they arrived back at the campsite, Dad and Chris had finished unloading the car. The tent bags were spaced out neatly on their designated spots, with Chris's tent already laying in pieces on the ground ready for assembly. Mom and Dad would be sharing one of the tents, with Evalyn and Rachel sharing the remaining one, much to Rachel's relief. She didn't want to be alone in a tent in the middle of the forest after nightfall.

"Well," said Evalyn, looking over at Rachel, "this tent's not going to build itself. We better get started."

"Alright," Rachel agreed as she knelt next to the tent bag Evalyn had already begun to unzip.

"I bet I can get my tent up way before you guys," Chris challenged.

"But you already have a head start," Rachel grumbled.

"Yes, but there's only one of me and two of you," Chris pointed out. "That evens things out, don't you think?"

"What do we get if we win?" Evalyn asked, pulling pieces of her's and Rachel's tent out of the bag.

"Hmm," Chris thought for a moment, "I know, how 'bout I gather all the firewood for ya tomorrow?"

"You're on!" Evalyn exclaimed.

"Hold up," Chris said, "what if I win?"

"Oh, you won't," Rachel butted in.

"But if I do?" Chris insisted.

"Oh, fine," Rachel replied, "we'll clean and debone all the stinky fish you and Dad catch."

"I'm good with that." Chris chuckled as he began working double time trying to get his tent up before Rachel and Evalyn put up theirs.

"*Rachel* . . ." Evalyn said in exasperation, "I hate deboning fish. Couldn't you have picked something else?"

"Don't worry," Rachel smiled, sorting tent pieces on the ground, "he's got nothing on us."

"Less talk, more work, fish girls," Chris teased as everyone frantically pieced together and staked their tents to the ground. Mom and Dad finished first, but they weren't part of the competition. Dad walked over and offered to help Chris with his tent, but Evalyn cried foul and Chris declined, saying he'd rather the girls smell like fish than get any help from Dad.

"Done!" Rachel and Evalyn shouted together as Chris worked feverishly to finish up his tent. He had always been much better at taking things apart than putting them together.

"Looks like you have some work to do tomorrow, firewood boy," Rachel mocked.

"No help from Mom or Dad tomorrow, either," Evalyn added.

"Yeah, yeah," Chris replied. "We'll see who can take down their tent the fastest when it's time to go home."

"You're on!" Rachel said, excited about another opportunity to cream her brother.

"Maybe," Evalyn corrected, not wanting to commit to any more challenges just yet.

The rest of the afternoon went by fairly quickly. Mom pulled out a book to read under the shade of a tree. Chris and Dad went fishing in the nearby stream, and Evalyn pulled out her nature journal, sketching everything she saw from birds to trees to squirrels. She had a real gift for drawing lifelike images of nature.

Rachel tried a little bit of everything, not because she wanted to, but mostly because she needed to do everything she possibly could to stay awake. She tried fishing for a bit with Chris and Dad but failed to catch a thing and was dying of boredom so she quit. She listened to the wind and the sounds of the woods, trying to imagine the firefoxes running through them to keep her thoughts away from less savory things. She sat by Evalyn and tried her hand at sketching, but her stick figure-like drawings were poor in comparison. She even tried to curl up with a good book, but her heart just wasn't in it.

After digging through her duffle bag, she pulled out a camera and began snapping photos, taking several shots of the campsite, Mom reading, Evalyn drawing, and Chris and Dad fishing. Eventually Mom took possession of the camera so she could get a few shots of Rachel helping Dad build the campfire in preparation for dinner. Once the fire was going, Rachel also helped Mom prep foil dinners to cook over the open flames.

Dinner was excellent, and as the day was drawing to a close, everyone sat around the campfire roasting marshmallows to make s'mores. S'mores were a family tradition the first night of camping each year, and Chris always made his especially gooey, sandwiching his chocolate between two sticky marshmallows instead of just the traditional one.

"I want you to know how much each of you mean to me," Dad said around the glow of the dying campfire. "This has been a fantastic day, and we couldn't have asked for better weather."

"It's been great," Mom chimed in, smiling at her children. "There's something very special about spending time out here together as a family. I know your dad and I aren't home very much these days, but we both want you to know that we love you very much, and we're proud of the young man and women you're becoming."

Evalyn, Chris, and Rachel all just sat in silence. It was embarrassing when Mom and Dad turned sappy on them. Rachel was pretty sure they just felt obligated to say mushy things once a year as some kind of morale booster to make up for being gone all the time.

"Alrighty," Chris said, breaking the awkward silence, "I'm beat. Bedtime for me."

"Same goes for me," Evalyn said, standing up. "'Night, Mom. 'Night Dad."

Rachel didn't want to be stuck alone with Mom and Dad so she promptly said goodnight as well and followed Evalyn back to their tent. The sleeping bags were already set up, although Rachel still had no desire to sleep. She squeezed into her sleeping bag, keeping her hoodie on for extra warmth since the nights were colder out there. She lay still on her side of the tent, trying not to bother Evalyn too much. She was tired, beyond exhaustion, but remained determined not to fall asleep. Her eyes burned as she struggled to keep them open.

She listened as the crickets chirped outside in the darkness. She could hear the sounds of nocturnal wildlife waking up all around. An owl's hoot echoed through the night sky, and there were scurrying noises and the snapping of twigs as unseen animals went about their nightly routine.

Hours passed. Her resolve to stay awake began to falter. She rolled over toward Evalyn who was still sound asleep and sighed. She wished she could fall asleep, too. The tent was still cool, but hints of soft, morning light began peeking through the zipper, lighting the walls with a pale hue. Dew still clung to the outside of the tent, and although Rachel was bundled up nice and snug in her sleeping bag, her body felt numb and cold with fear. The dread of falling asleep was the only thing left for her to cling to, but her eyes began to droop uncontrollably.

She stared at the walls of the tent, watching the pale light slowly intensifying through the blue vinyl lining as a few dewdrops dripped down the outer walls. Suddenly she heard a ruckus outside that sounded like something was rolling around on the ground not very far from where she lay. Sitting up, she reached her arm out from under her sleeping bag to the flap of fabric covering the tent window. Her hand shaking a little from over-exhaustion, she lifted the fabric just enough to peek outside.

At first she didn't see anything, but as her eyes focused in the direction of the noise, she caught a glimpse of something black no more than a stone's throw away, making her heart jump. She looked a moment longer, thinking it was a black wolf cub, when she saw a flash of its white-tipped, bushy tail. She knew instantly it was some type of fox. Its body was completely black, except for the white on its tail, but it definitely had a fox-like appearance, which eased Rachel's mind. It stopped moving and froze in place, lifting only its head as it stared directly at her through the tiny mesh tent window.

The fox kit lowered its head while keeping its eyes focused on Rachel as it began slowly creeping toward the tent, one foot in front of the other, walking silently until it came right up to where she sat, only an arm's reach away. Then it did something Rachel had never seen a normal fox do before. It motioned its head to the side, stopped to look at Rachel, and then motioned its head again and again, looking into her eyes through the mesh window after each swing of its head.

I think it wants me to follow it. The fox kit looked insistent, almost anxious. She felt certain this little fox was trying to communicate with her, but she had no idea why. It scratched at the side of the tent and whimpered, compelling Rachel to go out to see what it wanted, even though that went against everything she'd been taught about keeping a safe distance from wildlife. Maybe lack of sleep was beginning to affect her judgment.

She pulled her hand away from the window, letting the flap fall back down into place as she sleepily crawled out of her sleeping bag. Pulling fresh clothes out of her duffle, she slid on a clean pair jeans and a T-shirt before putting her hoodie back on. Evalyn stirred only a moment, then fell back into a deep slumber as Rachel crept out of the tent, stealthily zippering it closed behind her, before turning toward the fox kit that was still waiting.

The sun was still very low on the horizon, the grass wet with morning dew. Rachel stood outside of her tent and feeling a bit silly whispered to the kit, "Alright, you got me out. Now what?"

The kit motioned its head one more time and turned its body in the same direction, looking back at Rachel to see what she'd do.

"You actually understood that?" she gasped, so dizzy with fatigue she wasn't entirely certain the whole thing was not just some strange hallucination.

The fox just stared and waited.

"I must be going crazy," Rachel muttered, stepping toward the little fox, which began walking into the woods away from the campsite. She didn't want to stray too far, so as they walked she kept an eye on the tents, making sure they stayed in view.

"I hope we're close to what you want to show me," she told the little fox kit, "because I can't go much farther." The tents, though still visible, were shrinking from view, and Rachel had begun to stumble as her last few ounces of energy were nearly spent. Her eyes had become watery and her head heavy, filled with a sleep-deprived fog that made everything around her difficult to see.

They entered a muddy clearing where the fox kit finally stopped. It picked up a stick and began scratching something sloppily into the mud. This whole thing was becoming so bizarre, Rachel was beginning to wonder if any of it was really happening, or if this all wasn't just part of her imagination. When the fox kit had finished, it sat on the ground facing Rachel, waiting for her to see what it drew. Fading fast, Rachel strained her eyes to read words now written on the ground. There were only two, they read: *Danger* and *Run!*

But it was too late. She fell to her knees, overwhelmed by the intoxicating sensation of sleep that rushed over her body as she collapsed to the ground, splashing the side of her face into the mud and erasing the words etched in it as her body fell limply over them.

A moment later, she felt a renewal of her strength and pushed her body up off the ground. There was no more mud underneath her and the sky above was dark, completely overcast by a thick layer of black, threatening clouds. The air whipped around violently, forcing Rachel to hold her hair back tightly with her hands so it wouldn't sting her face and eyes. She squinted into the distance. North, South, East, West—it didn't really matter what direction she turned—everything looked exactly the same: dark, bleak, and dying. The sky loomed menacingly overhead; the clouds looked as though they were ready to burst at any moment into a torrential downpour, soaking Rachel to the bone but no drops fell.

The wind whistled and howled in an unsteady melody, causing Rachel's heart to beat stronger than was natural. Thunder roared through the sky as tiny branches broke and fell from the trees around her, twisting and turning, trapped in the wind's invisible grasp. Rachel knew where she was. She was back inside the nightmare that had been haunting her.

Off in the distance Rachel heard sounds even more deafening and chilling than that of the wind. Her heart began beating in a wild frenzy as panic flooded her body and tears leaked from the corners of her eyes. Frozen with fear, she couldn't will herself to move. Then she remembered the words that were written on the muddy ground the fox kit had brought her to. *Danger! Run!*

By some miracle, her body seemed to take over in an instinctive flight response, propelling her through the woods, away from the howls and growls, the snarls and snaps, the heartwrenching song of the shadow wolves on the hunt. Rachel knew who they were hunting. There was only one person who didn't belong in this strange world of her dreams. Only one person trespassing in their territory who had consistently slipped out of their grasp. They wanted Rachel, and she knew they wouldn't stop the hunt until they got what they wanted.

Rachel knew that very soon their hunt would end. It was only a matter of time before her luck would run out as each nightmare brought her closer to her ultimate fate. She shuddered at the thought of death. The howls were growing increasingly louder. Her lungs burned, and her legs ached. She knew she couldn't outrun them, but she had to try.

Running at full force through the trees, Rachel looked behind to see if the shadow wolves were in view, not noticing the drop just a few strides ahead. She turned her head forward, but it was too late. Her foot stepped off the edge into nothingness as her body, now airborne, came crashing down on a steep slope. She rolled and tumbled down a good distance, before landing with a thud onto her back.

Her head throbbed, and a small bead of blood dripped down her forehead. She opened her mouth for air, but her lungs wouldn't inhale. The force of the fall knocked the wind right out of her chest, causing a few excruciating moments of panic before her breathing resumed. Her body ached, and her head spun dizzily as she tried to make out the blur of trees overhead.

Dazed and confused, she lay on the ground until she heard the rumbling of paws headed her way. Her pursuers were close, much too close, howling with feverish delight. Rachel moaned, heaving her body back onto its feet, steadying herself with her hands, still slightly disoriented from the fall. She had landed on the bank of a wide, deep river that roared violently past.

A bloodcurdling snarl pierced the air, followed by a long, low growl coming from the ledge from which she had just haphazardly tumbled. She recognized the shadow wolf at once. It was Trebax, his sharp teeth gleaning as his lips curled up around the corners of his mouth, forming the wicked smile Rachel had come to loathe.

"You have nowhere left to run, little girl." His tone was gruff yet playful, like that of a cat toying with a mouse before the kill. His smile widened, allowing saliva to drip freely down his jaw.

Rachel's eyes flickered to the side, trying to spy the river without moving her head. Trebax, noticing, chuckled at her feeble attempt to find an escape.

"You can't get away!" he yelled to Rachel, licking his lips in anticipation. "Although I have to admit," he paused, a hungry look in his eyes, "it would be fun to watch you try."

The other shadow wolves gathered on the ledge next to him. There was Drenar, the overly large shadow wolf with the torn ear to his left, and Sanshir, the bony looking one on his right. A forth shadow wolf appeared on the ledge, a female shadow wolf slightly separated from the group, though not by much. This one Rachel had seen before but did not know her name. She had been blocked by Ember during the last nightmare Rachel had endured and was somewhat shorter than the other shadow wolves, with a solid build and a fit physique.

Lightning flashed in the sky behind them, followed by a deluge of rain that pounded down through the trees, soaking the ground and everything in between. They howled, charging down the slippery wet slope through the pouring rain toward Rachel, Trebax in the lead with the shorter one trailing closely behind. Drenar and Sanshir, a little more slowly, brought up the rear.

"Stay back, Vesper!" Trebax snapped angrily at the short shadow wolf who had nearly caught up. "This girl is mine!"

The river was her only hope. Rachel didn't know if she'd survive, but she had no other choice. She turned and pushed off the ground as hard as she could, her feet fumbling only slightly on the wet grass before she gained enough traction to lunge toward the river. Off the rocky bank she flew, plunging into the ice-cold water, becoming instantly submerged by the rush of the raging rapids.

The current pulled hard on her body as she struggled toward the surface for air, but before she could lift her head above the water, a large black figure plunged in after her, pushing her further down into the watery depths. It snapped at her hand as she reached toward the water's surface, and missing, caught hold of the coveted charm bracelet floating around her wrist instead.

Rachel's lungs screamed for oxygen. She thrashed frantically under the water, kicking away from the shadow wolf with all the strength she had left until the bracelet popped clean off her wet hand. Her head broke through the water into the air as she gasped for breath, pulling in a lung-full of oxygen, before getting dragged down under the watery swells again.

Tumbling through the rapids, fighting frantically for air, she could feel her life slipping away into darkness.

And then everything went black.

CHAPTER 7. MISSING

Evalyn woke up slowly, bathed in light shining through the walls of her tent. She yawned and squeezed her way out of her sleeping bag, turning and stretching as she reached out toward Rachel's bag.

"Rachel, time to get up," Evalyn said, rubbing her eyes. "It smells like Dad's already started cooking breakfast. Rachel?"

She tugged Rachel's sleeping bag before realizing it was empty.

"You could have woken me up. Seriously!" Evalyn muttered to herself as she pulled clothes out of her suitcase.

Outside, Dad had already started a campfire and was cooking eggs in a cast iron frying pan.

"Morning, sunshine," Dad said, smiling widely at Evalyn as she emerged from her tent. He prodded the eggs a few times with the spatula. "Is Rachel getting up, too?"

Evalyn was taken aback. "Rachel isn't in bed, Dad. She must have woken up before me. Maybe Mom or Chris has seen her?"

"I'm pretty sure Chris hasn't seen her," Dad said as he looked over at Chris's tent. "I can hear his snoring from here. Unless of course a bear got him in the middle of the night and fell asleep in his place." Dad chuckled heartily.

"Dad, you're terrible!" Evalyn laughed. "Besides, I'm

pretty sure Chris's snoring has scared away all the bears within a ten-mile radius."

"Probably true," Dad agreed. "Bears running for their lives." Evalyn giggled.

"So where's Mom?" Evalyn asked.

"Mom had to *relieve* herself, if you know what I mean. She's probably behind one of the trees out there," Dad replied, making a gesture with his spatula toward the surrounding woods.

"Aww, gross, Dad! TMI!" Evalyn scowled.

"Hey, you're the one who asked," Dad grinned, savoring the opportunity to gross out his teenage daughter. "Just wait until you have kids. There are a lot grosser things than taking a bathroom break. Trust me."

Evalyn groaned.

"Speaking of bodily functions . . ." Dad went on as if this were the most natural conversation in the whole world. ". . . are you hungry? Eggs are done." Dad scraped the eggs off the pan and plopped them onto a nearby plate.

"Starving!" Evalyn replied, overjoyed by the change of subject.

Dad cracked a few more eggs into the pan and began another ritual of shaking, poking, and prodding. Evalyn sat down on one of the campfire logs and began eating. The food was as delicious as it smelled. It wasn't long before Mom strolled back into the campsite, smiling.

"Mmm. Something smells good," Mom said, walking over to Dad and rubbing his back as she looked into the pan.

"Just in time," Dad said, smiling at Mom. "If you could just grab a plate, I believe these eggs have your name on them."

Evalyn watched, only slightly embarrassed, as her mom

gave her dad a thank-you kiss. In truth, she was a little envious of her parents and hoped someday she could meet a boy that she loved as much as her parents seemed to love each other.

"Oh, I almost forgot," Dad said, straightening his glasses before addressing Mom, who had already begun eating. "Have you seen Rachel yet this morning? Evalyn said she wasn't in the tent when she woke up."

"Rachel wasn't in the tent?" Mom asked with alarm. "I've been up for over an hour, and I haven't seen or heard her." Mom's usually pleasant face changed, a look of worry sweeping across it.

"*Rachel!*" Mom yelled, the words echoing through the woods. "*Rachel, honey, where are you?*"

Everyone froze in silence, waiting for a reply, but the forest remained still.

"*Rachel?*" Dad's voice called out, also echoing through the eerily quiet. "*Can you hear me?*"

Again everyone listened in quiet anticipation, but still there was no reply.

Mom turned to Dad, her worried expression growing quickly into panic. "It's not like Rachel to wander off—"

"No, that's not like Rachel at all," Dad agreed as he turned toward Evalyn. "Evalyn? Go wake up your brother. Hurry!"

Evalyn didn't have to be asked twice. She sprinted over to Chris's tent and ripped up the zipper as fast as she could, flooding light into the tent.

"Ahhh, it burns!" Chris hissed grumpily, throwing the pillow over his head to block out the light.

"Not now, you idiot!" Evalyn snapped, tearing the pillow off him. "Mom and Dad said get up now! Rachel's missing!"

Chris sat straight up in his sleeping bag, rubbing his eyes. "Wait, Rachel's what?"

"*She's gone! Missing!*" Evalyn yelled in agitation, throwing the pillow back at him. "Get dressed! I'm going to help Mom and Dad look for her!" With that, Evalyn stormed away from the tent and followed the sounds of her parents' increasingly frantic shouts.

"*Rachel, honey!*" Mom bellowed.

"*Rachel!*" Dad called, over and over again, that was until he saw Evalyn approach.

"Evalyn," Mom said, her voice shaking, "come help us look for her."

"Where's Chris?" Dad asked, looking around.

"He'll be here in a minute," she replied, "he's throwing some clothes on."

"I see," Dad said, calmly trying to mask any fears he might be feeling. "Well, we don't need anyone else to go missing. Evalyn you go with your Mom and search the south side of camp. I'll wait for Chris, and we'll take the north side." Dad's voice trailed off, his worried face giving away his otherwise calm demeanor. "Oh, and take this." He handed Evalyn a two-way radio. "Not much cell phone reception out here. Keep it on channel three, and let me know if you find anything."

"Okay," Evalyn said, grasping the radio securely in her hand.

"Sweetheart?" Mom inquired, grabbing Dad's hand in hers, her eyes telling him all the unspoken fears she couldn't vocalize.

"We'll find her," he replied in the most confident voice he could muster, giving Mom's hand a tight squeeze. "Now go, quickly. I'll head over to get Chris."

Evalyn and her mom walked, yelling and calling out Rachel's name over and over. They could hear Chris and Dad doing the same from a ways off. The forest was bright but fairly dense, so they had to walk slowly and carefully, making sure not to look over the same area twice.

The search didn't take very long. Evalyn and Mom stopped to listen to the crackly voice of Chris over the radio. "Eva, we found her . . ."

Evalyn held the button down on the radio and asked, "Where is she? What happened?"

But before Chris had a chance to respond, Mom snatched the radio out of Evalyn's hands. "Chris, it's Mom, can you put Rachel on the radio, please?"

They waited for a reply.

"I can't, Mom," Chris's voice shook a bit over the static. "She's . . . unconscious."

Mom, shaking, began to run to where her husband and son were, leaving the radio on Receive as Evalyn followed closely behind.

"We found her behind a few trees lying in a pile of mud just outside of camp." Chris's static voice continued. "We need to get her to a hospital. Meet us back at camp."

When they both arrived back at camp Dad was cradling Rachel in his arms like an oversized baby. Her skin was pale, and her body, partially caked in mud, hung limp and lifeless in his arms. Chris was already unlocking the car and opening the doors when Mom ran over to Rachel, gently lifting her head to look for any signs of life. "Rachel . . . Rachel?" Her eyes teared. "Dear God," she pleaded, closing her eyes, "please bring my baby back to me."

The ride to the hospital took an eternity even though

they were speeding down the road as fast as the car would go. Rachel lay heavily across Evalyn's and Chris' laps as they held her still through the winding turns. Mom called ahead to the hospital as soon as the cell phone found a signal.

The emergency personnel were waiting with a stretcher the moment the car pulled up. They lifted Rachel off of Chris's and Evalyn's laps and whisked her away, Mom running inside after them. Dad parked the car and walked hurriedly into the emergency room with Chris and Evalyn following behind. They were told to sit down and wait . . . and wait . . . and wait . . . as the doctors worked frantically to revive Rachel. Mom was too concentrated on the closed admitting doors to speak with the lady asking for assistance with some paperwork, so Dad sat down with her instead.

No one felt like talking. They sat in silence, watching as people came and went. Still no word from the doctors about how Rachel was doing. Finally, as Dad walked up to the desk for the twentieth time to find out what was going on, a doctor walked out to meet him and invited the family back to see her.

Following the doctor, the family walked into one of the back rooms to see Rachel. She was still unconscious, hooked up to a series of monitors. The doctors had run several scans and tests, but were unable pinpoint the cause of her coma and were unsuccessful at trying to wake her.

They did note, however, that they found a little extra fluid in her lungs, which seemed a bit unusual, and also pointed out several bruises on her body that they suspected were a result of her fall to the muddy, rocky ground where she was found. Aside from the minor bumps and bruises, there were no significant signs of injury that could have caused her current state. As far as the doctors could tell, the only thing truly wrong with Rachel was the fact that they couldn't wake her up.

"I'm so sorry," the doctor said, "everything looks fine medically. The only thing we can do for her now is make her comfortable and wait for her to wake up."

"She looks like she's asleep," Mom said, choking up a bit, gently brushing the side of Rachel's face.

"Some comas can be like a deep sleep," the doctor said, looking down at Rachel's medical chart. "There's definitely still brain activity. She's breathing on her own. Medically we've done everything we can. Aside from keeping her well nourished and safe, all we can do is wait."

Mom began sobbing, cradling Rachel's face in her hand, the doctor reassuring her again that since there was no apparent brain damage, the chance of her coming around was much higher for her than for other coma patients. Mom gently kissed Rachel's cheek and then took hold of her hand. The doctor's words were of little comfort.

Rachel was moved to a more permanent room where everyone sat and waited for her to come to. The nurses were kind and offered drinks and snacks to the family, but the only one who took them up on the offer was Chris.

Looking at her little sister, Evalyn couldn't believe how pale and still Rachel was. She was beginning to feel guilty for not waking up when Rachel had. No one knew how Rachel had ended up on the forest floor, but Evalyn felt certain that somehow she could have prevented it from happening if she had only been there with Rachel. But then again, how could she have known? How could anyone have known? Both Mom and Dad told Evalyn not to beat herself up. But Evalyn couldn't help but wonder if somehow she could have made a difference.

Mom wouldn't rest. She just sat, holding Rachel's hand, hoping and praying she would wake up. She talked to Rachel, telling her that everything was going to be okay, asking her just to wake up, to come home from wherever her mind had trapped her. Rachel continued to lay still, silent and unresponsive, but Mom refused to give up hope.

When night arrived, a nurse came in to ask the family to leave until visiting hours the next morning. Mom pleaded with the nurse until she finally agreed to let her stay the night. Evalyn, Chris, and Dad, however, had to go and find another place to stay until morning.

"Sweetheart," Dad said, putting his arm around Mom's shoulder, his face tired and sad, his voice cracking in exhaustion, "you've got to get some sleep tonight."

Mom leaned her head into his chest, equally exhausted, asking him and the children to do the same. Evalyn and Chris didn't want to leave, but the nurse shooed them out. Dad drove them back to the campground with the hope that the morning would bring good news about Rachel.

No one slept well. Mom did not sleep at all.

Morning at the hospital brought no change in Rachel's status and discussions arose about how long to wait before transferring her to a hospital closer to home. Mom dozed only a little during the day, and only when Dad took her place watching over Rachel.

After several days of waiting and watching, Evalyn and Chris finally helped Dad pack up the camping gear. Mom would stay with Rachel until she was transferred as Dad made the long, lonely trip home with Chris and Evalyn.

CHAPTER 8. TRAPPED

Rachel's whole body was sore, her head throbbing painfully. She was surrounded by darkness, as if sucked into a black void. She couldn't see, but she could hear, and the words she heard chilled her to the very core.

"Rachel!" her mother's terrified voice pierced the darkness. "Rachel, honey, can you hear me?"

"Mom!" Rachel yelled back, startled by the panicked cries. "I'm here! I'm right here!"

But those words never reached her mother. Rachel could hear Mom sobbing even though she couldn't see her. The torment in her mother's voice was gut wrenching.

"Please come home. Please wake up!" Mom's pained words echoed. "We need you, sweetheart. I need you! Don't leave us!"

"Mom!" Rachel yelled out again, "I'm okay. Please, stop crying!"

"Oh honey, what are we going to do?" Mom said, choking on the words.

Dad's voice broke through this time. "I don't know if there's anything else we can do."

"What if she never wakes up?" Mom cried, her voice muffled against what Rachel could only imagine was Dad's shirt.

"Mom! Dad! It's okay! I'm right here!"

It was no use. No matter what Rachel shouted, her voice just wouldn't reach them.

What's going on? Why can't they hear me?

Was she trapped in some sort of backward nightmare? Hearing her parent's anguished voices all because of her was the worst sort of punishment to endure. When was she going to wake up? What was this place?

In time the voices faded, leaving her alone in the dark. She could feel something stirring within her, a renewal of consciousness, which allowed her to finally open her eyes. But when she did, it wasn't Mom or Dad's face that she saw. Instead she saw the face of an enormous, terrifying, wiry-haired shadow wolf illuminated in a faint orange glow, staring at her from across the large, dark, dirty underground chamber in which she lay.

She could see other shadowy figures moving in the darkness on the outer rim of the chamber, only their eyes reflecting in the same low orange glow that lit up the monstrously large beast standing in front of her. It was by far the largest shadow wolf she had ever seen. His coat was thick, black and wiry like the rest, but his paws were larger and more sharply defined. His ears were erect and massive, and his jaw and muzzle were thick and wide. His tail was bushy and heavy, hanging low behind him, and he stood with an authoritative presence. Rachel knew this must be Umbra, the leader of the pack.

He stood, watching her as if he were waiting to see what she intended to do. The other shadowy figures, no doubt shadow wolves, paced along the walls waiting for their leader's command. On his right front paw hung the silver chain with little charms Rachel knew all too well. The fire charm glowed as it always had whenever it was dark, providing the only light that brightened this otherwise unlit chamber. Why did he have it?

Rachel stood, provoking hostile growls from the onlooking shadow wolves, though Umbra remained silent, watching.

"You're Umbra, aren't you?" Rachel's voice cracked as she spoke directly to the gargantuan shadow wolf wearing Aunt Jenny's bracelet.

"Ah, so you've heard of me?" Umbra said, his voice rich and deep, resonating through the air of the chamber.

"Only once," Rachel admitted, thinking about how carefully she needed to speak. One word from Umbra's mouth and the shadow wolves surrounding her in the darkness would surely leap out to engulf her.

"Then you know I am the leader of this pack?" Umbra asked, his voice sanguine yet dominating.

"Yes," Rachel replied, trying her best to stay calm despite the hungry stares of the other shadow wolves. "Why have you brought me here?"

"You don't know?" Umbra's asked, his voice masking a hint of surprise. "Certainly you know what world you are in." It wasn't a question really, but Umbra waited for a response.

"I'm pretty sure this is Calim," Rachel answered, watching his expression change from surprise to delight. Had she given away too much?

"Calim is indeed the name of *this* world," Umbra continued, beginning to pace as he spoke. "So tell me, what is the name of *your* world?"

"My world?" Rachel asked, not liking the direction the conversation was taking. She had just given herself up as an alien of sorts, and she didn't want to divulge any more information than she absolutely had to. "Why do you want to know the name of my world?"

"No reason, really," Umbra said casually, but Rachel didn't believe him.

"You're here," Umbra continued, "as the result of an unexpected side effect of the growing darkness. You see, the darkness requires the presence of someone like you to grow stronger and stretch further across the land."

Rachel did not like the sound of this at all. Was she going to be made into some sort of sacrifice to the darkness?

"The darkness lives and grows with only one purpose, to cover the world of Calim so we, the Shadai, may once again reign supreme over all the lands." Umbra stopped pacing to observe Rachel, looking intently at her face.

"With your help, little girl, our darkness will continue to grow until there is no light left for the other pathetic species on this planet."

Rachel shuddered as she remembered looking up at the impenetrable ceiling of black clouds that covered the sky each time she came to this world in her nightmares. She also thought about Incindia telling her how the darkness was working its way across the land. Her mind then raced to Torrens and especially to Ember, who had all been so kind and caring. She though of the other animals she'd observed, the sand kittens and the flying squirrels made of mist.

It was absolutely horrible what the Shadai were trying to do. Extinguishing all other life on this planet, destroying the beauty here for their own selfish purposes. This might not be Rachel's home, but she had grown to care for this world.

"I'll never help you!" Rachel shouted, her cheeks burning red with anger. "You won't win!"

"I'm afraid you don't really have a choice," Umbra laughed darkly. "Don't worry, we won't kill you just yet. For the moment, we still need you alive—but only just barely."

A sour taste entered Rachel's mouth. She swallowed hard to get rid of it. They weren't going to kill her, but that didn't mean they weren't going to hurt her.

"This world will be ours soon enough," Umbra snarled, glaring at Rachel for the first time with a mad look in his eyes and baring his gargantuan fangs. "It's only a matter of time. Nothing will stop the darkness now that it's begun."

"Incindia will stop it!" Rachel said, finding an ounce of courage as her anger grew.

"Incindia?" Umbra scoffed, the other shadow wolves barking with laughter. "A firefox cannot stop the darkness, and you'd do well to remember it."

He lowered his head, ears turned back in the all too familiar stance of a shadow wolf readying for attack. He growled loudly and viciously, erasing Rachel's momentary spurt of courage.

"Just for that," he snapped, continuing to growl, "I believe you need to be taught a lesson."

As he readied for the attack, a streak of fire came bursting into the chamber, surrounding Rachel on all sides. She was blinded a moment by the blazing light, then saw that the fiery wall was acting as a barrier between her and the shadowy monsters that held her captive. There were five firefoxes, two of which she recognized as Torrens and Incindia, circled around her, burning in an orange, white, and blue fury. They crouched facing outward toward the shadow wolves, the hair on their backs sticking up like a fiery inferno.

The chamber was completely lit with their flaming light,

reducing the shadow wolves to amorphous, wraith-like forms, shadow creatures distinguishable only by their outline, shape, and size. This was the true form of the Shadai, the reason they relied so much on the darkness. Without it, they were nothing more than silent, dark shadows dancing through the air and on the floors and walls.

Rachel could identify Umbra right away as he was the largest of the shadows in the room. Incindia stood between him and her as he ran right at Incindia then Rachel, charging past them both without any effect, trapped in his shadowy body. Other shadow wolves lunged at Rachel, too, but their efforts were also futile as they had been rendered completely harmless by the light filling the chamber. Umbra looked like he was howling in rage though he made no sound.

Into the chamber Ember ran, squeezing between two of the firefoxes to stand next to Rachel as an added layer of protection.

"Miss me?" Ember asked with a grin, standing with Rachel in the middle of the wall of fire created by the other firefoxes.

"You're okay!" Rachel exclaimed, feeling a rush of relief as the worry she'd been carrying for him melted away. When last she saw Ember he had bravely stayed behind to protect her from the shadow wolves that were hunting her.

"Of course I am!" he chuckled heartily. "Sorry I'm late!"

"Your timing couldn't have been more perfect!" Rachel smiled, feeling warm and a little more secure in the protective blanket of fire that surrounded her.

"They didn't hurt you, did they?" Incindia inquired while keeping her body postured to attack.

"No," Rachel replied, "I'm fine now, thanks to all of

you."

Incindia, still surveying the shadow wolves as they frantically ran across the chamber said, "Good, it looks like it's time to get you out of here. Rachel, I want you to follow Torrens as we walk. He'll be the one leading us safely out of this den."

Rachel turned to look at Torrens as he gave a nod of approval to Incindia and began slowly walking, leading the whole group outside of the chamber and into a series of narrow tunnels. Incindia, bringing up the rear, walked backward, keeping a close eye on the shadow wolves as they rematerialized once a safe distance from the bright light of the burning flames. As they walked, Incindia warned Rachel not to get too close to any of the firefoxes except for Ember, who had remained only warm to the touch as he walked dutifully next to her.

The further they went down the narrow tunnels, the more the howls filled the air as shadow wolves who were just outside the reach of the blazing, bonfire-like light, regained their solid forms. Umbra, now far enough away from the flaming light, screamed with rage. "*Incindia!*" shaking the ground and walls with his mighty roar.

Rachel could see the cave entrance now, which led out into the woods still covered by the darkness. Black clouds filled the sky as they had in every one of her nightmares, and the air outside was chilled, hanging with a low-lying mist.

The shadow wolves were easier to see now. The light of the firefoxes was much less potent out in the open air, allowing the shadow wolves to creep closer and closer without being reduced to shadows, remaining solid and lethal.

"Almost there," Torrens said as the mist in the air became first heavy and thick, then so unbearably saturated, Rachel almost felt like she was going to choke on the moisture. Her eyes were tingling and visibility was almost nonexistent as the fire surrounding her vanished from view. She couldn't feel the warmth of the fires anymore; all she could feel was the wet, cold condensation forming on her skin.

"Watch out!" Ember shouted, leaping in front of her to knock a shadow wolf out of the way right as it charged into view. The shadow wolf, taken by surprise by the little firefox, tumbled back into the mist and out of sight.

Rachel could hear the stomping of hooves and the neighs of horses filling the air followed by the snaps, yelps, and whimpers of shadow wolves in pain.

"Quickly!" Torrens beckoned through the mist, Rachel and Ember following his voice. "There's not much time."

Walking a bit farther through the whiteness that enveloped them, they came out of the fog and into a sizable clearing that felt like the calm center of a raging storm. There was howling and stomping and biting and whinnying all throughout the surrounding mist as an unseen battle raged beneath its cover. One by one, the firefoxes walked out of the mist with Rachel, their flames low and uneven across their bodies, with patches of fur so dampened by the fog, it extinguished parts of their flames.

In the middle of the clearing stood a magnificent unicorn, stark white with dark eyes and mist trailing off its body.

"Rachel," Incindia said, rushing over to her and Ember, looking much less stunning than she had in the cave with bits of singed fur and sparking flames struggling to reignite,

"I need you to go with Caligo. He'll take you to safety. The shadow wolves will break through the mist at any moment. No time to waste!"

"Caligo?" Rachel asked, seeing no other animals or people around except for the misty unicorn in the clearing. "You-you mean the unicorn?" she asked.

"Yes, that's Caligo, but he's not a unicorn. He's a mysticorn. Now hurry!" Incindia said forcefully, pushing Rachel forward.

"But I don't know how to ride a horse, let alone a mysticorn," Rachel protested, resisting Incindia's insistent nudging.

"He'll take good care of you. Just trust me. Now go!" Incindia yelled, giving Rachel one last shove with her snout before turning to block the first shadow wolf that had found its way through the mist. Running across the clearing with Ember following closely beside her, Rachel stumbled a bit, catching her balance as she sprinted toward Caligo.

Shadow wolves began to emerge from all sides of the clearing as Caligo galloped to meet Rachel. He was a tall mysticorn stallion, too tall for Rachel to climb onto on her own, but by some miracle she felt her body lift, something boosting her up just high enough to grab ahold of his neck and swing her body over his back. She saw Ember down on the ground, looking up at her. He was the one that had helped her mount the magnificent mysticorn, pushing her up with all his strength as she scrambled to climb on top.

She held on as tightly as she could, grabbing handfuls of Caligo's mane to steady herself as he galloped away at full speed, leaving Ember, Incindia, Torrens, and the other fire foxes far behind, to deal with the shadow wolves alongside the herd of mysticorns that Rachel now understood had been part of the plan all along to get her out safely. Mist trailed behind him as he galloped, streaming off of his tail and mane.

As she rode, further and further away, she could hear the enraged howls of Umbra as he chased behind, unable to keep up with Caligo's swift feet. He had lost his prey, the girl he had hoped would help him cover the world in darkness.

"The bracelet!" Rachel shouted, looking back, the shadow wolves, mysticorns, and firefoxes no longer in sight. She knew it was too late and much too dangerous to turn back for her bracelet, but it still made her sad to have lost it. She wondered how upset her dad would be when he found out Aunt Jenny's bracelet was lost forever—though he would probably never find out it was a shadow wolf that took it.

"Is everything alright?" Caligo asked, an ear twisting back in response to Rachel's unexpected outburst as he continued to run.

"Yeah," Rachel said, not going into any of the details. She didn't want to distract him or worry him about something over which neither of them had any control. The bracelet was gone, and that was the end of it.

Rachel was surprised by how easy it was to ride on Caligo's back. His gait was smooth, nearly flawless as he sped over broad fields of grass and through patches of woodlands. She could feel his body shift slightly beneath her, keeping her balanced on his back with very little effort on her part. Incindia had never told Rachel where Caligo would be taking her, but she had to trust it would be a better place than the one from which they had just escaped.

Blue skies shone over the horizon, the end of the

darkness swiftly approaching with each stride of Caligo's hooves, the forest changing from sickly and black to beautiful autumn woods bursting with color. Rachel recalled her first dream in an autumn wood in a forest much like this one, teetering on the edge of the darkness, a beautiful forest, but also dying with the encroachment of the black and ominous sky. It was also the first time she had come to Calim to meet a firefox named Incindia.

As they rode on through the autumn forest, the dark sky faded to blue. Once under the clear blue sky, the appearance of the forest changed again, the leaves green, lush, and vibrant with the forest itself now bustling with life. This was the type of forest in which she had met Torrens, a forest that had not yet been affected by the darkness.

She looked back as they rode on, remembering the dark forest of her nightmares. It was a terrible place, one she hoped she'd never return to, but even in that awful place she held one happy memory, a memory in which she met a little firefox kit named Ember. She hoped Ember and the others were all right. They had sacrificed their safety for hers, and she didn't think she would ever be able to forgive herself if anything happened to them as a result.

Caligo slowed as they wandered deeper into the flourishing woods far away from the shadow wolves and the tincture of darkness that helped give them shape. He came to a stop in front of a stream where he gulped up several mouthfuls of water.

"Caligo?" Rachel asked, "where exactly are you taking me?"

"To the firefox dens," Caligo replied, lifting up his head from the water, his thirst now quenched and his body rejuvenated as his horn glowed white, a mist swirling up and around it.

The firefox dens were no doubt the home of Incindia, Torrens, and Ember as well as countless other firefoxes. Rachel had longed to see the firefoxes' home ever since she had first met them, for if there was one thing that made her feel truly safe in Calim, it was the fiery warmth of the firefoxes.

"Are we almost there?" Rachel asked, looking at the sky, which was beginning to darken as night approached. She was excited to go to the firefox dens until she remembered that the firefoxes she cared about most wouldn't be there yet, because she and Caligo had run ahead of the others.

"We'll be there soon," he assured her as he resumed the journey, walking through the forest this time instead of galloping.

"Why did you help me?" Rachel asked, remembering the thick mist and horse sounds that came from it. "It's just that I know you put yourself in danger for me, but I can't figure out why. You don't even know me."

"We may not know you personally, but we do know Incindia, and she has told us many things about you. She asked that we help. I couldn't turn her down."

What did Caligo mean by saying he couldn't turn her down? To Rachel, it sounded like there was more to the story, but she wasn't sure if she should pry.

"What sorts of things did she tell you about me?" Rachel asked, wondering what kind of gossip about her was being spread.

Caligo shook his head and neck as he walked, scaring away the many insects that had begun using him as a perch. "She told us that you came from another world, and that she believed you held the key to stopping the darkness."

"The darkness?" Rachel asked, surprised. Incindia thought Rachel was the key to stopping the darkness? That was totally absurd. Sure, she wanted to help put a stop to it, but that was more because she couldn't bear the thought of anything bad happening to the good creatures here. "What do I have to do with the darkness?"

"She hasn't told you yet?" Caligo asked. This time he was the one who sounded surprised.

"No," Rachel replied, somewhat annoyed, "she hasn't." Although in all fairness to Incindia every time she had tried to talk to Rachel about anything remotely important, Rachel woke up from the dream before Incindia could finish.

"Well," Caligo said, "if she hasn't told you yet, I don't think we should discuss it any further."

That was a disappointment, but then Rachel was getting used to not being kept entirely in the loop. When Caligo finally slowed to a stop, Rachel could see dozens of firefoxes jumping and playing in a large field of tall brown grass adjacent to the green woods out of which she and Caligo had come. They looked over at Caligo a moment and continued to hop around in the field, undeterred by his and Rachel's presence.

"There's so many of them!" Rachel said, unable to contain her excitement.

"There are indeed," Caligo agreed, watching one of them finally jump out of the grass to come over and greet them. It was a firefox kit a little bigger than Ember, but not black the way Ember was. This little kit had a blazing fiery coat of flames that burned white, blue, and orange like the rest of the firefoxes Rachel had met. In fact, now that she looked more closely at the firefoxes in the field, she realized that none of them had a black coat like Ember's.

"Hello," the kit said with some excitement, "you must be the one they call Rachel."

"I am," Rachel said with a smile, looking down at the little kit while still sitting high atop Caligo's back.

"Ember's told me all about you!" he said with an excited hop. "Are you really from another world?"

"I guess . . ." Rachel replied, hesitation in her voice, still trying to come to terms with the fact that to them she was the strange creature from another world and not the other way around. Word about her had sure traveled fast.

Caligo interrupted the conversation. "I need to be going," he said to Rachel, looking at the darkening sky as the evening began drawing to a close. "The other mysticorns may still need me. Can I leave you in the care of this little firefox?"

Rachel looked down at the kit, considering whether or not she was okay with being left in his care.

"Sure," she agreed, sliding off Caligo's back, "any friend of Ember's is a friend of mine."

"Take care of her," Caligo instructed before turning to run back into the woods from where he had come.

"I will!" the little firefox shouted after him before turning to Rachel and looking at her in awe.

"I'm Blaze," he said with a bow of his head.

"Nice to meet you, Blaze!" Rachel said with a smile, her stomach rumbling a bit. It was the first time in any of her dreams she had felt a hunger pang or thirst.

Blaze stared at her stomach as he listened to the churning sounds it made. "Are you hungry?" he asked, tilting his head to the side.

"Starving!" Rachel replied. "And thirsty, too. Is there anything for me to drink?"

She didn't know if firefoxes drank anything. And what did a firefox eat? The question had never really crossed her mind.

"There's some food and drink for you waiting in Ember's den," Blaze informed her. "Incindia had it put there specially. I'll take you there now if you want. It's where you'll be staying tonight."

Rachel liked the sound of that. Food, drink, and a little sleep was all she could ask for to finish off this crazy day in the best possible way. She wasn't afraid to fall asleep here in the warm protective dens of the firefoxes. Blaze agreed to keep watch over her throughout the night until Incindia and the others returned.

She wouldn't dream about shadow wolves tonight, not while she was already in the world of her dreams, and she half expected to wake up at home as soon as sleep overtook her. This dream, though incredible, was already becoming much too long, and she was ready to return home. With those happy thoughts she fell asleep in the warm confines of Ember's den.

CHAPTER 9. ASSIMILATION

Chris lay in bed for hours. It was the first time since Rachel's accident that he finally had a chance to get some real sleep, and yet sleep was the one thing that kept evading him. The house just wasn't the same without Rachel, and he couldn't help but replay over and over again in his head the image of her lying unconscious on the ground in the forest. That, followed by memories of Mom yelling as Dad held the limp body of his little sister in his arms.

He stared up at his bedroom ceiling. It was covered in an array of holes made by darts from his dartboard set that he'd thrown at the ceiling when he was bored or frustrated. Would Rachel ever be coming home? Not lying in a bed at the nearby hospital, but really home, at the house, awake and well? He sat up in bed, pulling the darts out of his nightstand, throwing a few more at the ceiling.

Fwap! Fwap! Fwap! the darts thudded against the ceiling and stuck in place. Chris sighed and leaned his head against the wall.

"You've really done it this time, Rae," he mumbled softly to himself, struggling to keep the tears from falling.

Hours passed. Chris tried to play video games but just couldn't seem to enjoy himself; he fiddled with the computer he'd disassembled until he decided it wasn't worth working on, and he even tried softly turning on the TV in his bedroom, so Dad couldn't hear it from the other room. Nothing good was on. It was like all the powers in the world were working on dragging him down.

He walked over to his door and pushed it open slowly so no one else would be able to hear it squeak. After slipping out into the hallway, he silently shut his door and snuck downstairs, making sure to step over the creaky parts of the stairs. There was a light on in the kitchen, and as he peered around the edge of the wall to see who else was up, he spied Dad and Evalyn both sitting down at the table drinking warm milk. It was the sort of drink Mom would make when someone was having difficulty sleeping. It was supposed to help, at least that's what she would always say.

"Chris?" Dad said, speaking softly, his voice strained as he wearily sat at the dining room table.

"How'd you know I was here?" Chris asked, stepping out from behind the wall.

"Call it a father's intuition," Dad replied, taking another sip of his milk.

"Oh," Chris said rubbing the back of his neck, "so, uh, can I hang with you?"

"The more the merrier," Dad said, making a pitiful attempt at a smile.

"Why can't we go back to the hospital, Dad?" Evalyn said. "It's not like anyone is getting any sleep around here anyway."

"I know how you feel," Dad said sympathetically, "but your mom is with Rachel right now, and she doesn't want anything bad to happen to either of you. She wanted me to bring you home so you could get some rest, and home is where we're staying."

"But, Dad . . ." Evalyn frowned.

"No buts!" Dad said, sounding exhausted but stern. "Visiting hours are over right now anyway. We can visit Rachel first thing in the morning."

Evalyn glared defiantly, standing up. Then forcefully pushing the chair back under the table, she stomped away in a huff, back up to her room, slamming the door behind her.

"Girls . . ." Chris said sarcastically, shaking his head, but Dad was in no mood to smile.

"It's really late, Chris. Think you can head back to your room and try to get some sleep?"

Dad looked really worn. Chris wanted to protest, but couldn't bring himself to do it. He knew as bad as things had been for him and Evalyn, they were so much worse for Mom and Dad.

"Sure thing," Chris replied.

His dad reached over and squeezed his shoulder gently, saying, "There's a good son. I'll see you in the morning."

Chris headed back to his room, not worrying about the noise he made on the way. He sat in bed again, this time grabbing ahold of the flat, smoky-brown crystalline scale he had found in his pocket days before. He didn't know where it had come from, but he had found it right after waking up from the weirdest dream about wolf-like kobolds digging for metal in a mine and dragons.

Rubbing the scale between his thumb and forefinger to feel its rough surface, he finally drifted off to sleep, his head swimming with all sorts of images and memories of his mom, his dad and his sisters. Then all those images swirled and molded into a gray fuzz that shifted into a crystal clear picture of a mountainside. The trees growing on the mountainside were tall and green, and the boulders looked like they were chiseled throughout the face of it.

Not too far off from where he stood, Chris could see the waterfall that hid the entrance to the kobold mines he had explored in his last dream with a dragon named Rucknar. He looked toward the woods in which Rucknar had run off and again began following the invisible path of the dragon. The forest was lush, green, and fairly dense with all sorts of shrubbery strewn about. After some climbing through trees and over thorny bushes he found a wide dirt path that swerved down the mountainside, leading to a large clearing bustling with the activity of dragons and kobolds.

Overlooking the clearing was a rocky ledge, over which Chris peeked from behind a nearby tree as he tried to stay as inconspicuous as possible. In his last dream he remembered Rucknar telling him if he were found by any of the other dragons or the kobolds, he'd be killed. The funny thing about that was that Rucknar, too, was a dragon but never made any attempt to hurt Chris. Rucknar's empty threats made it hard for Chris to believe that all dragons were bad, but just to be on the safe side he watched the clearing below with extra caution.

From behind the tree, Chris could see a multitude of kobolds scurrying about the clearing under the watchful eyes of some enormous dragons, many times larger than Rucknar had been. The kobolds had the hood on their tunics pulled up over their ears, to act as a shade for their faces, no doubt to keep out the brightness of sun now high in the sky.

The dragons towered over the kobolds, easily four or more times their height. They each had front and hind legs, two enormous wings, sharp claws, long tails, horns, and varying degrees of scaly, spiky hides with bony ridges. Each dragon was unique, though Chris could see a clear contrast between two different types of dragons in the field below.

One set of dragons was smaller than the other, with simpler, sleeker hides covered in dull brown, green, or gray scaly skin. The brown one reminded Chris a little of Rucknar, only bigger and not crystalline looking. The other set of dragons varied greatly in color and were bulkier and larger in stature and design. Their scales glimmered in the sunlight with more metallic overtones and colors that ranged from gold, silver, and bronze to all the colors of the rainbow.

Chris watched as a large, red, metallic looking dragon swiped his claws at a kobold who had strayed from the others, scaring him back to the center of the clearing where a mass of kobolds continued to work, busily chiseling away at a large, solid rock altar, easily ten or more feet high. After they finished up their work, a silver dragon rushed toward the crowd of kobolds, scaring them back into a cave entrance that must have been another opening into their mine, much like the one Chris and Rucknar had slipped out of from behind the waterfall.

The altar they left behind was exquisitely designed with a curved, smooth top that looked like a very shallow bowl made to hold some sort of offering. The base of the altar contained a very ornate carving of two intertwined dragons. One of the dragons in the carving looked slender and frail while the other dragon had a very muscular and domineering appearance.

The stonework around the dragons was embellished with various gems and metals. The larger of the two stone dragon carvings was generously accented with a shimmering, sliver-colored metal of some kind, while the frail-looking dragon remained plain and unimpressive. Chris wondered if this was for some weird dragon wedding ceremony.

As he surveyed the dragon's camp, he heard a rustling of branches in the foliage behind him. When he turned to look at the bushes he saw two black, beady eyes staring at him between the leaves. He froze in place, looking around for any sort of weapon he could use to defend himself. He spotted a sizable rock and slowly bent to pick it up, never taking his eyes off the bush or those haunting black eyes.

The bush rustled again.

Chris held the rock up near his ear, poised to hurl it at whatever came out of the bushes.

"I told you not to follow me," a familiar voice hissed from beneath the branches. Chris recognized the voice at once. It was Rucknar!

"I didn't follow you," Chris replied, but that was really only a half-truth. He had followed Rucknar into the woods, but then became sidetracked by the bustling activity in the clearing below, completely forgetting about his search for the dragon. "Besides, from where I'm standing it looks like you're the one following me. Are you spyin' on me, Ruck?"

Rucknar poked his head out from the bush, his beady black eyes looking up at Chris. "So what if I am?" he snorted, wriggling his body completely out from between the branches.

"How did ya know I was here?" Chris asked, trying to maintain the illusion that Rucknar was the one to blame for following him instead of the other way around.

"I didn't," Rucknar snapped, whipping his tail back and forth. "You're not supposed to be here."

"And you are?" Chris asked, watching how suspiciously Rucknar moved around, surveying not only Chris but also the clearing below and the sky above.

"Well, someone has to keep an eye on those kobolds," Rucknar snorted, scurrying around in front of Chris to get a better look at the activity below. "They're up to something, and I'm going to find out what."

Rucknar stared down into the clearing with his back now facing Chris. Even with the large rock that Chris held in his hand, Rucknar obviously didn't consider Chris much of a threat, so Chris decided to drop the rock. As he did, Rucknar turned to look back to see what the pathetic human was up to.

"Is that why you were in the kobold mine?" Chris asked, now that he had Rucknar's full attention again. "The first time we met, you were in their mine. Was it to spy on the kobolds?"

"That is what I was trying to do," Rucknar grunted, "but I didn't get a good chance to sneak around because *someone* got in my way." Chris knew that *someone* was him, so he let the conversation end there. Rucknar turned his head back toward the clearing, squinting as he stared down at the valley below.

The kobolds were out again, frantically scurrying around pushing rocks here and there, chiseling stones, polishing and decorating everything in sight. It looked almost like they were setting up a big party. The dragons all just stood around watching the kobolds do all the work, occasionally spouting out commands telling them what to do. For such crude creatures, the kobold's workmanship was surprisingly impressive, at least from a distance.

"So," Chris asked, "what makes ya think the kobolds are up to somethin'?" Aside from being scraggly and a bit scary Chris couldn't help but wonder why Rucknar was so interested in them.

"The kobolds," Rucknar began, "are always whispering to each other under their breath when they think none of us dragons are close enough to hear them. We do have some kobold spies among them that are supposed to report to us right away if anything bad is being said, but I don't trust any of them. Not even the ones that are spying for us. I don't like the way they look at us. The elder dragons tell me not to worry. But they don't hear the things I hear the kobolds say. And I'm still small enough to hide in places where the kobolds won't notice me."

"What kind of things do the kobolds say?" Chris asked.

"That they hate us dragons. They want to be rid of us. Some say they would kill us if they could just figure out how," Rucknar grumbled.

"Well, how *does* one kill a dragon?" Chris asked casually, half forgetting for a moment he was talking to one.

"Would you like to try to find out?" Rucknar snapped angrily, turning around to face Chris.

He spread his sizable wings and rose up on his hind legs, reaching Chris's height. Chris backed away. He knew Rucknar was a dragon, but never really thought he looked like much of one until now. Before, Chris had thought of Rucknar as more of a big, brown, oversized lizard, scurrying around on all fours. Rucknar always kept his wings folded flat against his back and his horns, though large, were short compared to those of the much larger dragons in the valley below. This was the first time Chris had ever seen Rucknar stand up. It was amazing!

"Cool!" Chris breathed, awestruck by Rucknar's awesomeness. Then, it hit him. *Cool* was probably not the best choice of words right at this moment with an angry dragon about to attack.

Rucknar lunged at Chris, just barely missing him, as Chris dodged, falling flat on his butt.

"Ah man!" Chris said, feeling the pain spread from his rear to his legs and torso.

Rucknar wasn't much better off. When Chris dodged, Rucknar took a tumble, too, landing smack on his back. Chris got up as quickly as he could and ran a short distance into the woods before ducking behind a tree. He didn't know if he could outrun an angry dragon, even if it was only a little one. And he couldn't climb up the steep slopes on the mountainside, most of which resembled walls of jagged rocks separating plateaus of trees.

Rucknar had followed close behind but didn't see exactly where Chris had hidden. He worked his way around the trees trying to find Chris. As he got closer to Chris's hiding spot he began taunting him, trying to coax Chris out of hiding.

"Where are you hiding, human?" Rucknar said, sounding annoyed. "I thought you wanted to find out how to kill a dragon." He hissed as he spoke, slowly creeping around the nearby trees. "Now's your chance. Unless, of course, you're too scared."

Chris was a little scared, but more than that he was angry at himself for getting Rucknar so riled up. He didn't want to hurt Rucknar, and he certainly didn't want to get hurt. So instead of waiting for Rucknar to find him he stepped out from his hiding place and said, "You've got me all wrong Ruck—" but before he could finish his sentence, Rucknar bolted toward him.

Chris ran, then grabbed the trunk of a slender tree with smooth bark with one hand and swung around it facing back in the direction from which he had come. Rucknar, unable to turn as quickly around the trunk of the tree to follow, lost his footing and slid into another tree. "You'll have to do better than that!" Chris shouted, taunting Rucknar, weaving in and out of the trees to try to keep a safe distance away. "I don't want to fight you, Ruck. Heck, I don't really need to know how to kill a dragon. Besides, you're the one who brought it up in the first place."

Rucknar lunged at Chris again, but not before Chris took another sharp turn, dodging the dragon's assault, causing him to crash into yet another tree. Chris's body was aching; he knew he wouldn't be able to keep up this pace much longer.

"Okay, I'm sorry Ruck! Please stop and at least talk to me about this." Chris could hear Rucknar slowing down. He, too, was panting and Chris could hear a loud purring resonating from Rucknar's chest with each breath. It wasn't a happy purr like that of a cat, but rather a loud rhythmic rumble, drumming loudly and then softening with each breath as Rucknar came to a halt. Chris stopped, too, and bent over in a little coughing fit before catching his breath.

"Geez, Ruck!" Chris coughed a couple more times, his heart still throbbing. "I really thought you were going to kill me."

"I would have," Rucknar replied icily, "if those trees hadn't gotten in my way."

"Ya know, that was pretty amazing!" Chris said, grinning.

"What?" Rucknar asked, laying down exhausted over a flat rock.

"Well, you of course," Chris beamed. "I mean, when you stood up, wings spread, teeth bared . . . you actually looked like a *real* dragon."

Rucknar just stared in disbelief. "Are all humans as stupid as you?" he asked, annoyed.

"What?" Chris replied innocently.

"I *am* a real dragon, so of course I look like one. You really should be more careful about the things you say." Rucknar huffed, stretching his wings out one last time before folding them against his back again.

"Whatever," Chris said, brushing off Rucknar's comments.

"Don't you have any common sense?" Rucknar asked.

Chris shrugged. "Beats me. So are we friends now?" he asked, grinning widely before adding, "I did apologize after all."

"I don't know," Rucknar said, tilting his head to the side and staring at Chris. "Asking a dragon how to kill a dragon is not very bright." He whipped his tail through the nearby plants, cutting off the tops like a lawnmower.

"Well, you're the one who brought it up," Chris frowned. "You said the kobolds were tryin' to figure out a way to do it. You know, a way to kill dragons. And I was just wonderin' if there was a way. You're right, though, I probably shouldn't have asked."

"Probably?" Rucknar snorted.

"Well, sure," Chris replied. "If I hadn't asked you, I wouldn't have gotten a chance to see just how awesome a dragon you are, Ruck. Those kobolds would sure be stupid to try and take on a dragon like you."

"The kobolds!" Rucknar broke in. "I almost forgot. The ceremony is about to begin." He glared at Chris. "It's your fault I missed spying on them this time, too."

Rucknar scurried off, back toward the ledge overlooking the clearing in the valley below. Chris followed, not wanting to miss anything. Rucknar crouched low by the ledge, and Chris did the same, keeping a healthy distance away from the reach of Rucknar and his whip-like tail, just to be safe. The hustle and bustle had changed. The kobolds were no longer frantically rushing all over the valley. In fact, Chris could no longer see any kobolds at all, unless he counted their faint outlines at the entrance to the mines.

Instead, the valley was filled only with dragons talking loudly with one another. Chris couldn't make out just what they were saying from his perch on the mountainside because there were too many talking all at once, but he could see what they were doing, and he watched with interest as the larger, more powerful looking dragons walked around the enormous altar, forming a large, perfect circle.

Their scales gleamed fantastically in the sunlight in all sorts of metallic hues. Some dragons were blue, some purple, some gold — each dragon its own magnificent shade of color. There were silver dragons, copper dragons, orange, green, and red dragons. Looking down at the dragons in the circle was almost like looking down into a brand new box of crayons, the colors varied so widely. Chris could hardly believe his eyes. They all looked so amazing and at the same time so intimidating.

Near the center of the circle, forming a straight line in front of the altar, were three smaller, dull looking dragons. These dragons weren't nearly as small as Rucknar; they were gigantic in comparison. They looked thinner and much plainer than the surrounding dragons. Their skin and scales ranged from green to brown to gray and had no sheen at all, their colors were flat and dull.

Chris spied something in the bowl-shaped altar that hadn't been there before. It was filled with three large chunks of metal that sparkled and glistened in the sunlight.

"What's going on down there?" Chris asked, directing his question to Rucknar who was obviously ignoring him. Rucknar continued to stare down at the entrance to the kobold mines, ignoring the dragons down in the valley — and Chris.

"Hey," Chris said, inching over to Rucknar, poking him with a finger in the shoulder, his scales rock solid, "what's wrong? You think the kobolds are gonna attack or something?"

"I doubt it," Rucknar replied, breaking free from the trance he had been in while turning his head and squinting his eyes to give Chris a nasty glare. "The kobolds wouldn't have a chance. They've rebelled in the past, and it always ends the same."

"The same?" Chris asked.

"It always ends in a slaughter. They still haven't managed to take down a single one of us," Rucknar finished.

"Hmm," was all Chris said. He looked back down at the valley below. There wasn't a single dragon the size of Rucknar in the whole place.

"Why aren't there any dragons like you down there, Ruck?" Chris asked.

"I'm still a youngling," Rucknar replied, diverting his eyes from the kobold mines to finally look instead at the circle of dragons. "We younglings aren't allowed to go to the assimilation ceremony. It's forbidden."

"So there are more small dragons like you?" Chris asked, wondering where the other ones could be.

"Sure, tons," Rucknar said. "But during the ceremony, we have to stay holed up in a boring cave."

"Yeah, because of the whole forbidden thing, right?"

Chris asked, finally understanding why Rucknar had been sneaking around the way he was.

"Yes," Rucknar agreed.

"So if it's forbidden what are you doin' up here?" Chris pried.

"Spying, of course. They can't keep me cooped up in a cave," Rucknar snorted.

"Don't any of the other dragons notice you're gone?" Chris asked, wondering if it was even possible for Rucknar to go unnoticed.

"Not really," Rucknar admitted. "I found a way out of the cave a long time ago. The other younglings don't know about it and just think I'm off exploring somewhere deep inside. The caves are pretty complex. Sort of like the kobold mine, only larger." Rucknar began staring suspiciously at the kobold mine again.

"So what's goin' on down there anyway?" Chris asked, again diverting Rucknar's attention from the kobold mine. But before Rucknar could answer, the sounds of dragons talking in the valley below began to die down, capturing both Rucknar and Chris's attention.

Each dragon in the circle standing in front of the altar fidgeted just slightly before resting, frozen in what appeared to be an assigned place. Chris peered down, captivated by the shapes below. A feeling of absolute awe came over him as though he was witnessing something so powerful, so sacred that no human eye was worthy of seeing it. And yet, there he was, lowly and human.

A low hum emanated through the air. First softly like the buzz of a fan and then slowly growing in strength and volume. The dragons all stood perfectly still as if they had become statuesque figurines like the carvings on the altar they surrounded. The music was unlike any Chris had ever heard. The sounds and notes blended together in a surreal melody that felt like it was piercing Chris's being.

He didn't understand the words that were being sung, but he didn't have to. The music was so powerful it transcended all barriers of understanding, completely absorbing Chris in its melodic sways. Coming out of a gigantic cave opening many times larger than the kobold cave entrance and on the opposite side of the clearing, was an enormous black dragon. His scales looked neither metallic nor plain, but instead sparkled in the sunlight and looked crystalline.

The black dragon had two large horns, which were long and protruded out of the back of his head, twisting slightly in opposite directions yet remaining symmetrical to each other. His physique was bulkier and stronger looking than any of the other dragons in the valley below, including the metallic ones, and his wings were large, half-stretched open as he walked.

The other dragons, still motionless, continued their song as the black dragon walked to the decorated altar and turned around to face the weak and scrawny looking row of dull dragons.

Maybe this isn't a wedding ceremony, Chris thought to himself, watching the brown, green, and gray dragons bow slightly to the black one towering over them. Was this some sort of sacrificial offering?

"Who's that big, black, crystal-looking dragon?" Chris whispered to Rucknar.

"Adamas, the dragon king," Rucknar answered quietly. "And he's not a crystal dragon, he's a pure *diamond* dragon. The only one left."

Chris recognized the dragon king's name from somewhere. Come to think of it, he remembered hearing something about a diamond dragon, too, but he couldn't pinpoint when and where. His brain recently had been so full of worry for his little sister Rachel, he was having difficulty focusing on anything else.

"So what's goin' on down there?" Chris quietly asked.

Rucknar let out a low groan, apparently not wanting to take the time to explain anything more to the annoying human beside him. "Just watch. They're nearly ready – "

"Ready for what?" Chris pried, still wanting an explanation. Rucknar ignored him.

The song of the dragons died down, and the dragon king stood up tall on his hind legs in front of the stone altar, his wings now fully outstretched in a magnificent display. Chris couldn't believe he was seeing this. The dragons were all so incredible!

Adamas lifted a large purple chunk of metal from the bowl on top of the altar and holding it up with his claw, he said in a booming voice that echoed throughout the valley, "Ragorock!"

Chris didn't know what that meant, but he got goose-bumps just hearing this dragon king's mighty voice. A small, plain looking dragon with brown scales stepped out of line and approached the altar.

Adamas looked over the brown dragon a moment and then continued. "Today, Ragorock, you have earned the highest honor of the Allorum. On this day you take on your new armor and new name. You have earned the right to become one of us forever."

Chris's eyes widened with understanding. This wasn't a marriage ceremony at all or a sacrificial offering. It was some kind of dragon coming of age ceremony. The smaller dragons were finally ready to take their place among the elder dragons as full blown members of the clan.

Adamas held the shimmering purple chunk of metal out toward the weakly brown dragon adding, "You shall no longer be known as Ragorock. Henceforth, you shall be known as Chaq, defender of the Allorum. Now take this offering, Chaq, and begin your assimilation."

The brown dragon reached out meekly toward the dragon king and accepted the metal, holding it gently in his claws. After coddling it for just a moment, the wispy brown dragon lifted it up in the air above his head, tilted his head back with his eyes shut tight, and dropped the chunk of metal into his mouth, swallowing it whole in one swift gulp.

"Whoa, he ate it!" Chris gasped, staring down intensely at the brown dragon, wondering what would happen next.

The brown dragon's skin began changing color, much like a chameleon would. It changed slowly from brown to dark blue and then faded into a purple shade the exact same color as the metal he had eaten. But that wasn't all that was happening to him. His scales protruded slightly from his body, becoming thicker and more defined. His muscles began bulging out all over as he grew several feet in size. His claws fattened and sharpened, and his wings enlarged in all directions. His horns even grew denser and slightly longer, and his face became wider and well defined.

His scales glistened purple metallic in the sun, and he no longer looked at all like the scrawny brown dragon he had been. He looked just as brilliant as any of the other Allorum posed in the ceremonial circle. If Chris hadn't seen it with his own eyes he wouldn't have believed it was the same dragon. When the transformation was complete, Chaq bowed down to the dragon king, fanning out his magnificent wings, and then arose and left the altar, taking his place among the other dragons in the circle.

Only a moment more passed before the dragon king called another dragon up to the altar. This one was the gray dragon named Korimar. This time the dragon king pulled a large silver chunk of metal off the altar and began the same ritual for this dragon as he had for Chaq, saying, "Today, Korimar, you have earned the highest honor of the Allorum. On this day you take on your new armor and new name. You have earned the right to become one of us forever."

Holding the shining silver metal out toward the gray dragon, Adamas continued. "You shall no longer be known as Korimar. Henceforth, you shall be known as Janikvi, protector of the Allorum. Now, take this offering, Janikvi, and begin your assimilation." Just like the previous dragon had, Janikvi took his offering from the dragon king and swallowed it whole. His body expanded in all directions. Metal spikes shot up out of his spine and ran all the way down his back to the tip of his tail. His horns curled down as they grew, and silver metal oozed up and over his scales until his entire body was coated in a magnificent silver sheen. He, too, took his place in the dragon circle, and the ceremony went on.

Chris stood amazed as he watched the last dragon go through the same ritual, finally, leaving no more scrawny dragons in the clearing below and no more offerings on the altar. One by one they had each transformed before Chris's eyes into magnificent yet terrifying creatures.

He looked over at Rucknar who was still watching the ceremony and began imagining what kind of dragon he would become when he finally assimilated. Each dragon's transformation had been so unique. Chris didn't know if it was the type of metal that affected how the dragons transformed or if it was something hard coded into each dragon's DNA.

With the ceremony ended, Adamas, the black diamond dragon king, bellowed with his mighty voice, "Now we feast!"

All the dragons roared with delight, opened up their enormous wings, and flew up into the sky, scattering in all directions. Rucknar looked over at Chris, alarmed. He had forgotten about this part of the ceremony. "If you value your life, hide!" Rucknar hissed as he ducked back into the same bushes Chris had first found him in.

Chris looked up into the sky and saw several dragons heading his way. He didn't blend in well with the forest like Rucknar did, and his spiky brown hair with dyed blond tips and bright red T-shirt didn't help any, either. He knew a bush like the one Rucknar had jumped into wasn't going to hide him very well, and the ones nearby were covered with sharp thorns. He began to run, looking frantically for a hiding place.

The dragons flew very fast, and Chris hadn't run very far before he was spotted by a large red one, followed by a bronze and a silver one.

"Oh crud!" Chris yelled, running as fast as he could.

But the dragons were much faster.

The red dragon came slamming onto the ground in front of him as Chris skidded to a halt and turned around, running back the way he had come. The bronze dragon landed next, breaking a number of trees and shrubs in the process, thwarting Chris's progress as he scrambled to run in yet another direction. The silver dragon landed last, blocking his path, shaking the ground so violently Chris lost his balance and fell down smack in the middle of the three dragons. The dragons were huge! Much larger up close than they had appeared while in the clearing below. They towered above Chris, looking down on him.

"What have we here?" the red dragon laughed, surveying the little human that had fallen to the ground.

"A spy!" the bronze dragon hissed in accusation.

"Can I kill him?" the silver dragon asked hopefully.

"No!" the red dragon snapped as the silver dragon inched closer and closer to Chris. "Adamas will be the one to decide what happens to him."

Without another word and with great speed, the red dragon snatched up Chris in one of his large claws and took off into the air with the other two dragons following closely behind. Their flight was a blur. Chris hung down below the red dragon's belly, held tightly in his grasp. The air rushed by so swiftly Chris could scarcely keep his eyes open. He felt the weight of his whole body hanging loosely in the air. And then, in no time at all, the dragon had landed, tossing Chris onto the ground like a rag doll.

Chris tumbled a few times before landing face down in the dirt, his clothes, hair, and face now dusted with soil. He lifted up his head and saw the base of the large stone altar used during the ceremony. The intricate carvings were even more incredible than he had imagined, and he now knew the significance of what they represented.

Pushing up to his feet, Chris brushed off the dirt from his clothes as best he could. The silver and bronze dragons were no longer in sight. The red dragon watched Chris with a wide sneer across his face, showing his unnervingly sharp white teeth. The dragon didn't say a word to Chris; he just stared at him with his cold, black, merciless eyes.

It wasn't long before the silver and bronze dragons came into view and landed nearby. The silver dragon walked around anxiously, whipping his tail around much like Rucknar had. He was the smallest of the three dragons but was still enormous. Chris knew this dragon. It was Janikvi, one of the three that transformed during the ceremony. He had one of the more unusual sets of horns of any of the dragons Chris had seen. His horns twisted down and bent slightly outward. He also had blue eyes, something Chris hadn't noticed during the ceremony as he watched from afar.

"Is he coming?" the red dragon asked the others, maintaining a watchful eye over Chris as he spoke.

"Yes," the bronze dragon said, "Adamas is on his way back as we speak."

None of the dragons said a word to Chris; they just kept watch over him and the sky. Chris, standing near the large stone altar, looked up at the sky as well. He could see some of the other dragons flying back to the valley, among them was Adamas, the dragon king. He was the only black dragon in the whole clan, so he was very easy to spot against the bright blue sky.

The dragons guarding Chris roared with delight at the sight of Adamas, their king. He let out a similar roar in reply as he landed in front of Chris, shaking the ground even more violently than Janikvi had, causing Chris to fall over again.

Chris stared up in awe at the dragon king. He was an immense dragon both in size and stature. His glistening black scales were large, each one easily larger than Chris's hand. They were thick and solid, too, made of fine black diamonds, the likes of which Chris had never seen.

"My dragons say you were sneaking around. That you are a spy from the city of Maldin," Adamas said in a confrontational tone, his voice booming across the valley. "Do you deny this?"

Chris opened his mouth to speak, but the words just wouldn't come out. His heart pounded so hard in his chest it felt like it was going to explode. Looking up at the great dragon king was both awe inspiring and terrifying. When he finally did muster up what little courage he had to speak, he blurted out, "I'm no spy! And I've never even heard of the city of Maldin."

"So," Adamas continued, disregarding Chris's reply, "you're a liar *and* a spy!" His voice boomed even louder as he took one gigantic step toward Chris, his scales clapping against one another as his foot landed with a terrible crunch. Chris dared not move, his body shaking with fear.

"Who sent you here?" Adamas asked, looking over Chris with curiosity. Chris wondered if the dragon king was beginning to notice the same differences Rucknar had noticed when they first met. Chris hadn't seen any other humans in his dreams, but according to Rucknar, Chris was unlike any of the humans here. At the very least his hair and clothes were out of place.

"No one sent me here," Chris replied, determining honesty was the best policy. He didn't want to get caught in a tangle of lies, and he didn't know enough about this place to start making things up anyway.

Adamas paused. Chris could see the dragon king's expression changing. It didn't look like the dragon king was convinced Chris was telling the truth, but he was certainly a bit more curious.

"If you are not a spy, not from the metal city, and no one

sent you here then tell me, human, why *are* you here?" the dragon king asked, lowering his face down to Chris's to inspect him more closely.

Chris wanted to tell the truth, but he doubted the dragon king would believe him. Even so, what choice did he have, really? He looked into the king's large black eyes. They looked a lot like Rucknar's eyes but much more wizened and mature. Chris could feel hot dragon breath blowing over his face, and he could hear a rumbling in the king's chest as he breathed, moving in closer to Chris. Chris felt nervous having the dragon king's face so close to him. What if Adamas didn't like the answer Chris gave? He could easily gobble up Chris in one gulp. But, even so, Chris had to answer.

Chris gulped and then replied, "I don't know why I'm here. I just fell asleep and woke up here. Ya know? This is all just a dream."

Chris stared into the dragon king's cold black eyes, feeling the hot breath burning his skin and clothes.

Adamas lifted his head away from Chris and frowned in disappointment. "More human lies! There are no such things as dreams."

Chris could hear a long buzzing noise that was getting progressively louder.

"What's that?" Chris asked, looking around trying to pinpoint the noise.

The other dragons looked around, too, attempting to figure out what it was the strange human was talking about. But Adamas wouldn't be fooled. "No more lies, human. Or you will become the final feast to celebrate this day."

But before Adamas could say another word or the other dragons had a chance to act, Chris opened his eyes and was home, lying in his bed, his alarm clock ringing loudly in his ear. He rolled over sleepily and turned it off.

CHAPTER 10. BURNING DEN

As Rachel lay fast asleep in the warm confines of Ember's den, her head flooded with images of her family. Evalyn, Chris, Mom, and Dad all seemed to float in a black void, calling out to her, pleading with her to come home. Rachel tried to cry out to them, but they couldn't hear her. It was like she was a ghost, billions of miles away. Their voices were sad and strained. Rachel reached out into the darkness, but her arms wouldn't stretch far enough to reach them.

"Mom, Dad, I'm right here! Can't you see me?" her words echoed through the blackness, passing right through them without ever reaching their ears.

"Rachel, honey, everything's going to be okay." Mom's voice echoed shakily as she caressed the air in front of her like she was touching something very dear to her. "I'm here. I'm here, sweetheart."

Mom looked strange. Rachel had only ever seen her mom as a strong and powerful woman, one who could handle any situation, no matter how difficult, with grace and ease. For the first time in her life, Rachel saw her mom as a human being. Not a super woman but rather a person, scared and vulnerable.

"Rachel? Can you hear me, baby?" Mom looked as though she'd been crying.

"I'm here, Mom. It's okay. Really!" Rachel said, trying to

comfort the image of her mom projected in the darkness. She didn't like seeing her mom like this, scared and upset. Her mom didn't acknowledge her. Instead, Rachel's words just floated off worlds away from her family.

"Dear God!" Rachel's mom finally broke down quivering, tears streaming down her soft cheeks, smearing what was left of her makeup. "Please bring my Rachel home. Please bring her back to us."

Rachel woke up with a shock. Were her dreams ever going to get any better? She'd almost take being hunted again by the shadow wolves over seeing her mom like that. It had been a strange, long dream: the shadow wolves capturing her, meeting their leader, Umbra, then being rescued by firefoxes and mysticorns. She still couldn't figure out why her family had been part of it, but at least she was home now.

The room was much too dark for her to see, so she reached over blindly toward her lamp to turn it on and leaned into something warm and hairy. Rachel screamed as she shoved the hairy thing away, trying to get it off of her bed, causing it to let out a loud shriek in return. Crackling embers of fire shot out over all the room, dimly lighting it, allowing Rachel to see the room for the first time in the dying flames. It wasn't her room at all. In fact Rachel wasn't even in a room; she was still in the firefox den of a little black kit named Ember.

"Ouch!" a voice grumbled in the darkness. "Would it kill you to watch what you're doing?"

Rachel, surprised by the voice, replied somewhat defensively, "It's sort of hard to watch what I'm doing in the dark. You could have at least let me know you were there. You startled me!"

The voice replied smugly, "I startled you? Don't you mean *you* startled *me*?"

"Whatever," Rachel said. "Can you help me turn on a light or something, so I can at least see who I'm talking to?"

The den lightened to a low glow, and Rachel could see the crackly, burning body of a creature she recognized sitting down nearby, his fiery coat reminding her a little of hot coals in a dying fire.

"Ember!" Rachel beamed happily, reaching over to give him a great big hug.

"Careful!" he warned, and the den went dark again as Ember extinguished his flames just in time to prevent Rachel from getting burned as she gave him a tight squeeze.

"So what are you doing here anyway?" Rachel asked, surprised and pleased to see him.

"Well, this is *my* den after all," Ember chuckled. "But more important than that, I'm keeping you safe, of course!"

Ember smiled as he stepped back away from Rachel and again lit up the den with the dim light of his fur coat. "Wouldn't want those shadow wolves taking you back."

"You think they're going to come after me?" Rachel asked, feeling a nauseating sensation begin to rumble in the pit of her stomach at the thought.

"I wouldn't put it past them," Ember replied. "We did make them pretty mad, but don't worry, you're well protected. I'm here after all," he said with a wink.

"That's true," Rachel agreed with a smile. If there was one thing she knew about Ember it was how determined he was to keep her safe.

"So would you like me to show you around?" Ember asked, lighting the white flames on his ears, paws, and tail to brighten up the den even more than the charcoal glow of his body had.

"Umm, I guess so," Rachel replied, looking around the den with its dirt walls, dirt floor, and chunks of small, singed, wood pieces scattered about. The only other noticeable addition to the den was a large pile of leaves and long grass that Rachel had used as bedding.

"Alright!" Ember exclaimed cheerily as he stood up and stretched out his body. "Follow me!"

Rachel stood up too, and as she did, the sickening juices still swishing around her stomach after the talk of shadow wolves trying to capture her again changed into a squelchy grumble. She was hungry. Just how long *had* she slept? Rachel quickly grabbed the waterskin Incindia had left for her and tied it to her waist before picking up a loaf of bread left over from the night before. Food felt good in her belly and helped the nausea subside.

The walk to the den entrance was a short one. Leaves and brush covered the entrance so well that the light pouring over Rachel's face when Ember moved them aside was nearly blinding. The sun was high in the sky, confirming what Rachel's stomach already knew. She had slept for way too long.

"What time is it?" Rachel asked, not sure whether or not firefoxes kept time.

"About midday," Ember said looking up at the sun. "You slept an awfully long time."

"Well, I have been through a lot," Rachel said, frowning.

"That's true," Ember grinned, his fur dimming to black all over as the white flames extinguished in the sunlight.

Outside the den, the forest looked beautiful as the sun poured down through the leaves all around. Rachel could see firefoxes creeping out of foliage-covered holes here and there, and she wondered just how many dens there were. The one she stayed in was really quite quaint, with only one little tunnel leading to the cozy chamber or den in which she slept. She wondered if all firefox dens were that way or if some were more elaborate than others.

"This whole forest is our home," Ember said, walking beside Rachel through the trees. "The den you stayed in was mine, of course, but there are many others like it scattered throughout the forest. They're hard to find if you don't know what to look for, but that just keeps us better protected."

"Where does Incindia stay?" Rachel asked, hoping she would have a chance to thank Incindia for helping save her from the shadow wolves the day before. If it hadn't been for Incindia and the other brave firefoxes that broke into the shadow wolf den, Rachel would still be trapped there. She shuddered at the thought of what Umbra might have done to her if Incindia and the others hadn't found her just in time.

"Incindia's den is just north of here," Ember answered. "But there's really no point in going to it right now because she's not home."

"Not home?" Rachel asked with concern. Did she make it back safely after the encounter with the shadow wolves?

Ember, perceiving her thoughts, clarified by saying, "Don't worry, Incindia made it back safely. You'll have a chance to see her soon enough, but right now she's busy taking care of some important business."

That wasn't good enough for Rachel. She'd wanted to see Incindia for quite some time now, and when Caligo told her that Incindia believed Rachel held the key to bringing a stop to the darkness, it made her even more determined to speak with Incindia as soon as possible to find out what was going on.

"It can't be helped," Ember said, seeing the determined look in Rachel's eyes. "All we can do is wait for Incindia to return. But don't worry, I've got something special in mind to pass the time." He grinned widely, causing Rachel's determined expression to melt into a smile.

"Oh fine," she said. "What is it you had in mind?"

"It's a surprise," Ember replied, grinning even wider. "Are you up for a walk?"

"I guess so," Rachel agreed, shrugging her shoulders.

"It's settled then!" Ember said cheerily. "But before we leave I need to grab a bite to eat. Wait right here a minute."

Rachel watched as Ember bounded off toward a brown field of grass. It was the same field of grass where Rachel had seen all of the other firefoxes hopping around the night before. Ember was only gone a minute, and as he returned, Rachel could see him holding something brown and wooden between his teeth. It looked like a large, wooden mouse, though it wasn't moving at all.

Ember lay down on the ground, gently holding the wooden mouse between his paws as he began chewing at it until it caught fire. He continued to gnaw at it through the flames.

"You eat wood?" Rachel asked.

"Uh, yeah!" Ember said with a chuckle. "I'm a firefox after all. But this isn't just any wood, it's an Oakin."

"What's an Oakin?" Rachel asked, though she had a pretty good idea it had something to do with the mouse-like look of the piece of wood he was chewing.

"You don't know?" Ember said while devouring the last bits of the wooden mouse before standing up. "Don't worry,

I'll explain on the way. We'd better get going. It's a long walk."

Rachel followed closely behind, but all she could see ahead of her was what looked like miles of forest. As she turned back one last time to look at the dens as they were vanishing from view, a strange sense of déjà vu came over her, and she felt as though she had done this before, following a fox kit in a forest, but everything felt fuzzy in her mind.

"So," Ember said, continuing the conversation as the firefox homes vanished completely from sight, "the Oakin are the animals here that are born from the element of wood. Sort of like how we firefoxes are Fi'eri, born of the element of fire."

"You're a Fi'eri?" Rachel asked, trying to recall if that was a word she'd ever heard before. It sounded familiar. "Are their other Fi'eri beside firefoxes?"

"Sure," Ember said, continuing to walk through the woods. "But you know, I should probably start from the beginning. Did Incindia ever tell you about the Shadow Wars?"

"Shadow Wars?" Rachel repeated. "Nope, never heard of them."

"You see, it all began with the creation of Calim. No one knows exactly how Calim was created, but everyone knows it was a dark and desolate hunk of rock in the beginning. The whole planet was covered in darkness, and out of the darkness the Shadai were born."

"Like the shadow wolves, right?" Rachel asked.

"Exactly. The shadow wolves were some of the first Shadai to roam the planet, but they weren't the only ones. Remember when we rescued you from the shadow wolf den, and they all turned into shadows?"

"Yeah, I didn't know they did that before then," Rachel replied, remembering the shadow wolves running around the den, trapped in their shadow forms.

"That's because every time you saw them it was under the shadow of darkness. The thing about the Shadai is that they are only powerful in the absence of strong light. That's why we were able to rescue you from their den. They couldn't touch you in their shadow state, neither can any of the other Shadai. In the beginning, Calim was such a dark place because the whole planet's atmosphere was saturated with an obscurity that blocked out all light. No sun, moon, or starlight could penetrate the blackness. It was a very dark and cold place back then."

"But if the whole planet was covered in darkness," Rachel interrupted, "then how could the Shadai ever turn into shadows?"

"They didn't," Ember said, hopping over some logs that had fallen down in their path. "The Shadai weren't always shadows, or at least, they didn't realize they were. Under the cover of the darkness the Shadai were always in their solid form, so they never knew what their true nature really was. The reason we firefoxes refer to that period of time as the Shadow Wars is because of the constant fighting that occurred between all the different species of Shadai."

"So the Shadai fought with each other?" Rachel asked, not entirely surprised, as she thought of Drenar, the large shadow wolf with the torn ear.

"Yes," Ember continued, "the Shadai take great pleasure in causing suffering and pain in others, and since at that time the Shadai were the only species roaming the planet, they only had each other to fight with. One day, during one of their many wars, a bright light pierced through the darkness hanging over Calim, transforming those nearby into shadows. Word traveled quickly, and all the Shadai tried to stay as far away from the mysterious light as they could. They didn't know what to make of it, and they had no power over it since it rendered them completely formless when they were within its reach. The light began growing, changing Calim with it. Luminaries burst out of the light and began covering the land."

"Lu-mi-nar-ies?" Rachel said slowly, careful to pronounce the word just right.

"Yes," Ember smiled, pleased Rachel was showing interest in what he was saying, "the Luminaries are those on Calim that are made of light. The Luminaries are the light elementals."

"Okay, so basically, Calim was pitch black and the shadows or Shadai lived there, only they didn't know they were shadows. Then one day a light broke through the sky revealing to the Shadai their true form, while at the same time releasing Luminary over all the land?" Rachel summarized.

"Well, yes, but that was really just the start of Calim's transformation," Ember explained. "Despite how terrifying the light was to the Shadai at first and the stories they had been told by those exposed to the light, some of them began venturing into it anyway to see for themselves. See, the whole planet eventually became drenched in that light, and there were very few places left for the Shadai to hide. It wasn't until each Shadai ventured into the light for themself that they truly understood what they were. Reduced to shadows, they couldn't touch anything or speak to anyone, even among themselves." Ember paused a moment, giving

Rachel a chance to chime in, but she didn't, so he continued.

"At the same time the Shadai were learning about their true nature, peculiar things were happening all over the land. New life was springing forth. First were the Luminaries, of course. Then came the plants in all their different forms, textures, and sizes, which we now call the Oakin. Territories naturally developed, and climates fluctuated across the land. Legend has it we firefoxes were first born out of a raging fire that swept across the land, leaving a permanent scar where it torched the ground that still exists today. We walked right out of the blazing inferno, or so the story goes, and so did a number of other Fi'eri."

"So the Fi'eri are those born of fire, and the Shadai are shadows. The Luminary are light, and the Oakin are like plants, right? So what are the mysticorns? Just mist?" Rachel asked, thinking about Caligo carrying her safely away from the darkness and the shadow wolves.

"They're actually called the Vapori, but yeah, they're made of mist, which is a part of the Aquari family of elements blessed with the element of water. They say the Aquari birds flew right up out of the newly formed seas and rivers during Calim's awakening, and there were even dragons that crawled out of the volcanoes, and rocky bears that rolled off the mountainsides coming to life and breaking free of the planet itself. Well, you get the picture. The Shadai had finally learned their true nature, shadows in the light, solid and black in the darkness. You can almost always tell who's a Shadai by their color." Ember said. "Though there are a few exceptions to that rule."

"Like you?" Rachel asked, looking over Ember and his black ashen fur. "You're certainly not a Shadai, but you don't really look like a firefox, either."

"Yeah, like me I suppose," Ember said with a wink. "Actually, most young firefoxes go through a color changing phase. We start out orange, turn black like coal, and then slowly turn orange again. It's not until our second orange phase that we get our true flame. Really young foxes can't create a very large fire, so they have to stay close to the den until they get their second orange coat. They certainly can't defend themselves against something like a shadow wolf."

"When will you turn orange?" Rachel asked.

"I'm . . . uh . . . special," Ember replied with a slight blush of orange glow burning on his cheeks. "I'll never be orange in the same way the other firefoxes are."

"Why not?" Rachel asked, a look of genuine concern in her eyes. "Is there something wrong with you?"

"No, nothing's wrong really," Ember assured her, but Rachel could tell the conversation was beginning to make him feel uncomfortable. "Anyhow, I haven't finished telling you about Calim's transformation."

Rachel sighed, "Okay, continue." She was slightly disappointed, but Ember seemed grateful to continue with the story.

"The Shadai became more angry and spiteful than ever before after the other species took over the vast majority of the land, and they formed a pact with one another that they would never again kill one of their own kind. They all agreed that Calim's newer species like the Luminari, Fi'eri, Ai're, Aquari, Calimin, and Oakin were intruders taking over a world that should belong only to them. The shadow wolves are especially strict about keeping the ancient treaty. They no longer hunt or kill other Shadai. Instead they focus on terrorizing all the other species on Calim. They believe the Shadai are the rightful owners of this world, and they want to take it back."

Rachel was beginning to understand why Umbra had told her the Shadai would reign once again. If they were the first species on this planet, it was no wonder they felt as though they had a right to rule over it, however awful that would be for everyone and everything else.

"You just mentioned a species called an Ai're and another one called a Calimin, but you haven't told me about those yet," Rachel remarked, thinking through all of the different elementals Ember had just taught her about.

"Oh, that's right. It's hard to keep everything straight sometimes. The Ai're are those that are blessed with the element of air."

"Like those weird fish that look sort of like bubbles?" Rachel asked, recalling the airy looking fish that swam in the stream where she and Incindia had first met.

"Exactly!" Ember said excitedly. "You're catching on. The Calimin are the elementals made of rock or sometimes even metal. They are, in a way, part of the planet itself, born from the very crust of Calim."

They had walked for quite some distance now and Rachel was beginning to get thirsty. She polished off the last bit of water in the waterskin and tied the empty bag back onto her waist as Ember stopped to look around.

"We're nearly there," he announced, ears perked up and attentive.

Rachel couldn't help but wonder where he was leading her. She followed him around a steep hill covered in trees, which hid a very wide creek that was shallow enough in parts to walk through without becoming completely submerged under water. The whole area, including the creek, was brimming with wildlife. There was a bear swiping at fish in the water, a raccoon plucking berries off a bush, a red fox lapping up water with its tongue, a rabbit chewing on vegetation, a squirrel scurrying up the side of a tree with an acorn in its mouth, and many other animals doing the things animals do. There were birds, too, up high in the trees and flying through the air.

The fact that all of the animals seemed to be carrying on with their own business, ignoring each other, was certainly unusual, but it wasn't the strangest part of this place Ember had brought Rachel to. The strangest part was that not one of the animals was unusual in any way, at least not by Earth standards. All of the animals looked absolutely ordinary, and after getting to know some of the exotic species on Calim, these animals looked completely out of place here.

"So," Ember said, "notice anything different?"

"The animals here aren't elementals," Rachel said, though that was only one of the many subtle differences she was beginning to notice.

"That's true," Ember agreed. "Notice anything else?"

"These animals all look like they're from Earth," Rachel added, watching a hawk swoop down through the air to catch a mouse that did *not* look like it was made of wood.

"That's true, too," Ember smiled. "I want to show you something. Stay right here."

"Where are you going?" Rachel asked, slightly alarmed as she watched Ember bolt straight toward the large brown bear that only moments earlier had used its massive paws to snag a couple of fish from the water. As Ember reached the bear, Rachel watched, eyes wide, as it swiped a paw right at him—and then Ember was gone.

"Ember!" Rachel squeaked, both confused and horrified, trying to muffle her cry so as not to draw the bear's attention. The bear let out a mighty growl and turned its back toward Rachel as it hunched over and began ripping and tearing at something that Rachel hoped wasn't her friend.

"It's alright!" Ember's voice called out from beyond the bear. "Come here and see."

Rachel couldn't see Ember, but she could see the large bear still sitting with its back turned toward her.

"Come on!" Ember coaxed. "You're going to miss it!"

"Miss what?" Rachel whispered, still wary of the bear.

Ember, realizing that Rachel would require a little more persuading, poked his head out from beside the bear. "She won't hurt you. She's just an Echo."

"A what?" Rachel asked, taking enough courage from seeing Ember's face to make her way closer to where the bear sat.

"An Echo," Ember repeated, ducking back out of view.

Rachel gulped hard, looking one last time over the bear, which was entirely too close to her. She stepped softly around it, trusting that Ember knew what he was doing and saw what Ember was so anxious to show her. There were three bear cubs playing around a few saplings and small trees. One of them had managed to climb so far up a particularly skinny tree, it caused the trunk of the tree to arc. A second club, climbing up the same tree to follow its sibling, dangled by one paw in the center of the arc trying desperately to hold on. As the cubs played, the mother bear tore at an especially rotted log, digging for fat-rich grubs and other bugs, ignoring Rachel as she stopped next to Ember.

"They're playing," Ember said, watching the two bear cubs both fall from the bended tree, which sprang back up straight and tall once free of their weight. The third bear cub rushed over to tackle the other two, causing all three of them to tumble to the ground. The mother bear, looking up at her cubs while making a loud grunting noise, stood up and began walking away from Rachel and Ember with the little bear cubs trailing behind.

"I guess that's it," Ember said, apparently wishing there had been more time for him to show Rachel the bear cubs before they vanished from view.

"Is that what you brought me out here to see?" Rachel asked.

"Not just the bears," Ember replied as he looked around at the other animals that remained. "Although those cubs *were* pretty fun to watch," he added.

Rachel looked around, too, at the trees and the animals. "You wanted me to see this place? It is beautiful, but why?"

"I heard you last night," Ember admitted, "talking in your sleep. I heard you crying out to your family, and I figured you must be homesick."

Rachel thought back to her dream in the black void calling out to her mom. Ember was right. She had been feeling a little homesick, though she thought she had hidden it pretty well. This dream had gone on much longer than any of the ones she had before, and she couldn't understand why she hadn't woken up from it yet.

"The Echoes that come here are dreams from Earth. I thought if you were feeling a little down they might help cheer you up a bit," Ember said with a smile.

"These animals are all just dreams?" Rachel asked.

"Sure," Ember said. "They can't see us, hear us, or even touch us. They just come here for a little while to live out their dreams. Then, when the dream ends, the Echoes disappear. Sort of like you do."

"Am I an Echo, too?" Rachel asked, watching the

animals, so peaceful and beautiful, but also seeming somewhat detached from this world, unlike herself and Ember.

"I'm not sure," Ember said, lifting up his head. "I think you're an Echo, but you aren't exactly like the others. You're much more real than they are."

If Rachel was an Echo it was obvious she was very different from the ones Ember was showing her. She was aware of her surroundings, and she could see, hear, and touch everything in this world in a way that seemed very real—at least to her. The idea that there were animals from Earth whose dreams made it all the way to Calim was intriguing, opening up a world of possibilities in her mind.

Were there other dreamers from Earth like her? People who came to visit here the same way she did? Or was she just an oddity, alone in this strange world?

She looked at Ember, appreciating his thoughtfulness for bringing her here and teaching her about Calim's history and inhabitants. This place *was* peaceful, and it did give her comfort, because it was a little bit of home brought here to Calim.

"Thank you," she said, giving Ember a warm smile, "for bringing me here."

"My pleasure," Ember grinned, giving Rachel a low bow in return. "It's about time we headed back. Get some water if you need to, it's pure and clean here. The Aquari take very good care of it."

Rachel drank her fill of water and filled up her waterskin in preparation for the trip back. She noticed Ember sniffing at the cool creek flowing past, but he didn't drink.

"Aren't you thirsty, too?" she asked, realizing she hadn't seen him drink anything all day.

Ember let out a laugh. "Fire and water don't exactly mix."

"Oh, I didn't think about that," Rachel said, slightly embarrassed for not having realized that on her own. "So you don't drink anything ever?"

"Nope," Ember said, a hint of firefox pride in his voice, "I don't have to. I get all the nourishment I need from the forest. Even the leaves on the ground help sustain me when I burn them properly."

Rachel thought back to the trails of ash she had followed when she first came to Calim. Were those trails burned into the forest floor a firefox's way of taking a drink? Or had they been more purposefully placed than that? They did lead her straight to Incindia, which was either by dumb luck or destiny. Rachel still wasn't certain which.

Incindia . . . Rachel needed to speak with her. To ask her what the mysticorn Caligo meant when he said Rachel was the key to stopping the darkness, and what Umbra meant when he said he needed someone like her to help the darkness grow.

CHAPTER 11. SECRET DREAMS

Chris sat at the breakfast table picking at his food, trying to prolong the morning meal as much as possible before dragging himself out the door to head to school. A new school year had begun without Rachel, who was still spending her days in a hospital bed, unaware of the time slipping past. Breakfast wasn't the same anymore, not without a little sister to pick on. Nothing was the same anymore.

The minutes ticked past with little progress made in finishing his food. He didn't have an appetite this morning, which for Chris was unheard of. His mind drifted to the strange dreams he'd been having about dragons and kobolds. Normally he'd blame Rachel for his weird dreams, coming up with some crazy excuse as to why they were her fault. But she wasn't here to blame, and he was beginning to worry that she might never come back.

"Chris, it's time to go!" Evalyn shouted from the entry foyer, swinging a keychain with a car key on her finger ready to drive to school.

"Hurry, Chris! Or we're going to be late," Evalyn barked as she watched her brother move like molasses to get out of his chair and put his backpack on.

As they got in the car and headed toward school, Evalyn, fuming, finally blurted out, "What's wrong with you today? You're not acting normal!"

"Oh, and you are?" Chris shot back grumpily, giving her an ice-cold glare.

Since the accident, Evalyn was more easily angered and agitated, lashing out at everything and everyone who crossed her path, a drastic change from her normally cheery self. Chris on the other hand was just the opposite. He felt somewhat depressed and withdrawn, not enjoying things nearly as much as he used to. Evalyn knew Chris was right, that Rachel's absence from the family had changed things for everyone, which is why instead of irritating him further, she chose to drive the rest of the way to school in silence.

After school, as Chris rode down the street on his skateboard to spend time away from the house and get his mind off Rachel, he spied Ryan following him on a bike, holding a Welcome Home card and a stuffed animal.

"Chris!" Ryan shouted, waving the stuffed animal in the air.

For a moment Chris pretended not to hear him, but it was too late, he'd already looked Ryan's way. So instead he resolved to just get the conversation over as quickly as possible.

"What's up Ryan?" Chris asked, cracking a half smile while stopping his skateboard.

"I have something for you . . . well, for you to give to Rachel when she comes home," Ryan clarified, stopping his bike next to Chris.

"When she comes home?" Chris asked, a little startled that Ryan would have the audacity to act like he knew what was going to happen to Rachel when *no one* knew what was going to happen to her: not the doctors, not his parents, and least of all Ryan. "You know she's still at the hospital, right?

She hasn't woken up yet."

"I know," Ryan replied, undeterred, "but when she does wake up and comes home, I want this to be in her room waiting for her. Do you think you could put it there for me?"

Chris sighed, looking at the card and the stuffed animal. Just because he wasn't feeling all that great didn't mean he had to drag Ryan down with him. Besides it *was* a very nice gesture.

"Yeah, sure," Chris agreed reluctantly, taking the card and stuffed animal from Ryan's hands before hopping on his skateboard again to head home.

The house was quiet. Evalyn was out with friends, no doubt trying to take her mind off everything going on at home the same way Chris had been. Mom was at the hospital visiting Rachel again, and Dad was working late, leaving Chris all alone. He made his way up to Rachel's room, but as he touched the knob to open the door, he paused.

No one had gone into Rachel's room since the camping trip, not even Mom, and Chris wasn't sure if anyone was even allowed in her room. Staying out of Rachel's room seemed to be an unwritten rule that everyone just obeyed. It didn't feel right, the thought of going in, not when she wasn't able to enter herself. He looked at the card and stuffed animal he was still carrying, and although it went against his better judgment, he turned the knob and gently pushed the door, swinging it open.

Inside, clothes were thrown about the room, books lay all over in disarray, and to anyone unaware of the situation the room would look like it was well lived in. But for Chris, the room seemed lonely. He walked over and sat down on Rachel's bed, setting the card and stuffed animal on her nightstand. As he did, he saw the corner of a book poking out from underneath her pillow. He slid his hand under to pull it out, figuring it was probably the last book Rachel had read when life was still normal.

As he turned the book over in his hand, he instantly recognized it: It wasn't a storybook, it was her diary, the one Mom had given her for her last birthday. If entering her room had seemed wrong before, then what he was considering to do next was even worse, but he couldn't resist the urge to crack open the diary and look inside. The first word read *Firefox*.

"Well, that's bizarre," Chris said aloud, wondering why Rachel would have written something like that to start off her diary. Maybe it was a code word for something else, but as he read on it became abundantly clear it wasn't a code word at all. Rachel had been keeping a record of her dreams. It said so right in the book, describing her dreams in excruciating detail—and her dreams were really, really weird.

After browsing a bit, Chris decided to return the diary and leave Rachel's room the way he had found it. After all, Mom and Dad would be home soon. Just as he began to close the pages a word caught his eye that triggered an intense rush of adrenaline. The word was *Shadai*, followed by the words *shadow wolves*. Chris knew those words. He'd heard them before, digging them out of his mind like a distant memory that had nearly faded to extinction.

Rucknar had mentioned the word *Shadai* once; Chris was certain of it. And regarding shadow wolves, the kobolds had said something about them, too. At least he thought they had. *But it was impossible.* Why would Rachel have written *those* words in her diary? He had never mentioned his dreams to her, and what was more, she had written down all sorts of things about the Shadai and the shadow wolves that Chris knew nothing about.

He went to his room, bringing the diary with him to avoid risking the wrath of Mom or Dad should they find him in Rachel's room when they arrived home. They would know eventually that someone had gone in there once they saw the Welcome Home card and stuffed animal sitting on her nightstand, but Chris felt certain "eventually" didn't mean anytime soon, and they probably didn't know about the diary, either, so it wouldn't be missed.

He sat at his desk and pulled out the crystalline scale from his pocket, the one that looked just like Rucknar's scales. Holding the scale in one hand, feeling the rough texture between his fingers, he continued to read the diary, this time more carefully, looking for clues that might help explain what had happened to Rachel that awful morning at the campout.

There were too many strange things going on for Chris to brush off everything as mere coincidence anymore. He was onto something; he could feel it with each pulse of adrenaline that rushed through his body as he uncovered Rachel's secret dreams. The dreams became worse as Chris read on, transforming from the happy and beautiful memories he could tell his sister cherished to dark and terrifying nightmares. She was scared and upset. How could he not have noticed?

But he knew exactly why he and the rest of the family had no clue about what was going on in Rachel's life. They were each so absorbed with their own plans and their own lives they were blinded from seeing what was happening to her. She had been silently suffering as the nightmares intensified, but no one saw or knew. Rachel had endured everything alone.

After he finished reading, Chris wasn't satisfied. There were too many questions and not enough answers. The firefoxes were a place to start maybe; if Rucknar knew about the Shadai then it was entirely possible he knew about those things as well. As crazy as it seemed, Chris had a suspicion that he'd see Rucknar again in his dreams, and if he did, it was possible there might be a chance, however small, he'd be able to find Rachel there too.

He looked at the scale between his fingers. There was no concrete proof of its origin, only the remnants of a dream, but after reading Rachel's diary he wondered. Was he really holding a dragon scale? How was that even possible? He tucked the scale back into his pocket and slid the diary into a desk drawer.

After dinner, which consisted of a boxed meal and some microwave popcorn, Chris finished up his homework and went to bed. It took some time to fall asleep because he was both excited and nervous about continuing the dream he had left off. In his last dream, the dragon king Adamas was interrogating him. What if Rachel was right about the dream world being real, and he found himself confronted by the king once more? He banished the thought from his mind. Whatever happened next, Chris had to know if Rachel's diary and his dreams were connected, or if he was just losing it because he had lost his sister to an unending sleep.

The trees were tall and the terrain was rough and heavily sloped. Chris didn't recognize this place, but he was definitely back inside his dream. He skidded down some boulders to reach a much more level terrain and detected the scent of burning fire off in the distance. As he made his way toward the smell's origin, he saw flashes of light dart across the sky through gaps in the leafy canopy above him.

I wonder if those are Luminary? he pondered, remembering the moth-like creatures he had seen in the kobold mines. They reminded him a little of those moths, though he could have sworn that one of them looked just like a bird, spreading its wings wide open as it glided past.

The smell of the fire was very close now. Was it possible he had found one of Rachel's firefoxes so quickly? He tried to step as quietly as he could up to the spot where the smell of smoke still lingered. There was no fire and no firefox, much to his disappointment, but there was something else on a large patch of singed earth.

"Ruck!" Chris said enthusiastically, waking the young dragon from his slumber. Seeing Rucknar made Chris feel much more like himself again.

"You're here?" Rucknar snorted grumpily in disbelief, still groggy. "How did you find me?" he asked, looking around as if to make sure Chris was alone.

"I dunno," Chris replied, scratching the back of his head. "We just keep bumping into each other."

"Why did you come back?" Rucknar hissed, standing up and stretching his wings to help him finish waking up. "Do you have a death wish or something?"

"Whaddya mean?" Chris asked innocently. He and Rucknar were still friends, weren't they? "Of course I don't!"

"You caused quite a stir at the ceremony. The dragons are furious! They don't know how you got away, but they are looking everywhere for you," Rucknar huffed.

"They are?" Chris asked. It made sense. His alarm clock had saved him from the dragon king's clutches just in time. Evading the king was sure to have put him in a bad mood and in turn, all of his dragons.

"You'd better leave," Rucknar said, folding his wings flat against his back again, squinting at Chris. "They won't be nearly as friendly this time."

Chris appreciated the warning, but he had business to take care of, and he wasn't going anywhere until he got some answers.

"I can't leave, Ruck, not yet. We need to talk."

Rucknar looked up toward the bits of sky he could see, through the leafy green canopy of the trees. "They're coming," he said, alarmed, backing away from Chris.

"Who's coming?" Chris asked, watching Rucknar's tail whip back and forth in irritation.

"The dragons," Rucknar hissed, giving Chris a sharp glare.

"For me?" Chris asked, wondering how they could've known so quickly where he was. He hadn't even had a chance to ask Rucknar about the firefoxes or the shadow wolves.

"No," Rucknar replied, backing away even further, "they aren't coming for you, they're coming for me."

"For you?" Chris said, surprised. "Why would they be after you?"

Rucknar didn't answer. Instead he slinked even farther away, turned around, and began to run.

"Wait up!" Chris called, chasing after him as fast as he could through the trees. Just when he thought Rucknar had given him the slip, he saw a smoky-brown tail with crystal-looking scales slide underneath an enormous, flat, boulder in a small clearing where the trees had thinned. Chris looked to the open sky but didn't see any dragons. He rushed through the clearing to the boulder as well and ducked underneath it, crawling military style into the dark space.

"Ruck!" Chris called, unable to see clearly underneath the large rock.

He heard a shuffling noise and then nothing but silence. He had almost called out to Rucknar again when a loud boom sounded out as something large landed on the boulder above, shaking the ground beneath it, along with Chris, who froze in place. Then another loud booming sound shook the ground again, and Chris could hear heavy footsteps and dragging noises across the boulder above him.

"Are you sure he went this way?" a strong masculine voice asked. It wasn't Adamas' voice, but it was definitely one of the dragons.

"I think so," a second voice replied, sounding every bit as much like a dragon as the first. "I was certain I saw something this direction."

"Let's keep searching," the first dragon directed. "He can't be much farther. He's still just a youngling, so his wings aren't strong enough to carry him yet, and Adamas will be even more furious than when he lost the boy if we don't bring Rucknar home soon."

Rucknar was right. The dragons were searching for him, but why? In the dark space beneath the rock, Chris waited silently for the dragons to leave. They tarried only a few moments more before Chris could hear the boulder creak in relief as the weight of the dragons lifted off. It was some time before Chris felt safe enough to speak, let alone move. It wasn't until he heard a slight shuffle in the darkness again that he felt certain the dragons were truly gone.

"Ruck," Chris whispered out, "I really need to talk to you. It's about my sister."

The shuffling halted, then changed direction, drawing

closer until Chris could make out Rucknar's face staring at him beady eyed through the darkness.

"Your sister?" Rucknar hissed quietly. It had never occurred to him that this human was part of a family.

"Yes," Chris said, "I have two of them actually, but one is in trouble, and I want to help her if I can."

"What sort of trouble?" Rucknar asked, squinting suspiciously at Chris while whipping his tail behind him. Chris couldn't see Rucknar's tail, but he could hear it thrashing across the ground.

"She's fallen asleep and won't wake up," Chris summarized, "and I need you to tell me how to find the firefoxes and the shadow wolves."

"Why would you want to do that?" Rucknar asked, his curiosity piqued, though he remained cautious of the strange human's request. "Humans have no dealings with *shadow wolves* or *firefoxes*."

That was exactly what Chris had been hoping to hear. Rucknar had just confirmed that shadow wolves and firefoxes both did exist in this dream world. There was only one more piece of information he needed to be certain of to confirm that he and Rachel were dreaming about the same place.

"Ruck, my sister met with some firefoxes and was being chased down by shadow wolves under something she called the darkness."

"What would a human be doing in Shadai territory?" Rucknar asked, sounding as if the world as he knew it was being turned upside down, and this was only the beginning.

"So you know where it is?" Chris asked hopefully.

"Not really," Rucknar admitted, "but I've heard the elders talk about it."

Chris's heart sank. If Rucknar didn't know how to find the shadow wolves or firefoxes, how was he going to?

"There was one more thing my sister mentioned," Chris continued, hoping to get a little more information out of Rucknar while he was still in a somewhat agreeable mood. "She said the darkness was growing and soon it would engulf all of Calim."

"Impossible!" Rucknar protested, not even flinching at Chris's mention of Calim, which was the last piece of information he needed to confirm that he and Rachel really were dreaming about the same world. "The darkness doesn't grow, it can't. All dragons know the tale of the sentinels who banished Skia to the darkness to maintain the balance of the elements."

"The balance of what?" Chris asked, realizing the conversation was morphing from a discussion on how to help his sister into a dragon history lesson. "Look, Ruck, I don't really want to argue about the darkness with you. I just want to help my sister."

"How could your sister have told you so much if she's asleep?" Rucknar inquired suspiciously, wondering if Adamas had been right about humans and that Chris was just a liar trying to trick him.

"It doesn't really matter," Chris said, exasperated, not wanting to get into a long discussion about the diary, the camping trip, and everything else that had happened. "The point is, I need to know how to find the firefoxes, to see if they know what happened to my sister. And you're the only one I know who can help. So will you help me or not?"

Rucknar considered. He had no intention of going back home any time soon, and he did believe Chris, despite having reservations about the human's story.

"Follow me," Rucknar directed, turning around to scurry out from under the large boulder into the open air. Chris followed, thinking about the two dragons that had come so close to finding the both of them. If Rucknar felt safe enough to be out in the open again, then Chris felt certain, at least for now, it must be safe.

"I heard something once," Rucknar said, as Chris followed closely behind, not knowing where Rucknar was taking him. "I overheard the elders talking about a people in the windlands called the Evarance Keepers who protect all the histories of Calim. Not just the human histories, but the histories of all species, including us dragons. Though they look human the elders don't believe they are. Most humans are bad and seek the destruction and enslavement of my kind, but there is something different about those who live there. One elder said they had powers that were both unnatural and at the same time beautiful. Powers unlike anything he had ever seen."

"And do you think they might know where my sister is?" Chris asked, trying to suppress the hope rising in his chest. Chris recognized the word *Evarance*. It was also one of the words in Rachel's diary. Speaking with Rucknar had been everything he had hoped it would be and more. It was as though the pieces of a puzzle were slowly coming together.

"If anyone could help lead you in the right direction I think it might be them," Rucknar concluded. "At the very least they would know where you could find the firefoxes."

"Do you know how to get there?" Chris inquired.

"I think so," Rucknar hissed. "I haven't been there before, but it shouldn't be too hard to find."

Chris needed to convince Rucknar to help him. It was

his only hope of finding Rachel—or at the very least of finding out more about what had happened to her here. If the other dragons were looking for Rucknar, and he didn't want to be found, which was apparent from the way he had reacted when the two dragons came looking for him, there might be a chance he would take Chris to the Evarance Keepers.

"Hey, Ruck," Chris said, still following Rucknar as he scurried onto a dirt path carved out in the middle of the woods.

"Yes?" Rucknar hissed, continuing to walk forward without giving Chris so much as a sideways glance.

"Do you, well, I mean . . ." Chris struggled to ask the question, realizing that if Rucknar said no, he'd be at a complete loss as to what to do next. "Do you think you could take me there? To the Evarance Keepers, that is. Or at least point me in the right direction?"

Rucknar stopped in the middle of the path and turned around to look at Chris, cracking a dragonish smile. Chris had never seen Rucknar smile before, so he couldn't tell if it was a good thing or a bad thing.

"We're nearly there," Rucknar said, smiling even wider.

"We're *what*?" Chris asked, still processing what it was Rucknar had just said.

"The windlands are just up ahead, with Divarus, home of the Evarance Keepers, about a day's journey in. I can take you there, unless of course you want to stay here and wait for the other dragons to find you."

"Of course I want to go with ya, Ruck!" Chris said, smiling back. "Why didn't you tell me you were headed that way?"

"You never asked," Rucknar snorted, his smile fading

back to his usual serious expression as he turned and began walking again.

Chris continued to follow, but as they walked he couldn't shake the feeling that his dream was going to end soon, long before he would be able to make it to Divarus to meet with the Evarance Keepers.

"Ruck?" Chris asked, thinking more and more about the dream ending as they walked. "If I, say, disappeared while we were on our way there, like I did when Adamas was questioning me, what would you do?"

"Continue to Divarus," Rucknar replied without so much as blinking an eye. "I'm not just going there to help you. I have business I need to discuss with the Evarance Keepers, too."

That surprised Chris. What business did Rucknar have with them? And why were the dragons looking for him?

"I was wondering . . ." Rucknar said, hitting the end of the forest path and stepping out into a large valley covered in green grass, "how *did* you escape with Adamas and the other dragons completely surrounding you?"

"I don't really know," Chris said, shrugging. He wasn't sure if he should tell Rucknar that this was all just a dream for him and that he had woken up just in the nick of time.

He had told Adamas about the dream, but Adamas didn't believe him, calling him a liar, refusing to give credence to the existence of dreams. What if Rucknar was the same and turned on Chris at the very mention of it? At the same time, Chris had been curious about what Adamas had implied. If Adamas didn't believe in dreams, did that mean dragons didn't have dreams?

"Ruck, do dragons dream?" Chris asked. He knew that he was going to wake up soon. He could already feel himself beginning to come in and out of consciousness in his bedroom back at home. He would have to explain to Ruck about the dreams, even if he felt hesitant about it. It was the only way to help Rucknar understand why Chris was about to disappear again.

"No," Rucknar replied, "we dragons don't dream. But I heard what you told Adamas, and I believe you."

That was the last thing Chris heard before his alarm sounded, telling him it was time to get up and get ready for another day at school.

CHAPTER 12. TOKENS

It had only taken one night, one dream, for Chris's demeanor to completely change. Evalyn noticed it as she watched Chris scarf down mounds of freezer waffles, orange juice, and microwave sausages for breakfast.

"What's gotten into you?" she asked, not sure how to react to her brother's newfound appetite and energy.

"It's Rachel!" Chris said with a smile, slurping down the last drops of orange juice in his cup.

"What about her?" Evalyn questioned warily. She had been up late speaking with Mom and Dad about Rachel's condition. To her knowledge nothing had changed. Was it possible that something had happened this morning that Chris knew about and she didn't?

"I think I might be able to find her," Chris said as he cleared his plate off the table, dumping it in the sink.

"What do you mean *find her*?" Evalyn inquired, taken aback, panic flooding her mind as terrible thoughts raced through about what might have happened to Rachel in the short time that had passed since she last spoke with Mom and Dad. "Did she go missing?"

"Umm. No," Chris replied, realizing that he and Evalyn weren't even communicating on the same plane of thought.

"Well, then what in the heck are you talking about?" Evalyn demanded, feeling what little patience she had swiftly fleeing.

"So it's like this," Chris said, trying to think of a way to explain what was going on without freaking out Evalyn in the process, "I started having these really weird dreams—"

"Oh, Chris," Evalyn sighed, brushing off what he had just begun to say, "I thought you were talking about something *important*. You scared me, making it sound like someone had taken Rachel from the hospital."

"Eva, it *is* important!" Chris countered. "Would you just hear me out?"

Evalyn remained skeptical, but seeing the determined expression on Chris's face she considered giving him a chance to explain himself, however ridiculous it might be.

"Oh fine," Evalyn agreed reluctantly, "you can explain it to me on the way to school. We have to get going or we're going to be late."

Once in the car Chris watched Evalyn for clues that she might be ready to hear what he had to say. She didn't look his way, but she also didn't turn on the radio, so he took that as a sign that she was at least amenable to hearing him out.

"So . . ." he began, "I've been havin' these really weird dreams. At first, that's all I thought they were. I had a dream about a mine full of these kobold things that looked sort of like short wolf people and I met a dragon named Rucknar who helped me escape. The dream felt so real, you know? But dreams aren't real, right? So after I woke up, somethin' rolled out of my pocket onto the floor. Only it looked just like somethin' I had picked up off the ground in my dream."

"Chris, you aren't making any sense," Evalyn said, pulling up to a stoplight as the light turned red.

"Look!" Chris said insistently, grabbing the crystal scale from his pocket and holding it in front of Evalyn's face.

"What is it?" Evalyn asked, taking the scale and turning it over in her hand before handing it back.

"I think it's a dragon scale," Chris replied.

"A what?" Evalyn balked, wondering how Chris expected her to take him seriously after saying something like that.

"A dragon scale," Chris repeated as if Evalyn hadn't heard him the first time.

"And what's a *dragon scale* got to do with Rachel?" Evayln asked, humoring her brother a little longer just to see what sort of crazy connection he would come up with. The light turned green, so Evalyn continued driving.

"It's not so much the dragon scale, Eva. It's what the dragon scale means. It means my dreams are *real*."

"That's ridiculous," Evalyn said dismissively, speeding up to pass the slower vehicle traveling beside her. "Dreams aren't real."

"Yes, they are," Chris asserted, "and I can prove it!"

He whipped Rachel's diary out of his backpack and held it up. Evalyn briefly glanced over to see what stunt Chris was trying to pull now when she saw the diary and recognized exactly what it was. It was Rachel's, and Chris had no business taking it. Infuriated, Evalyn pressed her foot down even harder, but when she refocused her eyes on the road, she saw a series of red tail lights speeding toward her.

"Watch out!" Chris shouted, looking over as they sped forward toward the stopped cars.

Evalyn's foot fumbled as she tried to hit the brakes and she pulled the steering wheel hard, just missing the car in front of her as they rumbled down the curb, screeching to a halt.

Her heart pounded painfully in her chest and her hands,

still holding the wheel, shook. As the shock of the near accident set in, tears began filling her eyes.

"Chris! How could you!" Evalyn snapped, wiping the salty wet tears from her cheeks as they dripped down, thinking about her little sister. "That diary is Rachel's. How could you invade her privacy like that? Especially with things the way they are right now?"

"It's not what you think!" Chris said. "This is more like a dream book than a diary. It's a record of Rachel's dreams. She was having some pretty crazy ones before the accident, and I'm havin' dreams just like them."

"Chris, just stop," Evalyn pleaded, feeling her anger transform into despair as she lifted both hands off the steering wheel, still shaking, to cover her face in an attempt to prevent more tears from dripping onto her pants. "Rachel's in the hospital, and there's nothing we can do about it!"

"But there is," Chris insisted. "Ruck is takin' me to the Evarance Keepers. He thinks they might be able to help me find Rachel."

"The *what*?" Evalyn asked, sniffing and drying her eyes with her shirt sleeve.

"The Evarance Keepers," Chris said again, and as he did Evalyn's eyes grew wide with surprise.

"How did you know about that?" Evalyn asked, her heart no longer pounding from the sudden stop of the car, now pounding because of something else entirely.

"What, the Keepers?" Chris replied.

"No, the Evarance," Evalyn clarified, wiping her eyes one last time as the tears subsided.

"Oh, well Ruck mentioned the Evarance Keepers to me, and Rachel wrote all about the Evarance in her diary," Chris said, shrugging his shoulders as he tried to read Evalyn's face to figure out what was going through her mind. "Wait," he continued, "you've heard of the Evarance, too, haven't you?"

It was true. As much as she wanted to deny it, especially after reacting the way she had, she couldn't. She remembered her dream about a handsome boy named Kendrick, a boy who taught her about the Evarance and the dreamers.

"But that's impossible," Evalyn gasped. "It was just a dream."

"I know, right?" Chris agreed, passing the diary over so Evalyn could see for herself the things that Rachel had written.

Evalyn looked down at the diary on her lap, not touching it, just staring at it. "But . . ." she began to protest. The thought of reading Rachel's personal thoughts still felt very wrong.

"Please read it, Eva," Chris said with all the sincerity he could muster. If Evalyn was having the same sort of dreams he was, then there was an even better chance of finding out what had happened to Rachel. It meant they were all connected, and if that were true, Evalyn could help.

Picking up the diary firmly in her hands, Evayln cringed as she opened it to the first page. "I can't believe you're making me do this," she said, giving Chris one last glance of uncertainty before reading the first word: *Firefox*.

Evalyn continued to read, flipping through the pages, losing track of time and place. Many of the things Rachel wrote weren't familiar to her, but then she found it: the word *Evarance* written in Rachel's own hand.

"There was a boy in my dream," Evalyn said to Chris, looking thoughtfully at the pages of the diary. "He told me about the Evarance. What it was and how it worked. He said it was a path that we travel through when we dream, and he called the dreamers Echoes. He thought I might be an Echo, too, a dreamer visiting from another world. He told me his world was called Calim. But unlike the Echoes he showed me, which were ghostlike and distant, I was there and somehow I was real. I know it sounds crazy."

"No crazier than me meeting a dragon and takin' one of its scales home," Chris replied with a laugh.

"I guess not," Evalyn agreed, cracking a smile. "There was something else that happened in my dream. I was given something by the boy. A flower that looked and smelled so beautiful. He called it an andalyn and said it was an echoprint left behind by a little girl. He gave it to me and asked me if I would keep it." Evalyn's thoughts trailed off as she recalled the dream burned into her memory.

"And when I woke up, there was a flower in my hand," she added, letting out a gasp as she realized what that might mean. She had brushed off the flower as a gift from a secret admirer or a prank pulled by Chris. She had never *actually* entertained the idea that it was really the same flower as the one given her in the dream.

"Chris, we have to go home!" Evalyn exclaimed, handing the diary back to him before returning her hands to the steering wheel, turning the signal on as she got back on the road.

"But what about school?" Chris asked. "Mom and Dad will kill us if we don't go."

"I've just got to know if the flower is still there," Evalyn argued, flipping a U-turn at the earliest spot available. "Besides, we're already late. Our best bet is to get home and call Mom and Dad to tell them we're both sick today before the school calls to say we're not there."

"Lyin' about being sick, skipping school . . . who are you and what have you done with my sister?" Chris joked. He'd always wanted to play hooky and skip school for a day, but Evalyn, being the goody-goody that she was, made that nearly impossible – at least until now.

When they pulled up to the house Chris ran in and called Mom, giving her his best fake sick voice before handing the phone to Evalyn, who confirmed that they were both too ill to go to school. Thankfully Mom bought it and was too busy having just returned to work to take off to tend to them, leaving Evalyn and Chris free to explore the mysteries of the diary.

Evalyn rushed to her room, searching for the flower, which had been in the vase on her nightstand. After the camping trip, in all her anger and frustration, she had knocked several things off of her dresser and nightstand while trying to cope with the loss of her sister. She found the vase empty on the ground, the spilled water now completely evaporated with the passage of days.

Checking beneath her nightstand, Evalyn spotted a long green stem and grabbing it, pulled the flower out along with some dust that clung to its petals. The flower was still alive, and more than that it was as beautiful as ever, smelling every bit as heavenly as it had in her dream. Even without water and sunlight, the flower showed no signs of bruising or wilting.

"Did you find it?" Chris asked, walking into her room, backpack put away but with Rachel's diary still in his hand.

"It's here," Evalyn replied, showing Chris the flower as she gently brushed off the dust, revealing the brilliant white and red coloring. The petals felt like silk and radiated with strength and life. "I can't believe it's still alive."

"I can," Chris said, no doubt in his mind that Evalyn's flower was just like his scale: a token of some sort from the dreams.

"I still don't really know if I believe it, though," Evalyn said, twirling the flower between her fingers as she sat down on her bed. "How could Rachel have known about the Evarance?"

"The same way you do," Chris said, handing the diary again to Evalyn. "You need to read the rest," he added, wanting her to see for herself the nightmares Rachel was having and what those nightmares implied.

Evalyn opened the diary, returning to the page she had left off. She read on, past the Evarance and into the darkness, where shadow wolves were hunting her little sister and a black firefox named Ember was risking his life to protect Rachel from the monstrous wolves.

Upon reaching the last page, Evalyn's heart sank. "Is that it?" she asked Chris, hoping by some miracle he knew more about what had happened to Rachel than what the book presented.

"Afraid so," Chris replied. "But look," he directed, flipping back a few pages, pointing at the last date entered in the diary.

"That's . . ." Evalyn breathed as she now understood why Chris had been so anxious for her to read the diary to the end.

". . . the morning of the campout," Chris finished. "Her last dream before the accident. The shadow wolves were after her, and they were so close. What if they actually got her?"

Evalyn didn't want to entertain that thought. She could

feel the fear and pain Rachel had been going through while she read the diary. But she couldn't handle speculating about what horrible things might have happened to her sister after that last entry.

"I'm gonna to find her," Chris said with that same determined look on his face that had convinced Evalyn to hear him out on the way to school. "Or at least find out what happened to her."

"Do you really think that's possible?" Evalyn asked as doubt and disbelief still plagued her mind despite all of the evidence in front of her.

"I know it is," said Chris. "The world Rachel dreamed about, it's called Calim. Eva, it's the same world you and I dream about, too. We're all connected to it. Ruck and I are almost at the Evarance Keepers, and according to him, if anyone can help us find Rachel it's them."

"I want to believe you, Chris," said Evalyn. "I really do. But it just seems so impossible."

Chris thought for a moment. There was nothing more he could say or do to convince Evalyn of what he already knew to be true. He pulled the dragon scale out of his pocket and looked at it along with the flower Evalyn was holding. The only time he could remember dreaming about Rucknar, with the exception of his first dream, was when he fell asleep with the scale on his person. Other nights his dreams were either uneventful or nonexistent. Maybe it worked the same way with Evalyn and the flower.

"I have an idea," Chris said, holding up the scale, looking at it with the light that shone through Evalyn's blinds.

"The times I dreamt of the world Rachel wrote about I had the scale with me when I fell asleep. Maybe it's the same way with you and your flower. If you fall asleep with the flower maybe you'll see that Ken guy again."

"Maybe," Evalyn agreed. "I guess it wouldn't hurt to try."

"Do you think you can trust him?" Chris asked.

"Of course," Evalyn said, without a moment's hesitation, "he was so nice to me, and he *did* give me this flower. If it helps me dream about that place again, I guess I could ask him about the Evarance Keepers. He seemed to know a lot about the Evarance."

"Alright, it's settled then," Chris concluded. "I'll go with Ruck to the Evarance Keepers, and you can try to meet me there."

The plan sounded like it might work *if* Evalyn dreamed about that boy again *and if* that dream was connected to both Rachel's and Chris's dreams. It still seemed like a long shot in Evalyn's mind, but she resolved at least to try. She kept the diary in her room and read over it several times, committing to memory as much as she could about the world of which Rachel wrote. If Chris was right about their dreams being connected, she had a feeling that the record of dreams in Rachel's diary would become vital in their search for her.

As the day passed, Mom called home several times to make sure both Chris and Evalyn were doing okay. By evening, when Mom and Dad were finally home from work, Chris and Evalyn both felt miraculously better. Dad decided they both must have caught a 24-hour bug. Mom wasn't so sure and was a little skeptical of their so-called illness, but she didn't pursue those suspicions further.

When it was time for bed, Evalyn took the flower out of the vase, which was once again situated atop her nightstand,

and held it in her hand. She lay in bed and placed her hand and the flower close to her face as she drifted into a deep slumber, breathing in the flower's intoxicating scent. When she opened her eyes, she was on a bed in a quaint wooden cottage with an old-fashioned fireplace actively burning, keeping the whole house toasty warm. She knew this home; it was Kendrick's.

"I'm back," she breathed, sitting up in the bed, amazed that falling asleep with the flower had actually worked. Not only had the flower brought her back to Calim, the world of her dreams, it had also come with her, still clasped in one of her hands. Her cheeks grew warm and tingly as a familiar face appeared through the doorway, handsome as ever, with chocolate-brown eyes that sent her heart aflutter.

"Evalyn," Kendrick said, smiling with both bewilderment and elation. "You've returned!"

"Yeah," Evalyn replied, twisting her hair bashfully with her fingers, trying to inconspicuously comb it so he wouldn't see how messy it had become while she had been in bed. She didn't want to be seen by anyone, especially Kendrick, looking like a mess.

Kendrick's smile widened as he looked at her. "To what do I owe the honor?" he asked, giving a slight bow at the waist.

This made Evalyn's cheeks burn even more as she struggled to answer his question, unable to think straight. Then she remembered Rachel and the diary. It was just enough to bring her back to her senses.

"It's about my sister actually," Evalyn said as she stood up, keeping the flower close. "I think she might be here in Calim, and I was hoping you might be able to help me find her."

Kendrick looked both surprised and intrigued by the idea that another girl like Evalyn had come to visit his world. "Do you know where she is?" he asked, trying to gauge how difficult the task of finding Evayln's sister was going to be.

"Not exactly," Evalyn admitted, refusing to stare too deeply into Kendrick's eyes again lest she become lost in them. "But I have an idea of where to start looking."

"So where do we begin?" Kendrick asked, tilting his head down slightly to try and recapture Evalyn's gaze as she averted her eyes.

It's not that Evalyn didn't *want* to look at him. In fact she would have been quite happy spending hours doing just that. But she had a job to do. She needed to find out as much as she could about this world to see if Chris was right about Rachel and the dreams. Looking up, she focused all her energy on the task at hand, trying hard not to be swayed or distracted by Kendrick's well-meaning gestures.

"Have you heard of a people called the Evarance Keepers?" Evalyn asked, hoping beyond hope that Kendrick was familiar with them.

"Of course," Kendrick affirmed with a smile. "They live in the windlands not very far from here. In the city of Divarus."

"Really?" Evalyn asked excitedly, having a newfound respect for her brother Chris *and* his stubbornness. He had been right about their dreams all along, which meant there really was a chance of finding out the truth behind what had happened to Rachel. "Could you take me to them?"

"I don't see why not," Kendrick said, still smiling. "Do you know how to ride an aquamare?"

"A what?" Evalyn said, taken off guard by the unfamiliar word.

"An aquamare," Kendrick laughed lightly. "Don't worry, I can teach you. They're quite gentle. Let me pack a few things for the trip, and we'll be on our way."

"Are you sure it's alright?" Evalyn inquired, wanting to be absolutely certain she wasn't imposing. "I mean, taking me to the Evarance Keepers? You don't have any other plans?"

"I'm honored to bring you there, Evalyn," Kendrick reassured her. "There's nothing I need to do here that's more important than helping you find your sister."

Evalyn had thought he might be amenable to helping her, being the gentleman that he was. But even so she was amazed at how quickly he was willing to drop everything he was doing to cater to her every request. She watched as Kendrick packed a couple of sacks with food, bedding, and clothing. He also pulled a sword from off his fireplace mantle and slipped it into a sheath attached to a belt around his waist.

"That should be everything," Kendrick announced, tying up the sacks and briefly looking around the room to make sure he hadn't forgotten anything for the trip. "Now if you'll follow me to the stables I'll introduce you to Tempest."

"Tempest?" Evalyn asked, the pitch of her voice raising slightly as she spoke, uncertain of whether or not she liked that name for something she was supposedly going to ride. Tempest sounded more like the name of a chaotic storm on a raging sea than the gentle creature Kendrick spoke of, and she was already nervous about learning to ride an aquamare in the first place.

Kendrick could sense her uneasiness. "It'll be alright,"

he said, reaching out his hand for hers. She hesitated a moment before placing her free hand in his, allowing him to guide her out of his home and onto the dirt street that led back to the marketplace where the stables were. The sky outside was clear and blue, and the air was filled with the crisp, clean scent of morning.

Kendrick and Evalyn walked hand-in-hand down the road toward the stables. His touch was soft, gentle, and warm, causing her heart to beat a little faster and her face to begin feeling a little flush. Not wanting to be swept away again into another world and another state of being, she slipped her hand out of his once they reached the stables and breathed in slowly, regaining control of her emotions, which had started running away with her again.

In the stables they walked past several vacant stalls before Kendrick stopped at one, turning to face Evalyn.

"Evalyn, meet Tempest," Kendrick said with a grin, gesturing his hand toward a large wooden gate, fastened closed in front of the stall. Evalyn peeked inside, and her jaw nearly dropped as she saw an enormous semi-transparent horse that looked like it was made entirely out of water.

"Nnn-nice to meet you, Tempest," Evalyn said timidly, giving a nod to the aquamare as it stared back at her. "What's it made of?" she asked Kendrick, keeping her eyes on the mysterious creature as it stepped toward her, stopping with its nose only inches away from her own.

"Primarily water," Kendrick replied as he watched Tempest begin to rub her nose up against Evalyn's cheek. "She's a pure Aquari, not a mixed breed."

The aquamare felt neither wet nor cold but rather warm, rubbery and smooth, almost like a water balloon but not exactly. It was a sensation unlike anything Evalyn had ever felt before, the sensation of the horse-like animal nuzzling her cheek and hair with its muzzle. Though still intimidated by the sheer size of this large creature, Evalyn could feel a sense of calm wash over her as Tempest continued to caress Evalyn's face with her own. Evalyn returned the gesture by stroking Tempest's muzzle and cheek.

"She likes you," Kendrick noted, his attention now focused on Evalyn, intrigued by every movement she made. He had never seen anyone so unfamiliar with his world before. It was fascinating to him to watch her amazement and awe at everything he showed her, which to him seemed rather ordinary.

"So are you ready to go?" Kendrick asked, unlatching the gate while making a clicking noise with his mouth to coax Tempest out of her stall.

In truth Evalyn wasn't ready at all, and she doubted she ever would be. She was dreading taking a trip on anything that even slightly resembled a horse. Tempest seemed well behaved and mild tempered enough, just like Kendrick had said she was, but she also looked so large and *powerful*. How was Evalyn supposed to ride something like that? She had only had one experience on horseback. She was a kid at the time, and it hadn't even been on a big horse.

The pony at the fair was short and sweet tempered, too, but somehow Evalyn managed to fall off of it, landing right in the middle of a muddy wet puddle, soaking her clothes and hair and getting traumatized in the process. She didn't know if she could handle getting back up onto a horse again. Even if an aquamare wasn't exactly a horse it was horse-like enough to cause feelings of anxiety to build up in her chest. Especially now that she wasn't touching Tempest directly and the calming effect the aquamare had on her had worn off as quickly as it had come.

Kendrick took the two sacks he had packed and draped them over Tempest's back so one hung down on each side of her body. Then stepping onto a wooden stool for added height, he mounted onto the back of the aquamare and held out his hand again toward Evalyn.

"We'll ride together," Kendrick smiled, still holding out his hand. "Tempest and I will keep you safe. I promise."

If getting back onto a horse, or an aquamare in this case, was what it would take to get to the Evarance Keepers and find out about Rachel, Evalyn had to do it, even if her body trembled at the very thought. *Ready or not* . . . she said to herself, closing her eyes only a moment, taking in a deep breath to calm her nerves. Then taking Kendrick's hand she stepped up onto the wooden stool and with his help, managed to get onto Tempest's back, sitting securely in front of him.

The aquamare felt squishy, a little like sitting on top of a waterbed, though not nearly as flimsy. As Evalyn sat on Tempest's back, the calming sensation returned and the anxiety she had felt completely melted away. She was going to be okay. Everything was going to be okay. She looked at the flower still in her hand and glanced around to see if there was somewhere safe to put it during the ride when she had an idea.

"Kendrick?" she asked, turning her body to try and look at him.

"Yes, m'lady?" he asked with a smile.

"Do you have something I can use to tie my hair?"

Kendrick thought a moment and reached down into one of the sacks, pulling from it a leather cord. "Will this do?" he inquired, reaching his arm partly around Evalyn to show her the dark-brown cord.

"It's perfect!" Evalyn exclaimed, taking the cord from his hand, then setting the andalyn down in its place. "Would you hold that for me a minute?"

"Certainly," Kendrick replied, gently holding the flower while leaning back to give Evalyn more space as he watched.

She lifted both hands to her head and fashioned a lovely braid, twisting the leather cord into her hair and using the ends of it to tie off the braid securely. She then reached her hand back for the andalyn, which Kendrick promptly gave her, and she weaved the stem of it into her braid until it rested snugly in her hair with the blossom decoratively displayed.

"Are you ready now?" Kendrick asked, smiling and sitting upright.

"Ready as I'll ever be," Evalyn replied, both hands now free to hold onto a rope tied loosely around Tempest's neck.

Kendrick reached his arms around Evalyn's, grabbing the same rope, and with a slight squeeze of his legs Tempest began walking forward out of the stables and onto the dirt road.

"How do you control her without reins?" Evalyn asked, feeling how freely the rope around Tempest's neck moved.

"She listens to my body," Kendrick said matter-of-factly. "I communicate with her using light pressure from my legs. It doesn't take much to direct her. She's sensitive to my movements and I to hers."

Evalyn admired Kendrick for his gentleness and skill in handling the aquamare. The calming effect given off by Tempest was so relaxing, Evalyn was actually enjoying the ride, which was surprisingly smooth. In no time they were not only outside the town but beyond the valley of the

Echoes where Kendrick had shown Evalyn the dreamers and picked the beautiful andalyn for her.

The hours passed like minutes as they approached Divarus, home of the Evarance Keepers. Riding with Kendrick felt like a dream—perhaps because it *was* a dream. A beautiful dream . . . warm and cozy, riding across the grassy plains wrapped in Kendrick's arms. But like all good things, it was finally time for the dream to come to an end.

CHAPTER 13. REVELATION

As Rachel and Ember walked through the woods, making their way to Incindia's home to which Ember had promised to take Rachel after showing her the Earth Echoes, Rachel felt something gnawing at her mind that made her feel uneasy.

"Ember," Rachel said, pushing a few tree branches aside as she walked beside him through the rich, green forest, "there's something Umbra said to me about the darkness that's been bothering me."

"Umbra?" Ember inquired, ears perked up with curiosity. "What did he say?"

"He said the darkness required someone like me to grow, and with my help it would cover all of Calim," Rachel replied.

"Did you tell Incindia about it?" Ember asked.

"I haven't seen her yet," Rachel reminded him.

"Oh yeah," Ember replied with a slight chuckle. "I suppose it's hard to tell her something without having seen her yet."

"Yeah, it kind of is," Rachel agreed. "And that's not the worst part. I told him I wouldn't help him, but he said I didn't have a choice. He seemed sure I was going to help him whether I wanted to or not."

"But that was *before* we rescued you, right?" Ember replied. "You aren't under his control anymore. He can't make you do anything you don't want to do."

Ember was right. Umber had no control over her, but the troubled feeling still lingered. She couldn't help but wonder if he knew something she didn't.

"Even so," Ember continued, somewhat more seriously, "you should tell Incindia what Umbra said to you as soon as we get to her den. She'll want to know about it. Anything that has to do with the darkness is important."

Rachel already knew that Incindia would want to know what happened to her while she was held prisoner in the shadow wolf den. It was one of the many topics Rachel planned on discussing with her. There were so many unanswered questions she had, and the more she learned about this world the more questions came to her.

"There's something else I've been thinking about," Rachel continued, trying to put her thoughts of Umbra aside at least for the moment, though the new thoughts weren't much better. "It's about the dream I had last night in your den."

"The one where you were calling out to your family?" Ember asked as he thought back to when Rachel had been tossing and turning in his den.

"Yeah, I had a dream about them: my mom, my dad, my brother, and sister," Rachel said, crinkling her nose to ward off the sadness she felt as she remembered the way their voices sounded.

"I could hear them calling out to me, begging me to come home. I yelled back, but they couldn't hear me. They sounded just awful, crying, shaking, sobbing, pleading . . . it was nothing like them at all. I've never heard any of them so upset in my whole life. Mom looked like she was having a nervous breakdown. And I couldn't help them, couldn't make them feel any better. I was right there the whole time and they had no idea . . ."

Rachel's eyes misted over a bit as she spoke, despite her best efforts not to let her emotions show.

"I hate to say it, Rachel, but I don't think you were dreaming," Ember said sincerely. "This world is your dream, not the other way around. I think you were hearing your family in your world exactly as they were."

"But why would they be that way?" Rachel asked. "It's not like my parents to cry like that. They spoke as though they were trying to talk to me, hoping I would hear them."

"You did hear them," Ember said.

"But they couldn't hear *me!*" Rachel rebutted. *Then she understood.* If this was a dream then that meant she was still asleep. And if she was still asleep and they were all awake, frantic for her to wake up, too, something had gone very, very wrong.

"Why haven't I woken up yet?" Rachel asked Ember. "The way my parents were talking it was almost as if they would never see me again."

Ember paused a moment, but he had no more idea what was going on than Rachel did.

"Maybe Incindia will know," Ember replied thoughtfully. "We're nearly there."

"I hope she does," Rachel agreed, unable to let go of the fear she carried but unwilling to let it consume her.

"Now can I ask *you* something?" Ember inquired, looking up at Rachel as they walked side by side through the last stretch of the luscious greenery leading to Incindia's den. His fiery coat was so low with flame the black ashen fur stuck out above it.

"I guess," Rachel replied, shrugging. She *had* been the one asking most of the questions up to this point; it was only fair that Ember have a turn to ask questions, too.

"Where do you fit in your family?" he asked light-heartedly, trying to keep her mind off her present worries. "You said you had a brother and sister."

"*My family* . . ." Rachel's words trailed off as she thought about Chris and Evalyn, then Mom and Dad. Not how they were in the black void of her last dream but rather how they were when she was still with them. She thought about the family pictures on the walls, how different she looked, and how different she was from everyone else.

"I suppose I *don't* fit in, not really," she concluded, but the confused look on Ember's face told her that wasn't enough of an answer so she continued. "I have a mom and a dad and an older sister and brother, but I don't look anything like them, not even a little bit. They all have blue eyes and dark brown hair. And my hair is, well, this . . ." she said as she pulled a few strands of her own strawberry-blonde hair over her face. "They all have perfect complexions, too, and my face is splotchy," she added, letting go of her hair and pointing her finger toward her nose, which was lightly dotted with tiny freckles that were barely visible.

Of course Ember could see that Rachel was exaggerating. Her face and hair were really nice for a human, but it was clear she didn't see herself the same way he saw her.

"Is that why you don't think you fit in? Because you look different from the rest of your family?" Ember asked.

"Well, yeah. I'll never have Evalyn's thick, beautiful hair or my Mom's gorgeous blue eyes," Rachel said, frowning. "My eyes look like dirty moss."

It was quite apparent this, too, was an exaggeration. Rachel had beautiful eyes, like a vibrant field of new grass. At least that's what they reminded Ember of whenever he looked at them.

"Does any of that really matter?" Ember asked. "Do you really think the way you look is the only thing that makes you part of a family? I mean, look at me! I don't look anything like the other firefoxes, but they're still my family, and I'm still a firefox, even if I don't look exactly like one."

Rachel thought a moment. All her life she felt so different, like she didn't belong, but was what she looked like really the only thing that made her feel so out of place in her family? No, there was more than just that.

"Well, my dad, he's just really smart in a way that I'll never be. And Mom," Rachel closed her eyes briefly imagining her mother's face as clearly as if she were standing right in front of her, "Mom is good at everything she sets her mind to. She's dedicated and organized, but I get totally distracted all the time. Then there's Evalyn, who's so creative and caring. She has such a beautiful heart and sweet spirit about her. But me, I'm so selfish and unladylike." Rachel would never be like Evalyn, no matter how much she wished she would.

"And last, there's Chris," Rachel said, pausing in thought for a moment. Her frustrations with her brother made it a little harder to see his good qualities, but she knew he had them. "Chris can be a pain at times, and he drives me totally crazy, but he's really good at tinkering with things, taking them apart, even if he can't always put them back together. He's good at skateboarding, too."

"What's that?" Ember asked, never having heard that word before.

"Oh," Rachel said. "Skateboarding is where you stand on top of a piece of wood that has four wheels attached. You ride it on hard surfaces like streets and sidewalks."

Ember tried to envision Rachel's description, but had a hard time doing so. Perhaps it was something he'd have to see to fully understand.

"And what about you?" Ember asked, skipping over fallen branches scattered across the ground.

"What *about* me?" Rachel said. "There's *nothing* good about me." And as the words left her mouth, she began to choke back a few tears because she knew deep down it was truly how she felt about herself.

"That's not true," Ember said, amazed that Rachel couldn't see just how incredible she was. "I may be different from the other firefoxes, but there's still a lot of good things about me, and even though you look different from everyone in your family, I know there's a lot of good things about you, too."

"Like what?" Rachel asked, wondering what Ember could see in her that she couldn't see in herself.

"Like you have a beautiful smile, as human smiles go. And you have a good heart, and you're brave and smart. Not many humans could have outfoxed the shadow wolves the way you did. In fact not many elementals could have, either."

"That was just luck," Rachel protested. "I didn't really do anything but run away, and they caught me in the end anyway, so what does it matter?"

"All I'm saying is that being different isn't always bad. You know, from the moment I met you I noticed lots of things about you that are really incredible. You stood up to Umbra and rode a mysticorn through unfamiliar woods—all while keeping your spirits up despite how scary it all must have been for you. You're an amazingly strong person, Rachel."

"Well, I had a lot of help," Rachel interjected.

"True," Ember agreed, "but the courage came from within you."

Rachel had never thought of it that way before. She didn't feel strong *or* brave.

"Just you wait," Ember said with a wink, "you'll understand someday."

"If you say so," Rachel said doubtfully.

"I do say so," Ember smiled, looking ahead through the forest of trees. "We're here! Incindia's home is just over that mound."

Rachel looked, too. She could see the mound and fiery ears poking out from behind it.

"Incindia!" Rachel shouted enthusiastically, running toward her den. Ember ran, too.

As they rounded the mound to her den entrance, it wasn't Incindia standing there, it was the firefox kit Blaze, who had shown Rachel the way to Ember's den the night before when Caligo had dropped her off.

"Blaze?" Ember said startled, expecting to see Incindia instead. "Where's Incindia? And what are you doing here? She should have been back by now."

"She couldn't make it," Blaze replied as he stepped forward, obscuring something from view, something he had been pawing at as Rachel and Ember had approached.

"What's that you've got there?" Ember asked as he stepped to the side to try and see what it was that Blaze had obviously tried to hide.

"It's something Incindia wanted me to give to you, well,

Rachel," he clarified pointing his nose Rachel's way. "But I think it may be a little more well done than she intended for it to be," he added sheepishly, moving over to reveal a half burned cloth sack filled with what had probably been delicious food before Blaze had fried it to a crisp.

"Oh, Blaze," Ember laughed, shaking his head as he picked up the burned sack in his teeth and handed it to Rachel. "You really need to learn to control your fire."

"And you really need to learn how to make one," Blaze countered jokingly as he boosted the intensity of his own flame to show off. "Incindia told me humans were flammable. How was I supposed to know their food was, too?"

Rachel gazed inside the blackened sack to see if there was anything edible remaining. Only half the food was damaged beyond recognition, the other half was still salvageable.

"It's okay, Blaze," Rachel said as she pulled out a toasted hunk of bread and took a bite out of it to show him not all was lost. "It's still good. Thank you."

"Don't thank me," Blaze said modestly, still embarrassed about having burned the sack. "Thank Incindia. Human food's not easy to come by."

"Where *is* Incindia?" Rachel asked. She couldn't thank her for the food or anything else until she found her.

"Elder Oakin called a meeting of the elements," Blaze replied, looking more serious than he had only a moment ago. "Incindia's there to represent the firefoxes, and she wants both of you to go there to meet her."

"She wants Rachel to go?" Ember asked, the flame on his coat intensifying slightly for a moment as his protective instincts kicked in.

"Yes, she wants *both* of you to meet her there," Blaze

confirmed as he watched Ember's flame flicker in agitation. "You know how to get there, don't you?"

"Yeah, I know how to get there," Ember replied curtly before looking over at Rachel. "Do you think you can walk a little farther?"

"Yeah, I think so," Rachel replied. "So where are we going exactly?"

"To the Oakin Glen to meet Incindia," Ember said flatly, obviously irritated by something, but Rachel didn't fully understand what. He had been so excited to take her to see Incindia before.

"We'll need to leave right away to get there before nightfall," Ember added before turning back to face Blaze. "Thanks for giving Rachel the food."

Blaze bowed his head slightly in response. "No problem. Good luck at the council."

He gave Rachel a slight nod as well and bounded off into the forest, burning a trail behind him as he went.

"Is everything alright?" Rachel asked, looking at Ember, feeling slightly alarmed by his sudden change in mood.

"I'll tell you on the way," Ember said uneasily, his mind deep in thought as he lead Rachel farther and farther away from Incindia's den into unfamiliar woods—unfamiliar to Rachel at any rate. After walking in silence next to Rachel for several minutes, Ember was finally ready to talk.

"It's called the council of elements because the elementals gather together to discuss issues important to all of us, like conflicts between species, managing territorial boundaries, and most recently the growing darkness," Ember said dryly, his voice absent of its usual light-heartedness.

"They rarely meet, but when they do, humans and other

non-elementals are forbidden from attending. Bringing you there doesn't feel right. Not because I don't want you to see and hear what goes on there, but more because I don't think it's safe. Not all of the elementals who attend are friendly toward humans," he said solemnly.

"Do any Shadai attend?" Rachel asked. She doubted they would based on her encounter with the shadow wolves, but they were elementals, too, so she wondered.

"They attended only one meeting, but that was a long time ago," Ember replied. "The Shadai used that meeting to execute an attack on the other council members. They never intended to participate really in the discussions, and they've been banned ever since."

Rachel walked silently next to Ember for a time, thinking. "What do you think they want to talk about this time?"

"I don't know. I'm *pretty sure* they want to talk about the darkness," Ember replied, looking up to the sky as they walked, which was growing darker, not due to the darkness, which was still a fair distance from where they were, but rather, due to the setting sun. "It's growing every day now, swallowing more of the land in its black shadow."

"And me?" Rachel asked. "Why does Incindia want me to go?"

"Maybe she doesn't have a choice," he replied. "If Elder Oakin or the other council members asked her to bring you to them, she would have to or risk damaging the alliances she's worked so hard to build. Of course, I don't really know if that's the case. I could just be getting worked up over nothing."

Rachel knew that if Ember had a reason to be concerned, she did, too. If humans were forbidden from attending the council but Incindia insisted that she attend, there *must* be something significant happening that included Rachel in some way. After all, she *had been* under the shadow of darkness *and* been in direct contact with the shadow wolves several times. Perhaps Incindia called her to the council to tell them what she knew about the shadow wolves' plans.

As the last traces of light dimmed, Ember and Rachel approached a clearing encircled with great pillars of light.

"Luminary," Ember said, pointing out one of the many pillars of light that lined the clearing in front of them. As they walked closer, Rachel could see that the pillars were actually composed of a kaleidoscope of beautiful yellow butterflies glowing with a golden light. She and Ember walked in between two pillars to enter the clearing, which was filled with more elementals than Rachel could count.

The masses of elementals that had gathered together were breathtaking but also a bit scary. There were large cats that looked a little like panthers but were made entirely out of water. Gigantic bears, made of hard stone, towered over Rachel, staring down at her with cold eyes. She saw an elemental that looked a little like a kangaroo with a body that constantly shifted and changed in appearance as spinning grass, leaves, and dirt filled its form, the swirling wind within it holding captive all the loose debris.

"That's an Ai're," Ember pointed out, noticing Rachel's fascination with it as she stopped to stare. He nudged her hand with his nose to keep her moving along as a way of preventing potential conflicts and to keep the focus on finding Incindia. None of the elementals confronted her directly, but all of them watched as she walked past.

As Rachel and Ember neared the center of the clearing the hum of conversation died down and was replaced by whispering. It was clear to Rachel that many of the elementals were trying to lower their voices beyond her ability to hear, but several others remained just loud enough for the sting of their comments to reach her ears.

"Is that the one?" a bush-like rabbit said in a hushed voice. Rachel recognized him immediately as an Oakin.

"How could something so small cause so much damage?" a large black granite bear inquired.

"Aquari killer!" another elemental cried out. Their voices rang like acid in Rachel's ears.

"Maybe they're wrong about her," a friendlier sounding voice chimed in.

"They're never wrong," a fifth voice cooed darkly.

The further they walked the worse the comments became. Rachel couldn't understand why the elementals would say such horrible things about her. Whatever the stories were that had circulated among them, they had to have been the worst kind of lies. She'd never done anything to harm any of them, but she was beginning to understand why Ember had been so hesitant to bring her.

She watched as Ember's flames sparked to life next to her as he, too, listened to the things the other elementals were saying about her. His ears and paws burned hot white, while the rest of his body pushed flames up above the tips of his black ashen fur, ready to protect Rachel at a moment's notice. If anyone was going to cause trouble for her they'd have to get through him first.

Rachel could feel all eyes upon her, heads turned in eager anticipation as she took her last steps to the center of the gathering where well-defined groups of elementals convened together in what looked like designated places.

"You made it!" Incindia called out with a smile as she stepped out from the group of Fi'eri gathered together on a large patch of charred soil and stepped over to greet Rachel.

Rachel was both happy and relieved to see Incindia. Her very presence made it easier to ignore the whispering that continued all around, but it didn't completely take away the feeling Rachel had that the other elementals still viewed her as the worst kind of uninvited party guest.

"Incindia, I'm so glad to finally see you!" Rachel cried out, being sure not to get *too* close to her as her flames burned brilliantly over her entire body. "What's going on?" Rachel asked. "Why did you need me to come here?"

"Follow me," Incindia directed, walking away from the crowds of onlookers that were still whispering and gawking at Rachel as she and Ember followed Incindia just far enough away to be out of earshot of the other elementals.

"They won't be able to hear us over here," Incindia said softly, stopping to look at Rachel. "I'm sorry I wasn't able to meet you at my den. An emergency meeting was called, and I had to come here right away."

"And Rachel?" Ember butted in. "Why did you want me to bring her here? Humans are forbidden from attending the council."

"Under normal circumstances that would be true," Incindia affirmed. "However, recent events have been *anything* but normal."

"What was the council called together to meet about?" Rachel asked, still trying to figure out how she fit in to all of this.

"It's the darkness," Incindia replied. "It won't stop growing. In the past it would grow a little bit then stop for a time before growing again. But now it's growing consistently with no slowing down and no stopping."

"But what's that got to do with me?" Rachel asked.

"Everything," Incindia replied.

CHAPTER 14. THE COUNCIL

Night had fallen over the Oakin Glen where scores of elementals gathered together to discuss ways of protecting each other from the encroaching darkness. The sky, now black, was filled with tiny dots of starlight that danced through the heavens above in constellations Rachel had never seen before. The clearing was also illuminated with birdlike Luminaries gliding overhead to light the glade below, while pillars of butterflies encircled everything, creating entryways of beautiful golden light for the elementals to walk through as they congregated near the center marked by a single oddly shaped tree with long, thick branches.

Rachel knew she was already running out of time to speak with Incindia as she watched the elementals so focused on gossiping about her redirect their attention instead to gathering around the unusual tree. Incindia and Ember sensed it, too; the council meeting was about to begin.

"Rachel," Incindia said hurriedly, "Tell me something. When was the last time you were home?"

"Right before the shadow wolves captured me," Rachel replied. "That's part of what I wanted to speak with you about. It's been awhile since I've gone home, and I'm worried something's gone wrong. I had a dream about my family. They were frantically trying to get me to wake up, but I'm still here, and I don't know why."

"It's as I suspected," Incindia said. "You and the darkness are both connected. It only grows when you're here. And since you haven't gone home yet, it's growing larger by the hour."

"Wait, what?" Rachel said in disbelief. The darkness taking over the land was all because of her?

"But I don't control the darkness!" she protested. "The only reason I even knew about it in the first place is because you and Torrens showed it to me. If I could go home right now I would. Believe me. But for some reason, I just can't. I don't know how to wake up from this dream."

"Which is why you were called to be a part of this meeting," Incindia continued. "The council members requested your presence. They've learned about your visits here, and they know the growth of the darkness seems to be directly linked to you."

That gave Rachel no comfort at all, and her heart beat fast as the gravity of what Incindia said began to set in.

"What's going to happen to me?" Rachel asked, growing more anxious every moment. "If everyone thinks I'm the one that's causing this darkness—"

"I'll protect you," Ember chimed in, boosting his flame as much as he could, unable to hold in the anger that had slowly begun to grow within him as he listened to Incindia. He turned to Incindia, posturing his body between her and Rachel. "They can't blame Rachel for this! I've watched her since she first arrived. There's *no way* she would cover our world in darkness!"

"Not intentionally," Incindia agreed. "Rachel, I don't believe this darkness is your fault. But the fact remains that you are somehow connected to its growth, and we need to understand what that connection is if we can. I'm sorry you had to come here under such circumstances. But please believe that I will do all I can to protect you, whatever the council decides."

"Do you really think any of them will listen?" Rachel asked doubtfully, replaying the whispering of the elementals in her mind. "They already think I'm guilty!"

"Don't worry," Ember said. "I'll protect you with my life if I need to."

"As will I," Incindia agreed. "But hopefully it won't come to that." Her ears twitched as the murmurings of the elementals grew quiet.

"It's time," she said. "We need to take our place with the others."

Rachel and Ember both reluctantly followed Incindia back to the large patch of charred ground filled with Fi'eri of all shapes and sizes. They stopped a fair distance away from the others, partially to keep Rachel safe from the heat generated by the massive gathering of Fi'eri, of which Incindia and Ember were a part, but also to keep her a secure distance from the other elementals who were giving her strange and unwelcome looks.

Silently they stood next to each other facing the massive tree, which began bending and warping right before their eyes into a magnificent wooden elk. The hooves of the elk made up the base of the tree, sunken into the ground with roots grown down so deep that they remained unmoved, anchored firmly into place. Its body was covered mostly in bark, moss streaking through the dips and curves of the rough hide. Horns grew out into long, thick branches decorated with autumn leaves that were beginning to fall in stark contrast to the lush green trees that surrounded the glade. The elk shaped tree appeared knotted and old, but the face of it radiated with a look of ancient wisdom.

"That," Ember whispered to Rachel, "is Elder Oakin. He leads the council meetings here, which all now take place in this glen. In his old age, the roots of his body have grown too deep for him to move around anymore."

Rachel watched as the wooden face turned her way. His eyes blinked several times, looking her over with curiosity before turning away to address the elementals congregated before him.

"Welcome," Elder Oakin said in a firm, rich voice that carried across the entire glen, "thank you all for traveling so far to meet here to discuss an important topic that affects the lives of each and every one of us. The darkness of the Shadai is continuing to grow at an alarming rate. If left unchecked, it will surely cover the planet and block out all light—except that light created by our dear friends the Luminary and the Fi'eri. But I'm afraid even their light will over time be snuffed out by the darkness, destroying all life on Calim as we know it, plummeting the planet back into the dark age."

Murmurings spread through each of the elemental groups, ranging from doom and gloom to shock and disbelief.

"It is for this reason we have met," Elder Oakin continued, "to discuss the darkness that is upon us and decide what to do to stop it before it spreads further across our land. And so I will open this discussion to any and all who have input to give."

The first to step forward was a large aquari cat, panther-like in appearance, whose dark purple liquid body refracted the light of the Luminary shining in the night air.

"That's Delusor," Ember whispered again to Rachel. "He's the high council member representing the Aquari at this meeting."

Delusor walked silently past each of the elemental groups, pausing only briefly in front of Rachel with a dark stare before finishing his round, coming to a halt near Elder Oakin.

"I'm sure by now all of you have heard the rumors," Delusor purred smoothly, addressing each elemental in the council. "Word sent down by our kin in the north confirms that the Evarance is indeed thinning. Without its protection, Calim will undoubtedly become consumed once again by shadow and darkness as all life on this planet, save the Shadai, withers into extinction."

At this, several elementals cried out, angrily protesting the darkness and the Shadai as whisperings spread, causing Delusor to give a hint of a smile.

"The Evarance," he went on, "is the life-giving light that brought each of our ancestors here. We *cannot* stand idly by and let it vanish as we succumb to the darkness."

"Hear, hear!" many of the elementals cried out in agreement.

Another much smaller creature, wooden in appearance and weasel-like in shape, stepped forward to interject, "But the darkness *has* stopped expanding before. It *may* stop expanding again."

"You're wrong," Delusor said, baring his feline fangs, scaring the weasel back into his place among the other Oakin. "It was no accident the darkness grew so unsteadily before, and it is no accident that it continues to expand unceasingly now."

"But how is it possible?" asked a giant calimin turtle

with a multicolored rock shell.

"If I may?" Incindia said, bowing her head to Elder Oakin as she stepped out in front, singeing the ground with each paw as she did, her fiery coat blazing strong and hot.

She knew Delusor all too well and wanted to be the one to explain Rachel's predicament in a way that wouldn't poison the other elementals against her any more than they already had been.

"Proceed," Elder Oakin agreed, nodding his head toward Incindia before Delusor had a chance to protest.

"Delusor's right," Incindia affirmed, much to the surprise of the other elementals who knew she and he rarely agreed on anything. "The growth of the darkness in the past and now are no accident. We don't know what the cause of the darkness is, but we do know there is a connection between it and the girl I've brought here tonight."

Incindia looked to Rachel as gasps of shock and horror filled the air from those who had refused to believe the rumors were true. The eyes of all the elementals were fixated on Rachel. Ember's fiery coat crackled like hot coals as he held his legs firmly in a defensive stance and lowered his head, ready to attack any that dared to harm Rachel. Delusor let out a slight laugh as he watched the reaction of those in attendance and took the opportunity to seize the dialogue back from Incindia.

"So what you're saying," he purred coolly, "is that this girl and the darkness share a special connection. If you would be so kind, please enlighten us."

Incindia's fur flickered in irritation at Delusor's smug tone. She looked to Elder Oakin, who nodded for her to continue.

"This girl is not from our world. She has come to Calim

through the Evarance from a world called Earth. Her visits here seem to allow the darkness to grow, and for a time her visits were relatively short and sporadic, so the darkness's growth reflected that. Whenever she visited it would expand a little further across the terrain, and when she returned back home its growth would cease."

"And now?" Delusor asked, savoring each word Incindia said.

"And now," Incindia continued, giving Delusor a sharp glance, "she seems to be trapped in our world and needs our help to get back home. I believe that somehow the shadow wolves learned of this connection between her and the darkness. They have found a way to exploit that connection by trapping her here in order to ensure that the darkness continues to grow without stopping. If we don't help her find a way back home, the darkness won't stop, threatening not only her existence but the existence of each one of us as well."

Silence fell over the elementals as each one, especially those not yet directly affected by the darkness, internalized the seriousness of the situation. Some wondered how it was possible the Evarance that gave them all life could also be the very thing that brought them to their doom. Delusor stepped out from beside Elder Oakin, standing evenly with Incindia.

"Very good, Incindia," he purred, pleased with the information she had presented, "but if I may, you failed to mention another, much quicker and easier way to stop the darkness for good. *Right here, right now.*"

His words stirred up both excitement and hope in the mass of elementals—excitement that there was a simpler way to end the crisis before them and hope that it would work. Incindia knew exactly what game Delusor was playing. He was manipulating the emotions of the others to get his way, but she wasn't about to let him get the upper hand, especially when Rachel's very existence was at stake.

"That's *not* an option, Delusor," Incindia barked aggressively, taking a slightly offensive stance toward him, her fiery coat blazing.

"Temper, temper," he mocked, giving a conniving smile. "The Elder Oakin himself said we were gathered together to *discuss* the darkness and what to do about it. How can any of us really make an informed decision without getting all the facts?"

Incindia turned her head to look at Elder Oakin, but he gave no impression that he was going to intervene. At least not yet.

"Clearly," Delusor said in an almost innocent tone, looking at Incindia and Ember who were both fired up, "the firefoxes' judgment has been clouded by this girl, preventing them from seeing her for what she *really* is. All of us here must not fall for her guise. I ask each of you to be willing to listen to a voice of reason in these *very* dangerous times."

Incindia wanted to protest to prevent Delusor from planting the seeds of hate and vengeance in the hearts of the others, but her actions would only add fire to the argument he had made against both the firefoxes and Rachel, so she was forced to remain silent and let him finish laying out *his* plan before the council.

"It's simple really," Delusor purred. "Think of how many of us have already been killed since this girl first came to our world. As the darkness grows, the Shadai come with it, attacking and killing without mercy or remorse. It is *her darkness* that's growing over *our land*.

"Think of how many of us are yet to die as we wait to find a way for this girl to return back to her own world. And what if after all our efforts and all of those lost lives, it turns out there is no way for her to return home? I propose a solution that will *guarantee* no more lives are lost to the darkness, one that will restore balance to our lands. We kill the girl, and with her the darkness dies."

It was as Incindia feared. Delusor had proposed the unthinkable. "We cannot sentence an innocent girl to death for something she has no control over!" Incindia cried out. "She doesn't want the darkness to overtake our lands *or* destroy our homes and families. Taking her life would be nothing short of murder!"

A few of the elementals yelled out in agreement, but the vast majority of them stayed quiet, considering Delusor's words.

"Is it murder really?" Delusor asked, looking out to the elementals over whom he still held sway. "I'd say it's justice and payment for the lives and land already lost."

As Delusor finished his argument, an airy-looking python, whose body shifted like the wind pulling grass and dirt into it as it moved across the ground, slithered out from the throng of Ai're who were standing together in the windiest area of the glen.

"It'sss the girl," the airy python hissed angrily, agreeing with Delusor. "Shhhheeee brought this darkness upon us. Shhhee's to blame for the Shhhadai uprising. Shhheee musst be punishhhed for what shhheee hasss done."

"She doesn't control the darkness any more than we do," Incindia countered. "There is a connection between her and the darkness which we don't yet fully understand, but it's the Shadai that are responsible for trapping her here. It's the Shadai who have destroyed homes and lives. How can we condemn her when they are clearly the ones to blame?"

"How can we not?" Delusor replied as though he were speaking on behalf of all of the elementals in attendance. "You say it's not her fault, but the darkness is still growing, and she's still here letting it. One girl is a small sacrifice to make for a world free of the darkness. Think of how many elemental lives can be spared for the price of one mere human."

"All life is precious," Incindia protested, "even the life of this girl. We cannot allow ourselves to sink to the level of the Shadai. We are a council of justice but also of mercy. Never before have we entertained the idea of taking an innocent life. It's not who we are, and I hope not who we are to become."

A large bear that looked like a statue carved out of rough gray and white stone came forward to speak, joining Incindia, Delusor, and the ai're snake. The bear, like Elder Oakin, looked old and wise. His rocky hide was worn and chipped, causing his movements to be slow.

"We Calimin can feel trembling within the core Calim itself as the darkness grows across the land, killing not only us but the very planet to which we cling," he said in a grizzly voice. "We need to take action, but it must be the right action. If this girl is innocent, as Incindia suggests, and not the true cause of the darkness that is upon us, would our time not be better spent seeking the truth *before* casting blame?"

"But time is the one thing we don't have!" Delusor argued fiercely, losing the cool disposition he had maintained as he began pacing, visibly agitated. "Every moment we stand here debating is another moment the darkness has to suck the life out of our lands. At this very moment more elementals are suffering and dying because of this girl! You say this girl is not the cause of this darkness, but the facts all point to her. When she is among us the darkness grows. And when she is away the darkness ceases. None of you can deny this!"

"Calm yourself, Delusor," Elder Oakin said, at last joining in the conversation. "Perhaps it is time we heard from the girl so the truth of this matter may be discovered. If there is indeed any truth to be found." He looked to Rachel, staring at her with his dark, wooden eyes.

All of the elementals fell silent, looking, too, waiting for Rachel to speak. Even Delusor held his tongue, though he remained visibly perturbed, pacing back and forth as he stared at Rachel with angry eyes.

"You're on," Ember whispered to Rachel, extinguishing the flame on his head, shaking the ash from his fur to nudge her forward near Incindia as he followed dutifully behind to ensure that she remained protected.

Rachel felt her face begin to flush red as she nervously looked out over all of the elementals who were watching her. Her breathing became shallow and uneven as she struggled to find the words to say. And then it came to her, the only thing she could say that was truly of any value at all.

"I'm sorry," Rachel said, as she looked out to all of those different eyes and faces, feeling their anger, their fear, and their pain as clearly as if it was her own. "I don't know where the darkness came from or why it's growing over your land. Until coming here tonight, I didn't even know I was a part of it."

"Liesss . . ." the airy snake hissed before getting a stern

look from Elder Oakin.

Clearly Elder Oakin wanted Rachel to say more, but what he wanted her to say was still a mystery.

"I've come to love your world in the short time I've been here," Rachel continued, "and if there was anything I could do to make things better for all of you I would. I know what an awful place this will become if the darkness triumphs. I've seen it, trapped beneath its blackened sky, being hunted by the Shadai that worship it, watching the life of everything it touches being sucked away until nothing is left. I don't want that for any of you. If I could go home right now I would."

"And why can't you go home?" Elder Oakin asked.

"I don't know," Rachel replied, shaking her head. "I haven't been home since I was captured by the shadow wolves. They chased me to the edge of a river. I jumped in to escape them, but they followed me and must have caught me because the next thing I remember was waking up in their den, completely surrounded."

"Did they do anything to you or say anything to you while you were there?" Elder Oakin asked, trying to determine the extent of the shadow wolves' influence over Rachel.

"Umber told me that he needed someone like me for the darkness to grow. He told me I was going to help him with it. That I didn't have a choice. He also said he needed me alive." As Rachel finished her last sentence, the renewed gasps of the elementals made her realize, too late, that she had said too much.

"See!" Delusor cut in, unable to hold his tongue any longer. "The girl admits to conspiring with the shadow wolves. Umbra himself said he needed her alive to keep his precious darkness growing over our land. If Umbra wants her alive then we really have only one choice. To end this now before Umbra gets what he wants!"

He charged at Rachel, taking matters into his own paws as it was clear to him the council was too weak. Ember stood ready to take the brunt of the impact head on as Incindia rushed to his side, but before Delusor could execute the attack, a golden eagle shinning with a brilliant light swooped down, hovering between the firefoxes and Delusor, temporarily blinding him with a pulse of light, stopping him in his tracks. Delusor hissed at the Luminary that blocked him from his prey, but neither advanced nor attacked.

"Enough, Delusor!" the shinning bird cried out, touching its feet to the ground and folding its wings onto its back. "The council will decide what happens to the girl, *not you*."

Delusor shook his head, freeing his eyes from the blinding light that had stunned him. When his vision returned, he looked to the other elementals, but none spoke out in his defense. Disgusted with their incompetence, he turned away, flicking his tail as he walked sourly back to the patch of grass and fallen leaves from which he had come.

The golden eagle looked out to the elementals. "The Evarance is unstable. This girl's very presence is proof of that. We must find a way to restore balance to the Evarance if we can ever hope to be free of the darkness. It's the Evarance that has brought her here, allowing the darkness to consume our lands. How can we be sure that with this girl gone another dreamer won't come and take her place until this world is only fit for the Shadai to live in?"

"If I may," Incindia said, stepping forward next to the golden eagle, "I believe that this girl is not the true cause of the darkness, but rather a symptom of it. Taking her life will not end it, but *it will* stain this council with the blood of an innocent."

"I agree," the mysticorn Caligo brayed, walking out from among the Aquari, his misty mane and tail gently flowing behind him as he stopped to stand with Incindia. Rachel was happy to see him again. "How can we be sure that taking the life of this girl would in fact make the darkness go away? What if when the girl is gone the darkness remains? I have not yet seen definitive proof of this girl's guilt. Without that it is not our place to condemn her to death."

Elder Oakin, who had been patiently waiting to hear all sides of the argument before adding in his own input, finally decided to speak.

"I don't know if killing the girl would stop the darkness or not, but I agree with Incindia that we are not murderers. The evidence indeed weighs heavily against the girl, but the circumstances surrounding that evidence tell a different tale. I believe we should help her return home if we can before considering more drastic and permanent actions."

"Calim isss dying," the airy snake warned. "Delusssor isss right, there isss no time to wassste!"

His words caused a spark, igniting arguments among the divided onlookers about the fate of the girl. Delusor, who had regained his composure after his unintended outburst, watched in eager anticipation as the discussion became increasingly heated. He listened to the voices around him, calculating if the majority of them were in favor of *his* plan or the ridiculous firefox Incindia's. When it became clear to him the council as a whole was leaning heavily toward helping the girl instead of holding her accountable for the darkness, he stepped forward once more to address them, carefully crafting his words to regain their trust.

"I wish to apologize," Delusor called out over the voices of the elementals, persuading even the most vocal of them to fall silent to listen to his admission of guilt, which for him was very uncharacteristic. "My rash actions earlier were uncalled for and I, like all of you here, will honor the will of the council whatever decision is made. In light of the evidence and lack thereof, I would like to propose a compromise. What if we give the girl time to return safely home?"

His words shocked almost everyone, especially those who had grown in favor of punishing Rachel, but Incindia knew Delusor wasn't finished yet.

"However," he continued, "should the girl fail to return home in an allotted amount of time, and should the darkness continue to grow, then the girl's life will be forfeited."

His words caused a stir among the elementals again. This time the focus was less on what to do about Rachel and more on how much time she should have to find a way to return home. To most, his words sounded both reasonable and just because they allowed the girl a chance to return home, while keeping alive the promise of stopping the darkness for good before it was too late. It seemed like a perfect compromise.

Incindia, Caligo, and Ember, however, could see Delusor's plan for what it really was, despite its enormous appeal. If taking Rachel's life was wrong now, it would be equally wrong later, but Delusor's words had successfully swayed the hearts and minds of the council members so completely that they were no longer able to see the deception weaved in. The majority reasoned that giving the girl a little time to find a way home was enough—and her death would be justified if she failed.

After putting Delusor's plan to a vote, where it passed with overwhelming support, Elder Oakin had no choice but to nod in agreement. As he did, his great tree-like horns shook with such force the Luminary that were perched upon them scattered into the night sky, and the loosest of the dying leaves fell to the ground. The council gave Rachel just two weeks to find a way to successfully return home, causing the clock of her life to begin swiftly ticking away.

CHAPTER 15. DIVARUS

Evalyn awoke feeling warm and tingly all over. She could still feel the sensation of Kendrick's arms wrapped gently around hers. It was hard to believe her dream had been real. Chris was right about the flower and the dream world—all thanks to the diary Rachel had left behind.

"Chris!" Evalyn shouted enthusiastically as she leapt from her bed and rushed to his room, unable to contain her excitement. He was still sound asleep, snoring with the covers pulled halfway over his face. "Chris, wake up!" she coaxed, pulling the blanket down to his shoulder and shaking him hard.

"Five more minutes . . ." he responded groggily, pulling the blanket back up over his head.

"You were right!" Evalyn continued, ripping off the blanket entirely so he'd have no choice but to wake up. "Right about everything! I did dream about Kendrick again, and he's taking me to the Evarance Keepers. We're nearly there!"

Chris yawned widely, then opened his eyes, still feeling somewhat disoriented. Just moments before his rude awakening, he, too, was dreaming of Calim, standing with Rucknar just outside a tall city wall made of polished stones where a wide archway sat adorned with flowering vines and veiled in colorful flowing drapery that masked what lay beyond. He and Rucknar had reached Divarus, home of the Evarance Keepers.

It was in that moment when he had stretched his hand out to move the silky, curtain-like fabric aside, that he heard it, Evalyn's excited shouts echoing through the air. "Chris, wake up!" her voice called out. He shouted back, asking for more time, but it was already too late. The dream had fizzled away before he could see what lay inside the city wall. He was back in his room, reaching for his covers which were no longer there.

"Eva, why'd you have to wake me up?" Chris asked grumpily, yawning once more as he sat up in bed.

"I already told you!" Evalyn replied, still giddy with excitement. "Kendrick and I are on our way to Divarus to see the Evarance Keepers!"

"Well, Ruck and I just arrived—" Chris began.

"You did?" she asked anxiously. "What was it like?"

"I don't know yet. We were just about to enter the city when *someone* pulled the covers off my bed!"

"Oh . . ." Evalyn said, her enthusiasm waning several notches as she realized what she had done. Chris's dreams were every bit as important as hers with regards to finding Rachel. "Sorry."

"Eh, it's alright," Chris said nonchalantly, giving his arms a good stretch. "I remember what it was like when I found out Rachel and I were both dreamin' about the same place and there was a chance I might be able to see her again. I couldn't wait to tell you, either, even though I knew you weren't going to like it so much. So I get it. But do me a favor and don't wake me up next time. Wouldn't want to miss out on anything important."

"True," Evalyn agreed. "So Divarus. You weren't able to

see it?"

"Nope," Chris replied. "The only thing I saw was a long wall that I think surrounded the city and a big entrance covered with curtains. I'm not a hundred percent sure the city of Divarus was on the other side of that wall, but Rucknar seemed to think we were in the right place. What about you? How'd things go with Ken?"

Evalyn's face began to turn a light shade of pink. "Well, *Kendrick* said he would be more than happy to help me find Rachel. And we did ride for some time before I awoke from my dream, so I'm pretty sure we're close to the city, too."

"Wait, you *rode* to the city? Like on a horse?" Chris asked, trying unsuccessfully to suppress a snicker. He remembered Evalyn's mishap on the pony ride.

"Yes, we did," Evalyn said smugly. "And it wasn't a horse. It was an aquamare."

"An aqua what?" Chris interjected.

"An aquamare. It's a little like a horse only made out of water," Evalyn replied.

"How can you ride somethin' made out of water?" Chris asked, trying to envision what an aquamare might look like. "Do you swim in it or something?"

"No!" Evalyn retorted. "I'll show you when we meet up in Divarus."

"Alright," Chris agreed. "But for now let's go get some breakfast. I'm starving!"

"You're always starving!" Evalyn said with a laugh before leaving Chris's room to let him get dressed.

It was Saturday, but Mom hadn't cooked Saturday morning breakfast since Rachel's accident, leaving Chris and Evalyn to fend for themselves while Mom and Dad both slept in. They were exhausted from the long week and still depressed about Rachel's condition, which hadn't improved. After Chris and Evalyn had finished their breakfast, Mom and Dad finally awoke just in time to take Evalyn and Chris with them to see Rachel in the hospital for the start of visiting hours. They were already fully dressed, so they went to the car to start it while Chris and Evalyn remained in the house, still working their shoes onto their feet.

"Eva," Chris whispered, tying one of his shoelaces as he looked up at her. "I'm going to tell Rachel what we're doing."

"But she can't hear you," Evalyn remarked.

"You don't know that," Chris argued. "I've been thinkin' about when you woke me up this morning. I heard your voice right before the dream ended. What if she can hear us, too? If we let her know we're going to Divarus maybe she'll find a way to meet us. We can at least try."

Evalyn considered. When she was reading Rachel's diary there were a few entries that talked about her dreams being prematurely cut short. There was even one in particular in which she mentioned hearing Chris yell at her in her dream to wake up for breakfast as the dream came to an end. Chris's idea was crazy, right?

"Alright, we'll try," Evalyn agreed, grabbing her purse as the car horn sounded from outside. "So what *exactly* do you plan on telling her?"

"I don't know yet," Chris said, shrugging. "I'll think about it more on the way. You think of somethin', too. It'd be better if we both talk to her. At least I think."

The car horn sounded a second time, prompting Chris and Evalyn to rush outside the house, slamming the door behind them. They hopped into the backseat and listened to Mom and Dad talk about their week.

As they got closer to the hospital, Chris thought more and more about what he was going to tell Rachel. First off, he thought he would mention Divarus and the Evarance Keepers. She'd never written about them in her diary, so it was likely wherever she was she hadn't heard about them yet. He thought it would be worth while telling her about Rucknar, Evalyn, and Kendrick, too, so she would know who to look for if she was actually able to meet up with them somehow.

The car stopped in the hospital parking lot. Within a few minutes they had arrived, standing outside the too-familiar door where Rachel lay. Upon entering, everyone's heart sank at the sight of her still in bed. Though the monitors hooked to her body displayed vital signs that reassured the family Rachel's condition hadn't worsened, they also showed no indication she was getting any better.

It was always this way whenever they came to visit Rachel. Her hospital room always brought with it a feeling of sadness accompanied by an overwhelming sense of helplessness.

This time, however, was different. Chris and Evalyn still couldn't get around the feelings of sadness that permeated the very walls of this place, but for the first time since they had lost their little sister to the coma, the helplessness they had felt when they looked at her was gone, replaced entirely by something else. *Hope*. The hope they felt was empowering. They didn't know how or when they would see Rachel whole again, but they had a plan and enough faith to see it through.

Mom and Dad spent the better part of the morning by Rachel's side until one of the doctors called them out of the room to discuss Rachel's progress — or lack thereof. Once they were gone, leaving Evalyn and Chris alone with Rachel for the first time, Chris walked over to Rachel's bedside. Looking down at her he put his hand over hers. It felt clammy, cold and lifeless, but he had to believe she was in there somewhere and the message he was about to give her would be heard.

"Rae," he began, stroking her hand with his thumb while looking at her face which remained frozen as if in a deep sleep, which is exactly what he thought she was.

"You've gotta listen to me. Eva and I, we're havin' these strange dreams about a world called Calim. I met a dragon there, well a youngling actually, named Ruck. And Eva met this guy named Ken who's helping her reach the city of Divarus. It's a city that's home to a people called the Evarance Keepers. If you can hear me, please, go to Divarus. Eva and I are looking for you."

Chris paused a moment, trying to regain his composure. The sadness of seeing Rachel lying trapped in a hospital bed was starting to overcome him. "I've just got to believe you're okay in there, Rae. Mom and Dad can't take much more of you being gone. So please Rae, please, go to Divarus. Ruck said the Evarance Keepers would be able to help us find you. So please don't give up, wherever you are."

He let go of Rachel's hand and took a few steps away from her bedside, making room for Evalyn to step in so she would have a chance to speak with Rachel as well before their parents came back.

"Rachel," Evalyn said softly, looking into her sister's pale still face, "I don't know if you can hear me, but if you can, listen to Chris and come to Divarus. Kendrick and I are on our way there now and should be arriving soon. We all miss you so much, but we haven't given up hope that you'll come back to us. Things just aren't the same around here without you. I hope you're still okay. Please come home if you can. And if you can't, don't lose hope. We're coming for you!"

Their parents stepped back into the room. Their meeting with the doctor had ended. Dad offered to take Chris and Evalyn home while Mom stayed by Rachel's bedside talking and singing softly to her. At the day's end, Evalyn and Chris both agreed not to leave the city of Divarus until they found each another and with any luck learned some new information about Rachel that would help them find her.

As Chris lay in bed his mind wouldn't stop racing at the excitement of seeing Evalyn on the dream side and finally meeting the Evarance Keepers in the mysterious city of Divarus. It took some time, but sleep finally came.

Looking around, Chris felt certain he was back in Calim, but Rucknar was nowhere to be seen. He stood near a tall wall made of polished stone that looked just like the one surrounding Divarus in his last dream. Only this time he was inside the city wall, not outside it. He looked about and saw people talking one with another and walking on smooth cobblestone streets wearing long and flowing colorful garments nearly brushing the ground.

The people looked happy, peaceful, and prosperous, and the streets of the city were clean and well kept. The buildings were both beautiful and as colorfully diverse as the people who walked past. Some buildings were tall, others short, and most were made of brick or stone, but there was also a fair amount of wooden structures. As Chris stared, people watching, a man with red hair wearing a bright blue and white robe came up to him.

"Can I help you?" the man asked.

Chris remembered how Rucknar had said the Evarance Keepers were kind to the dragons so he didn't think there would be any harm in telling the man that he was looking for his friend.

"Actually, I'm lookin' for someone," Chris said. "A dragon youngling named Rucknar. Have you seen him?"

The man thought a moment, "I haven't," he replied, rubbing his chin. "But Serena might have. Serena handles all communications with the elementals and nonhumans. If your dragon friend is here Serena would know."

"Think you could point the way?" Chris asked.

"Of course," the man said with a smile. "Her home's just around the corner. Can't miss it."

Chris thanked the man and walked in the direction he pointed out, rounding the corner. The home was large and wooden with wind chimes hanging above a wide front porch made of a long, wrap-around deck that disappeared from view as it swept around the backside of the house. The house was painted purple and decorated with large murals of elemental looking animals. One of the murals was that of a magnificent dragon, reassuring Chris that he had reached the right place.

Walking up the porch steps, he reached for the knocker, which looked like a brass cat curled up sleepily in a ball with a hinge on its tail hanging down in a J shape. Holding firm to the brass cat's tail, Chris knocked three times and waited. A little wooden door slid open between the cat and the curve of its tail revealing two brown eyes and part of a dark face.

"Yes?" a female voice asked from behind the door, "is there something I can help you with?"

"Hi. I'm looking for a dragon, a youngling named Ruck.

Have you seen him?"

The little peephole slid shut as shuffling noises came from behind it, followed by large dragging sounds like furniture being pulled across the floor. A moment later the main door flung open and a short, dark-skinned woman, not nearly as tall as Chris, with curly black hair pulled back into a bushy bun and tinted goggles resting snuggly on her head beckoned him in.

"You're Chris aren't you?" the woman asked, not allowing time for Chris to respond before directing him to follow her, which he did. He didn't know how the woman knew his name but suspected Rucknar had something to do with it.

She lead him down a hallway lined with oddly shaped doors that were lightly sculpted and beautifully decorated. As he followed he caught glimpses of what lay beyond the doors looking through the stained glass windows that were built into and around them. Through the glass he spied what looked like elemental animals of all shapes and sizes much like the ones Rachel had described in her diary.

"Come along, dear," the woman coaxed as she observed Chris slowing down to get a better look through the stained glass. "I don't normally deal with humans, that's Genevieve's job. But seeing as you're a friend of the dragon, I've decided to make an exception. Rucknar is quite special," she continued, "very different from the other dragons I've met."

"Different how?" Chris asked as he picked up the pace behind the woman he had determined must be Serena.

Serena halted, looking over Chris in bewilderment as she tried to understand how he could be so blind to things that in her mind were obvious. "You're his friend, aren't you? And you don't know?"

"Know what?" Chris asked, beginning to feel irritated.

"He's the heir of the Allorum. Son of Adamas, last of the diamond dragons."

"Ruck is Adamas' son?" Chris said. "But if Adamas is the *last* of the diamond dragons how is that possible?"

"Rucknar is a half-breed," Serena clarified, continuing down the long hall, passing by several adjacent hallways. "Half Allorum, half diamond. He is the embodiment of the best of both species, possessing the most desirable qualities from each clan."

Chris had never thought to ask Rucknar why his scales looked crystalline when the scales on the young dragons at the assimilation ceremony were flat and dull in comparison. It made sense. The son of a diamond dragon would have to be diamond, too, wouldn't he?

He remembered the mighty dragon king standing in front of him with crystal clarity, and the more he thought about it the more it made sense. There *were* subtle similarities between Rucknar and Adamas that he hadn't picked up on before, and the crystal scale he'd snatched off the ground during their first encounter wasn't really crystal at all; it was diamond! Chris reached into his pocket and pulled out the scale to take a second look. This whole time he'd had in his possession a sizable diamond!

Serena stopped at the end of the long hallway at a large door. Chris shoved the scale back into his pocket while Serena fiddled with a locking mechanism, the likes of which Chris had never seen before, causing the door to pop wide open the moment the lock was released. A rush of warm air blew into the house and light poured in with it revealing an elaborate garden outside the confines of the strange home.

Stepping out into the sunlight, Chris followed Serena,

who continued walking toward a large stone carving of a dragon painted with exquisite detail much like the altar had been at the dragon assimilation ceremony. Poking out from behind the statue a brown dragon tail shining with smoky-brown crystalline scales, which Chris now recognized as diamonds, flicked back and forth across the ground.

"Ruck!" Chris shouted, excited to see his friend again, prompting Rucknar to scurry out from behind the statue into full view.

"Chris!" Rucknar hissed happily in reply, seeming in high spirits. "How did you know where to find me?"

"I have my ways," Chris said with a wink. "Ruck, why didn't you tell me Adamas was your dad?"

"You never asked," Rucknar said with a snort.

"Oh, like I would know to ask somethin' like that," Chris said sarcastically, grinning. "So if you're the son of the dragon king, doesn't that make you like a prince or something?"

"An heir," Rucknar replied somewhat grumpily, clearly wanting to talk about something else.

"Alright, an heir then," Chris said. "So did ya get all your questions answered?" He didn't know what Rucknar and Serena had spoken about, but whatever it was it had to have been important. Why else would Rucknar sneak away from his clan?

"Yes, I think I have all the answers I need," Rucknar hissed, giving a dragonish grin, clearly relieved to be talking about something other than his dragon lineage. "Serena and I have had lots of time to talk."

"Are you ready to go then?" Chris asked, anxious to find Evalyn and with any luck Rachel as well.

"I think so," Rucknar replied, nodding.

"Good," Chris continued. "We need to meet up with Eva. She's come here, too, to help find Rae."

Rucknar turned his attention to Serena. "Thank you for helping me."

"Anytime," Serena said with a warm smile, stroking Rucknar from the cheek to the tip of his horn in farewell. "You are always welcome here. But be aware: The path you are choosing to follow will alter your destiny forever in ways you won't expect and may not like."

"I know," Rucknar replied, "but this is how it must be."

"Thank you for taking care of him," Chris said, reaching out to shake goodbye, which she politely declined, instead pulling him into her arms to give him a strong hug.

"Any friend of *this* dragon is a friend of mine. Don't be a stranger. And keep Rucknar safe."

"Will do," Chris replied with a laugh, returning the heartfelt hug.

"Come on, Ruck," Chris said with a nod. "Evalyn's waiting."

Chris still had hope Rachel would somehow make it to the city, as unlikely as that was, but it was Evalyn he was most anxious to meet. That's because meeting her would make all of the dreams and all of the talking about dreams absolutely real, washing away any remaining doubt by proving once and for all that they both weren't somehow making up this whole "dreams being connected" thing.

Chris was about to turn and walk away with Rucknar when he realized he had no idea where to go. Even if he wandered the city for hours, there was no guarantee he would bump into Evalyn or even Kendrick. Without a plan, any efforts he made to find her would be futile. If he had been smart, he would have told Evalyn to meet him at the city entrance, but it hadn't occurred to him to make a plan that specific until now, and now that he was already back in his dream, it was too late. He looked back at Serena hoping she may be able to help.

"Serena, there's one more thing. I need to find someone in the city. She doesn't live here, she's just visiting. Can you tell me the best way to find her?"

"Ah, yes," Serena said with a quirky little smile, "I told you already, Genevieve is the one who deals with human issues. She's an Evarance Oracle. If anyone can help you find your friend, it's she."

"And where can I find her?" Chris asked.

"Up the hill, just past the fountain," Serena said, pointing in the direction he and Rucknar should go, then describing the house in detail so they would know what to look for.

She lead them back through her home, saying one more goodbye on the front porch before pulling the goggles resting on her head down over her eyes to work with a Luminary that couldn't control its light, shutting the door behind her as she went back inside.

"Well," Chris said with a grin, "here goes nothing!"

He and Rucknar left Serena, walking down several streets in the direction she recommended before coming upon a large crowd gathered around a tall fountain. Chris and Rucknar pushed through the crowd to see what all the commotion was about. There he saw Evalyn and a guy he assumed must have been Kendrick in the middle of the crowd sitting on top of a large horse made entirely out of water.

"So that's an aquamare," Chris breathed, looking at the massive mare in awe. It looked squishy and fluid like a water balloon, and Chris couldn't help but wonder what would happen if it burst. He shook the nefarious balloon popping plans that had begun formulating from his mind, focusing instead on uniting with his sister to continue the search for Rachel.

"Eva!" Chris yelled out from the crowd.

Evalyn, hearing her name, turned her head to look his way when someone in the crowd shouted at her, pointing.

"See! There it is!"

"It's an omen," another said, gasping at the sight of Evalyn. "We're all doomed!"

Chris could feel the crowd becoming increasingly agitated and dangerous by the moment with Kendrick and Evalyn trapped at the very center of it. He looked beyond the fountain and saw the home Serena had described to him. It was large and white with a dome shaped section of roof and a high metal fence surrounding connected to an open gate. The gate, like the door in Serena's home, had a peculiar lock on it. That gave Chris an idea.

"Ruck!" Chris said, leaning down toward Rucknar, who was rather enjoying the spectacle the humans were creating around him. "I need your help. We have to make a path to that white house over there before things get out of control."

Rucknar understood. He stretched out his wings, forcing people away from him and Chris, hissing menacingly at the crowd as he walked.

"Eva, Ken, this way!" Chris shouted over the confused crowd of people who were backing away from him and Rucknar.

Kendrick nodded at Chris in acknowledgement. Rucknar thrashed his tail and flapped his wings, picking up his pace through the scattering crowd, making a wide path through which Kendrick and Evalyn on the aquamare could escape. Tempest followed closely behind Chris and Rucknar, Kendrick and Evalyn still riding her, until all of them stood together inside the fenced surrounding. Chris ran to the gate and slammed it shut, popping the lock into place using what he had learned while observing Serena.

"Wow! Way to make an entrance, Eva!" Chris said. "You've got the whole town riled up!"

"Not now, Chris," Evalyn said, still concerned about the crowd that was now gathering outside the gate. She looked to Kendrick who had remained as calm as a mountain in a storm. "What should we do?"

Kendrick looked around to determine the next best course of action. Although they were momentarily safe, they were also trapped even more so than they had been amid the crowd. While Kendrick thought, Chris acted, walking up to the door of the white house, knocking loudly, breaking Evalyn's focus from Kendrick and Kendrick's focus from the growing crowd. He wasn't about to wait for Kendrick to come up with a plan, because he already had one.

"We need to go inside," Chris called out, keeping his body facing the door as he waited for someone to answer. Rucknar, who had been terrorizing the crowd through the gate just for the fun of it, gave one last loud hiss before scurrying up to the door beside him.

Evalyn, following Kendrick's lead, slid off Tempest's back onto a paved walkway leading up to the front porch.

"Will Tempest be okay?" she asked Kendrick, stroking the side of the aquamare's neck. She worried about the crowd getting through the gate.

"She'll be fine," Kendrick replied before walking with Evalyn to the front door where Chris and Rucknar were still waiting.

The moment their feet touched the porch landing the door to the white home opened.

CHAPTER 16. DUSK TO DAWN

Rae . . . Chris's voice echoed in the air, piercing through the darkness in which she stood, the very same darkness she had been accused of creating, which swirled around inside her like an endless storm raging through her mind. She heard him again, though his voice was uneven, muffled by the howling winds that whipped past.

Listen to me . . . Strange dreams . . . Calim.

Those were just a few of the words she made out before the storm raged louder and more fiercely than before. How could Chris possibly know about Calim? Or the strange dreams that caused her to be trapped here? Surely she was hearing nothing more than her own voice wrapped in the guise of her brother's. It was a cruel trick for her mind to play.

Go to Divarus. His voice came again, reaching out to her through the storm. *Eva and I are looking for you.*

Evalyn and Chris were looking for her? Rachel couldn't believe it although she desperately wished it were true. Even if they wanted to see her, how could they? She was trapped worlds away with no way to return home and time working feverishly against her. Two weeks to live was nothing when compared with the fullness of life she still wanted to experience. The thought of her demise plagued her mind, nearly causing her to become lost in the traumatic storm, when she heard Chris's voice again break through, bringing her back to her senses.

Rae, please, go to Divarus. Don't give up wherever you are.

Divarus? His voice sounded genuine, but that only made it harder for her to believe that what she was thinking and feeling was real. After all, Chris wasn't the type to be so serious or encouraging. At least not when he was speaking directly to her. She almost dismissed the voice, again reasoning it to be nothing more than a figment of her imagination, when the storm lessened, allowing Evalyn's voice to reach out to her, too.

Rachel . . . I don't know if you can hear me, but if you can, listen to Chris. . . . Come to Divarus. . . . Don't lose hope. We're coming for you!

With Evalyn confirming the validity of Chris's words the voices in her head were harder to deny. If what they said were really true, and she was beginning to believe that they were, then she had to go to Divarus, wherever that was, to find her brother and sister before time ran out. The storm around Rachel ceased, leaving nothing but silence and darkness. Chris and Evalyn's voices were quiet, too, leaving Rachel with only one clue to follow. But maybe one clue was enough. She sat down in the darkness trying to calm her thoughts. Even though she was alone, she no longer felt alone, and hope now swelled within her.

Soft, sweet music rang out through the air, wrapping around her like a warm blanket on a cold winter's night. She recognized the song and the one who sang it, the melody filling her body with both sadness and joy. Through the music she could feel her mother near as tears began to drop gently from her eyes. She didn't want her mother's song to end, but it did, and when she awoke she found Ember beside her keeping her warm and safe in the confines of his den.

His den looked different than before, lit up brightly by a hawk-like Luminary named Lux who perched on a tree root sticking out from the dirt wall. It was just one of the many precautions put in place by Elder Oakin after the council had agreed to ensure Rachel's safety while she searched for a way home. Since time was limited, Caligo, the mysticorn stallion, volunteered to be Rachel's legs since he could travel much farther and faster than she could on her own. He carried her back to Ember's den after the council meeting to let her rest for the journey ahead, while Torrens took on the role of night watchfox, standing outside the den entrance to guard against the Shadai until daylight came. Rumors had spread that the Shadai were on the move, their territory spreading farther and faster than ever before.

Rachel was wide awake now, but had no concept of time as she lay in the small den lit up as brightly as if it were noon. Ember and Lux remained still, resting in the quiet tranquility of the den, sound asleep. Rachel didn't want to disturb them, but she also didn't want to wait any longer than she had to before asking Ember about Divarus and making her way there. She rolled away from Ember, slowly and quietly, creeping to the den entrance without disturbing him or Lux to get a better feel for the time of day.

Rachel moved away the branches of leafy foliage that disguised the den's entrance, peering out into the darkness that proved to her that morning had not yet come. Crawling out into the night air she looked for Torrens, who was supposed to be watching over the den, but didn't see him anywhere.

"Torrens?" Rachel called out in a hushed voice. But she heard no reply and saw no signs of his fiery coat.

It was still much too early to wake Ember, but something didn't feel right, and Rachael felt he should be made aware that Torrens was gone. Brushing the branches aside again, she began to crawl back into the safe confines of Ember's den when suddenly something grabbed hard and fast onto her shoe, pulling her away from the den. She screamed as the unknown assailant dragged her swiftly away, across the forest floor, and into the darkness of night. She thrashed and yelled, kicking and twisting her body hard against the rocks and twigs that littered the ground, trying to grab hold of something.

As she watched Ember's den shrink from view, she could see a low glow of flames emerge, Ember's flames, followed by a light that shot up into the night sky — no doubt the light of Lux acting as a warning beacon. Other fiery lights appeared, too, dotting the dark forest with their orange auras. Her screams had stirred the firefoxes from their dens, but she was too far away now for them to see her, masked by the darkness of the forest and sky, dawn not yet having broken over the horizon.

How could she have been so foolish as to leave the safety of Ember's den? She screamed out again, hoping to draw the attention of Ember and the others. If they could not see her, perhaps they could still hear her. The shadowy figure pulling her body remained unmoved by Rachel's feeble attempts to call out for help, moving even faster as he pulled her body beside his, dragging her more violently across the ground. She could see her captor now, his eyes filled with a chillingly familiar, wild, bloodthirsty look, a look she had grown to loathe. Trebax had her in his clutches, his mouth clamped down hard over her shoe like a vice painfully squeezing her foot.

Light beacons like the one Lux made began lighting up the now dark-gray sky. Each one appeared in response to the one before, signaling Rachel's abduction to the elementals scattered throughout the woods who had been tasked with keeping her safe until the mystery of her entrapment could be solved or her time ran out. The calimin tortoises were the first to take action, rolling like boulders across the ground, hitting Trebax as he ran and causing him to stumble, nearly dropping Rachel's foot from his mouth.

Caught off guard by their assaults and losing ground fast, he regained his footing and tightened his grip on Rachel's shoe. He pressed forward with great haste, dodging their attacks until he was ahead of them. Even with Rachel in tow he was faster than the boulder-like tortoises were, and his mission couldn't afford to be delayed. Dawn was approaching, and with it came the light of day that would transform him into a shadow and force him to drop the precious prey he had worked so hard to obtain.

The firefoxes, running through the forest chasing after Trebax and Rachel, were drawing nearer, though they still remained far from catching up. The delay caused by the tortoises and the weight of Rachel's body prevented Trebax from running at optimum speed, giving them a slight advantage.

Many strides ahead of the others was Ember, who was closing in fast. Though small, he was quick, and had been the first of the firefoxes to bolt after Rachel, following her screams into the dark forest. Ember's coat crackled orange-hot, and his ears, feet, and tail tip burst into brilliant white flames, his protective instincts pushing his body to its limits. His orange, coal-like flames weren't bright enough in the gray of morning to render Trebax a shadow, but they were strong enough to burn him. Ember slammed his body hard into Trebax's side, singeing a large patch of the black, wiry coat that distinguished the shadow wolves from the other species of Shadai. But it did little to alter the shadow wolf's course.

The other firefoxes were drawing closer, burning fiery paths behind Trebax as they narrowed the gap between him and them. Bat-like Ai're joined them, flying above the flames burned into the forest by the firefoxes, absorbing the peaks of those flames and fanning them higher into the sky, creating massive walls of fire. Ember slammed into Trebax again but to no avail. Trebax was as determined to keep Rachel as Ember was to rescue her.

The morning sky was transforming from dark to pale gray with Trebax and Rachel nearing the dark cloud cover that marked the edge of the Shadai's growing territory, territory that had now become clearly visible against the changing sky. Once under the protection of the darkness he would have no fear of becoming a shadow under the light of the morning sun, or dropping the girl that Umbra so desperately desired.

Ember could see the darkness, and he knew he had to free Rachel before Trebax reached it. The light from his body might not be bright enough to transform Trebax into a shadow, but the blazing white light of his ears just might be bright enough to dissolve the one thing keeping Rachel trapped: his mouth. Ember rushed Trebax again, this time aiming for Trebax's jaw, letting the white, flaming light of his ears shine through the rock-solid muzzle that held Rachel captive. Trebax's face changed for only a moment, becoming part shadow as Ember's ears passed through. But a moment was all it took to free Rachel's foot from his clutches, and her body came to an abrupt stop on the ground.

Trebax, again whole, lifted his head to the sky and howled with a power and force so strong it reached deep into the heart of the Shadai's newly formed territory. Howls echoed back in reply from other shadow wolves that heard Trebax's call, their black forms lining the forest just underneath the shadow of darkness. Using the distraction created by the emerging wolves, Trebax cracked Ember hard across the face with his head, causing the little firefox to fall limply to the ground before turning back toward Rachel, anxious to reclaim his prize.

Rachel, sore and in pain from being dragged so forcefully across the ground, clumsily scrambled to her feet, determined not to let Trebax get ahold of her again. She wanted to run toward Ember, worried about his safety and wellbeing, but she also recognized he had put himself in harm's way to protect her, and falling right back into Trebax's grasp was the last thing he would want her to do. So she ran. Away from Ember, away from Trebax, toward the firefoxes and their burning walls of flame.

Trebax charged at Rachel in hot pursuit, but he was too late. The firefoxes and Ai're caught up with her first, burning flaming walls around her high into the air, reducing Trebax to a shadow of his former self as he passed through the flames and the girl he so desperately desired. Once away from the intensity of the fiery light, he became himself once again: solid, lethal and ready to act. He ran a second time toward the blazing wall of fire, but before he reached the fullness of its light—light that would reduce him again to shadow—something caught one of his paws, then another paw, and another, until his feet were firmly anchored to the forest floor.

Oakin weasels had wrapped their bodies around his legs, planting their feet deep into the soil and making it impossible for Trebax to break free. He snapped and bit at their wooden hides until another weasel grabbed ahold of his muzzle, rooting its body firmly into place, trapping Trebax's mouth and head against the cold, hard ground.

"So it *was* you," Incindia said as she walked out from the among the firefoxes who had shielded Rachel with their fiery light. Her golden eyes glowed brightly as she eyed Trebax, flames flickering in the cool morning air. "I should have known Umbra would send you to do his dirty work."

Trebax growled angrily, grunting as he struggled to free his mouth and legs from the Oakin ensnaring him. When it was clear to him that his attempts to escape were futile, he looked at Incindia with a cold, evil stare.

"You know nothing, firefox!" he snarled through clenched teeth, growling as though he were about to pounce, moving his stare from Incindia to Rachel, who he could now see through the wall of flames that had diminished around her. He wanted to be sure she was watching and listening to the words he spoke.

"You can't save the girl! She is already lost!" he growled. "And there is nothing you or anyone else can do about it."

Rachel didn't want to believe him. She couldn't believe him. Not after hearing Chris and Evalyn say they were looking for her. A newfound hope was burning within her, and she wasn't about to let go of it no matter what Trebax said.

Howls filled the air as the shadow wolves who had responded to Trebax's call drew near, stopping just short of the firefoxes' flaming light. Drenar and Sanshir stood among them, eager to attack, but Trebax knew they had come too late. The sky was changing again, rays of light peeking out over the horizon, brightening the area more and more with each passing moment. He stared at Rachel with angry eyes, growling in disgust at the girl who had evaded him once again.

"If you think you've won, girl, you're *wrong*!" he barked aggressively. "This war has just begun! *We will catch you*! And when we do, your fate will be even worse than that of those pathetic firefoxes who protect you!"

Rachel looked at Ember, whose body lay still on the forest floor. Then she looked back at Trebax, who gave a wicked smile before dissolving into his shadow form, which freed him from the Oakin that had ensnared him. Dawn had broken brightly over the horizon allowing the sun to shine brilliantly into the morning sky, transforming the shadow wolves into shadows. Trebax, now free, turned from Rachel and the firefoxes to run back with his pack to the dark territory they called home, howling into the air as they hit the cover of darkness that returned them to their solid states.

Rachel rushed to Ember, kneeling beside him and lifting his head into her arms while shaking his body gently to see if she could rouse him.

"Please be okay," she whispered in his ear, unwilling to allow thoughts to enter her mind that would suggest otherwise. She stroked his black ashen fur, covering her hands in soot as she turned his head to face hers and stroked his cheeks lightly with her thumbs. He stirred, slowly opening his eyes, looking up at Rachel and the bright morning sky.

"Ember!" Rachel said, pulling him into a warm hug, the ash on his fur rubbing into her gray hoodie and smudging the side of her face.

"That Trebax sure packs a punch!" he chuckled with a weak smile, lifting a paw to rub the side of his head where Trebax had struck him.

"He's gone now," Rachel said. "He and the other shadow wolves turned into shadows the moment the sunlight hit them. You saved me, you know. If it wasn't for you I'd be with them under the shadow of darkness, too. You're my hero!"

"Aww . . ." Ember sighed, his cheeks burning a light orange. "It was a team effort really. We all worked to protect you. But why did you leave my den in the first place?"

Rachel thought about her actions leading up to this moment. She had put everyone in danger even though her intentions had been innocent enough. She hadn't wanted to disturb Ember's or Lux's sleep. The fact that she knew Torrens was standing watch had given her a false sense of security. She had been careless.

"Wait, where's Torrens?" Rachel asked, alarmed, remembering that she had never had the opportunity to tell Ember he was missing.

She looked at the firefoxes still standing nearby, the ones who had saved her from Trebax with their flaming walls of fire. Incindia was there and several other firefoxes she had met briefly in passing, but Torrens was nowhere to be seen.

"Incindia?" Rachel called out. "Where's Torrens?"

Incindia perked up her ears and looked Rachel's way, cutting short her conversation with an Aquari goose who had just arrived to discuss cleaning up the fiery mess that still lingered throughout the forest. She looked around at the firefoxes who were present, but like Rachel, she didn't see Torrens anywhere.

"I don't know," Incindia replied, startled and a little confused. "I thought he would be here with us."

Another Aquari goose arrived, waddling up next to the first one. This Aquari was fat and large. It left a trail of puddles on the ground where it stepped and was clearly oversaturated with water it had picked up from a nearby stream, no doubt to help put out fires in the forest.

"Incindia," it said, somewhat fatigued from carrying around the extra water weight. "We found something by the stream you need to see."

Incindia nodded at the watery goose in acknowledgement and turned back to Rachel.

"Don't worry," she said, "Torrens will turn up. For now take Ember back to his den. I'll be there shortly to meet you."

Rachel agreed, and Incindia left in great haste. As she vanished from view, Caligo arrived to carry Rachel back to Ember's home. Rachel stepped gingerly onto a singed tree stump near Caligo, mindful to not put too much pressure on her foot, which was swollen from her encounter with Trebax. She then gently lifted Ember onto Caligo's back before pulling herself up behind him.

They arrived back at the den in no time, and with the light of day now streaming through the leafy canopy there was no fear of another shadow wolf attack until nightfall. Rachel sat with Ember outside of his den, squeezing the sides of her foot, which had begun throbbing, to try and ease the pain.

"Will your foot be alright?" Ember asked with an expression of genuine concern.

"I think so," Rachel replied, lifting her hand away and stretching out her leg to get a better look. She pointed her toes and rotated her ankle with relative ease. "It doesn't feel like anything's broken. It's just a little sore, that's all."

"Good to hear," Ember said, relieved. "Wouldn't want you traveling with an injured foot."

"And what about you?" Rachel asked. "Trebax hit you pretty hard. Are you going to be okay?"

"Of course I will," Ember said with a chuckle, boosting his flames as much as he could to show Rachel he was still ready for anything the shadow wolves had to throw at him. "It's going to take a lot more than a knock on the noggin to stop me!"

"I guess so," Rachel said with a laugh. She was relieved that Ember was all right and still in high spirits despite all of the trouble she had caused him.

"Hey, Ember?" Rachel said, remembering her dream. "There's something I've been wanting to ask you but with all of the craziness this morning I never had a chance."

"What's that?" Ember asked, yawning wide and stretching as he realized how early he had been awakened.

"I had another dream last night," Rachel continued. "It was similar to my last dream, but at the same time really different. I could hear my brother and sister calling to me in the darkness. They told me they were coming for me. Somehow they know about this world and've found a way to get here. They said I should go to Divarus to meet up with them."

"Divarus?" Ember said, surprised. "I know where that is. All elementals do. If your brother and sister know about Divarus they must really be here."

"How soon can we get there?" Rachel asked, excitement bubbling up within her at the prospect of seeing Chris and Evalyn.

"It's not that simple," Ember replied, hushing his voice while looking around to see who might be within earshot. "The shadow wolves are after you now, and the council is keeping a close watch over you. If we're going to get you to Divarus we need the council's help to safely travel there."

It made sense. After all, this wasn't a casual journey. Each night she would be vulnerable to shadow wolf attacks. And each day there was no guarantee she would make it safely to her destination.

"Don't tell anyone about your brother and sister," Ember whispered seriously. "Not even Incindia."

"But I trust Incindia," Rachel interjected.

"I do, too," Ember agreed, "but why do you think you attended the council meeting in the first place? Incindia was trying to do the right thing by informing the council about you and your connection with the darkness. What would the council do if they knew your brother and sister were here, too?"

Rachel hadn't thought about that. It was as much her job to protect her brother and sister as it was Ember's job to protect her. If the council knew that more dreamers like her were materializing in their world it was impossible to tell what would happen to Chris and Evalyn.

"I understand," Rachel said, nodding. "What do we do then?"

"The council wants answers, right?" Ember asked. "They want to know how to stop the darkness, and they want to get you back home, at least for the time being. Well, Divarus is the home of the Evarance Keepers. If anyone would know of a way to get a dreamer like you back home it would be them. We can make a case for going to Divarus without mentioning your brother and sister."

Ember's ears perked up. Then Rachel heard it, too. It was the sound of small paws running hurriedly across the ground. They both looked in the direction of the sound and saw Blaze jump straight through a bush, causing it to burst into flames. He looked alarmed and out of breath.

"Blaze, what's wrong?" Ember asked, waiting for him to catch his breath.

"It's Torrens," Blaze said, still breathing heavily. "They found him by the river. Trebax lured him there in the middle of the night. Incindia asked that I come get both of you."

There was no time for conversation. No time to speculate on the seriousness of Blaze's words. Rachel called over Caligo, who had remained nearby absorbing water from plants and shrubs on the forest floor. He came and swiftly carried Rachel and Ember to the riverside, following Blaze to the exact location where Incindia lay watching over Torrens, whose fire was weak and nearly extinguished. His body was soaked with water and blood, the few flames that remained struggling to stay lit. His white, black, and orange fur lay damp, dull, and cold against his skin.

Hopping off Caligo's back, Rachel and Ember rushed to Torrens' side. He was still alive but badly injured. His body shivered with cold despite the warmth of Incindia's fire. Rachel's breath caught in her throat and her heart stopped beating as she looked down on him. The kind, protective firefox she had come to love was now hurt because of her.

"This isn't your fault," Torrens breathed quietly, turning his eyes to Rachel, perceiving her thoughts. "It is I who failed you," he said, coughing in pain as he spoke.

Trebax's words echoed in her ears. *This war has just begun! We will catch you! And when we do, your fate will be even worse than that of those pathetic firefoxes who protect you!*

He was right. This was a war. But Rachel couldn't bear the thought of anyone else getting hurt because of her.

CHAPTER 17. VISIONS

Standing on the porch of a large white house in the city of Divarus, Evalyn, Chris, Kendrick, and Rucknar watched as the door before them swung slowly open. A woman stepped out from behind the door. She was tall and slender with eyes like a forest in the light of morning, and sun kissed, light-ginger hair that hung down to her waist in loosely cascading waves. Her face was fair and beautiful. The gown she wore was white and flowing with delicate beads sewn into breathtaking patterns across the bust. To Chris she looked more like an angel than a mere human being. He knew at once this must be Genevieve, the woman of whom Serena had spoken so highly.

She invited the strangers into her home, much to the dismay of the growing crowd of onlookers who gathered outside the metal gate surrounding her house. They wanted to see a spectacle. She quietly closed the door behind her guests after they were safely within the walls of her home, paying particular attention to Evalyn as she walked by. She led them to a room that looked like a small library with a couch, a couple of armchairs, and walls covered in bookshelves filled to the brim with books.

An oval coffee table with little drawers built into the sides sat in the middle of the room. On the table lay a silver platter filled with rolls, jam, and butter. Next to the platter was a matching pitcher filled with a honey-colored liquid and three empty cups laid thoughtfully out on the table. Two of the cups were placed in front of the couch and one in front of an armchair. It was almost as if she knew Chris, Evalyn, and Kendrick would arrive.

"My name is Genevieve," the woman said, with a lovely warm smile and a sweet gentle voice. She gestured to the furniture, stretching out her hand in welcome. "Please make yourselves at home. I have something to attend to, but I'll be back shortly."

She promptly left the room, and as quickly as she had Rucknar scurried around the back of the couch to look at the books lining the walls. Chris claimed one of the armchairs, plopping down on top of the cushiony seat before kicking off his shoes and propping his feet up onto the coffee table. He stretched out his arms then pulled back his hands, placing them behind his head, spreading his elbows wide.

"Chris!" Evalyn said in an agitated, yet hushed voice, looking both embarrassed and appalled that her brother would act in such a way in a stranger's home.

"*What?*" Chris asked, wiggling his back snugly into the chair. "She *did* tell us to make ourselves at home."

"I don't think *that's* what she meant!" Evalyn countered, taking one last glance at her brother's stinky feet kicked up on the coffee table before rolling her eyes and focusing her attention instead on Kendrick who gave her a warm smile.

"Ladies first," Kendrick said, gesturing to the couch in much the same way that Genevieve had, causing Evalyn to blush ever so slightly. Now Chris was the one rolling his eyes at the icky-sweet way Kendrick and Evalyn looked at each other.

Evalyn sat down and Kendrick followed, sitting down

on the cushion next to her. They were both being way too polite and proper for Chris' taste.

"Well," Chris said, taking his feet off the table, leaning forward to look at the tray of food in front of them. "I'm starving. How about you, Ruck? Do you want a roll?"

Rucknar just snorted in reply, clearly more interested in the books than the food on the table.

"Alrighty then," Chris continued. "Guess that means more for me!" He grabbed a roll, slathered butter and jam all over it, then scarfed it down, licking the sticky jam residue off of his finger before picking up another one.

"Hey, Eva, want one?" Chris said with a grin, knowing full well she wouldn't touch it after he had just slimed his fingers with saliva.

"I think I'll pass," Evalyn said, wrinkling her nose in disgust.

"Your loss." Chris grinned wider, covering the new roll with butter and jam before devouring it as well.

"I'll take a roll," Kendrick said.

"Uh, yeah, okay," Chris replied, his grin clearly fading as he grabbed a roll and tossed it Kendrick's way. It was not that Chris hated Kendrick or anything, but seeing the way Evalyn looked at the guy just didn't sit right with him.

Kendrick caught the roll and broke it open, taking a bite of the soft warm bread.

"So," Kendrick said still addressing Chris, "who's Genevieve?" He had been wondering how Chris knew this house would be a safe place to go.

"She's some sort of oracle, I think," Chris replied, coming to the conclusion that having a conversation with Kendrick was better than watching him and his sister make goo-goo eyes at each other.

"Someone told me that she could help," he said. "I was told she could help me find Evalyn in the city, but now that we're here and I've already bumped into Evalyn and you, I'm really hoping she can help us find Rachel."

"An oracle?" Kendrick asked, looking thoughtful.

"Well, somethin' like that," Chris affirmed. "*All I know is* she's the one to talk to around here when a person needs help."

Evalyn was just about to join in the conversation when she felt something sliding between her feet, pushing her shoes apart. It was brown and scaly, and at first glance it looked like a snake. She squealed, jumping up onto the couch in a flash and grabbing onto Kendrick with both arms, nearly knocking him over in the process. The whole couch rocked forward as something hit the back of it with a loud thud. Evalyn's body trembled as she squeezed Kendrick tightly. Continuing to move, the couch scooted forward several inches before stopping. Another loud thud sounded, this one resembling the sound of a large heavy book hitting the floor, and Evalyn squeaked, closing her eyes tightly.

Chris, having watched the whole thing from the comfy confines of his chair, burst into laughter at Evalyn and poor Kendrick whom she was smothering.

"It's only Ruck, Eva!" Chris explained, still chuckling at his sister who clearly couldn't tell the difference between a dragon tail and a snake.

Evalyn opened just one of her eyes, and then the other, loosening her grip on Kendrick and blushing a bright shade of red. She had forgotten about the dragon.

"Whatcha doin', Ruck?" Chris asked, lifting his eyes to peer over Evalyn's now vacant side of the couch.

Rucknar picked up the large book he had freed from the

shelf and dragged it around to the front of the couch, placing it down in front of Chris. While Chris examined the front of the book, Kendrick pushed the couch back into place and Evalyn returned to her side of it, mortified about getting so excited over such a little thing—although Kendrick hadn't seemed to mind one bit.

Evayln couldn't help but look at Rucknar. He was about the size of a large dog but longer from head to tail, with huge wings folded flat against his body and a giant skull that held two large horns that arched slightly out from the back of his head. A line of spikes ran down his spine and tail, and he was completely covered in smoky-brown, crystal-looking scales. If Evalyn had been the least bit interested in reptiles, she would have found him fascinating to look at, but she wasn't, and he really grossed her out, so much so that she turned her face away to avoid becoming sick to her stomach.

Ignoring Evalyn's apparent squeamishness Chris ran his fingers across the cover of the book Rucknar had brought him, feeling the texture of it. It was old and cracked. It had a green leather binding with golden writing across the front in a language Chris couldn't read. He flipped through the pages, of which there were many, all written in the same peculiar language.

"What's this, Ruck?" Chris asked, closing the book and turning it toward Rucknar.

"It's a history," Rucknar hissed, "of Calim since the beginning."

"The beginning of what?" Chris pressed.

"The beginning of the world and the beginning of the dragons," Rucknar replied. "It's written in dragon tongue."

Chris's eyes grew wide as he looked at the writing on

the book. "Can you read it, Ruck?"

"I can't," Rucknar huffed, sounding somewhat disappointed in himself. "It's in an ancient tongue. Only the Elders can read it."

"Ruck, can I take a look?" Kendrick asked, reaching out his hand.

Rucknar squinted his eyes, peering suspiciously at Kendrick over the tabletop.

"It's Rucknar, not Ruck!" he hissed grumpily, giving Kendrick a sharp glance. The only one he would tolerate calling him that ridiculous nickname was Chris; he still had a healthy distrust of humans. He pulled the book off of the table and dragged it back around the couch, making Evalyn feel rather unnerved about having such a large lizard shuffling around behind her.

Before Rucknar came out from behind the couch to bring Chris the book, she hadn't really paid much attention to him. She had been so focused on Kendrick, his chocolate-brown eyes, his brown hair, his heartwarming smile . . . she had scarcely noticed anything else. But the more she thought about the dragon shuffling around behind her, the more uneasy she became. Scaly creatures creeped her out, and Rucknar was no exception.

"Way to ruin the moment, Ken," Chris complained, kicking his feet up onto the table again and leaning back into his chair just as Genevieve walked back into the room.

"I see you've made yourselves comfortable," Genevieve commented, a hint of laughter in her voice, as she looked at Chris lounging in her armchair before turning to look at Evalyn, taking a particular interest in the flower Evalyn wore in her hair. "The townspeople are gone now, and your aquamare is safe."

Is that what Genevieve was doing? Evalyn wondered. *Calming down the townspeople to ensure not only Tempest's safety but our own?*

Genevieve sat down in the vacant armchair, looking at Chris then back at Evalyn.

"I know why you're here," she said, leaning down to one of the coffee table drawers, sliding it open to pull out an extra cup stored inside. "You're looking for someone."

"Yes, our sister Rachel," Evalyn confirmed. "She's lost. Somewhere with the firefoxes, we think. Can you tell us where they are?"

"I can do more than that," Genevieve replied with a twinkle in her eye. "But before I show you where your sister can be found, please, have a drink."

She took the pitcher and poured the honey colored liquid into each of the cups, beginning with her own. Setting the pitcher down, she lifted her glass to her perfectly shaped lips and took the first sip.

"What is it?" Evalyn asked, gently lifting up her cup as Chris and Kendrick took theirs, too. Chris downed his in a flash, emptying the whole thing within a matter of seconds.

"Whatever it is it's really good," Chris interjected, licking the remnants off his upper lip.

"Thank you," Genevieve said with a smile, gracefully accepting Chris's compliment. "It's called bellarune. It comes from the nectar of a flower grown here."

"I know that flower," Kendrick said, perking up. "My village grows it along the riverside."

"Do you live in Teran?" Genevieve asked, looking over Kendrick's clothing. She recognized the craftsmanship sewn into his white collared shirt and dark, olive-green waistcoat. Even his pants and boots had a quality about them that hinted of his little village.

"I do," Kendrick replied.

"And by what name are you known?" she asked.

"Kendrick Knight," he replied. It was the first time Evalyn had ever heard his last name. *And what a fitting last name it is,* she thought. He was, to her, like a knight in shining armor, aiding her on a quest to find her sister. She was surprised she hadn't thought to ask him about his last name before, but it had never really come up.

"And what are your names?" Genevieve asked, turning to Chris and Evalyn.

"My name is Evalyn, Evalyn Summers," Evalyn said, speaking out before Chris had a chance. She wanted to give Genevieve a proper introduction without the silly nicknames that Chris was so insistent on using. "And this is my brother Christian, but he prefers to be called Chris."

"And where do you two come from?" Genevieve inquired, looking at Chris's and Evalyn's clothes, which were unlike anything worn by the people of this village or the neighboring regions.

Chris and Evalyn looked at each other, unsure what they should tell her. In the silence of their uncertainly, Genevieve closed her eyes as if she were in a momentary trance, breathing in and out slowly, allowing her chest to rise and fall noticeably.

"I know what you are," she declared calmly but definitively, opening her eyes. "You're Echoes, dreamers from another world."

"How did you know?" Evalyn asked. She was aware that she and Chris looked out of place here, but Genevieve hadn't learned enough about them yet to come to that sort of conclusion.

"I'm an Evarance Keeper and an oracle, too, so I asked the Evarance if it knew where you were from," Genevieve replied with a hint of a smile.

"You can speak to it?" Evalyn asked.

"In a way," Genevieve confirmed. "My people have dedicated their lives to understanding and protecting the Evarance and the dreamers who travel through it to our world. We have a special connection to it. I don't speak to Evarance with words, I reach out to it with feelings, and it responds back to me with impressions. The impressions the Evarance sends to me aren't always clear, but even so they can be very enlightening."

"Are there other dreamers like *us* here?" Evalyn asked.

"Not that I'm aware of," Genevieve said. "The dreamers who come here, the ones we call Echoes, are only ghostlike reflections of dreamers from other worlds, nothing more. Certainly nothing as real as you and your brother."

She paused again, staring at Evalyn with fascination.

"That flower in your hair, where did you get it?" Genevieve asked, trying to understand how Evalyn and Chris had managed to come to this world as more than just ordinary Echoes. She speculated that perhaps the andalyn Evalyn wore was an echoprint of her own making that somehow allowed her to fully manifest herself in this world.

"Oh this?" Evalyn asked, pulling the andalyn out of her braided hair, holding tightly to it with both hands. "It was a gift," she continued with a smile, "from Kendrick."

Genevieve looked at the young man.

"So tell me Kendrick," Genevieve began, her manner becoming a bit more serious than it had been, "your village is known for their abundance of flowers and herbs. What type of flower is Evalyn holding?" It was apparent she was trying to make some sort of point.

"It's an andalyn," Kendrick replied. "Surely an Evarance Keeper such as yourself knows what an andalyn is. The flower I picked was an echoprint made by one the Echoes that regularly visits my village. A little girl who likes to come and play in our flowery fields."

"I *am* aware of what it is," Genevieve said, with a nod of both agreement and understanding. "I just wanted to see if *you* knew."

She leaned forward as she had once before to pull out another item from within the coffee table drawer. It was a small, blue, drawstring pouch with silver strings wrapped tightly below the rim of the bag. She untied the bag, placing her thumb and forefinger inside, and drew out a large pinch of fine, clear crystal granules, almost powderlike in texture, which she sprinkled into the palm of her hand, leaving the pouch to rest on her lap.

She blew the tiny crystals from her palm out into the air where they froze, suspended above the table where everyone could see. Even Rucknar peeked his head around the couch, curious about what the human oracle was doing.

"The people of this city believe that the andalyn is a sacred flower," Genevieve explained as a flower looking just like the one Evalyn held appeared within the particles of the crystal dust, floating in the air and looking very much like a three-dimensional hologram.

"Its rarity and beauty make it highly sought after," Genevieve continued, motioning her hands in a circle as the crystals shifted, rotating the image of the flower. "It is the essence of a dreamer left here to linger in our world."

As she spoke, the crystals moved again, changing into a little boy holding his hand over the top of his heart, pulling something from within himself and planting it into the ground.

"It is these sacred flowers that connect us to the dreamers of other worlds," she said, pointing to the boy, who was clearly an Echo and the flower he had planted, which was now growing in the ground next to him.

"Some believe it to be a symbol of eternal love and devotion, as the andalyn, once picked, reflects the emotions of the giver in much the same way an Echo reflects the dreams of a dreamer."

The crystals danced in the air, revealing a love-struck couple holding hands and growing old together. The flower remained pristine and beautiful for as long as the couple lived and remained true to the love they had for each other. This made both Evalyn and Kendrick smile as they watched the romantic notion of which Genevieve spoke.

"While it is true that the andalyn has the ability to show the pure emotions and feelings of the one who picks it," Genevieve continued, "as proof of their love for another, few within the walls of *this* city are tolerant of such a view. Andalyns are much too sacred to be picked for such frivolous things as love and romance."

The crystals showing the couple collapsed, laying flat across the air as if awaiting Genevieve's next command. Evalyn looked at Kendrick, who was beginning to look distraught over the harshness of Genevieve's words. He had, after all, been the one who picked the flower for Evalyn, not knowing that it was offensive to the Evarance Keepers.

"Some believe that picking an andalyn is the most heinous of crimes, symbolizing the death of both a beautiful dream and part of the dreamer who made it," Genevieve went on.

The crystals swirled again in the air, showing a thief in the act of plucking the flower at night, causing it to wilt before tossing it into a bag. Then they showed the thief exchanging the bag with the flower for money before the image dissolved before them, causing the crystals to again lay flat in the air.

"Because of their rarity and their value, many andalyns are harvested for profit and greed, destroyed by the selfish emotions in the heart of the one who picked it and sold to the highest bidder as a cure for otherwise incurable illnesses. There's no proof the flower has any curative properties, but that doesn't stop people from buying and selling them. Most of the people here in Divarus are superstitious about picking an andalyn, saying it carries with it a curse for both the one who picked it and the one who keeps it."

Evalyn's eyes grew wide as she listened to Genevieve's words, wondering if Kendrick had unknowingly doomed them both by picking and giving her the flower. No wonder the townsfolk seemed upset with her. They must have thought she was bringing a curse upon their city when they saw her wearing it in her hair.

"Does that mean Kendrick and I are cursed?" Evalyn asked, deeply concerned.

"I don't believe so," Genevieve said reassuringly. "I'm not one to put much faith in superstitions, but you would be wise to keep that flower hidden from view. Many will view it as a bad omen. Others may try to take it from you."

Evalyn nodded, and Kendrick, heeding Genevieve's words, took the flower from Evalyn's hands and wrapped a piece of fine leather around it to keep it both safe and concealed.

"I will not judge you for the choice you made,"

Genevieve said, now addressing Kendrick as she watched him finish tying a cord around the leather wrapping to hide the flower. "That flower is still vibrant and beautiful, so I know your intentions are genuine. However, that flower will also forever hold a piece of the girl who made it. It is a part of her soul, left here to beautify our world. It is too late to undo what has been done, but you and Evalyn are both responsible now for keeping it safe and protected."

"We will," Kendrick said, handing the wrapped flower to Evalyn for safekeeping.

"Now then, about your sister." Genevieve closed her eyes, this time drawing with her fingertips blindly into the air, causing the crystal particles to swirl and dance again until a picture of a girl running through a forest wearing a dark gray hoodie formed above the table. The hood she wore covered the top of her head, and strands of strawberry-blonde hair fell out from underneath it, obscuring part of her face as she ran. Beside her ran a small, black and white firefox, and behind both of them, poised to attack, crouched an adult firefox that burned with a blazing blue, orange, and white fiery light.

Chris and Evalyn recognized Rachel at once. She was wearing her favorite hoodie and running next to the little black firefox she had described in her diary. On a nearby cliff in the light of the moon a black shadow wolf with wiry hair howled into the air, calling his pack into action. The crystals turned in the air, revealing more black wolves scattered through the trees, running toward the firefox that had stayed behind with Rachel to protect her.

"Your sister is in great danger," Genevieve said, opening her eyes to look at the images that now showed Rachel and the little black firefox approaching a large cave guarded by two giant stone bears.

"See here," she said, twisting her hand in the air, zooming in on the images to reveal a stone slab set against the rocky mountainside beside the cave. Carved into the slab was writing: *Be warned, oh traveler, when day is spent and the light of the moon shines high, this cave will close and not open again until touched by the beams of sunrise.*

"She is heading toward the Calimin Cave," Genevieve said uneasily, "to seek refuge from the shadow wolves. But I fear she doesn't know what that cave holds. Without you there to aid her she might not make it through the night."

"Is all of this happening right now?" Evalyn asked, worried it was already too late for them to help.

"No," Genevieve said, "what you are seeing has not yet come to pass. But it will."

She closed her eyes a long moment again as if she had caught a glimpse of something more, then opened them.

"There is something called the iridium sphere in that cave. It is the most precious and rare of all the metals found in this world."

Rucknar perked up at the sound of this, coming out completely from behind the couch, flicking his tail back and forth in excitement. Any metals, especially precious ones, were never far from a dragon's mind.

"You need the sphere," Genevieve said simply. It was just one of the many impressions she felt as she delved deeper into the mystery of the Rachel's whereabouts. Then as the vision faded she ended with one more thought. "Follow the sphere. Its path will bring her home."

The crystals collapsed, falling from the air and scattering over everything beneath them. The visions were over and so was the dream as Chris and Evalyn felt the pull of their bodies on earth bringing them back home.

CHAPTER 18. RESOLUTION

In the light of the afternoon sky Rachel rode on Caligo's back. The mysticorn stallion's white mane and tail moved gracefully in the air as cool droplets of mist flew off his body, gliding behind him in a foggy trail. Next to him and Rachel, Ember walked, and in front of them all, Lux soared through the air, leading the way through the woods with his shimmering light. Though the misty air pouring off Caligo felt both damp and a little cold when brushing past Rachel's face, it had no effect on the warm, wet fluid dripping down her cheeks.

Her face was moist with newly formed tears at the memory of seeing Torrens lying by the river. When she left him he was injured and weak, struggling for breath and shivering with cold. Incindia lay by his side, using her fire to keep his alive, though his flames were sparse and barely visible. Rachel had wanted to help him, but there was little she could do. As word traveled throughout the forest, firefoxes gathered en masse, creating heat much too intense for her delicate human body to endure, forcing her to reluctantly leave his side.

He said he had failed her, but in her mind the opposite was true. She was the one who had put him in danger. Not only because of the shadow wolves who hunted her, but also because of the darkness she brought with her by virtue of her very existence.

Torrens had been there for her from the beginning. He was there when she was still new to this world, teaching her about the darkness that threatened it. He had helped her to safely escape from the shadow wolf den and nearly lost his life trying to protect her from the same shadow wolves that had imprisoned her. He was more than just a firefox, he was like a big brother to Rachel, keeping watch over her in the darkness of night, the unsung hero who had so selflessly fought for her with everything he had.

Too many lives would be endangered if she didn't find a way to return home. It was this knowledge that drove her to continue on even when she desperately wanted to give up. It was the reason she left Torrens behind to rest and heal in Incindia's care despite her own selfish desire to stay by his side. He wanted her to go on, to find a way home, not just to stop the darkness from destroying this world but also and more importantly to keep Rachel safe from the will of the council that threatened her life.

Days had passed since Trebax's attack, but the pain and guilt Rachel carried as a result of that attack caused her to spontaneously burst into tears. It was within one of these moments that she now found herself as she focused her eyes on Lux's shining light, trying to block unhappy thoughts from her mind as she used the sleeve of her hoodie to dry her face. She was on her way to the city of Divarus to seek council from the Evarance Keepers that lived there and find her brother and sister.

Ember was right, it didn't take much to persuade Elder Oakin to allow them to journey there. He wanted them to find answers to the mystery of the darkness and the cause of Rachel's entrapment. So it was with his blessing they left on their journey to seek the Evarance Keepers' guidance. In light of what happened to Torrens and at Rachel's request her traveling companions were limited to Caligo, Ember, and Lux. She needed Caligo to help her travel with haste and Elder Oakin insisted Lux be their guide. He was a migratory hawk, traveling far and wide, and knew how to lead them along safe paths to places where Rachel could wait out the dark nights. Lux would also act as a beacon in times of need as he had when Trebax snatched Rachel from Ember's den. His light would call the aid of nearby elementals who had been directed by the council to help.

Rachel didn't want Ember to join her. She was too afraid that what had happened to Torrens would happen to him, too, but he refused to leave her side, so she reluctantly gave in. Truthfully, she was grateful to have him around. He brought her comfort and hope. He lifted her spirits and was the only one who knew about Chris and Evalyn. She needed him to help her find them.

The past few evenings were spent hiding in elemental homes, staying with them during the darkest hours of night, hours in which the shadow wolves would no longer be shadows. Each night Ember would lay next to Rachel as she slept, keeping her warm with the heat of his body. Lux would shine his light brightly through the night, keeping it much too bright for any Shadai to endure. His light was a protection for her and another reason that Elder Oakin had asked that he join Rachel in her travels. Caligo didn't care for confined spaces, so during the nights he stayed outside, dissolving into a low-hanging mist as the cover of darkness fell over the land.

Ember looked up at Rachel as he walked beside her and Caligo, watching her use her sleeves to dry her tears. He knew she was thinking about Torrens again.

"It was a close call," Ember said as he walked, breaking Rachel free from her thoughts. "You know, if the fire burning within Torrens had been snuffed out completely he wouldn't have survived. But his flames were still burning when we left him, so I think he'll be alright."

Rachel appreciated that Ember was trying to cheer her up, but it was hard to let go of the worry she carried. She just couldn't think about anything else.

"I know something you don't know," Ember said with a grin, hopping around to the front of Caligo, then walking backward so he could still see her.

"You do, huh?" Rachel asked with a smile, wiping the last tear from her eyes and deciding to play along.

"Yep," Ember said, hopping around again to Caligo's other side, turning his body once more to face forward while looking up at Rachel. "I've been to your world."

"You have? But when?" Rachel asked surprised. How was that even possible? There were no Echoes back home — at least none that she knew of.

"Do you remember your last day on Earth?" Ember inquired, a mischievous look in his eyes.

"Well, sure," Rachel said, recalling the campout and how exhausted she had been. She had struggled to stay awake all night in her tent for fear of falling asleep again. "I'd never been so tired in my whole life!"

"Do you remember the fox kit outside your tent?" he asked, grinning as he watched Rachel's expression changed from surprise to confusion.

"Wait, that was you?" she exclaimed.

"The one and only," Ember said with a wink and a chuckle.

"But how?" Rachel asked.

"I don't know," Ember replied. "Incindia told me to watch over you, because you always seemed to show up wherever I was. Like when you first came to the autumn woods standing on the burned leaves."

"But how did you know about that?" Rachel said, not remembering anything or anyone being there with her except for the dying trees and the ashen trail.

"I was watching you," Ember replied, "trying to figure out if you were friendly or not."

"And when I met Incindia and Torrens?" Rachel went on.

"I was there, too," Ember said. "You even followed me to the beach. It was weird."

Rachel thought back on her dreams but had difficulty believing Ember had been there for each and every one of them.

"Why didn't you ever introduce yourself or let me know you were there?" Rachel asked, surprised Ember had been keeping something so big from her for so long.

"Well," Ember said thoughtfully, "at first Incindia asked that I just watch you. She wanted to know how often you showed up and what you were doing here. But even if she hadn't told me to keep my distance I didn't really know what to say. I'd never seen a girl like you before. But when I saw you run into the vines to hide from the shadow wolves chasing you I just had to help!"

Now *that* Rachel did remember. It was the first time she'd ever seen Ember, nearly mistaking him for a shadow wolf because of his black fur.

"And the message written in the mud?" she asked, recalling her last moments on Earth before becoming trapped in this world.

"I wanted to warn you," Ember explained. "More than anything I wanted to warn you about how close the shadow wolves were so you'd know if you came back to run away the moment you got here. I fell asleep with a burning desire in my heart to tell you to stay home, and when I woke up I was there in your woods looking right at you through the window of your tent."

"But if I was following *you* every time I dreamed then why did I start waking up in the darkness? I mean, what were you doing there?" Rachel asked.

"Oh, that," Ember said, blushing a light orange. He hadn't intended on taking this conversations so far that Rachel would find out that her early encounters with the shadow wolves were partly his fault.

"I was spying on the shadow wolves for Incindia. The darkness was starting to grow over the land, and she asked me to see if the shadow wolves had anything to do with it. Because I'm small and black and don't have a big flame, I can camouflage myself in the darkness much easier than the other firefoxes. Once I was there it was really hard to leave because you had returned, and the shadow wolves caught wind of you. And then they caught wind of me."

The pieces were falling into place in Rachel's mind. The whole time she had thought her dreams were random and not entirely connected, but now she understood that they had always been connected. She had always been connected to this little firefox. But why?

Lux's light flashed brightly in the air, catching Rachel's eye as he took a sharp turn through the trees, picking up speed.

"Hang on tight," Caligo directed as he ran through the

forest, following the Lux's light into a large, grassy plain.

Rachel held fast to his white flowing mane, and Ember ran at full speed by their side, igniting the flames on his back to a low orange crackle, preparing for whatever might come.

"What is it?" Rachel asked, looking around but not seeing anything that would warrant the abrupt change of pace.

"It's a shadow wolf," Caligo neighed, increasing his speed to keep up with Lux, who was flying feverishly through the air.

"But it's still daylight!" Rachel protested, looking back across the grassy field, her hair blowing across her face as she spied a wolf-shaped shadow emerging from the woods.

"It's following us," Ember said, struggling to keep pace with Caligo. "A shadow wolf's sense of smell is dulled in its shadow form making it difficult for them to track their prey. This shadow wolf must have been following us since this morning, probably to find out where we're sleeping tonight."

"Do you think there'll be another attack?" Rachel asked.

"I wouldn't put it past them," Ember replied, his breath growing heavy as he ran. "But if we can lose it in the woods up ahead it might have difficulty picking up our trail again until after nightfall."

They cleared the grassy field, entering more woods as Lux zigzagged through the trees, making several more sharp turns, putting a good distance between the shadow wolf and them. Ember began to slow, tuckered out by the long sprint. His flames died down, too, leaving his body warm but harmless to touch. Caligo slowed down beside him, letting Lux fly off into the trees out of sight.

"Do you think we lost it?" Rachel asked Caligo, reaching

down from Caligo's back to pull Ember up with her.

"I'm not sure," Caligo replied, walking once more in the direction Lux's light had last been seen.

Rachel looked around, but the shadowy wolf was nowhere to be seen. A shadow wolf so close to them was concerning, especially since the sky was beginning to change. The light of afternoon was fading to evening with shelter still nowhere to be seen. Lux hadn't returned, either, which made Rachel that much more nervous. Perhaps he was scouting ahead for shelter, or maybe he had circled back to make sure they had lost the shadow wolf.

"Do you know where we're staying tonight?" Rachel asked Caligo.

"The Calimin will be our hosts tonight," he replied, clearly having spoken with Lux. "They have a cave in the mountain. But we must get there before it shuts."

"What do you mean before it shuts?" Rachel asked as Ember perked up his ears while sitting in her lap, having rested enough to get a second wind.

"I've heard of that cave," Ember broke in. "The Calimin Cave closes sometime in the early hours of night and doesn't open again until morning."

"Well, that's fine by me so long as it keeps the shadow wolves out!" Rachel said, pulling her dark-gray hood over her hair to keep the chill out as a cold wind began to blow, adding to the already cool mist streaming off Caligo's body.

"Look, it's Lux!" Ember shouted, seeing the golden light of Lux's feathers shining ahead.

Caligo began to gallop again through the forest, following the golden light of the Luminary. Darkness was falling fast over the land now, and it wouldn't be long before the Shadai were no longer shadows. After riding some distance they were approaching another clearing, this one leading to the Calimin Cave that had become faintly visible in the distance.

As the light of the sun disappeared from the sky, howls filled the air to welcome the moonlight that shone over the trees. The shadow wolves were coming. By the sounds of them there were many running through the dark forest, having clearly picked up Rachel's scent. Rachel looked back to see how close they were, but only one was in view, trailing behind and moving fast. It was Trebax. He must have been the one that followed them during the day, still determined to get Rachel back.

At the edge of the forest where the clearing began, free of the trees that slowed his progress, Caligo ran with all the speed that he had. He was growing fatigued by the long day's journey, and Trebax was closing in fast. A few more strides, and Trebax was in range. He lunged into the air and bit down hard onto Caligo's hind leg, forcing the mysticorn stallion to cry out in pain and vanish into a puff of mist, dropping Ember and Rachel to ground. They tumbled to a stop and scrambled to their feet as Trebax growled vehemently, aiming for them next. Suddenly out of the forest came not another shadow wolf but a fiery mass that Rachel recognized at once to be Torrens.

"*Run!*" Torrens barked at Rachel and Ember, facing Trebax with a growl, his fire blazing stronger and more brilliantly than Rachel had ever seen it burn before.

She ran as Torrens instructed, with Ember by her side as Trebax's loud angry howl echoed through the air behind them. She didn't understand how Torrens was there, but she dared not look back for fear of slowing her pace. She ran with all her strength toward the rocky, tree-scattered mountainside that held a cave opening guarded by two gigantic calimin bears. Lux had already flown inside, his light shining out to Rachel, beckoning her to follow.

A chorus of howls broke out into the air behind her as the shadow wolves broke free of the tree line, flooding the grassy plain like a dam of water bursting open. The rocky bears before her creaked and cracked, moving to face each other. Their bodies began molding together, creating the beginnings of a stone seal over the cave entrance. The cave was closing!

"Ember!" Rachel yelled, pointing to the shrinking opening between the two bears, her heart beating hard as she ran with all her might toward the gap that remained. She reached their rocky hides and slid her body sideways through the narrowing space. Ember slipped in behind her as the bodies of the bears crushed together, completing the seal over the cave entrance.

It was dark inside the cave, even with Lux's light dancing over the rocky surfaces. The stalactite covered ceiling was unnervingly high, and the walls were so widespread it made Rachel feel very small. In the distance she could barely make out what looked like several paths branching out deeper into the mountain. Her eyes had not yet adjusted to the darkness.

Her breathing slowed, but her heart still beat fast as anger at Trebax built up in her chest. She was mad at what he had done to Caligo and mad at what he was probably now doing to Torrens. She pounded her fists hard against the rock walls in frustration and anguish.

"Torrens!" she screamed, her voice echoing through the caverns as she lifted her face, causing the hood over her head to slide off, tears welling up in her eyes. "You aren't supposed to be here!"

She fell to the floor and burst into tears, covering her face with her hands at the thought of what might be happening to him. Seeing Torrens had been bittersweet. On the one hand, she was relieved he was still alive and surprised his flames were burning so strong and bright, but on the other, he had put himself in harm's way again, and it was all because of her. He was supposed to be back at the firefox dens, resting and healing from his wounds, but instead he was now trapped outside with an enormous pack of shadow wolves surrounding him.

"It'll be alright," Ember said, putting a paw on Rachel's shoulder. "Torrens looked great, and with a fire that strong, the shadow wolves won't be able to touch him."

Rachel wanted Ember to be right, and more than anything she wanted Torrens to be safe. She couldn't bear carrying the weight of responsibility for him anymore. She was overcome by fear that he might be injured again or killed, and it was more than she could handle.

"But why?" Rachel asked, her lips quivering as a flood of emotions came over her. "Why would he come back after all that I put him through?"

"*You* didn't put him through anything, Rachel," Ember said reassuringly but firmly. "Torrens made his own decision to help you. Just like Caligo and I. No one forced us, you know."

The more Rachel thought about what Ember said the more she understood. Torrens had *chosen* to help her again. It was *his* choice, and he knew the risks. Instead of wallowing in self-pity and remorse, what she really needed to do was be thankful he was there. Without him she and Ember would have never made it to the cave in time, and

Trebax would have certainly captured her and killed Ember. He had made all the difference.

"How do you think he healed so quickly?" Rachel asked, wiping the tears from her eyes.

"I bet it was because of the other firefoxes," Ember said. "They must have used their heat to dry off his fur and their flames to seal up his wounds. Being surrounded by such an intense blaze of fire must have rejuvenated him and his flames. Firefoxes are pretty tough."

"I guess they are," Rachel agreed, placing her hand on the back of Ember's neck and giving it a good long rub. "Thank you for putting up with me. I know it can't be easy."

"No worries," Ember said with a smile, "you keep my life interesting. I wouldn't want it any other way."

Rachel understood the lesson Ember was trying to teach her. She couldn't keep blaming herself for things beyond her control. Torrens, Ember, and Caligo had all known what they were doing when they volunteered to help her. And in the end it was their choice to make. The best way to honor their kindness and efforts was to be grateful for them and show it. Rachel didn't know if she'd see Torrens again, but if she did she was resolved to let him know how much he meant to her and how much she appreciated him for everything he'd done. In the meantime she'd have to start where she was, in a dark cave with a little firefox and a luminary hawk to be her guides.

Standing up, she looked around the cave using Lux's light to better decipher her surroundings. Then she heard it: a low rumble and a scraping sound followed by a thud. The sounds were faint at first, repeating again and again, but with each iteration they grew louder and more intense, like nails dragging down a chalkboard and the sound of a drum letting out a slow steady beat.

Ember's demeanor instantly changed, his coat bursting into a crackly, coal-like glow with orange flames spurting out from his black ashen fur. The hairs on his back stuck up as he moved, his body poised to attack as he growled with his teeth bared. Rachel's heart beat hard in her chest, thumping in unison with the hideous noise. A raspy groan echoed through the air, making it clear they were not alone.

CHAPTER 19. CALIMIN CAVE

It was morning again, and Chris had already made his way down to the kitchen to warm up some breakfast. He sat at the table drizzling syrup all over a mound of freshly heated freezer waffles and microwave sausages, taking extra care to fill each crispy waffle indent to the brim with the sticky, sweet brown liquid. He had just cut and stabbed a huge chunk of waffles with his fork, lifting them to his mouth, when Evalyn walked in looking very worried.

"What is it, Eva?" Chris asked before shoving the fork full of waffles into his mouth.

"It's Rachel, of course," Evalyn replied, watching Chris chow down the oversized bite. "Seriously, Chris, how can you eat like that right now?"

"Well, *it is* breakfast time, you know," he answered nonchalantly after finishing his mouthful, taking another big bite, this one including sausage.

"But Rachel's in danger. We have to do something!" Evalyn said, becoming more annoyed at Chris with each passing moment.

"I think Rachel will be okay —" Chris began.

Evalyn cut him off. "You don't know that! What if by the time we go back to Calim it's too late?" she snapped.

"I don't think it works that way, Eva," Chris responded before washing down the remnants of waffle with a large glass of milk.

"But what if it does?" Evalyn continued, clearly worried something bad might be happening to Rachel at that very moment. "That woman, the Evarance Oracle, she told us Rachel wouldn't make it through the night in the cave without us."

"True, but she also said Rachel wasn't at the cave yet. She was showin' us the future," Chris said, trying to reason with Evalyn. "Look, Eva, I want to help Rachel just as much as you do, but the dream ended when it did and where it did for a reason. What are we supposed to do? Just go back to sleep?"

"Yes!" Evalyn replied, exasperated. "That's exactly what we need to do!"

Chris thought a moment. He wasn't even a little tired, but what if Evalyn was right? What if by the time night rolled around and he and Evalyn went to bed it was too late to help Rachel?

"Alright," Chris agreed skeptically, eating the last of the food off before putting his dishes into the sink. "I'll give it a try if you will."

Thankfully it wasn't a school day, and their parents had already left to visit Rachel at the hospital again so they wouldn't be at all suspicious about Chris and Evalyn going back to bed so soon after waking up. Chris felt silly climbing back into bed, when his room was so brightly lit with sunlight. But, staying true to his word he closed his eyes, pocketing the smoky-brown diamond scale as he attempted to fall asleep again.

He tossed and turned for quite some time, but his body refused to cooperate. After about an hour of struggling he did manage to doze off for a short time, mostly out of sheer boredom, but the nap was short and didn't produce any dreams. All it did was make him feel groggy and grumpy when he awoke. So he gave up trying and went to Evalyn's room to check on her.

He cracked her door open slowly and quietly to be sure he didn't wake her if she had managed to get back to Calim, but she wasn't asleep. She was wide awake, too, sitting on her bed looking down at the andalyn as she twirled it between her fingers.

"No luck, huh?" Chris asked as he walk into her room and sat on her bed next to her.

"I just don't understand," Evalyn said, her voice and eyes still directed at the flower, but her words clearly meant for Chris. "I fell back asleep, holding the flower in my hand just like before, but there were no dreams. None."

"Then we wait," Chris said. "Did you see how excited Ruck got when he heard about the iridium sphere? I'll bet he's on his way to the cave right now, which means tonight I'll be there, too."

"But what about me?" Evalyn asked.

"Ken will get you there, won't he?" Chris replied. There were still many things that neither he nor Evalyn fully understood about their dreams, but there was one thing that had become clear. When Chris woke up in Calim he was always with Rucknar, and when Evalyn did she was always with Kendrick. Neither of them knew for certain what would happen if their companions chose to follow a path that led away from where they wanted to go.

"What if Kendrick's gone home back to Teran?" Evalyn fretted, stopping her fingers from twirling the flower to refocus her attention on Chris.

"Did he tell you he'd help find Rachel?" Chris asked.

"I guess . . ." Evalyn said.

"Then you've got nothing to worry about, Eva," he reassured her. "I saw how that guy was looking at you, and there's no way he'd bail on you. I mean look at the flower he gave you, it's still, uh, pretty and all, so it means he still likes you, right?"

That made Evalyn smile. It was sweet Chris was trying to cheer her up, especially when she could tell he didn't like Kendrick very much.

For Evalyn the day dragged on and on, and even though Chris had told her not to think about Rachel too much, it was all her mind could focus on. If she was too late, if she didn't get to Rachel in time, how would she ever be able to forgive herself?

Despite the underlying fears that nagged at her, she managed to make it through the day and into the night, relieved when her head finally hit the pillow. Hopefully this time she would return to Calim. As soon as she closed her eyes she opened them again, but when she did nothing looked familiar in any way. Thick, green forest surrounded her, with light shining down at her through the canopy above, dancing all around her in leafy patterns across the trees and ground. Her senses felt heightened as she listened to the subtle sounds of the woods, jumping each time she thought she heard a noise.

This forest felt wild and intimidating, and to make matters worse she felt lost and alone, not knowing which way she should go. *Did Rachel feel this way when her dreams carried her to strange woods all alone?* Evalyn wondered, revisiting Rachel's diary in her mind.

This wasn't like the town of Teran or city of Divarus, the sort of places Evalyn had been growing accustomed to waking up in with walls and streets filled with people and Echoes. And it wasn't like the forest her family would camp out in every year. That forest was familiar. The camp ground, fire pit, and trails were all things she'd known ever since she was small. She never felt lost in those woods. Then again she had never strayed too far from camp or her family.

The air smelled clean yet heavy and rich at the same time, filled with the aroma of soil and wood blended with the fragrance of flowering plants. It reminded her of the andalyn, fresh and clean, but not nearly as sweet and intoxicating. Evalyn glanced down at her hand to be sure the flower was with her, which it was, but the brown leather wrapping Kendrick had gently placed around it to keep it concealed was gone. The wrapping never made it back to Earth with her when her last dream ended, only the flower did. Perhaps that was another limitation of this dream world. Nothing given to her except for the flower would stay with her once she awoke. Even her brief time spent with Kendrick was, after all, only temporary.

She heard a sound, a rustling in the distance, but couldn't tell where it was coming from. Then she heard it again, much closer to her than before, but she still didn't see what was making the noise. Her heartbeat accelerated as she surveyed the surrounding forest, trying to pinpoint the sound that was evading her, but it fell quiet, almost as if it were mocking her. She saw nothing but felt that something, or perhaps someone, was watching her.

"Kendrick?" Evalyn whispered nervously, hoping it was nothing more than her paranoia causing her to feel so tense.

"He just left," a nearby voice hissed. Then she saw it: a lizard-like face hidden in the foliage of some nearby plants.

It was Rucknar. Her brother's creepy dragon friend, but

Chris was still nowhere to be seen. The color of her cheeks drained from a fleshy tone to a pale white as she watched Rucknar shimmy out from between the large leaves that had hidden him from her sight. To Evalyn he looked enormous! His smoky-brown, crystalline scales shimmered as bits of sunlight peeked through the leafy canopy overhead, reflecting off them. He glared at her with a suspicious expression, causing a feeling of panic to overcome her.

"N-nice dragon," she said nervously, holding her palms out toward Rucknar while stepping slowly backward to give herself some distance from the humongous reptile.

He watched her, tilting his head slightly to one side, then the other, squinting as he looked over her. Her mannerisms were nothing like Chris's, and the only obvious similarity between the two of them was their dark-brown hair and blue eyes.

"There you are, Ruck!" Chris shouted with a big grin, walking out from behind a tree, diverting Rucknar's attention away from Evalyn. "Oh, hey, Eva," Chris added, finally noticing her, too, as she lowered her arms to her sides and let out a big sigh of relief. "Everything okay? Where's Ken?"

"He's gone," Rucknar butted in before Evalyn had a chance to speak, giving her one last sideways glance of suspicion before ignoring her. "I followed him here to the Calimin Cave. It's just up ahead."

"That's fantastic, Ruck!" Chris exclaimed, anxious to see the cave for himself. "Can you take us there?"

"I suppose," Rucknar huffed, walking between Chris and Evalyn to lead the way and cracking a slight dragonish smile as he saw Evalyn put her hands over her mouth to stifle a fearful squeak. Being praised and being feared were two things dragons rather enjoyed and expressing fear was something Evalyn was quite good at.

Chris followed behind Rucknar with Evalyn following behind him, determined to stay as far away from the oversized lizard as possible. The woods opened up into a large clearing that lead to a rocky mountainside where two gigantic stone bears stood, the same bears Chris and Evalyn saw in Genevieve's vision. One bear stood on each side of a large cave entrance, so perfectly still that neither Chris nor Evalyn recognized them for the living creatures that they were. Tempest was outside the cave, too, laying in the grass to rest. As Rucknar, Chris, and Evalyn approached Tempest lifted her head in acknowledgement right as Kendrick walked outside of the cave to join her. It was so perfectly timed it was almost as if he had been expecting them.

"Kendrick!" Evalyn called excitedly, even happier to see him than she had been to see Chris after finding herself alone with Rucknar.

"You're back!" Kendrick said, walking up to her, smiling warmly as he watched her twist a lock of hair around her finger.

"I am," Evalyn replied, her knees feeling weak as she looked deep into his eyes. The whole world felt better with Kendrick around.

Kendrick caught a glimpse of the andalyn in Evalyn's hand and pulled the leather wrapping from his pocket.

"May I?" he asked, reaching out for the flower.

"Of course!" Evalyn said. "It doesn't seem to stay wrapped when I go back home."

"I noticed," Kendrick said, grinning. "When you left, the piece of leather I wrapped the flower in stayed behind. I've been saving it for the next time we saw each other."

He wrapped up the flower and handed it back to

Evalyn, brushing his hand gently against hers as he did. The touch of his skin made Evalyn's heart flutter.

"Here," Kendrick said as he walked over to Tempest and pulled a small, empty satchel from a sack on her back, handing it to Evalyn. It was very purse-like in appearance. "You can use this to carry it."

Evalyn took the satchel and gently placed the andalyn inside before pulling the strap over her head onto her opposing shoulder to keep it safe and secure. She thanked Kendrick and had almost become lost in those beautiful eyes and smile again when Chris started clearing his throat as loudly as he could, which was his not so subtle way of pulling both her and Kendrick back to reality.

"So," Evalyn said, tucking the lock of hair she had been fiddling with behind her ear. "We're staying in here tonight, right?"

"That's the plan," Kendrick said. "This is where Genevieve said your sister would be."

"And we're not too late?" Evalyn asked, wanting to be sure none of her earlier fears had come true.

"Not at all," Kendrick replied. "After you left I asked Genevieve if she could tell me what day her vision of Rachel took place, and thankfully she knew. Today's the day. Based on what we saw, Rachel should be arriving soon."

The afternoon sun was still high in the sky, but it was descending rapidly, which meant night was not far behind. Evalyn was growing excited at the prospect of seeing her sister again. It had been far too long since they had spoken with each other.

"So," Chris broke in, "are we going into the cave or what?" He could see how restless Rucknar was becoming.

Rucknar was crouched low to the ground, swishing his

tail forcefully across the grass as he moved his neck and head to look deeply into the cave. He glanced up at Chris and then rushed inside before another word was spoken. He didn't want or need a human's permission to enter, and he was anxious to find the iridium sphere. Besides, he liked caves and other deep, dark, damp places.

"Wait!" Kendrick said in warning as Rucknar rushed past the stupid human.

Once inside his eyes quickly adjusted to the darkness where he saw a large cavern with a high ceiling filled with stalactites. At the back of the cavern seven pathways branched into deeper and darker parts of the cave. He chose the far left path as the first place to explore, scurrying deeper into the darkness.

Chris tried to chase after Rucknar, watching him vanish into the dark, but Kendrick caught Chris, holding him back.

"What's the big deal?" Chris snapped angrily, shoving Kendrick's arm away. He wanted to stay with Rucknar and wasn't about to let his sister's pseudo-boyfriend stop him.

"There's something I haven't told you yet. Something you need to know before entering the cave," Kendrick said. This just made Chris more agitated as he could feel the distance between him and Rucknar grow with each passing moment. He preferred the company of Rucknar to Kendrick any day and wondered what Kendrick could possibly have to say to him that was more important.

"There was something else Genevieve told me after you and Evalyn left," Kendrick continued, ignoring the angry look Chris was giving him. "The iridium sphere is guarded by something large and very dangerous. If any of us, Rucknar included, stumble upon the creature and disturb it it could mean the end of all of us."

Knowing something dangerous was in the cave gave Chris all the more reason to find Rucknar right away, before anything bad happened to him. He ran into the cave, leaving Kendrick and Evalyn behind, heading into the left-most pathway, which was the last place he had seen Rucknar go. As he went the cave became dark. So dark he could scarcely see which way he was headed and stumbled over some rocky growths on the ground.

The air became more moist the farther in he walked and with the last adjustment of his eyes, he could make out shallow pools of water to his left and his right, pools that glowed with the pale light of tiny fish swimming inside them. He heard a swish followed by a cracking sound against one of the rocky walls, and he knew without a shadow of a doubt it was Rucknar's tail.

"Ruck," Chris called out softly into the still, dark air. "Where are you?"

He heard a scurrying sound, and a moment later Rucknar's face distinguished itself from the darkness in the light of the glowing pools.

"Let's go," Rucknar instructed begrudgingly, deciding it was less work to drag Chris along with him than to try and leave him behind again. Rucknar had never met anyone more determined and stubborn than Chris, but, Chris did make for some interesting company. He turned to hurry away again, Chris following behind without a moment's hesitation, making sure to stay as close to Rucknar as he could so he wouldn't lose sight of him in the darkness. As they walked the walls began to glow, dotted with the white light of luminary moths just like the moths found in the kobold mines.

"Interesting," Rucknar hissed to himself out loud, so

Chris could hear him, too.

"What?" Chris asked, noticing that the cave was growing lighter and lighter the farther they went.

Rucknar didn't answer Chris. He was too deep in thought to waste his time answering silly questions. He knew that where there were luminary moths there was fresh air. They weren't the type of species to dwell in the deepest and darkest parts of a cave. These moths were attracted to the underground pools' moisture. They were also attracted to cave entrances and exits where the air was fresher and flowed more freely. Rucknar knew these moths could not have come from the main cave entrance because he and Chris had explored much too deep into the cave without having seen any of them until then. And that could only mean one thing.

He moved forward swiftly as Chris struggled to keep up. Then he stopped suddenly to look at something on the wall. Chris looked, too. There was a tunnel-like opening, not terribly large but not all that small, either, where rocks had eroded away allowing sunlight to shine through. It was just large enough that Chris imagined he might possibly wriggle his way through if he really tried, but for fear of getting stuck he had no intention of trying.

"Guess this cave's not as secure as the sign made it seem," Chris laughed, trying to lighten Rucknar's all too serious mood, but Rucknar ignored him, clearly focused on something else.

The youngling sniffed the air and rushed down a dark pathway that had no watery pools or Luminary lighting the way. His breathing changed to a more rhythmic rumble as he scurried along, excitement building up in his body, which began to radiate a yellow and orange light shining dimly through his diamond scales. The light came from a fire that was churning inside him, building in both brightness and intensity.

"Ruck," Chris said, never having seen Rucknar do anything like this before, "you're glowing!"

"Shh…" Rucknar hissed in an attempt to hush Chris up. "It's just up ahead. Be quiet."

"What's up ahead?" Chris whispered back. But then he saw it.

They had entered another large chamber, this one illuminated by sizable clusters of crystals that gave off a radiant and colorful light scattered throughout. There were six pathways leading out of the chamber, seven including the pathway Chris and Rucknar had just come from. Chris wondered if all of the paths eventually led back to the cave entrance from where they had come.

At the back of the room there was a huge white rock column complemented by curtain-like mineral deposits that hung down from the ceiling behind it. In front of the column a stalagmite grew out several feet from the ground, with the top sliced off to make a flat, table-like surface on which an iridescent metal sphere, no bigger than a tennis ball, lay. To Rucknar's eyes it looked just like the offering table back home, the metal ripe and ready for the taking.

The fire in his chest grew stronger, his desire to keep the metal for himself swelling within him. The metal called out to him, enticing him to take and to hoard it. It was the greatest temptation he had ever felt. For a dragon there was no more precious metal to obtain, and for an Allorum, no greater offering. But he couldn't have it for his own, as much as his body ached to assimilate with it. He needed the metal for another reason, a reason only he knew anything about.

In his clan, assimilating with a metal, becoming completely saturated in it both inside and out, was the most perfect way to hoard the metal so no one else could have claim over it. It was a hoard that became part of you and went with you everywhere you went. As younglings in the clan came of age, they would be gifted with their own precious metal in a sacred ceremony and rite of passage that moved them into adulthood and full clan membership. The metal offering was something to be earned, not taken. And assimilating with a metal prematurely or taking an offering meant for another were the most heinous of crimes. Crimes that brought with them punishment, exile, and sometimes even death.

Rucknar tried to clear his mind, pushing away the greedy thoughts. He needed the sphere, but he had to be very careful not to succumb to its temptation. He slowed his breathing, cooling the fire inside him until the glow of it had completely left his body. He was in control again, not the metal, and he was ready to make his move.

"Stop!" Kendrick said quietly but forcefully as he and Evalyn walked out of the shadows from behind Chris and Rucknar, having come after them when they had carelessly rushed into the cave.

"Stupid human," Rucknar grumbled defiantly, darting into the large chamber and heading straight for the iridium sphere.

"Wait, Ruck! Stop!" Chris shouted, realizing he had never told Rucknar about Kendrick's warning. But Rucknar didn't hesitate. No human was going to keep him from this metal, not even Chris.

The ground began rumbling, and Rucknar had only made it about half way across the chamber when giant chunks of rock broke free from the walls in sections, crashing down all around to reveal what had been a perfectly camouflaged calimin dragon nearly five times Rucknar's height. It finished pulling its body free from the wall, taking some of the illuminated crystal clusters with it, which still clung to its rocky hide and feet.

"Who has awakened me?" the dragon groaned in a raspy voice almost as if it were in pain, moving its body in front of the iridium sphere and completely blocking it from Rucknar's view.

The dragon looked old, its eyes clouded with milky-white mineral deposits that obscured its vision. As it strained to see who was there it spied Rucknar standing in the middle of the chamber.

"A dragon?" its voice said gruffly in surprise, as if seeing another dragon was something completely unheard of. "What clan are you from?"

Rucknar hesitated to answer, still soaking in all the details of the rock-like dragon before him. He had never seen any other dragons outside of his clan before and was fascinated.

"The Allorum clan," he finally replied, watching the massive dragon start heavily sniffing the air.

"And what is a dragon from the Allorum clan doing with filthy humans?" the dragon asked in a raspy voice, still unable to see Chris, Evalyn, and Kendrick but recognizing their unmistakable stench. "I may not be able to see your friends, but I know they are there."

"The humans are *not* my friends," Rucknar said defensively, squinting. "They're a curiosity to me. Nothing more."

"A curiosity?" the great dragon wheezed with a laugh.

"Well, if they mean nothing to you, surely you won't mind if I go and crush them."

Rucknar didn't care much for Kendrick or Evalyn and wasn't overly concerned about their safety or wellbeing. Chris, however, was a different story. Chris had managed to wiggle his way into a small piece of Rucknar's heart, and Rucknar didn't like the idea of watching Chris die.

"The humans are after something," Rucknar said, trying to distract the large dragon from pinpointing Chris, Evalyn, and Kendrick's whereabouts as they quietly and slowly stepped back into the shadows of the dark pathway from which they had come.

"After something?" the large dragon said, coughing out some rocks onto the ground. "Let me guess. They want the sphere."

"Yes," Rucknar hissed, trying to win this dragon's trust and buy Chris a little more time, "which is why I came to warn you."

The calimin dragon looked at Rucknar suspiciously, lowering its head to Rucknar's level and looking at him face to face.

"So those humans are *not* your friends?" the rocky dragon asked one more time to be sure of where Rucknar's allegiance lay.

"Of course not," Rucknar said, which was partially true since Chris was the only one he would consider remotely close to a friend. "What dragon would want a human for a friend?"

The calimin dragon read Rucknar's face then moved his head back up.

"You're a poor liar," it said, unconvinced, "but if what you say is true why not help me dispose of those filthy humans? Then after they are gone we can discuss the *real* reason you are here."

Rucknar looked back at the tunnel but saw no sign of Chris, Evalyn, or Kendrick. Surely they were on their way back to the cave entrance.

The calimin dragon sniffed the air once more, noticing the human smell was fading. "I'm going after those little non-friends of yours," he said, watching Rucknar become flustered.

"Don't!" Rucknar hissed, the desperation in his voice revealing with certainty that he had feelings for the humans. "I need them—"

The large dragon laughed. "Funny thing is, I need them too. Only dead. No one tries to steal from me and lives to tell the tale."

Rucknar watched as the calimin dragon focused in on the pathway that led to Chris, Evalyn, and Kendrick, having determined where the strongest traces of human scent still lingered. He looked as though he were ready to move and go after Rucknar's human companions when he paused and stopped to listen to something. Rucknar listened, too. There was a faint sound echoing through the cave like large boulders being pushed across the ground.

"It's closing," the large rock dragon said softy, keeping keenly tuned in to the noise. He wanted to go after the humans, but he knew now they had nowhere to go. It was only a matter of time before they were his. The calimin bears who guarded the cave entrance had begun their nightly ritual of sealing the cave opening. Once completed, the humans would be trapped inside.

"Your friends cannot leave now," he said, tilting his head to listen to something else that piqued his interest.

Rucknar heard it, too. It was the distant howls of shadow wolves followed by the crushing sound of the calimin bears as they finished the seal over the cave entrance, silencing the sounds that came from outside. Then a girl's scream echoed through the air in the cave, calling out a name Rucknar didn't know. It didn't sound like Chris's sister Evalyn, which led Rucknar to one conclusion. Rachel had arrived.

The calimin dragon turned to Rucknar, giving him a mischievous smile. "I'm going to teach you a lesson, youngling," he mused in a soft, raspy voice. "Dragons and humans are not meant to be friends. I will show you what happens to a human that crosses a dragon's path. Your lesson will begin with that girl and end when every human in this cave is dead."

He dragged his heavy rock tail across the cave floor, creating a rumbling sound that echoed through the cave. His feet crunched in a slow but steady rhythm, one after the other, as he dragged a crystal cluster across it with each step, making a screeching noise. He grunted and moaned, letting out a raspy groan as he moved the weight of his rocky body across the floor, determined to get the girl.

CHAPTER 20. THE GIFT

The Calimin Cave had completely sealed, leaving Rachel, Ember, and the luminary hawk Lux trapped inside, as a raspy groan echoed through the air, drawing nearer to them with each shrill scrape and resounding thud. The ground rumbled, causing tiny fluctuating vibrations and making Rachel feel unsteady on her feet. Ember stood by her, his coat crackling like hot, fiery orange coals rising out over his fur. The hairs on his neck and back stood as he postured his body defensively, baring his teeth with a growl.

"What is that?" Rachel whispered, her heart beating in sync with the hideous noises, though she doubted that Ember knew.

Ember stopped growling and watched Lux as he flew anxiously across the cavern, dipping in and out of the tunnel-like paths to see which one the sounds were coming from. He settled in front of the rightmost passage, flickering his light to signal Ember and Rachel to follow.

"Whatever it is," Ember said in a hushed voice, dousing his flames to hide the light and minimize the fiery smell, "it doesn't sound friendly. I think we should follow Lux."

Rachel didn't hesitate. She ran to the far right pathway, following the light of the luminary hawk as Ember sprinted by her side. The deeper into the cave they went, following a naturally carved path into the mountain, the quieter the sounds became. As they traveled Rachel caught glimpses of incredible rock formations revealed by Lux's passing light. The path twisted and turned many times and then opened into a large chamber with crystal clusters radiating colorful light.

The ground of the chamber was littered with piles of rocks, and parts of the wall looked as though they'd been torn to pieces. At the back of the chamber there was a white column with curtainlike mineral deposits draped behind it. In front of the column, a broken stalagmite presented a strangely iridescent metal ball.

A whipping sound followed by a rock-shattering crack reverberated through the chamber, causing both Ember and Rachel to jump. Ember's fur burst once again into crackling, coal-like flames as something, hidden from their view, moved in the shadows. Rachel's heart beat hard in her chest as Lux darted across the room to shine light into the darkness on whatever was lurking beneath the shadows. His light hit its target as a dragon the size of a large dog, only longer, with smoky-brown crystalline scales and wings folded tightly against its back, scurried into the chamber, avoiding the blinding light.

Ember maneuvered his body in front of Rachel, determined to protect her from the dragon, even if it meant his life.

"Rachel?" the dragon asked suspiciously, squinting to look over the girl who, to his surprise, looked nothing like Chris or Evalyn.

"You know my name?" Rachel replied timidly.

"Chris told me," the dragon hissed, not wasting any time. "He's here in this cave looking for you."

Rachel couldn't say another syllable, though she tried. She was so full of emotion the words caught in her throat. Her heart still beat hard but now with shock not fear. She didn't think she'd see Chris until she made it to Divarus, and even then the chances were slim. Was it really possible? How did he get here?

"We don't have time for this," Rucknar snapped, not willing to wait for Rachel to come out of her self-induced trance. "Your brother and sister are looking for you. They went to the entrance to find you, and the dragon that's headed there won't show them any mercy if it finds them."

Coming back to her senses Rachel asked, "There's another dragon? Wait, Evalyn's here, too?"

"She won't be for long," Rucknar snorted in frustration, "and neither will Chris if you don't get to them fast!"

Rachel wondered if the groaning, screeching, pounding noises that were headed for the sealed cave entrance were coming from the other dragon. Surely it had made its way to there by now. Was it too late for her brother and sister?

"What do we do?" Rachel asked, feeling a panic overcome her for fear of what might happen to them. She'd never seen a dragon in this world before this one, and couldn't figure out what it had to do with Chris or Evalyn, but it knew their names and hers, so she felt as though she could trust it.

"Take the path behind me," Rucknar directed, motioning his head to the same route that had brought him and Chris to this chamber the first time. As he did a raspy roar echoed through the air. This time Rachel had no doubt it was the other dragon reaching its destination.

Rachel looked to Ember, who nodded his head in agreement. They both sprinted for the tunnel, hoping they wouldn't be too late as Lux flew ahead, keenly aware of the danger but anxious to help. He flew much faster than Rachel or Ember could run, making it to the entrance before they did, and it was a good thing! A girl and a boy were trapped by a massive calimin dragon made of rock. Its body, tail, and wings wrapped around them, creating a wall-like structure they couldn't escape.

A man was there, too, young and tall, in a waistcoat. He was holding a sword, swinging it at the dragon's rocky hide, while yelling to distract the monstrous creature, but his efforts had little effect. The dragon remained focused on the girl, eagerly anticipating her demise.

"I'll get to you soon enough, human!" roared the calimin dragon in response to the feeble attempts made by the young man and sounding rather pleased with himself. The girl screamed in terror as the dragon opened its mouth wide, preparing to swallow her whole.

Lux darted toward the dragon's face, pulsing his light directly into its eyes, causing it to wince in pain as it lifted its wing to shelter itself from the blinding light, freeing the girl and boy.

"Evalyn! Chris!" a voice called across the chamber.

Then they saw her. Rachel stood at the edge of the far left path next to a small black and white firefox burning with a fiery light that crackled like embers on dying fire. "Hurry!"

They ran toward her, and had nearly made it when a large cluster of shining crystals hurled from the dragon's rocky tail, shattering against the large stalactites hanging down from the ceiling, breaking them free. The large icicle-shaped rocks, mixed with a shower of broken crystals, fell down, crashing onto the ground between them and Rachel, closing off the pathway with an impenetrable wall of rock.

"Don't worry about us, Rae!" Chris shouted through the rock mound that separated them from her. "We'll find another way!"

The calimin dragon charged at them but once again failed to shield its eyes from Lux as he gave it another blast of light, causing the dragon to stumble as Chris, Evalyn, and Kendrick made it safely onto the next pathway over. This one was much narrower than the previous pathway, making Evalyn feel a little claustrophobic. They ran in single file with Kendrick bringing up the rear, not looking back for fear of slowing down. The crushing sound of rock scraping against rock followed them as the dragon pushed its body through the confined space in hot pursuit.

Following the path they came upon an even tighter section of wall that required extra maneuvering to get through. Evalyn felt the blood drain from her face as the walls of the cave closed in all around her. Evalyn wondered if they were headed toward a dead end and couldn't bear the thought of being trapped in a space like this with her only way out blocked by that hideous lizard.

"Evalyn?" Kendrick said, pushing through the cramped space behind, noticing her start to flounder as if she were about to collapse. "It'll be okay. We're nearly there. Just take a deep breath and keep your eyes on Chris."

The reassurance in Kendrick's voice was the only thing that helped her push thorough until she came out the other side of the narrowing passageway, breathing a big sigh of relief as it opened wide, leading out into the giant chamber that held the iridium sphere.

Except now the iridium sphere was missing.

"Come on!" Chris shouted, running back down the tunnel that lead to Rachel as an anguished roar echoed throughout the cave, the calimin dragon still struggling between the narrowed walls unable to follow. They didn't run far before Rachel and Ember met them, as anxious to make sure they were safe, as they were to find her.

"Chris!" Rachel cried, waisting no time as the crumbling of rock echoed through the air matched by the groans of the still struggling rock dragon. "Your friend Rucknar told me to bring you to him. He thinks there might be a way out."

It wasn't the joyous reunion they had expected. There was no time for catching up or happy tears. That would have to wait for later. At the moment there was only one thing that mattered: staying alive. So on they ran, up the dark path following Rachel and the golden light of Lux. The pathway swerved, moving around pools of water with raised rock edges that housed the luminary fish shining with pale light. Then the air grew thick with white glowing moths fluttering as if in a feverish frenzy. Chris focused his eyes through the white lights of the moths and saw something move in the distance.

"Ruck!" Chris shouted, running ahead of Rachel, pushing his way through the eclipse of moths as everyone else followed. Already the horrible sounds of the calimin dragon echoed through the air, communicating that it had finally broken through the narrow passage.

Rucknar didn't acknowledge Chris. There was no time. Instead he continued to feverishly dig to widen the hole in the wall. It was the same hole that he and Chris had found earlier that gave the luminary moths passage in and out of the cave. His sharp diamond claws broke away the rocks and dirt like a knife cutting through soft butter. Once the hole was sufficiently dug out, he wiggled his way into it, pushing his body through and squeezing it up and out into the night air.

"Let's go!" Chris called out, climbing into the tunnel-like hole to follow.

"But the shadow wolves are out there!" Rachel protested as the ground began to rumble under her feet, the calimin dragon drawing nearer.

"I don't know about you, Rae," Chris shouted back over his shoulder as he continued to climb up through the rocky tunnel, "but I'd rather deal with a couple of dogs over that enormous dragon."

Chris was right. Not about the shadow wolves but about the dragon. This was no time to argue. Rachel climbed in after him, followed by Ember as the the light of the glowing crystals on the dragon's rocky hide came into view. Kendrick raised his sword, pointing it at the dragon as it hobbled toward them, giving Evalyn the chance to climb in next. She took a deep breath climbing into the tunnel, her heart beating hard as she felt the claustrophobic panic come over her again, keeping her eyes on Ember to distract her.

At last she pulled her body out into the cool, dark air as the raspy groans of the dragon and the clash of Kendrick's sword against rock traveled through the tunnel and reverberated in the night sky. She looked back into the hole, but there was no sign of Kendrick, and an anguished roar bellowed from the cave, stopping Evalyn's heart as she feared the worst.

Moments later a light flew out of the tunnel up into the sky, where Lux stretched open his wings and flew across the open air. Evalyn looked again back into the tunnel where the harrowing sounds of the dragon still bellowed. And then as if in a miracle, Kendrick surfaced from the hole in the ground soaked in water and partially caked in mud.

"What happened?" Evalyn asked, filled with relief at the sight of him, as he sat down on the ground, catching his breath.

"I made a bit of a mess down there," Kendrick said with a laugh, pulling his sword out of its sheath to wipe off the dirt.

"A mess how?" Chris broke in. Rachel and Ember gathered around him, too, while Rucknar watched silently.

"Well," Kendrick said, "as the dragon was coming I swung my sword at one of the pools of water, cracking open the thin rock that held it. Water gushed out all over me, knocking me to the ground and spilled out over the floor making it too slippery for the dragon, allowing me to escape."

"Do you think it can still come after us?" Rachel asked, looking down at the hole in the ground and listening to the moaning and scraping below as if it was trying to dig its way out.

"I don't know," Kendrick replied standing up, "but it's probably best if we don't stay here just in case."

He whistled into the air for Tempest, letting her know where they were. She was still outside when the cave entrance closed, but she could handle herself and knew how to avoid danger when needed. They walked down the mountainside too tired to run, looking for anything they could use as shelter for the night. Kendrick continued to whistle on occasion with the hope that Tempest would find them. Rachel looked at everyone as they walked, still soaking it all in. It felt like a dream within a dream, seeing her brother and sister again.

"So," Evalyn said, walking up to Rachel and wrapping one arm over her shoulder, giving it a squeeze. "Haven't seen you in a while. You doing alright?" It was as good a way as any to break the awkward silence that had fallen over the group in the wake of the dragon attack, while at the same time letting Rachel know that she had been missed

"I'm okay I guess," Rachel replied with a shrug, not sure if now was the time to get into a discussion about the elemental council's decision to impose a pending death sentence on her or talk about the darkness growing over the land because of her.

"You know, Rae," Chris chimed in, walking up next to Evalyn and Rachel, "we've all really missed you. Especially Mom and Dad. They go to visit you every day in the hospital. The doctors say you're in a coma."

This surprised Rachel. She knew after coming to this world and having the bizarre reverse dreams where she heard her family calling out into the darkness that she must still be asleep. But she didn't realize she had been asleep for so long that it required her to be hospitalized.

"How long has it been?" Rachel asked, trying to understand just how bad things were back home.

"About a month," Chris replied, adding, "you've missed a lot of school. You're gonna have a *ton* of makeup work when you wake back up!"

"You're probably right," she said, smiling. She never thought she'd admit it, but it was good to hear Chris's voice in person again.

"So," Evalyn said, looking down at the black and white firefox kit walking next to them, "that's Ember, right? We've never been properly introduced."

"Oh," Rachel replied, "yeah, that's Ember and up there is Lux." She didn't want to forget anyone. "Wait, how did you know his name?"

"Simple," Chris said, giving a mischievous grin, "we read your diary."

"You did *what?*" Rachel snapped, feeling both shock and anger begin to bubble up inside her. "How could you? That's private!"

"Well, it was sort of an accident," Chris rebutted. When he first picked up the diary he had thought it was just one of her storybooks.

"So, what? It just accidentally fell open in your lap, and you just accidentally decided to read what was inside?" Rachel asked sharply, rethinking her earlier thought about being happy to hear Chris's voice.

"It just happened, okay?" Chris shot back. "And it's a good thing, too, because we used what we read to help find you."

That struck a chord, softening Rachel's heart again. She had been wondering how they knew about this world and why they were looking for her here, but it was all starting to make sense. She still didn't understand how they got here, but she suspected it was in exactly the same way she had. They must be dreaming, too. She almost decided to apologize to Chris for being so quick to judge, but then she thought better of it. The last thing she wanted to do was to inflate his ego any more than it already was.

"I almost forgot," Evalyn said, grabbing Kendrick by the arm to pull him closer. "This is Kendrick. He's the reason I'm here. He offered to help me find you, and without him I would never have made it."

That made Chris feel somewhat annoyed. It bothered him that Evalyn kept giving Kendrick all of the credit. Sure, Kendrick helped some, he supposed, but he was the one who found Rachel's diary, and he was the one who had told

Evayln about it. Evalyn would have never known Rachel was here if not for him.

"Nice to meet you Rachel," Kendrick said with a slight bow. "Your sister's told me a lot about you."

"Wow," Rachel let slip, surprised at Kendrick's formality. "Well, I hope whatever she told you wasn't too terrible." She snickered.

"No, it was all good," Kendrick replied heartily before looking at Evalyn with a smile, making her blush. For Rachel, seeing Evalyn with a boy wasn't all that surprising, but still, it did take some getting used to.

"So Ember, where do we go?" Rachel asked, turning to Ember while growing more tired and cold by the minute. "After all that craziness back at the cave, we have nowhere to stay."

Ember perked up his ears to listen, but he didn't hear any shadow wolves. Perhaps they had given up trying to get Rachel once the cave closed. Or maybe Torrens had led them away. He listened again and heard something clapping softly against the ground.

"Tempest!" Kendrick said excitedly, seeing her trot toward them as he walked over to the beautiful aquamare to meet her. Like Rucknar and the calimin dragon, this was another animal Rachel had never seen before, but after attending the elemental council not much surprised her anymore. Besides she had seen plenty of Aquari in different forms and colors. Tempest shook her head up and down playfully at Kendrick, taking a couple of steps backward.

"She wants us to follow her," Kendrick translated. So they did.

She lead them down a small path to a rocky outcropping that acted almost like a small cave just big enough for everyone to lay under. Kendrick pulled blankets out of the sacks slung over Tempest's back, and Lux positioned himself so if any shadow wolves did come they would be hit by his light and transformed into shadows long before they reached Rachel or the others. Rucknar didn't join them. He felt uncomfortable sleeping too close to the humans.

"You've been awful quiet, Ruck," Chris said, walking over to sit down by him. "Everything okay?"

Rucknar looked to Chris then opened his mouth, letting the iridium sphere roll off his tongue and into his claws.

"Never better," Rucknar replied with a dragonish grin, looking down at the metal sphere.

"No way!" Chris said with such enthusiasm the others looked over to see what was going on. "You got the sphere?"

"You mean that ball of metal from the cave?" Rachel interrupted, watching as Rucknar turned the iridescent metal sphere in his claws, captivated by it. "What's so special about that?"

"What's special about it?" Chris repeated, acting almost offended by the question, while Rucknar drew the metal in close to his chest, squinting menacingly at Rachel, clearly insulted.

"It's only the rarest metal on this planet. And your ticket home, Rae," Chris continued. "When we visited the Evarance Keepers in Divarus, their oracle told us we needed the iridium sphere to get you back home."

"That thing?" Rachel asked, looking rather perplexed. "How's that supposed to get me back home?"

It was a good question, one that neither Chris nor Evalyn knew the answer to. After glancing at each other, they looked back at Kendrick, who looked as clueless as they did. They all heard Genevieve say they needed the iridium sphere, but she hadn't told them what to do with it once they got it.

"Ruck?" Chris asked, turning back to Rucknar, hoping he may have picked up on something while at the oracle's home that everyone else had missed. Rucknar's eyes widened, surprised yet again by how stupid humans really were.

"Weren't any of you listening?" Rucknar hissed grumpily in disbelief. This was yet more proof to him that what the Elder dragons said about humans was true. They really were an inferior species when compared with dragons, because dragons have excellent memories and never forget what they are told.

"The human oracle said, 'Follow the sphere. Its path will bring her home.' It's not the sphere but the journey of the sphere that will bring this human girl home. All you need to do is follow it wherever it goes, which really means just follow me," Rucknar hissed, still holding the metal tightly. It was lucky for everyone that the oracle had said what she did, because Rucknar had no intention of surrendering the sphere—especially to these stupid humans. He had been tempted to run away with it and abandon the humans altogether, but he knew how much it meant to Chris to help his sister return home, so he had stayed.

"Well then, I guess that settles it. Tomorrow we follow Ruck," Chris said with a wide yawn. "Thanks for getting' the sphere, Ruck." To which Rucknar snorted, acting as if he didn't care about the compliment from Chris, laying his head down next to the sphere to go to sleep.

Chris left Rucknar and walked back over to Rachel and the rest of the group to settle in for the remainder of the night, wrapping himself in the blanket Kendrick had set out for him. In time everyone fell quiet, drifting into a much needed slumber.

But for Rachel that slumber was shortlived. It was still the wee hours of the morning when she awoke, night canvasing the sky with only the slightest hint that dawn was approaching. As everyone lay quiet in the stillness of morning Rachel was unable to fall back asleep. She lay on the ground looking out at the stars with Ember curled up by her side, thoughts racing through her head about all that had happened.

She looked out into the darkness, watching as Lux's light bounced softly off the surrounding trees. Then in the dark forest beyond his light she thought she spied two eyes glowing in the distance.

"Ember," she whispered softly, gently shaking him to wake him, but he was in too deep a sleep to be so easily roused, so she gave up trying. As long as she stayed where she was, covered by the light of Lux, she knew she was safe, at least from the Shadai.

The eyes moved closer until Rachel saw who they belonged to. It was a black, female, wiry haired shadow wolf with a solid build but no taller than a fully grown firefox, which was short by shadow wolf standards, but intimidating nonetheless. This shadow wolf Rachel had seen a couple of times before, and from what she remembered it was a shadow wolf Trebax didn't seem to get along with. It had been a while but she also thought she recalled Trebax calling this shadow wolf by the name of Vesper, though she didn't understand what their relationship was.

The shadow wolf eyed Rachel but didn't growl or act as though it was going to attack. It kept its body just outside the range of Lux's light, walking and watching as if it were planning something. It was outnumbered, and as far as Rachel could tell there weren't any other shadow wolves around. In the past the shadow wolves had always been very vocal when they were on the hunt, howling into the air to signal their intentions whenever they caught wind of her. She briefly thought about waking the others but didn't, not wanting to cause unnecessary panic—especially with Evalyn and Chris there.

"Umbra thanks you for the gift," Vesper said quietly, but Rachel didn't understand what that meant. She walked over to Rucknar who was sleeping outside the protection of Lux's light and lowered her head near the iridium sphere.

"There's a very special dragon king waiting for an offering," Vesper added softly, picking up the iridium sphere with her teeth from between Rucknar's claws and face, doing so with such stealth and speed Rucknar slept on completely undisturbed. Then she ran away as silent as a shadow.

"Wait!" Rachel yelled, realizing too late the mistake she had made by not waking the others. But Vesper was already gone and the sphere was, too, her only hope of returning home gone with it.

CHAPTER 21. SACRIFICE

In the dark hours of early morning Rachel watched as the shadow wolf Vesper took the iridium sphere from Rucknar as he slept. She had realized too late what the shadow wolf was up to and had waited too long to wake the others.

"Wait!" Rachel shouted, as she watched the shadow wolf take off with the sphere, vanishing into the forest under the cover of darkness.

"Ember, Chris, Evalyn!" she yelled, shaking Ember first to wake him before turning to Chris and Evalyn who were both no longer there. Their blankets lay empty on the cold, hard, ground with only a satchel where Evalyn had once been, telling Rachel they must have gone home.

"What's wrong?" Ember asked, yawning widely.

"It's the sphere!" Rachel said as Rucknar too began to stir. "It's gone. A shadow wolf took it!"

"What's gone?" Rucknar hissed groggily, blinking sleepily as he looked down to check on the sphere in his claws, but it was missing. He jumped frantically to his feet, feverishly searching the ground all around.

"It's no use," Rachel said, trying to calm him down. "I saw a shadow wolf run into the woods with it. The sphere's already gone."

That was not an answer Rucknar was willing to accept. He looked at Rachel and then at the blankets on the ground behind her, seeing that Chris was no longer with them. Kendrick awoke, too, to see what all the fuss was about, as Rucknar scurried off into the woods in search of the shadow wolf and the precious metal it had stolen. Ember followed, knowing how important the sphere was to getting Rachel back home. Rachel would have gone, too, if she thought it would help, but she couldn't leave the protective light of Lux. Not with the shadow wolves still out there wanting to capture her—especially if this was just a trap to lure her away from the safety of Lux's light.

Ember chased after Rucknar, struggling to keep up with him as he ran haphazardly through the woods. Finally, after some time, Rucknar slowed, unsure where to go. He could feel the distance between him and the sphere growing, making him anxious and irritable. Ember sniffed the air, hoping to catch a whiff of shadow wolf, but there was nothing to be found.

"I think Rachel's right," Ember said, not wanting to admit defeat but knowing that without a way to track the shadow wolf, there wasn't much more they could do.

"The sphere is gone, and there isn't a scent or trail for us to follow," he added, hoping to persuade Rucknar to return to camp with him.

Rucknar wouldn't listen. He continued to run through the woods, looking in every direction. He had been so close to bringing the sphere back home, and he desperately needed it to regain his father's trust. It was the only way to make up for the mistake he made when he had watched the assimilation ceremony with Chris. In the moments after that ceremony ended Rucknar had hid just before Chris was captured by the dragons and brought to Adamas, the dragon king.

Rucknar had never intended to come out of his hiding place. Not so long as there were dragons around that could find him. But when Chris was discovered and taken to Adamas, he just couldn't resist the urge to find out what would happen to the peculiar boy he had found in the kobold mines. So he made the mistake of leaving the shelter of the bushes that hid him to watch as Adamas began his interrogation. While Adamas spoke Chris had disappeared, vanishing without a trace, and before Rucknar could hide again he was spotted by one of the dragons flying overhead, standing suspiciously close to where they had found the boy.

After being found Rucknar took the place of Chris in the valley below and had to answer to his father, Adamas, in front of the other dragons, for disgracing him and the clan's traditions by watching the assimilation ceremony before he came of age. He was also to be punished for socializing with a human, which was strictly forbidden, though Rucknar never blamed Chris for that. He understood now more than ever that humans were much too stupid to know that talking with dragons was a bad idea. If anyone was to blame for having a conversation with a human it was he.

After being shamed and humiliated in front of what may as well have been the entire clan Rucknar ran away determined to find the most precious of all metals to present to his father as a means of regaining his honor and bringing himself back into the full acceptance of the clan. The iridium sphere was his chance to return home a hero, presenting his father with the one metal that would make him the mightiest of all the dragons.

Still wandering through the forest Rucknar searched high and low for the shadow wolf and the sphere, but the black and white firefox still following him was right. All traces of the shadow wolf and the sphere were gone. He thought about leaving Chris's sister, Rachel, to fend for herself but decided to return back with Ember to the makeshift camp on the off chance Chris had returned. It was, after all, still possible that being with Chris would somehow help to get him the sphere back. He knew this because Serena, the oracle of dragons, elementals, and other non-humans, whom he had met back in the city of Divarus, had told him so.

While at her home, she had said something to Rucknar that made him choose to stay with Chris longer than he had intended. She said that for Rucknar to obtain that which he most desired he needed to stay with the human boy and see the boy's journey through to the end. She had been right that following Chris would help him get what he desired. After all, Chris had lead him to the human oracle's home where he learned the whereabouts of the iridium sphere, the very thing he had been seeking. Was it possible that if he journeyed with Chris a little longer he would get the sphere back? After all, Chris's journey wasn't complete until his sister returned home.

"Any luck?" Rachel asked as Ember and Rucknar arrived back at the makeshift camp. But she knew right away when she saw the expressions on their faces that the sphere and the shadow wolf were gone.

"There was no sign of the shadow wolf or the sphere," Ember replied, slumping down on the ground next to Rachel.

"Why don't you tell them what you told me?" Kendrick said, gathering up the blankets and other supplies, packing them back in the sacks on Tempest's back as dawn began to break over the horizon.

"Oh," Rachel said, realizing what Kendrick was getting at. Rucknar was a dragon, so it was possible that he knew about the dragon king of which Vesper spoke. It was certainly something worth mentioning. "The shadow wolf that took the sphere said something before she ran off. She said something about an offering for a dragon king. But I didn't really understand what she meant."

Rucknar did. There was only one dragon king he knew that had yet to find the perfect offering to assimilate with. It was his father. But dragons had no dealings with shadow wolves, and it didn't make sense for them to bring an offering to him. Rucknar didn't understand what game the shadow wolves were playing, but at least he knew where the sphere was headed.

"We have to go back to my home," Rucknar hissed, perking up at the information Rachel had provided. He thought perhaps having her along, at least until Chris retuned, would prove useful. "The dragon king is there, which means the iridium sphere will be, too."

He hoped he would be able to get the sphere back from the shadow wolf before it was taken to his father. After all, he wanted to be the one to present the metal offering, and if they hurried there still might be a chance for that to happen.

Rucknar's words gave Rachel hope again. She no longer needed to go to Divarus to seek the guidance of the Evarance Keepers. Chris and Evalyn had already done that for her. And she didn't have to go to Divarus to find her brother and sister anymore, because they had found her first. Time was running out for her to find a way back home, and if what Rucknar had said was true then she needed to follow him back to his home, wherever that may be.

"Lux," Rachel said, turning to the luminary hawk as he preened his feathers getting ready to start another day's journey, "I know we were supposed to go to Divarus, but Chris and Evalyn have already been there, and they found a way for me to go home. We need to follow Rucknar now if I'm going to be able to leave this world."

Lux lifted his wing, cleaning the last of his shining feathers before giving Rachel a swift nod in understanding. He didn't care which way they went as long as it helped Rachel return home and stop the darkness that was taking over the land. He flew up into the sky, no longer needing to protect Rachel from the threat of the Shadai since daybreak had flooded everything with morning light, and he flashed a series of lights in the air, not as a beacon to call aid during times of danger but instead as a signal to send a message back to Elder Oakin and the other council members to communicate the change of plans.

After completing his message he flew back down, landing on a nearby tree limb as the sound of galloping hooves drew near. They weren't coming from from Tempest, who was still standing calmly next to Kendrick. Instead they were coming from a white mysticorn stallion whose body trailed a cool, white mist.

"Caligo!" Rachel shouted happily, relieved to see that he was okay. "After the shadow wolf attack I didn't know if you'd be coming back."

"I'd never leave without you," Caligo neighed, stopping in front of Rachel, overjoyed to see that she, too, was okay. "I promised to help you find a way home, and a mysticorn must keep his promise."

"What about your leg?" Rachel asked, looking over Caligo who seemed to be standing just fine. "Did Trebax bite you?"

"It's just a little sore," Caligo replied, leaning his head toward the leg in question, "but no serious harm was done. I changed into mist just in time to prevent any permanent damage. For my kind changing into mist can be very healing, and most injuries repair themselves rather quickly."

Caligo looked past Rachel and noticed the others, surprised to see a human, aquamare, and dragon standing nearby.

"Are these your friends?" he asked confusedly. He hadn't realized Rachel had any human friends here, and dragons weren't known to tolerate anyone outside of their own kind very well. The aquamare, too, was unusual, at least for these woods.

"In a way," Rachel replied. "This is Rucknar, Kendrick, and Tempest," she continued, pointing to each of them in turn. "Rucknar will be leading us back to his home."

"What about Divarus?" Caligo asked, growing even more perplexed. Could so much really have changed in just one little night?

"There's no need to go there anymore," Kendrick interjected, stepping forward to address Caligo. "I've already been to see the Evarance oracle, and she spoke of a way for Rachel to return home. There's something called the iridium sphere being carried by a shadow wolf to this dragon's home. Going after the sphere is the only way we know of to return Rachel back to where she came from."

"It's true," Ember said, seeing the confusion on Caligo's face. "I know it sounds strange, but you just have to trust them on this one."

Caligo nodded, staying true to his word that he'd help Rachel return home if he could, though he didn't like the sound of going into dragon territory. Rachel stepped up onto a large boulder that lay on the ground to help her climb once again onto Caligo's back. Kendrick followed, mounting Tempest, resolved to continue on the journey with Rachel because he knew it's what Evalyn would want.

"Is everyone ready?" Rachel asked, still tired but wanting to move on.

"I was born ready!" Ember said with a grin and a hop, anxious to get going.

"Alright Rucknar," Rachel said, prepared to once again go and face the great unknown, "lead the way!"

Rucknar squinted at all of them, looking over each and every one of them with his beady black eyes. "If we do this," he hissed, still very uncomfortable with the idea of leading these humans straight to his home, but not having any other choice if he wanted to get the iridium sphere back, "we have to stay out of sight, and we have to move quickly. The dragons will kill you if they find you, and I won't protect you if they do. Don't get the wrong idea. I'm only helping you to help myself. And I won't stick around if there's trouble."

"Fair enough," Rachel agreed, just grateful he was willing to be her guide—at least for the time being. She wished Evalyn and Chris were there, too, but her time was limited, so she couldn't wait for them to return.

"Keep up if you can," Rucknar snorted, taking off into the the woods to lead them to his home, which by his calculations was less than a day's journey away.

Ember ran fast, keeping up with Rucknar, while Rachel and Caligo followed behind next in line, with Kendrick and Tempest bringing up the rear. Lux flew just about everywhere, weaving in and out of the trees overhead, enjoying the freedom of being one of the followers this time instead of having to lead the group.

The day was long and the journey tiresome. Ember took turns riding on Caligo's back with Rachel whenever he needed a break. Rucknar was tough and not as easily winded so long as he traveled at a manageable pace that allowed them to make good time without wearing himself out too much. On occasion, he stretched out his wings and flapped them, testing them to see if they were strong enough yet to carry the weight of his body, which they weren't; but they were getting close. When he moved his wings up and down he could feel the front half of his body rise up off the ground. It was a sign that he was coming of age, and soon he'd be ready to join the clan in an assimilation ceremony of his very own. That was assuming, of course, that the clan would welcome him back after he retrieved the iridium sphere and presented it to his father.

Kendrick told Rachel all about how he and Evalyn had met to pass the time. He told her about the Echoes in his village and went into greater detail about Divarus and the Evarance Keepers. He even told her about the andalyn he'd given to her sister. What it was, what it meant. It was really sweet actually to hear how much he admired Evayln, and Rachel could tell that every word he said was genuine. Rachel in return told him about the shadow wolves, the reverse dreams, and the darkness. She even mentioned to him the elemental council, and he was fascinated by every detail.

The terrain gradually changed from flat forest to green mountains, where Rucknar led them through paths in the woods that climbed upward on a mountainside until they could all hear the rumble of rushing water. They walked beside large slabs of stone, which climbed up the mountain beside them creating a natural wall-like structure. Rucknar slowed to a stop, hushing everyone, listening intently for something before peeking his head around the corner to make sure they were still alone.

As he peered around the wall of rock beside him he spied a wolf-shaped, black shadowy figure slip into an opening behind a tall waterfall — a waterfall that concealed a side entrance to the kobold mine. He had intentionally led the group around the mountain in such a way that they could slip past the other dragons unnoticed, but it meant coming back to this place, the place where his and Chris's friendship first began.

"What's going on, Ruck?" Chris said from behind Rucknar, startling him as he was watching the waterfall with suspicion.

"Chris?" Rucknar hissed quietly, turning around to see him while noticing that his sister Evayln had returned, too. "A shadow wolf just went into the mine."

"What mine?" Chris asked softly in reply, naturally changing the volume of his voice to match Rucknar's. He always felt a bit disoriented when waking up.

"The kobold mine!" Rucknar huffed in frustration. It was draining trying to keep all of these humans up to speed on what was going on.

Chris peeked around the corner, too, as Rucknar looked again, but he didn't see any shadow wolves *or* kobolds for that matter. Everything looked pretty quiet aside from the roar of the waterfall hitting the pool below. For Chris it felt good being somewhere familiar again.

"What's a shadow wolf doin' in the kobold mine?" Chris asked as he and Rucknar pulled back behind the rock again to stay out of sight in case a kobold or a shadow wolf emerged from the mine.

"Maybe the shadow wolf gave the iridium sphere to the kobolds," Rucknar speculated.

This caught Chris off guard. He didn't know that the sphere had gone missing.

"How'd a shadow wolf get the sphere?" Chris asked, interested in knowing what he and Evalyn had missed while they were away.

"It stole it while everyone was sleeping," Rachel jumped in, sliding off Caligo's back to stretch her legs as she walked up to join Chris and Rucknar. "It was just after you left, and we're trying to get it back."

That was all Rachel could tell Chris before a chorus of mighty roars echoed through air, reminding them all that they were in dragon territory. Rucknar lifted his head in alarm, uncertain why the dragons all sounded as if they were rejoicing. Was he too late? Had his father already gotten the sphere? He sprinted out into the grassy field in front of the kobold mine and ran around the pool at the base of the waterfall into the trees beyond.

Chris ran after him, and Rachel ran after Chris with Ember running by her side. Kendrick dismounted Tempest, leaving her to stay behind with the mysticorn, Caligo, as he took Evalyn by the hand to follow. Lux went last, flying past Kendrick and Evalyn to catch up with Rachel and Ember. They ran through the trees and came to a rocky overlook that gave them a perfect view of the clearing below. Chris looked down over the open field and could see the kobolds preparing for another assimilation ceremony as the sun was beginning to set over the land.

The king . . . the dragons said to one another, their voices echoing across the plain. *The king will assimilate! It's a time for great joy. . . . Now he will officially be one of us . . . a true Allorum and the mightiest of all the dragons. . . .*

Their cries of excitement continued as Rucknar looked down in disbelief. The sphere was supposed to be his gift to the king! He watched as the kobolds carried out the iridium sphere, placing it in the center of the altar. There wasn't a dragon alive, at least not an Allorum, that wouldn't be envious of the metal the king was preparing to absorb. It was the strongest and most powerful of all the metals. The only metal truly worthy of a king.

As the dragons excitedly carried on speaking of the king and the metal, Chris recalled a memory. Not a true memory, but the memory of a dream. The first dream he had when he came to this strange world. King . . . metal . . . "Poison!" he said aloud, looking over at Rucknar urgently.

Rucknar flicked his head toward Chris in confusion. "Poison?" he hissed. "What poison?"

"It was somethin' I heard before we met," Chris said, beginning to understand what was really going on down in the valley below. "I didn't think it was important then, but I'm sure it is now."

"What do you mean poison?" Rucknar pressed, irritated Chris was dodging the question. He squinted to give Chris the most suspicious looking glare he could make.

"It's somethin' I overheard in the kobold mine. Somethin' about the king and a poisoned offering," Chris went on, the memory coming back to him with crystal clarity. "They want to kill the king!"

Rucknar stared at Chris, his suspicious looks changing to disbelief. He had always suspected that the kobolds were up to something, but this was much too bold a move—even for creatures such as they.

"I know of no poison that could kill a dragon," Rucknar countered, attempting to brush aside Chris's concerns. "We dragons are strong both inside and out. No poison can hurt us let alone kill us."

"But," Chris continued, certain he was right about the danger, "the kobolds said they found poison in the mine that was strong enough to kill a dragon. They even said they tested it!"

Rucknar thought a moment, shaking his wings and shifting his shoulders uncomfortably. He did recall a youngling disappearing a while back, but the dragons had never suspected the kobolds of any involvement. They had always blamed the humans for any disappearances, because humans were known to capture and enslave younglings that wandered too far from home.

"It is possible . . ." Rucknar hissed thoughtfully. "Not long ago one of the younglings went missing, but we never thought the kobolds would do such a thing." Which was true. Kobolds were aways considered inferior and extremely stupid creatures when compared with the dragons, incapable of such sophisticated thoughts or actions.

"But . . ." Rucknar continued, growing very uneasy, his words trailing off as he seriously considered what Chris had told him, "if you're right about all of this, then my father is in danger."

He knew Chris wasn't very bright, but he'd never known Chris to be a liar. And he didn't believe Chris had any reason to make up something like this. It had to be true.

Rucknar looked down as night began to fall over the land, watching the dragons set torches afire, scattered across the land below, dimly lighting the ground. He knew that his father was running out of time, but he also knew there was nothing he could do to convince him of the danger. If he tried to reason with his father and warn him of the poison, his words would certainly fall on deaf ears. All dragons, especially his father, were much too stubborn and proud to ever take seriously anything a youngling had to say.

Rucknar felt his heart speed up as he instinctively whipped his tail back and forth across the grass, coming to the the full realization of what he had to do. Words wouldn't be enough to keep his father from taking in the poisoned sphere, and he knew he wouldn't be able to snatch it and run. There were far too many dragons gathered below, preparing for what they thought would be the greatest assimilation of all time, eagerly watching as Adamas entered the clearing making his way to the altar. But when Rucknar saw him all he saw was his father inching closer to death with each step.

"I have to save him!" Rucknar hissed, watching anxiously as Adamas drew nearer to the sphere.

He shifted his body and stretched out his sizable wings, pumping them up and down with all the strength that he had, moving them faster and faster until his body began to lift off the ground.

"You're flying, Ruck!" Chris said, unable to contain his excitement, his eyes growing wide as he watched Rucknar dive down through the air into the clearing below. The dragons grew quiet, rooted in place, watching in confusion as Rucknar landed next to the altar, stopping even the great Adamas in his tracks at the sight of his son who had been lost. Rucknar felt the pull of the iridescent sphere as he gazed at his reflection inside it. Wishing there was another way but knowing that there wasn't, he picked up the sphere, holding it firmly in his jaw as he sadly looked his father in the eyes before swallowing it whole.

CHAPTER 22. VESCUS

Rucknar had done the unthinkable. He swallowed the poisoned iridium sphere to protect his father from a painful death. No one saw it coming, not even Chris, who yelled Rucknar's name over the roar of the angry dragons who thought they had been betrayed.

The transformation began instantly as Rucknar fell to the ground, writhing in pain, his skin stretching and bubbling over his body as it grew until he was double his size. Chris had seen assimilations before, but none resembled what was happening to Rucknar, his body twisting and convulsing on the ground as he struggled back to his feet. The dragons rushed him to try and pin him down, but he knocked them away with newfound strength as the metal of the sphere pulsed through his veins.

Chris rushed to a dirt path that led down the mountainside, into the clearing below. He ran with all the strength that he had, sliding and stumbling on the steeper parts of the trail.

"I'm coming, Ruck!" he yelled, no thought of his own life or the danger the dragons posed.

Rachel ran after Chris with Ember by her side, unwilling to let her brother go alone. She followed him closely down the dark, dirt path, slipping and stumbling behind him in the blackness. Night had fallen, and with it came a howl, piercing the cool, dark air. It was a howl Rachel knew all too well: the howl of a shadow wolf calling to its pack. The single howl was met with many in return. So many it startled Rachel, causing her to trip and tumble at the end of the trail. She bumped into Chris, knocking him down, and they fell to the ground together, laying at the base of the mountain.

Beside them, a tall, rough, rocky surface covered the mountainside, towering above them and stretching out to the entrance of a mine. A multitude of howls infiltrated the air, growing in number and sounding as though they were coming from everywhere, as if the entire valley were surrounded by shadow wolves. Rachel climbed to her feet and Chris did, too, watching as a rush of kobolds burst from the mine, pouring into the valley before them. The wolflike kobolds were armed with mining tools sharpened for cutting through hard rock and stone. They scattered across the flat terrain, not noticing Chris or Rachel as they ran, attacking the dragons that were distracted by Rucknar as he continued to thrash on the ground.

Using the light of the torches in the valley below, Kendrick and Evalyn watched from the rocky ledge as the kobolds swarmed from one end to the other, attacking everything in their path. They heard the calls of the shadow wolves drawing nearer and looked to each other, unsure what to do. Chris and Rachel were still nowhere to be seen and even Lux seemed tense as he flew up into the sky, letting out a pulse of light that radiated through the air like a brightly shining beacon. Kendrick didn't know if the light was a warning or a call for help, but one thing was sure: Events were quickly escalating out of control.

"We have to find your brother and sister," Kendrick said

to Evalyn as she continued to watch the chaos below, feeling ill at the sight of the monstrous lizards and the wolflike creatures climbing onto them. Kendrick listened over the wailing cries of the dragons as they fought the attacking kobolds. He heard the sounds of fast-moving creatures running through the forest as more howls broke free into the air.

"We have to go now!" Kendrick said, pulling Evalyn by the hand down the same dirt path Chris and Rachel had taken.

When they reached the bottom they found Rachel and Chris standing against the rocky crust of the mountainside, tucked against a part that was sheltered from view, watching helplessly in horror as Rucknar continued to transform. His scales bubbled and popped as they grew larger in size, oozing yellow puss from the cracks between them like an infection seeping out of a wound. He tore at his stomach as if in severe pain before spewing acidic yellow bile from his mouth, burning the ground all around him.

A silvery-white liquid metal carrying an iridescent shine poured out over his diamond scales, coating them roughly and incompletely. They didn't look smooth or clean like the scales found on other dragons but were instead cracked and disfigured with a hardened yellowed crystalline substance filling in the gaps in the metal that streaked down each scale. His diamond scales changed from smoky-brown to foggy yellow, getting horribly discolored by the poison. His wings stretched high and then bent back down, warping as they did into an uneven shape.

Chris's heart ached, tightening in his chest as he watched his friend suffering through the most hideous of transformations. If only he'd kept quiet, not mentioning the kobold's poison, but it was much too late to undo what was done. Ignoring the danger he ran into the clearing, waving his arms to get Rucknar's attention.

"Ruck!" Chris screamed, but it was as if his friend, trapped in the writhing agony of his own wretched body, could no longer hear. Rucknar turned sharply, nearly hitting Chris with his wing. "You've gotta throw up the sphere!"

Even if Chris's words had touched Rucknar's ears the assimilation couldn't be stopped. Rucknar continued to roar with pain, whipping his tail at Chris, knocking him away. Chris got up and ran back to him again as Rucknar flailed his body like a wild beast, fighting the poison within. His horns lengthened and the spikes down his back thickened and cracked, nearly completing the transformation. He was much larger now than he had been before but still very much undersized compared with others of his kind, the poison circulating through his body stunting his growth.

Chris leapt out of the way of several furious tail swings and ducked down, just missing another wing as it sliced through the air. He was certain Rucknar wasn't intentionally trying to harm him. His uncontrollable thrashing was all the poison's doing, which really meant it was the kobold's doing. Rucknar had been right all this time to be suspicious of them.

A few nearby dragons, still crushing kobolds and knocking them away, noticed Chris as he ran around Rucknar. They recognized Chris as the boy who had disappeared shortly before Rucknar ran away and were resolved to take care of him once and for all, certain Rucknar had fallen prey to the human's lies and deceit. Coming at Chris they were knocked forcefully away as Rucknar still twisted and turned in confusion and pain. Chris continued to dodge and duck Rucknar's swings, using him like a living shield as the dragons continued their advance.

The dragons tried again to take out the boy but were unable to withstand Rucknar's overpowering blows, beaten back by his volatile movements. Even poisoned, Rucknar, with the strength of the iridium sphere inside him was much too strong for the other dragons to overcome.

Rachel and Evalyn watched in horror as it looked to them like their brother was being engulfed by the angry dragons. Kendrick pulled his sword from his sheath, on the verge of running out to help Chris when a rush of air mixed with a chorus of howls flew past them as the shadow wolves spilled out into the clearing from all sides to aid the kobolds in their rebellion.

Chris dodged Rucknar's whiplike tail again and ducked under his wing as it swept toward him. The dragons backed away to deal instead with the shadow wolves who had rekindled the determination of the kobolds.

"Ruck!" yelled Chris again, trying to get through to him while at the same time accidentally catching the attention of a couple of shadow wolves. Kendrick, Evalyn, and Rachel watched as Chris narrowly missed being hit by another uncontrollable slash of Rucknar's wing, unaware of the danger that was approaching him.

"I'm sorry, Evalyn," Kendrick said, looking toward her, "but your brother needs me, and if I don't go now it may be too late."

Evalyn nodded, still in shock as she watched the terrifying scenes of shadow wolves, kobolds, and dragons fighting everywhere.

"Take care of her for me," Kendrick said, looking at Ember and Rachel before running off toward Chris and

Rucknar, fighting off kobolds along the way. Before he could reach Chris, a shadow wolf lunged Chris's way but was knocked unconscious by a fortunate whip of Rucknar's tail, which Chris had just barely avoided.

Kendrick arrived not a moment too soon, knocking a second shadow wolf away as it tried to attack.

"Chris, are you okay?" Kendrick shouted over the Rucknar's anguished roars.

"Never better!" Chris said sarcastically. "Thanks for the help, by the way!"

"My pleasure," Kendrick replied, ducking with Chris as another of Rucknar's wings flew overhead, hitting a kobold running past. "But you know," he continued, growing more serious, "I really think it's time we got out of here."

"But I can't leave Ruck!" Chris said stubbornly, another shadow wolf leaping their way.

This one hit Kendrick, knocking him to the ground, bitting at him viciously with blood streaked teeth that Kendrick blocked with the flat of his blade. Kendrick held the blade firmly in his hands between him and the shadow wolf. He pushed the blade against the shadow wolf's throat, using it in much the same way as he would a shield to keep its teeth as far from his face as possible.

Chris picked up a pickaxe that had dropped to the ground near him and swung it as hard as he could, hitting the side of the shadow wolf on top of Kendrick with such force that he fell to the ground and scampered off with a whimper.

"I'm not leaving you, Ruck!" Chris shouted again, showing Kendrick just how stubborn he could be.

"Can't you see?" Kendrick said insistently. "Rucknar is beyond our help! And from the looks of it he can't be harmed by the dragons or any other beasts. What he's battling now is the poison inside him. We can't cure that."

Distracted by trying to persuade Chris to leave Kendrick was slammed hard by Rucknar's body and flung to the ground.

"Ken!" Chris cried out, rushing over to Kendrick, grabbing his arm to try and pull him safely away from Rucknar who was still flailing about.

Evalyn watched as Chris struggled to drag the weight of Kendrick's body safely out of Rucknar's reach.

"Kendrick!" she screamed, unsure if he was alive or dead, running out into the clearing that now more closely resembled a bloody battlefield, giving no prior thought to the danger, her mind focused on Kendrick alone.

As Ember and Rachel watched Evalyn run, it became apparent she wasn't going to make it. Kobolds had spotted her, changed their course, and were gaining on her.

"Ember!" Rachel cried. "My sister! You have to do something!"

Ember hesitated a moment, torn between staying with Rachel to protect her or running after Evalyn to keep her safe from danger as Kendrick had asked.

"Please!" Rachel pleaded, knowing she couldn't go and risk being captured again by the shadow wolves, which in the end would just hurt everyone else. Ember obeyed, bursting into crackly coal-like flames to run after Evalyn, shouting back at Rachel to stay where she was. Rachel stepped backward a few steps, pressing her back firmly against the stony wall, keeping as far out of sight as possible.

Chris continued to drag Kendrick's body away from Rucknar, whose erratic movements were much too dangerous to be around as Ember made it to Evalyn, just in time to distract the kobolds away from her so she could safely reach Kendrick and Chris. As Rachel anxiously watched, a gigantic copper dragon crashed down lifeless to the ground in front of her, blocking her view of the others. Kobolds and shadow wolves dropped down off the enormous dragon, moving to their next target, oblivious to Rachel tucked against the wall.

But there was one that noticed her.

Having been the one who inflicted the finishing blow, Umbra jumped down off the dragon's metallic hide. He was as massive as ever, with a large muzzle, erect ears, and sharply defined paws on which still hung the silver charm bracelet that he had stolen from Rachel right before their first encounter, its light shining brightly out into the darkness from the little fire charm.

Umbra growled as he stepped toward Rachel, licking the blood off his teeth, a testament of his latest kill, and bent down in front of her poised to attack.

"I guess I should be thanking you," Umbra said darkly. "You are, after all, the one who brought the darkness to this world. The time you've spent here has been very helpful to us," he added licking his lips. "But all good things must come to an end. I hope you've enjoyed your stay, because it's over now. We don't need you any longer. It's time to say goodbye, little thorn in my paw."

He howled deeply, shaking the ground, and leapt at Rachel to end her life.

He was caught in the neck mid-jump by Torrens who had minimized his flames to prevent Umbra from changing into a shadow when their bodies touched. Umbra and Torrens crashed to the ground, but Umbra struggled back up, smashing Torrens' body against the rocky mountainside to break free of him. But Torrens held fast, refusing to let go, his fangs sinking deeper into Umbra's throat. Umbra stumbled back and fell to the ground, struggling for breath as Torrens clamped down, squeezing even harder until Umbra had no more breath in him. Torrens let go only after he was certain Umbra was dead, then reignited his flames into a blazing light.

"Torrens!" Rachel said with relief, thankful he was still alive and grateful he had once again saved her life. The tide was turning as the clearing filled with other firefoxes and elementals who had heeded Lux's call. The light beacon had worked.

Torrens bent down over Umbra's body and pulled the silver charm bracelet off with his teeth before dropping it into Rachel's hands.

"I believe this belongs to you," he said, recalling how she used to wear it long before she had been given the countdown to her death. She looked at the bracelet and fit it to her wrist, rubbing the little fire charm between her fingers. But seeing it made her feel sad. She couldn't look at it without thinking about home, the place she longed for.

A shout came from the clearing, catching the attention of Torrens and Rachel. It was Ember struggling to protect both Evalyn and Kendrick as Chris, holding another mining pick, swung recklessly through the air trying to keep away the kobolds and shadow wolves who were closing in on them. Torrens ran to aid them, and Rachel stepped out to follow, knowing by the words Umbra had spoken that the shadow wolves no longer needed her, which meant there was also no more reason to hide for fear of being captured. She began to move forward to go after Torrens, but her way was blocked by a black, wiry haired shadow wolf with a wicked smile and bloodthirsty eyes.

She knew this shadow wolf; it was Trebax. Just the sight of him made her feel sick to her stomach and elevated her heartbeat to a pounding so intense that it caused her body to tremble. He walked methodically toward her, pausing only a moment to glance at Umbra who lay deceased. Seeing Umbra's lifeless and limp body only made his smile wider, because Umbra's death meant he was no longer constrained by the rules and demands of the former leader of the pack.

"Wake up! Just wake up already!" Rachel's head screamed as he approached, growling low and viciously, his lips curled up showing razor sharp teeth dripping with saliva and blood.

"You have nowhere left to run, little girl," he snarled with a wicked grin, crouching low, readying for the attack.

Rachel took one step backward before her back pressed hard against the solid rock wall. She closed her eyes tightly, waiting for the blow that would certainly end her life.

There was a time before the horrible nightmares began that she found solace in her dreams. To Rachel her dreams were an exciting escape from the boring life she once lived. But now more than anything she just wanted the dream she had become trapped in for so long to end.

Trebax lunged, snapping hard to kill the girl once and for all, but his bite met nothing but empty air as he hit the rocky surface of the mountainside against which she had stood. The girl was gone, vanished, taking with her the bracelet Umbra had worn as a trophy of her capture. He howled in angry rage, catching the attention of the shadow wolves across the valley. He looked around at the battle that was still raging. The kobolds were losing against the dragons, even with the the shadow wolves' aid. The elementals that had spread across the field were an unexpected addition to this fight, and the fact that the dragon king was not dead or greatly weakened as expected put the odds overwhelmingly against them.

Trebax howled loudly and long, taking the place of Umbra as leader of the pack. He called the shadow wolves to retreat and took off into the woods to lead them back to their territory under cover of darkness. They had hoped to take over this land with the kobolds' aid to use it as a strategic location to further the rise and reign of the shadows. The vastness of the caves in these mountains made them the perfect place to house more Shadai as they spread their darkness across the land. They had lost this battle, but the war was far from over. Darkness was coming, so the land was still destined to be theirs—just not quite as soon as they'd hoped.

Chris and Evalyn watched as the shadow wolves began their retreat, causing the kobolds to panic and scatter, rushing back into the depths of mine for shelter from the wrath of the dragons who remained. With the shadow wolves leaving and the kobolds dispersed, the elementals also withdrew. Their fight was with the Shadai, not the dragons or even the kobolds, so there was no more need to fight. During the mass retreat at the battle's end Chris and Evalyn, with the help of Torrens, had managed to pull Kendrick safely off the field under the sheltering cover of the trees while Ember ran off in search of Rachel. Kendrick stirred, opening his eyes in time to see Evalyn's silhouette shining in Torrens' fiery light.

"Kendrick!" Evalyn said, hugging him hard as tears began to flow freely down her face. "I thought you were dead!" Smiling, he raised his hand to wipe the tears.

It warmed his heart to see how worried she was. He sat up and coughed, his body aching all over; otherwise he had no serious injuries. Then he rose to his feet, taking Evalyn by the hand to join Chris as he looked out over the wartorn field littered with the bodies of the dead. Rucknar lay still, slumped down in the middle of the field, causing Chris's heart to sink. There was so much more that he had wanted to say to Ruck, but now it looked as though he would never have the chance.

Adamas walked toward Rucknar and towered high above his collapsed body, spitting in disgust at his treacherous son who had stolen his glory. He still didn't know that the offering was poisoned and supposed Rucknar's disfiguring transformation was the result of the treason. He pushed Rucknar's body and it began to stir, surprising Adamas that he could still be alive after going through such a hideous change. Rucknar stood up shakily as the remaining dragons gathered around, gasping in horror and utter disgust at his mangled body. Adamas looked down at his son and with anger pouring over him he spoke in a roaring voice that echoed over the plains.

"You shall no longer be known as Rucknar," he boomed, his voice carrying across the valley is it did during a traditional assimilation ceremony. But this was no cere-mony. His words were a mockery of what Rucknar's ceremony should have been and an insult for everything he believed Rucknar had done. He blamed Rucknar for not only the theft of his offering, but for all the deaths that occurred thereafter.

"Henceforth," he declared, "you shall be known as Vescus the vile betrayer. You no longer have any place within these mountains or with your kin. For your sin of stealing and assimilating with the most precious of metals that was meant for your father and king, you will be left to live in the awful and wretched state you now find yourself. May you always live in the misery you brought upon yourself and know that you are no longer my son or heir. You are banished forever to live out the rest of your miserable days in pain and suffering."

Adamas had thought about killing Rucknar, now Vescus, but decided not to because he felt that leaving him alive was a far worse punishment. Rucknar wanted to explain, but didn't know what to say; the harshness in Adamas's eyes said it all. His heart was cold and black, like the diamond scales on his body, with no more room left in it for his son.

Chris could see Rucknar's body throbbing in pain, his eyes expressing the deepest sorrow Chris had ever seen in anyone. Disgusted by the grossness of his appearance none of the dragons dared touch him. Instead all including Adamas turned their backs on him, thereby beginning his banishment and exile. Rucknar tried desperately to flap his wings to carry him far, far away, desirous of wallowing in shame and loneliness, but they were bent and broken, no longer beautiful or functional, and he was unable to fly. He waddled away into the forest and out of sight. Chris ran after him, angered by Adamas' blinding selfishness.

He ran through the woods following Rucknar's trail, a fair distance away from the group. The trees were especially thick in this part of the woods before opening up to a star covered sky under which Rucknar lay sulking on a massive boulder, wings twitching as the pain of the assimilation started to pass.

"Ruck?" Chris said cautiously, seeing if the transformation had changed more than just his appearance. Rucknar turned to look at him.

"Stupid human," Rucknar sniffed, his body trembling more from sorrow now than pain, "I am not Rucknar anymore. My name is Vescus. Vescus the vile, the deformed, the traitor."

He shimmied his body around the boulder, turning away from Chris, but that didn't deter Chris. Chris walked around the massive boulder, climbing up to sit next to Rucknar's face, which lay against the cold hard stone on which they sat. Chris now could see clearly the cracks in Rucknar's scales and the hardened yellow crystalline streaks that ran across them. He put his hand on Rucknar, feeling the rough metal that partially coated them and stroked his hand over one of Rucknar's bent and misshapen wings.

"No," Chris said sternly, refusing to let Rucknar believe the horrible things his father had said to him. "You are Rucknar. Rucknar the hero. You saved my life and your father's life, too. Rucknar the good. Helping me find my sister and staying with her even after I had gone. Rucknar the brave. Swallowing that sphere to protect someone you loved, knowing that by doing it you would probably die. Rucknar the strong. The strongest of all the dragons, so strong you survived death. You are Rucknar, not Vescus, and don't ever tell yourself any different, no matter what anyone else says."

Rucknar stared in disbelief at the silly little human whom he now recognized as his dearest friend. His father had disowned him, his clan had abandoned him, but deep in his dragonish heart he knew Chris was right. He was good, even if he didn't look it. Although his father would never know the truth about what Rucknar had done for him, Rucknar knew and Chris knew. Maybe, just maybe, he thought, humans weren't so stupid after all. Chris gave Rucknar a hug and as he did, the world around him changed, bringing him back home.

CHAPTER 23. A NEW DAY

Rachel slowly opened her eyes, seeing only a blurry white light above her as her eyes adjusted to the room. Was she dead? She couldn't remember anything after Trebax had pinned her against the mountainside and lunged, snapping at her with his ferocious fangs. If she was dead he'd made awful quick work of it because she didn't remember feeling anything. The blur in her vision started to clear. Above her was a ceiling with lights shining brightly and white walls with pictures on them she couldn't quite make out. She heard a beep repeating at a slow and steady pace, and struggled to turn her head to the side to see what was making the sound. She felt weak and fatigued.

Where was she? She looked around the room as her eyes finally came into full focus and saw that she was in some sort of bed with medical devices at her side. She looked to the corner of the room and saw an armchair with someone sleeping in it. Someone who looked just like her mother.

"Mom?" she said softly, her voice cracking as though it hadn't been used in a long time. She tried to sit up, but her body felt like a lead weight that despite her best efforts was impossible to lift up on her own. Even her arms felt numb and heavy, but she did manage to move a few of her fingers to feel the bedsheets underneath them.

"Mom . . ." she said again weakly, trying to rouse the

woman sleeping in the chair. As she struggled even harder to get up the beeping beside her accelerated.

The woman awoke, looking at Rachel with an expression only a mother would give after seeing a lost child return home. She hurried over to Rachel's bedside, tears welling up in her eyes and then overflowing onto her face as she embraced her child in the warmest, most loving hug Rachel had ever felt. It was just like a dream, too good to be true after all the terrible things Rachel had gone though. Without letting go of Rachel's hand, her mom pressed the nurse's call button and excitedly called her husband to let him know Rachel had returned to them.

Dad brought Chris and Evalyn to the hospital with him, where they were all relieved to see Rachel awake. As they smiled and laughed and joked, not talking about anything in particular, Rachel felt some of her strength returning to her, and she managed to use the bed's electronic controller to sit up. Mom and Dad left the room to discuss with the doctors what steps were needed to bring Rachel home. Chris and Evalyn sat by her side, quiet at first, waiting to be sure that Mom and Dad were out of earshot before speaking about what only they and Rachel would understand.

"That was some dream, huh?" Chris said with a quirky half smile. "I still don't understand what brought you back home, though."

Rachel looked at her wrist, seeing the beautiful silver charm bracelet. Thankfully neither Mom nor Dad had noticed it was there. She didn't know for certain, but she felt as though her coming back home had something to do with the little fire charm that still glowed with a beautiful orange light. Evalyn looked at the bracelet, too. It wasn't a piece of jewelry she remembered ever having seen before.

"It's beautiful," Evalyn said. "Where did you get it?"

Rachel glanced at the door to be certain her parents were still busy with the doctors.

"It's Aunt Jenny's," Rachel told them quietly. "I found it right as the dreams began. Please don't tell Mom and Dad about it." She had no desire to get into any trouble, though she imagined if she did her parents would be much more lenient with her than before she had slipped into a coma.

"No worry, Rae," Chris said with a grin and a wink. "Your secret is safe with us."

None of them had known their Aunt Jenny very well. Evalyn and Chris were so small when she was around they could scarcely recall what she looked like.

"I think," Rachel said, wanting to answer Chris's question about how she was able to return home, "the bracelet is what brought me here. I was wearing it when the shadow wolves caught me. They took it from me. I was trapped in Calim ever since."

What Rachel was saying made Chris wonder. He reached into his pocket and pulled out the dragon's scale from Rucknar that now served as a reminder of how Rucknar had once been and in his mind still was. For Chris it was a little bittersweet to look at. He rubbed the scale between his fingers, feeling the rough texture and held it up to Rachel to show her.

"You know, Rae," Chris said, handing Rachel the scale so she could feel it, too. "Eva and I each have somethin' that we brought back from Calim. Since then our dreams have been directly connected to these items. Without them we don't go back, but with them we do. For me my dreams always take me back to wherever Ruck is, and for Eva she always finds Kendrick nearby. I wonder if your bracelet does the same thing."

Rachel slowly held up her wrist, her eyes widening with the realization that it was in fact Aunt Jenny's bracelet that brought her to Calim and kept her returning there. There was something she had been connected to every time she returned there in her dreams. It was Ember who told her she appeared near him wherever he ventured, but she never knew that it was the bracelet that connected them to each other. Perhaps her bracelet, like the tokens Chris and Evalyn had, worked two ways. The tokens allowed them to go to Calim and were needed to return back home. At least that was the theory. The more she thought about it the more she realized that the Evarance oracle with whom Chris and Evalyn had spoken had been right: following the iridium sphere led her to Umbra, allowing her to get her bracelet back, which ultimately brought her home.

"Do you think Aunt Jenny's ever been to Calim?" Rachel asked, pulling the bracelet off her wrist to look at it one last time before handing it to Evayln for safekeeping.

"I think anything is possible," Evalyn said, looking over the bracelet before putting it in her pocket to bring home for safekeeping at Rachel's request.

Rachel didn't want her parents to see the charm bracelet, which was part of the reason she took it off, but she also couldn't afford to wear it anymore in case what Chris had suspected was true. She was sad not to see Ember or Torrens again, and she had never gotten the chance to properly say goodbye to Incindia, Caligo, or Lux, but going back was dangerous, and the time the council had given her to leave their world was nearly expired. If she returned she didn't know if she'd make it back alive. Besides, with her gone there was always a chance the darkness would stop its encroachment.

The hospital kept her several more days before she returned home to find a present from Ryan sitting on her bed. This was an unexpected surprise. After talking with Chris about what Rucknar had gone through, she was beginning to think she should start focusing more on the good in people than just on the way they looked. School began for her shortly thereafter, and like Chris had joked, there was a significant amount of makeup work waiting for her. She got back into the routine of normal life, school, reading, and picking on her brother, because after all he just couldn't stop himself from picking on her.

Things had basically gone back to normal, but they would never really be the same. Chris and Evalyn kept their tokens put away when they slept, agreeing with Rachel that it was for the best—especially after hearing her stories about the elemental council and the darkness she had brought into that world. Not using the tokens was hardest on Evalyn, who longed to see Kendrick again, but for now she had to rely on the beauty of the flower he had given her to know that he was safe and well.

One night after Rachel finished reading an especially exciting book she reached into her nightstand drawer to pull out the silver charm bracelet and look at the fire charm as it shone through the darkness of her room. She put the bracelet on her wrist and rubbed the little charm, watching the flames while thinking back to her time in Calim. And then she heard it: a soft voice whispering in sync with the light of the little fire as it flickered.

"Rachel . . ." the voice called out to her. She knew at once it was Ember. "Something's happened. I need you!" And those were the last words she heard before she drifted into a

deep sleep, the silver charm bracelet shimmering on her
wrist.

ACKNOWLEDGMENTS

Special thanks to everyone who helped turn my dream of becoming a novelist into reality. Thank you Dad, Mom, my sister Juventa, my daughter Mia and my husband Frank for your hours of proofreading and encouragement. Thanks also to my other family and friends who previewed the novel and provided valuable feedback.

I would be remiss if I didn't thank my content/line editor Lisa Rojany for helping make my novel truly shine, and my cover artist Renata Lechner whose beautiful cover art brought my characters to life.

Special thanks to Jeff Edwards for being a friend and mentor to me through this process and letting me become part of the Stealth family, and also to Jason Wright for the fantastic writing workshops that helped keep me on the path to publication.

Thank you to all of my family, friends, co-workers and fans for encouraging me along the way. This has been a tremendous undertaking and I couldn't have done it without you.

Most important, a special acknowledgement to my husband Frank, for your many hours of caring for our children Mia, Toby, Kira, Lara and Lily while I worked feverishly to complete this book. Thank you also to my children for surviving many hours without a mom and supporting me along the journey to publication.

ABOUT THE AUTHOR

Bonnie Clark lives in West Virginia with her husband and five children. She worked at a comic shop as a young adult, attending Japanese Anime conventions where she participated in cosplays, art shows, and sold merchandise. She has a passion for writing, achieving her dreams, and helping others achieve theirs. She loves gardening, nature, animals, and has dreamed about firefoxes since her early teens. She also loves getting back to basics by learning self-sufficiency and emergency preparedness skills. She graduated from BYU-Hawaii with a degree in Information Systems and currently works as a Cyber Security professional. To learn more, visit her website at www.evarance.com.

EVARANCE – RISE OF THE SHADOWS is her debut novel.